THE COLLECTOR

JOHN MAHER

INKUBATOR
BOOKS

For my Daughter
Róisín

1

THE BEND OF THE RIVER BOYNE

IT WAS A WARM SUMMER'S NIGHT ALL ALONG THE BOYNE VALLEY, with the shades of the ancient dead flitting around among the megalithic stones. The only sound Lukas Petraskas could hear through the muggy memory of the day's heat was the hooting of an owl on its lonesome night patrol. He watched it dip low over a ditch as it slowed down, and he smiled in salute. A night hunter, like himself.

Solitary, stealthy, silent.

The innocuous-looking silver Avensis, stolen to order the previous night in West Dublin, pulled up softly just down from the entrance to the Visitor Centre. Adam Bielski, the young Polish man at the wheel, pointed out the window. 'River is that way... small bridge.'

But Lukas didn't reply. He took out his mobile and swiped the professor's number. The silk-smooth voice of the old man answered at the other end of the line. The voice he had been monitoring silently for the past week.

'Hello? Who's speaking? Hello?'

Lukas checked the location tracker on his phone. The old man was exactly where he was supposed to be. He mentally rehearsed the route in his mind again, and the layout of the site. Excellent.

The voice at the other end spoke again. 'Hello?' Lukas could almost sniff the alcohol in the voice now. Even better. He switched off the phone.

Adam Bielski turned to Lukas. 'You sure about meeting place?'

But Lukas was already out the door. He crouched down in the field until the car pulled away, then pulled the backpack straps tight and made for the footbridge at the far side of the Visitor Centre. The river wasn't as fast-flowing as he had expected, after several weeks of sun. The wetlands of Lithuania didn't change that much, winter or summer. The water there had nowhere to go, of course, not like this river.

He headed for the bend in the river, where the older archaeological sites were situated. And the new site, where he would find the stupid old professor guy who couldn't shut his big mouth. That was why he was here, all the way from Spain. And to pay off the drug debt he had incurred when he tried a little private coke business behind his Russian boss's back. And lost big.

The sooner it was all done, the better. No professor, no more drug debt.

He slipped down onto the riverbank. Now he had his bearings. Good Soviet training from the old days: hard winter manoeuvres and forced marches on low rations. The young Polish driver from Dublin – there must have been at least thirty years between them – couldn't read a map, of course, unless it was a Google one. But he, Lukas Petraskas, a long-time Lithuanian transplant in the Spanish underworld, had the map of the area in his head: the start of the river bend, the main roads, the narrow access tracks, and the farmhouses where a dog might bark.

It was easy to see why people had settled here thousands of

years ago. Flowing water: drinking, fishing, washing, travelling. He slipped in beside a ditch to relieve himself and gazed up at the clear sky. No moon, but a spread of stars twinkling in the warm air. This professor man was the head of the new site and was making a big deal of the ancient dead buried there. Lucas could bring them to Lithuania and show them hundreds of places and thousands of graveyards from the Second World War. But those places and those dead weren't ancient, so no one cared. Not dead long enough.

He set off slowly. As he hiked along the riverbank, he tried to picture the professor again from the photograph he had been given. The well-fed face, the thinning hair, the dark eyes.

Idiot...

Sixty-something. Alone. Drank a lot. Started talking too much about things he shouldn't have talked about. The professor guy should have more sense at his age, with one foot already in the grave. But then, no wife, no children – only his own stupidity for company. A wife might have tamed his tongue for him.

So be it. Another day or two, and Lukas would be back on the east coast of Spain, among his own again. He just needed to do a tidy job tonight and make a professional exit.

Ahead, the river dipped south, and he could make out the start of the bend. He was close to the site now where the three portacabins should be. One for site finds, another for the diggers, and the largest, the one with the blue stripes, where Professor Carlton would be enjoying the warm summer night, along with his books and his bottle.

He sat by the ditch, took off his backpack, and checked again: maps, phones, money, the Glock and two passports. Then the little make-up bag with the syringes and the ampoules. It was easy to get syringes these days – or heroin – but getting the prescription drugs was harder. Funny old world. He put on the backpack and took off again.

A short while later, he saw what he was looking for: the three portacabins with the arc light and the little generator humming away, covering any noise he might make approaching from the blind side. The side without a CCTV camera. A movement to his left made him freeze, but it was only a badger trundling along by the ditch on its night mission: food. Eat or be eaten. The basic rule of life everywhere. Lukas braced himself for the encounter. This wouldn't be the usual routine, springing out of a car and shooting somebody at ten metres. Or taking someone out as he lay snoring after a bellyful of sex and cheap beer. No, this was something different. Smarts were needed here. That was why they hadn't farmed it out to some local lunatic with a drug problem. He took a deep breath and prepared to meet this strange old professor. He would get it over with as fast as possible, then cut and run.

He started to walk slowly towards the main portacabin.

INSIDE THE PORTACABIN, Professor Philip Carlton was at his desk, deep in thought. Although he had downed a third of a bottle of Redbreast, he still wasn't drunk. He felt a little light-headed, however, as he hadn't eaten since midday.

He considered himself in the abstract for a moment: sixty-three years of age, failing health, and a widower and divorcee with no official offspring. A graduate of University College Dublin, with a DPhil from Oxford and visiting research fellow-ships in half a dozen American universities. Books, monographs, endless articles, even a Festschrift published on his sixtieth birthday, with contributions from scholars of ancient Irish history and archaeology, far and wide. The fount of knowledge for all things pertaining to the Boyne Valley civilisation and early Celtic and pre-Celtic Ireland.

Ho-hum...

He poured himself another shot of whiskey and spoke softly to himself, as though to an invisible listener, a sudden wave of remorse sweeping over him. 'So why did you have to drag up those dodgy dealings in the past, dearest Philip? Wasn't the archaeology of five thousand years ago good enough for you?'

Because, in his sunset years, he had decided to make a clean breast of things, even if it cost him in prestige. He wanted to leave the world as he had entered it – with a clear conscience. Or something like that. He still really wasn't sure why. Maybe it was really nothing more than drink and the onset of dementia.

He couldn't deny the relief the revelations had brought him though, even if it was on a closed online forum. The sort of place only arcane archaeologists like himself could cross the threshold. Now, in the silence of the night, however, he just hoped that he hadn't ruffled too many feathers before contacting the special investigations unit in Harcourt Square.

He thought again of the detective's words on the phone a couple of weeks earlier. 'This is a very sensitive situation, Professor Carlton. You haven't told anyone else about your intentions?'

'No. Of course not.' Which was not an outright lie. But he had mouthed off on the closed forum website, in his cups, then regretted it all the following morning, in the fug of a hangover. He prayed silently again that he hadn't raised any hackles anywhere.

'So radio silence until we meet, then, Professor Carlton.'

He glanced at the calendar on the wall. Tomorrow evening he would meet with this detective in Dublin and bring along whatever evidence he had. Maybe then his conscience would be laid to rest. And the remorse – was it really some unnamed fear? – would stop.

He took a sip of the whiskey, picked up the phone and

spoke into the voice-activated app. He adopted an official tone as he carried on with his overview of the newly discovered site. *'With respect to the preliminary dating of the henge itself, a conservative estimate would suggest...'* The dig had all been a matter of luck. Luck and good weather. The five-thousand-year-old ring-shaped bank with its ditch had been exposed by the eagle eye of a drone during the scorching summer the previous year. It would now start yielding up its secrets, under his firm guidance.

And he, Professor Philip Carlton, would have one last stab at posterity before he finally snuffed it.

What was that rustling sound outside? He closed the recorder app and cocked his ear. A fox maybe or a roaming dog? Once upon a time, when the henge was new, it might have been a wolf or an elk of some sort. He closed his eyes a moment, feeling the whiskey course through his veins, bringing him back boozily to the scene in the Boyne Valley thousands of years before. The time of ancient Egypt and Anatolia and Mesopotamia.

He pictured a young woman sitting in front of a fire under a shelter made of branches, leaves and fern, the sound of children running around. He could smell the roasting meat: rabbit? Fowl? Fish? The young woman called out to the children in some pre-Celtic language that would never see writing. He smiled at his own imaginings, comparing them to the sober academic account he had just dictated into the phone. A mixture, he decided, of the melancholy musings of age, the twelve-year-old Redbreast, and a warm summer's night by a silent river.

Another noise broke his reverie then. It sounded closer now. Who or what could be out there at this time of night? Maybe a couple of the student volunteers canoodling in one of the other portacabins. Carlton smiled. The bend of the Boyne had seen all sorts of lovemaking and war-making over thousands of years. One more anonymous night of passion would hardly cause much damage.

He reached out for his walking stick, the one with the fancy ferrule he used to limp about the site, then came out from behind his desk. Hobbling over to the portacabin door, he stood out on the steps.

'Who's there?'

No one answered. Philip Carlton walked slowly down the steps and stood on the dry, firm earth. The smell of the past came to his nostrils from the freshly turned soil. He was half-tempted to wander over to the site for the hell of it. Then he cautioned himself. 'That's right, go and break a leg, Philip, and lie there for the night with the rats nibbling at your nethers.'

He turned slowly and made his way back up the steps, leaning heavily on the walking stick. Back behind the desk, he took another sip of whiskey. The little fold-up bed over by the wall suddenly seemed very welcoming now, but he would get another couple of paragraphs in before retiring.

He took up his phone and opened the voice app once more. '*A conservative estimate would place the henge much earlier than the adjacent burial chamber.*' He turned around and ran his finger over one of the site diagrams on the corkboard. He stabbed with his index finger at a point on the diagram and spoke softly to himself.

'That's where we'll make the second cut, next week.'

Out of the corner of his eye, Carlton saw the door to the portacabin open, ever so slowly, behind him. He swung around and peered over his lunettes to see a man in a dark jacket and cap standing there. A man who looked like he meant business. Bad business. The sort of business that ended up with one party being hurt. Badly. The alien eyes stared out at Carlton, smiling strangely. It was the sort of smile you might see in the schoolyard bully as he leaned into your face to clarify a point.

Yes, the pitted skin and the lean face all added up to one thing – threat.

Before he could open his mouth, the stranger spoke. 'Good evening, Professor Carlton.'

'Who are you, sir?' Carlton stared down at the stranger's feet and the set of disposable plastic booties covering his shoes. They looked like the sort of thing a forensic scientist might wear.

'And what are those galoshes on your feet, if I might ask?'

The stranger shut the door and walked over to him. 'Sit down, Professor Carlton. *Now.*'

Carlton hesitated a moment, then did as he was ordered. Up closer, he had a chance to observe the stranger better. Slim but fit-looking, with a face that bespoke a tough life. Probably in his fifties but look as fit as someone twenty years his junior. Military pedigree. Had to be. Maybe this was just a robbery. But what was there to rob here? Hardly grave goods or inscribed ten-ton stones. This wasn't the Nile Valley or Mycenae, after all.

The stranger reached down and took Carlton's phone from the desk, shoving it in his pocket. Carlton watched as the stranger slipped off the backpack and laid its contents out on the table. 'We can do this easy way or hard way. If I would be you, Professor Carlton...'

Carlton stared down in mute horror at the plastic syringes and tiny bottles of translucent liquid.

For a moment, Philip Carlton was overcome by a terrible dizziness. He closed his eyes as though he could somehow make it all go away. Images flashed through his mind now. A sunny day on a beach in the South of France, somewhere near Perpignan. A golden chalice glistening in a museum glass case. His long-gone wife smiling at him from the far side of his old study. All gone now. All gone with the days. He opened his eyes slowly again, half hoping, like a little child, that the bad man would be gone. But he wasn't. He was still there, with that lizard-like smile on his face.

Philip Carlton reached out suddenly for his walking stick. But the stranger was too quick for him. Grabbing it, he placed it out of Carlton's reach.

'You want hard way, then?' the stranger continued. 'You know how long time this will take, Professor?' He reached inside his jacket and took out a fearsome-looking knife with a long serrated edge.

Philip Carlton bit his lip. His vain little life was over. He knew that to be a fact now. Whatever love had come and gone was over. And his lofty name in the annals of academe. All vanity and a waste of breath. Like all the lives before him, along the valley of the Boyne river. He felt a terrible sense of loneliness envelop him all of a sudden, like a small child watching its mother walk away silently in the rain. He reached for the glass of whiskey as warm, silent tears started up in his eyes. 'One last sip?' he asked.

The stranger nodded, then pointed at the syringe and the vials. He smiled at Carlton. 'Easy way, always it is the better, Professor Carlton.'

2

THE WOODEN-HULLED MERMAID DINGHY CALLED *BETSY* SWUNG to starboard as the wind bit into the foresail and nosed eastwards, towards the Rockabill lighthouse and the open sea. They would circle the lighthouse, then head back west towards Skerries harbour for home, up in the farmhouse in the Blackhills.

Lucy O'Hara ran her hand through her long auburn hair, and her eyes fixed on the horizon. She glanced over her shoulder at her eight-year-old daughter in the bright yellow windcheater at the tiller. At the mop of blonde hair trailing in the wind. The little blue eyes were fixed steadily on the horizon. 'Steady, Saoirse. *Betsy* doesn't like sudden movements. She's too old for that, like me. Alright?'

'Are you really as old as *Betsy*, *Maman*?'

'Close.'

The child laughed that bright little laugh that reminded Lucy of her father, Gerhard, in Hamburg. Was good humour genetic? Maybe. Everything else seemed to be these days. A light wind had sprung up, and when she looked north towards the Mourne Mountains, she could see a band of rain sitting there, ready to drop south. They would be well back in harbour by then, though.

She opened the lunchbox and smiled at the little feast. Fruit, bread rolls, cheese and a couple of rosy apples. Her mother had even slipped in a bottle of St. Emilion, despite Lucy's protestations. Not that she was going to open it on the high seas with an eight-year-old in her care. Even a bottle of decent French wine had to wait for dry land.

'Right, let's see what we've got here, Saoirse.'

'Hope it's not all that healthy stuff.'

There was a sassiness in the smile that always amused Lucy. A sort of knowingness beyond her years. It was there from the day she was born: that wariness of the world, tempered with an overlay of irony. And that quick-on-the-draw tongue. Saoirse could shoot from the hip from the day she spouted her first phoneme. That time she threw a tantrum at the winter fair in Dublin because she wasn't allowed on a merry-go-round.

'Why are you behaving like a child, Saoirse?'

'Because I am a child. Ne c'est pas?'

She passed Saoirse a bread roll filled with salad and cheese and watercress – her mother's little touch along with her grandmother's insistence on using French with the child when they were together. 'Come on, let's eat, sweetie.'

Thank Christ for boats and horses and dogs, though. It sometimes felt to Lucy as if these were the only bonds between them: water, wind and the company of animals. She felt guilty every time the idea occurred to her. But guilt was saltwater soluble, thankfully. It vanished as soon as the sea was on the air and the wind on the coast of North Dublin filled the sails. They would knock a few more years out of this togetherness. Her French mother doing the heavy lifting while she sped up the coast and soldiered on in the garda station in Boynebridge.

Lucy reminded herself, for the umpteenth time, to stay in the day. That the present would soon be the past, and her daughter would soon enough be circling around her own heart's desires.

She leaned back and kissed Saoirse on the forehead.

The child frowned comically. 'What was that for?'

Lucy smiled. 'For luck, love. For both of us.'

They were rounding the Rockabill lighthouse when the phone rang. Lucy saw the name on the screen and frowned. What did Reese want with her? 'Saoirse, keep your eye on the horizon. Steady on the tiller now.' She hit the little green icon on the phone: Superintendent Reese.

'Lucy, is that you? George here.'

'George...Superintendent Reese...long time.'

'Yes, it is. Look, there's something big up your way and I want you in on it, ASAP.' Reese's voice was steady.

'Go on.' She moved back down the boat and took the tiller, wrapping her fingers firmly around the cold wood. Her back arched as the boat nosed forward into the wind, a little too close to the rocks near the lighthouse.

'The Carltons. Name mean anything to you?'

Lucy eased the tiller to the left and the boat swung southwards towards Skerries harbour. 'You mean *those* Carltons, I assume?'

'Our very own Kennedys, you might say. The eldest one, Philip, the archaeologist, has been found dead at a new dig in the Boyne Valley.' Reese sounded strangely uneasy.

'Suspicious?'

'No immediate indication of that, but the body was only found a couple of hours ago. He was a diabetic. Lots of medical issues. But I want it treated by you, unofficially for the moment, as a suspicious death.'

'Unofficially. Am I allowed to know why?'

'Well, Philip Carlton has been on our radar recently in Harcourt Square. I can't say anything more on it at the moment.

And there may be absolutely no connection. But... on the other hand...' Reese stopped himself.

'Right. So what do you need from me?' Lucy glanced over her shoulder at the lighthouse and checked her course.

'Get up to Boynebridge as soon as possible. The buckshees are already on the site, securing it. Peter Brosnahan, Anna Crowley and young Sheehan will be working with you.' Reese paused a moment. 'There's something else you need to know, Lucy.'

'What's that?' Lucy steadied the tiller and cast a glance back at Saoirse.

'Superintendent McHugh is senior investigating officer. Temporary SIO, that is. It's a holding operation. You're the jam in the sandwich between him and local until I sort out someone new.'

Lucy took a deep breath. She could picture McHugh's beady little eyes staring at her, the perma-sneer fixed to his lips. The Bateman case was back in her thoughts again, and all the trouble it had caused her.

'Cut him a little slack, Lucy. He doesn't need to know anything about our suspicions. He's just there for the optics and because he has an in with the Carltons. I'll send you the map link. How soon can you get there?'

'I'm out in the boat with Saoirse. It's going to be a couple of hours.'

'Say an hour and a half?'

'I'll do my best.'

The phone knocked off, leaving her mind momentarily full of the previous couple of years: investigations around the country as a newly appointed forensic linguist, promoted from the ranks with her glittering doctorate. The Hamilton sisters and the dodgy will in Leitrim, the stalker in Donegal stung by his own dialect, and the paramilitary informer blown through a barn door in

Wicklow with a double-barrelled shotgun. All cases that had hung on her specialist skills and training. Until the Bateman case and the tribunal of enquiry had busted her back down to local detective in Boynebridge, 'with special tasking, subject to demand.' In other words, *file under forget*. Reese was the only one who had her back. He came and airlifted her out every now and then, with the hope of getting her out of the boonies one day.

It couldn't come soon enough.

Reese didn't want to spook her, but it was clear that there was a lot riding on this. All might be forgiven, if not exactly forgotten. But was that likely? Maybe that was why Reese had put Superintendent McHugh in temporarily, too. It made a certain sort of stupid sense, sadly.

It was mid-July and Skerries harbour was chock-a-block with a mixture of the Dublin crowd, casual visitors and locals. When she pulled the boat in, she phoned her mother to take Saoirse.

Saoirse screwed up her face. 'How long will you be, *Maman*?'

'Back by this evening, love. *Mémé* will bring you to the beach.'

'You mean, I will bring *Mémé* to the beach. She always says it's too cold for her. *Pas pour moi!*' The little face contorted in imitation of her grandmother.

Lucy pulled out onto the road for the Black Hills a couple of miles outside the town of Skerries. 'Oh, I think you really have a soft spot for her, Saoirse.' She watched the little face in the mirror break into a stealthy smile.

'*Puede ser, Maman. Puede ser.*'

Lucy glanced in the mirror. 'What? Where's the Spanish coming from?'

The little face in the mirror smirked. 'It's a game I found on my tablet. I do it to annoy *Mémé* because she hates it when she speaks to me in French and I answer with a Spanish word.'

'Poor old *Mémé*! You little devil.'

THE BLACK HILLS area was just a short spin up from the windy coast road. A scattering of houses and farmhouses, near enough to be town and far enough to be country with access to the Belfast Dublin motorway, the sea and the coast road that snaked its way northwards to the Mournes.

Goldilocks's middle chair, geographically speaking.

In the car, Lucy turned on the radio to catch the headlines. '*The body of world-renowned archaeologist and expert on the Boyne Valley settlements Professor Philip Carlton has been found dead at a new dig near the River Boyne, in County Louth. Gardai are not looking for anyone else in connection with the discovery, at the moment...*'

She thought about the Carltons. Philip, she knew of from TV and the papers. His well-padded face regularly adorned cultural programmes. Then there was Joyce, who had once been a social queen, a lady who liquid-lunched at charity functions, a house-building programme in Africa, and disability organisations. There was a David, too, she seemed to remember, and a few others who had died tragically – two sisters and one brother.

Very Kennedy, alright. Very rich and influential.

And very dead. No, the stats weren't great for the Carltons. In fact, she couldn't think of any other family with such poor innings.

Lucy pulled out onto the coast road. In the distance, the band of rain had slipped south. She would be driving into it on her way to the Boyne Valley. A few minutes later, she turned off the coast road for her house in the Black Hills. When she pulled into the yard, the Peugeot was already in the farmyard, and she could see her mother through the window. She parked outside the house and they got out.

The horse was neighing in the back stable. The golden retriever, Polly, came forward to greet her. She stooped down to pet her. 'You poor old thing, you. Let's get you some water.'

Her phone rang. It was Dennis Sheehan, the junior detective, phoning from the site. 'Moyra Killanin has arrived, Lucy. She asked how long you would be?'

In her mind's eye, Lucy could see Moyra Killanin, state pathologist, bent over the cold body of Philip Carlton. Peering through her glasses as she went about her business meticulously. 'Tell her forty minutes, Dennis.'

'OK. By the way, Superintendent McHugh said to tell you he has already spoken with Joyce Carlton.'

'Keeping me away from them, obviously.'

In the house, she made herself a coffee, then googled the Carltons to refresh her memory. Six siblings. Philip now gone, Joyce above ground along with David, who lived with his husband, Michel, a graphic artist, in the South of France. Olwyn, killed in a car crash in Italy, Helen, dead of cancer. And Derry, the baby, a lush who drank himself to death a good few years before. Which left only Joyce and David standing.

No, not a great score at all.

TEN MINUTES LATER, she was on the motorway, heading north. The rain came down in swathes now, only clearing on the outskirts of Boynebridge. It was the sort of summer burst she remembered from her four years in Berlin, as the itinerant daughter of a senior Irish diplomat. France, Germany, UK, Spain. Hoovering up continental languages along the way. Until finally and fatally, Cairo, the curse of Christ on it.

The car swung left towards the bend in the Boyne as the GPS guided her along the narrow, nameless roads. A few minutes later, she spotted a couple of garda cars parked up against the ditch. Then three portacabins in an adjoining field.

Dennis Sheehan was at the entrance with his boy-band good looks. She pulled in behind one of the garda cars and got out. A young uniformed garda from the Boynebridge station nodded at her. 'Superintendent McHugh said to go straight to the first portacabin, Detective O'Hara.'

'Fine.' Lucy motioned to Dennis to join her. She popped open the boot and took out plastic overshoes, latex gloves and a shoulder bag. 'What's the story, Dennis?'

'Moyra Killanin is still in there with Superintendent McHugh.' Dennis watched for a reaction. She gave none.

'Right. Let's get started. Find who's working on the site and arrange interviews. Security staff, students, and anyone else.'

'Right.'

'And phone Peter Brosnahan. Get him to do a drive-by of the local farms and ask a few questions. Tell him to check any local CCTV. But play it down. Superintendent McHugh doesn't need to be bothered with these details.' She was mindful now of Reese's words: suspicious death. But why so? But no point in getting the rank-and-file rattled and causing ructions with McHugh.

Dennis glanced uneasily at the portacabin behind them. 'Am I missing something here?'

'What do you mean?' Lucy did a little eyebrow arching, but it was lost on the young detective.

Dennis looked awkward. 'Like, this is a suspected suicide, right? Not a crime scene. Superintendent McHugh said...'

'Superintendent McHugh is temporary senior investigating officer. If this turns out to be something else, we'll both be in the dock. A sin of omission is still a sin.'

Dennis did a chummy thumbs-up sign. 'Fair enough. Only saying, like.'

'Now, see that bunch of student types over by the fence? You can start with them. I'll see you when I've finished speaking to Superintendent McHugh.'

They walked into the field to where a uniformed garda was standing outside the first portacabin. Lucy knocked on the door and walked in. Inside, Superintendent Ambrose McHugh was standing in front of a huge corkboard with maps and sketches. The tightly trimmed grey hair and moustache made him look more like an ex-army man than a garda.

When he spotted Lucy, he pursed his lips like a mother superior about to strike. Hard cop, soft cop in the one putty-coloured face. 'Detective O'Hara. Good afternoon.' McHugh stretched out his hand formally.

Lucy shook the pinkish hand. 'Afternoon, Superintendent.'

Moyra Killanin looked over her glasses at Lucy and nodded towards the body of the late Philip Carlton sprawled across the desk. To his left, she could see an empty bottle of whiskey and, to his right, a syringe and a couple of vials of the type used for intravenous drugs.

McHugh pointed at the syringe. 'I think that's about it for me, Moyra.' He turned back to the corkboard and began to run his finger over the map. As though Lucy wasn't there at all.

Which, in a way, she suddenly felt she wasn't.

3

THE COLLECTOR LOOKED OUT OVER THE DARK GREEN TWEED OF the West Cork landscape and thought, *The only people mad enough to live in this Godforsaken place are the remnants of 1970s German hippies still alive and down-at-heel Irish pensioners.*

And me...

He started walking back along the cliff path, pausing at the turn to tighten the twine around the rabbits slung over his shoulder. Then he carried on slowly. *Not bad for a man in his seventies and still a good shot with a .22.* He didn't bother to check how many rounds were left in the clip – he had counted them out as he shot the two rabbits. One bullet high, two on target. But there was always something that made him keep a bullet in the breech until he was well inside the door of the house.

Caution, maybe.

He paused and looked back towards the sea as he reached the great house set into the clifftop. No one could have followed him up this far without being spotted. The previous owner had seen to that. Great chaps for fencing off other people's coastlines, the Germans, he mused. Denmark was full of them. Couldn't get away with that these days, mind you. Or planning permission for the house either. Have some semi-literate know-nothing from Dublin protesting about cultural vandalism and all that malarkey.

The shelterbelt of trees to the right of the house should have reassured him, but it always made him feel just that little bit uneasy. For a moment, he imagined figures in disruptive camouflage appearing out of the tall spruce. He raised the rifle to his shoulder slowly and pointed it towards the silent trees, feeling the weight of the dead rabbits cut into his flesh.

'Bang!'

He chuckled to himself and crossed to the patio doors. The Germans who had built the house had been thorough. There wasn't a wasted centimetre of space in the whole building. He opened the kitchen door, strode swiftly across the floor, and slung the rabbits in the sink. He would let them rest for a while before skinning them.

In the sitting room, he took up a magazine and began skim-reading an article about the Iranian situation as Lyric FM played a Beethoven sonata in the background.

The phone on the coffee table gave a little buzz, then two more, in quick succession. He left down the journal and stood up to stretch himself. Then he took the rifle from its cradle on the wall and made his way down the cellar stairs. He pulled the lever in the recess in the wall and watched the metal door open.

The door to the bunker.

It was built even better than the house above it. A nuclear, chemical and biological bunker, built during the paranoia of the Cold War. Just one of the many bunkers built across Western Europe to provide a fallback should the Soviets ever come West. This one, in West Cork, was the furthest west. The plan was that, when the alarm was sounded, high-ranking German army and government ministers would scatter across Europe to coordinate resistance. Like the Polish in Britain during the Second World War.

He tapped the wall beside him absentmindedly, feeling the reassurance of the cold concrete. The Germans had brought their own builders over with them, of course. Didn't trust the happy-go-lucky natives to build it without giving the whole game away in a pub at three in the morning. The Collector thought again of the paranoia in the form of mass concrete.

And he was strangely thankful.

He threw the light switch. The room was suffused with a soft light that revealed a large antechamber designed as a war room. But there were no tables or chairs or any sign of bureaucratic bric-a-brac here. No military maps on the walls either, or banks of dusty computers. Only glass cases and exhibition stands containing a selection of manuscripts and other historical artefacts. True, there were more exhibits in the other rooms. Gold torcs and bronze daggers and larger items. But this was the Collector's favourite room. Because his favourite exhibit was here.

The Genesis of St Fergal.

He crossed over to the glass case to his right and pressed the little red button. There was a hiss of compressed air as one of the pages of the twelfth-century vellum manuscript turned. He peered in through the glass and read Genesis 1:1.

In principio creavit Deus caelum et terram...

He uttered the sacred words to himself, *sotto voce*: In the beginning God created the heavens and the earth. Great opening line! He considered for the thousandth time the beauty of the zoological figures drawn around the illuminated sacred text. The colourful little dogs and cats and foxes. Later in the morning, he would pull over the study chair, adjust the lighting in the case and read his daily page, as he did every day. Intoning the sacred words in the sonorous voice of one of those long-forgotten, Latin-literate priests.

Not like the touchy-feely tree-hugging ignoramuses you had now.

The phone beeped once. He waited until it beeped twice more; then he crossed out of the anteroom to the first room on the right. A ham radio with a glowing digital interface was sitting in the corner on a low table. He sat in front of it and put on his headphones. Not that anyone would be able to hear down here, under thousands of tonnes of concrete.

'Good morning to you, Mr Arkens.' The Collector's voice was firm more than friendly.

'Good morning. Everything went as planned with Philip Carlton, as you know.' Jeremy Arkens's voice sounded nervous.

'Indeed it did, Mr Arkens. Our Lithuanian friend did a very tidy job. Well done! Poor Professor Carlton was ill and depressed, and he took the easy way out. I heard it on the radio, so it must be true!' The Collector gave a sardonic chuckle at his own joke.

'And what about David Carlton? What about his brother?' Jeremy Arkens sounded uneasy.

The Collector ran his finger along the barrel of the .22 as he spoke. 'Well, you need to meet with David Carlton when he arrives from France, and keep me abreast of any developments. We need to be sure that the suicide story holds. If the Carltons suspect, for one minute...'

'And this Saunders woman?' Jeremy Arkens voice suddenly reached a high pitch.

'I'm sorry?' The Collector's tone was curt.

'Violet Saunders? Philip Carlton's former lover... where is she now?'

There was silence for a moment. The Collector coughed politely at the other end of the line. 'Our Lithuanian friend is tracking her car and monitoring her phone conversations and emails.' The Collector's words were calm.

'And what if she decides to talk?' There was a new nervousness in Jeremy Arkens's voice.

'Our man will sort that out, too. The piece of software his

companion slipped into her phone with the email keeps us up to date on where she goes, who she talks to and what she says. One question, Mr Arkens...'

'Yes?'

Now, the Collector had Arkens where he wanted him. Squirming. 'Are you familiar with the concept of chain of command?' The Collector's voice was polite to the point of rudeness.

'Of course.' Jeremy Arkens just wanted to get off the phone now.

'Then you should look on yourself as the middleman. No more, no less. Now, good day to you, sir.' The Collector switched off the radio set and stood up. He took up the .22 and made his way back into the anteroom. He paused a moment in front of the manuscript to switch off the case light. 'Au revoir, dear St Fergal.'

Outside the bunker, he raised the handle in the wall, and the metal door closed again. Then, cradling the .22, he made his way back up the steps. He paused at the top of the steps to listen for a moment then carried on into the great kitchen, where the two rabbits were resting in the sink, a little pool of blood congealing just below their heads.

'Now, my friends. Let's undress you.' He wiped his hands on the towel and thought hard on the subject of Violet Saunders. If needs must, then so be it. She would have to be silenced like the father of her child.

Then he picked up a shiny Swiss Victorinox carving knife and grabbed the legs of the first rabbit.

'Ladies first...'

4

THEY ALL SEEMED TO BE STANDING ON ONE ANOTHER'S TOES IN the cramped portacabin. Lucy O'Hara stood back while the forensic photographer took his shots and considered Philip Carlton's jowly, well-lived-in face.

McHugh turned around from the corkboard. 'Moyra, can you explain the situation again, please.' He sounded like an old parish priest about to launch into a sermon.

Moyra Killanin glanced over at Lucy and continued. 'The evidence shows a massive overdose of insulin. In a diabetic like Philip Carlton, that would cause many issues. Hypoglycaemia is just one of them.'

'And probable cause of death?'

'Ultimately, it might be any number of things, or just simple cardiopulmonary arrest. But this is early days.'

McHugh came around the desk and smiled at Lucy. 'Right. I'll see you up in the station, Detective O'Hara.'

Lucy glanced over at the body of Philip Carlton again. 'Are we setting up an incident room?'

McHugh smiled sweetly at her. 'There is no incident. Sometimes deaths are just deaths. Or do you know something we don't?'

'It's not being treated as suspicious, then?' Lucy glanced over at Moyra Killanin.

McHugh nodded towards the corpse. 'No reason for that. Right, I'll see you in the station with your colleagues, as I've said.'

She waited until the door closed behind McHugh's broad behind. Moyra Killanin looked over at her.

'This is the suicide note. I thought you might like a look at it before it goes to forensics.' She handed over a sheet of typed paper in a see-through evidence bag.

Lucy scanned the suicide note into her phone, then started reading it. Straight away it struck her: it was like an Abba song that seemed slightly off-centre, linguistically. Right thoughts, right emotions, but just... awkward. Tenses used oddly.

But there was something more. She scanned the note again. High grammar and stilted syntax mixed with basic grammatical errors. How could that be? Was Philip Carlton really that drunk when he wrote this? Even drunks didn't get basic syntax wrong. Same way you remembered the pop songs of your teenage years even when you were bog-eyed with booze, years later. So deeply etched into the brain biochemically.

Lucy looked across at Moyra Killanin. 'Something's not right here. The language is all off... lopsided, you might say.'

'Your department, Lucy. I'll stick to corpses. I wouldn't say your Superintendent McHugh has much time for forensic linguistics though. Would I be right?' Moyra Killanin closed her briefcase.

Lucy looked up from the note. 'It's in the same box as folk remedies for gout and Morris dancing.'

'Anyway, I'm finished here. The late Professor Carlton will be going to the morgue in Boynebridge first, and then on to Dublin for the full Irish.'

'Anything else you can give me here, Moyra? Even off the record?'

Moyra Killanin angled her head. 'Like I said earlier, the overdose of insulin was the initiating event. Can't speculate on the rest just yet.'

'It doesn't seem right to me. The language... just a feeling.'

Moyra Killanin locked her briefcase. 'Feelings don't sit well in pathology reports. Look, it's probably exactly what it seems. A sad, lonely man, with a bottle of whiskey at his elbow, deciding to check out early. Like it says in the note.'

'Maybe. Maybe not.'

She waited until Moyra Killanin had left, then turned back for one last look at the body. Sad. Who would have known Philip Carlton best of all? His brother and sister? Former lovers, if they would talk. David Carlton, the only surviving brother, was due in from France. She would nobble him. If your own brother doesn't know you...

Lucy stepped out onto the bone-dry ground. It was another seriously hot summer, like the previous one. The one that had brought the henge to light in this field. She looked out across the burnt grass towards the site of the preliminary dig. Dennis Sheehan was talking to a couple of buckshees who were walking the site for stray evidence. A group of young men and women were standing over by a tent. A young blonde-haired woman was crying, and the others were comforting her.

Lucy walked over to them. 'I'm Detective Lucy O'Hara. You were all working on this site, I assume.'

A fellow with long hair and the whisper of a beard spoke. 'Aye, we're all volunteers, so we are. Deirdre here was very close to Professor Carlton. He was her thesis supervisor.'

The young blonde-haired woman sniffled a little on cue. One of the other women moved to embrace her.

Lucy turned back to the young man. 'Has someone spoken to you yet?'

'Detective Sheehan has arranged to talk to us all this afternoon.'

Lucy nodded over at the dig. 'How many are on this site?'

'There's six of us. Then there's a couple of security men who come and go.'

Lucy frowned and looked about the site. 'That's a very small number.'

'It's just a preliminary dig, Detective.' Long hair sounded like he was going to give a lecture.

'Right. I see. No one is to leave the site until you've given all your details to us. Clear?' Lucy stared hard at the Alpha male in wellies and flak jacket again. She imagined him sermonising his acolytes at three in the morning on global warming and the latest conspiracy theory. He had an eco-warrior look about him. Good bank manager material, down the line.

Lucy glanced over at the teary blonde with her head on the chest of a taller woman.

She walked over to where Dennis was standing with the uniforms. 'You deal with beardie, and I'll question blondie.' Lucy glanced back again at the little group. 'You don't think old Carlton was hitting on that young one, do you?'

Dennis smiled softly. 'Never know. Some ol' fellas are real rams, so they are.'

'Is that a fact, now? Contact Anna and get her to do the on-site cameras. Peter can do the local ones.' Lucy pointed at the cameras around the site.

'Right. Anything else?' Dennis pulled out his notebook and started writing.

Lucy nodded over at the little group of students 'This lot... interviews?'

Dennis glanced down at his notebook. 'I can do general overview this afternoon if you like. Detective Brosnahan is chatting to the staff in the hotel Philip Carlton was staying in when he wasn't kipping out here. The Valley Inn.'

Lucy turned back to Dennis. 'You do the overviews, then. Did Carlton stay out here a lot?'

Dennis grinned. 'According to the students, a couple of times a week. He used to hit the bottle and order food out from a Chinky in town.'

'I think you'll find we call it a Chinese takeaway in the twenty-first century.' Lucy smiled sweetly at Dennis.

'Right. Right. Chinese takeaway. Wouldn't like to offend anyone, Detective O'Hara.'

'I'm sure you wouldn't. What's the blonde girl's name, by the way?' Lucy pointed towards the little group of archaeology students.

'Deirdre Delaney. She's from Carlow town.'

Lucy looked back across the site at the little group. The blonde girl had stopped crying now. The show was over. They all seemed to be listening to the chap with the ponytail, who looked like he was giving them a pep talk.

'McHugh say much to you earlier?' She spoke to Dennis without looking away from the group.

'He expects it to be all done and dusted by tomorrow.' Dennis looked uncomfortable. The bearer of bad tidings.

'Does he indeed? OK, drop me back to the station. I need to keep on top of all this.' They started walking back towards the entrance.

They climbed into the Passat in silence. There was a grinding of gears. Lucy looked over at Dennis. 'You quite finished tearing the bollox out of this state property?'

'Sorry.' Dennis pulled out onto the road.

Further down, they could see an RTE television van. It wasn't Joe Bloggs who had snuffed it in the portacabin, of course. Professor Philip Carlton. Our very own gentry.

'Pull in there, Dennis.'

Dennis pulled up beside the TV van. A young man was fiddling with a boom at the side of the road. She rolled down the window and flashed her badge. 'Hello, there. What's the story here?'

'We want to do a piece to camera with the background of the site, Detective. All that Celtic palaver, you know.'

'Pre-Celtic palaver, actually. Remember, no traipsing around the site.' Lucy smiled sweetly.

'Is it a crime scene, then, Detective?' The techie stopped fiddling with the boom for a moment. Their eyes fixed on one another.

'No, it isn't. But a man died here this morning. So how about a little respect. Right?' Lucy rolled up the window.

THEY REACHED the station in Boynebridge a quarter of an hour later. There were more cameras there. It was the local boys this time. Dennis pulled up in the courtyard. 'McHugh has set out a room for us at the back for the incident investigation.'

Lucy ground to a halt and fixed Dennis with a stare. 'There is no incident. This is a high-profile family. We need to be seen to be especially attentive. That's all. That doesn't mean we don't investigate though. Quietly. Are we clear about that?' Lucy looked across at Dennis.

He smiled back, eager to please. 'Gotcha.'

Lucy slipped in by the back entrance to the station and helloed a few uniformed guards as she made her way upstairs. She could hear voices behind the door. Anna Crowley was talking about her CCTV footage. Her voice was clear as a bell. Lucy opened the door slowly. A few desks had been set up around the room with computers. McHugh was standing in front of an enormous whiteboard.

He turned to greet her. 'Ah, Detective O'Hara. As I was saying, we should be able to put this to bed as quickly as possible.'

Lucy glanced around at the others. 'Yes, sir.'

'I want forensics and pathology tied up ASAP.'

'And the Carlton family?' Lucy scrutinised the eyes carefully.

'David Carlton flies in from France tomorrow. I'm going to drop in on Joyce Carlton this afternoon when I get back to Dublin. We've already spoken on the phone, of course, and I've arranged to have a more detailed conversation with her about Philip. Sort of post-mortem catch-up, you might say, if that doesn't sound too morbid. I played rugby with their late brother in UCD, actually. Derry Carlton.'

The Old Boys Brigade. No outsiders need apply. Sealed South Dublin ecosystem.

Lucy smiled politely. 'So should I contact Joyce Carlton myself, protocol-wise? Maybe meet up with David Carlton when he arrives?'

McHugh pursed his lips for a moment and glanced over at the others. Lucy waited long enough for him to think it was his own bright, shining idea.

'Why not? Give her a buzz and introduce yourself. You can handle the meeting with David Carlton and save me the trouble.' McHugh popped his hat on and smiled.

Lucy nodded politely. 'Yes, sir.'

'Now, I have to get back down to Dublin. I expect you to update me this evening.'

McHugh paused at the door and spoke in a low voice to her. '*Festina lente.* Understand?'

Lucy lowered her voice. '*Make haste slowly.* I did study Latin and Greek in secondary school, sir. Didn't forget all of it.'

'Well, good for you. What I'm saying is, we wouldn't like another Bateman now, would we, Detective?' McHugh glanced over his shoulder to make sure no one was listening.

Lucy winced.

McHugh disappeared out the door. Anna Crowley sat back

in front of her computer and started going through the CCTV images.

Pete Brosnahan looked up from his desk. 'Interview schedule?'

'Stagger them. Site volunteers first. Anna, call out Joyce Carlton's mobile for me there.'

A noise made Lucy turn around. The door opened slowly. Lucy expected to see Dennis's laddish leather-jacketed figure in front of her. Instead a well-built man in his thirties filled the door frame. A rugby full forward decanted into a high-end Louis Copeland suit. A black briefcase was attached to his right paw.

There was a big cheesy smile on the face. 'Is this the Philip Carlton room?'

Lucy squinted in the low light. 'It is. Can I help you?'

'I'm Gerry Sullivan. National Bureau of Criminal Investigation, in Harcourt Square. And you must be Detective O'Hara.'

'That's me. What can I do for you, Detective Sullivan?' What was this bozo doing here now? Had Reese sent him up from Garda headquarters in Harcourt Square to keep an eye on her? Make sure she didn't blot her copybook again?

Gerry Sullivan glanced around him. 'A quiet moment, maybe?'

Lucy nodded at Anna and Brosnahan. 'Anna, Pete... give us five, lads.'

Sullivan waited until the door closed behind the two younger detectives. 'I've been asked by NBCI in Harcourt Square and Superintendent Reese to liaise and assist you.'

Lucy looked over Sullivan's shoulder, keeping an eye on the closed door. 'Assist me with what exactly?'

Gerry Sullivan moved closer to her. 'Second-level case management, analysis of evidence and statements, special tasking.'

'Special tasking? Like what?'

Gerry Sullivan had a smile strapped to his face now. A smile she was itching to wipe away with the back of her hand.

She repeated the question. 'Like what, Detective Sullivan?'

'Well...' Sullivan leaned against the desk. 'Special tasking for high-profile deaths. NBCI have quite an amount of experience in sensitive cases.'

'Really? Oh, so it's a case now, is it?' Lucy leaned forward.

'It's an unexplained death of a person of significance, more than a case, Detective O'Hara.'

Lucy ran her hands through her hair. 'Well, that's clarified that. I wouldn't like us getting off on the wrong foot.'

Sullivan beamed at her. 'And there are certain unexplained-death protocols. I'm sure you know all about those.'

Lucy frowned. 'That's not the message I'm hearing from Superintendent McHugh. Does the superintendent know about your role here, by the way? He is SIO on this unexplained death, after all.'

Sullivan glanced at his watch and grinned sweetly. 'And yes, he will know, in about five minutes or so when Superintendent Reese phones him.' Sullivan suddenly perked up. 'So, what can I help you with, off the bat?'

'You can call me Lucy, for starters, Gerry.'

'Right, Lucy it is.' Sullivan summoned up another stock smile.

'And you can hook up with Dennis Sheehan on the site-interview schedule. We can catch up later, when I've figured out what your role is here.'

Sullivan left his little briefcase down on one of the tables. 'Right. Fair enough.'

She gave him a little smile and headed off downstairs to the locker room, thinking to herself along the way: *Who are you, Mr Sullivan? And what are you really here for?*

. . .

IN THE LOCKER ROOM, she called Joyce Carlton's number. There was a delay; then a serene voice came over the phone.

'Joyce Carlton. Who's calling?'

'Ms Carlton, my name is Detective Lucy O'Hara.'

'Yes?' Joyce Carlton sounded like she was sedated. Not that strange – her brother had just died.

Lucy felt she was reading from a prepared script herself now. One that had special stage instructions for the likes of the Carltons. 'Let me first offer my condolences on the sudden death of your brother Philip.'

'Thank you. Is there something I can help you with, Detective?'

'There is, actually. Superintendent McHugh asked me to have a word with your brother David.'

'David?' Joyce Carlton sounded like she was having difficulty remembering her own brother's name. 'David? Oh, yes, Detective. Well, he's coming back from France tomorrow, you see...'

Lucy paused a moment before speaking. 'If you could ask him to phone me on his return.'

'Of course. Is it something important?'

Your brother has just died. Of course it's important. Lucy bit her lip and spoke softly and carefully. 'I want him to fill me in a little on Philip. On his life in recent years. I understand that Superintendent McHugh has already been in touch with you and gone over some background.' Lucy felt like she was speaking to an app now.

'That's right. As much as I can, at the moment, you understand. David might be a problem though.' There was a deep sigh at the far end of the line.

'A problem, Ms Carlton?'

'Well, you see, Philip hasn't really had regular recent contact with David and his new... husband, you know.'

'I see. Well, like I was saying, if David could phone me, I'd really appreciate it. And perhaps we could meet together over the next few days? I don't want to double up on what you're telling Superintendent McHugh, of course.'

There was a silence. Had she gone too far, too quickly? Peed on McHugh's patch?

'Of course. Of course.' There was a pause. 'I really can't believe Philip is gone.' Joyce Carlton's voice suddenly sounded faint now.

'I understand that. It's a very difficult time for you. I'll do my best to make things easier for everyone.'

'Thank you, Detective.'

Lucy knocked off the phone and slipped it into her pocket.

She made her way up the backstairs. When she entered the room, Gerry Sullivan was standing beside Pete Brosnahan as he worked on the computer, like he was in charge of the whole place.

Maybe he is, she suddenly thought. And she was the last one to hear it. The jam in the sandwich between McHugh and Sullivan.

Sullivan smiled across at her, but she said nothing.

5

THE LIGHT WAS STARTING TO SLIP FROM THE BABY BLUE SUMMER sky when Lucy O'Hara turned off the M1 for the coast of North Dublin. She drove slowly through the outskirts of Balbriggan and out on the sea road, against the remnant of the summer's evening traffic heading home. Families with cars full of sleepy, grouchy children. Parents anxious to get home before the smaller ones got a second wind and kept them up half the night.

As she drove along, Gerry Sullivan's Cheshire-cat smile kept taunting her. She resisted the urge to phone Reese, though. George Reese would expect her to read between the lines until such time... as what? She didn't like blurred lines, or trying to read between them, either. And she didn't want a loose cannon around the store when she was already watching her P's and Q's with snakes like McHugh, who would hang her in a heartbeat.

Why was Harcourt Square so interested in a lonely old archaeologist's apparent suicide, anyway?

One thing was sure: Sullivan was a player. But it galled her that she didn't know the game.

Yet.

She pulled up an Egyptian radio station on the internet radio. A couple of elderly men were discussing one of Naguib Mahfouz's novels. The one set in Alexandria during the Nasser era. Her mind was sucked into the half-dialect of their conversation and the high Arabic of the reading. For a moment, she was back in Cairo again. Walking through the ancient market of Khan al Khalili with its shiny brassware and glazed pottery. The cries of the merchants and the swirl of bodies scurrying to and fro.

The little linguistic diversion did the trick, as it usually did: Sullivan's smiling presence had been erased by the reverse-engineered Arabic swishing around her brain.

SHE PULLED into the farmyard in the Black Hills a short while later. The dog barked as she drove in, recognising the engine of the ancient Volvo estate that she just couldn't bring herself to part with. She could hear her mother playing backgammon with Saoirse in the big sitting room. In the kitchen, there was a smell of herbs on the warm evening air. She helped herself to a small plate of ratatouille, poured herself a glass of wine and joined them.

She looked over at Saoirse. 'Have you fed Polly, love? And watered Chantal?'

Saoirse smiled. 'All done.'

Lucy took a sip of Bordeaux. Her mother had a knack for nosing out half-decent French wine in Irish supermarkets. Lucy looked over at Saoirse. 'Bedtime. I'll be in to read you your story in five minutes.' Saoirse disappeared.

Her mother looked up from the paper. 'Lots on the radio about your Professor Carlton today. He was a big noise, it seems.'

'Suspected suicide.' Lucy took another sip of wine.

Her mother looked over her reading glasses at her. 'Suspicious suicide?'

'No. Suspected. There's a very big difference.' There was no point in getting into it with her mother. Lucy took out the iPad and opened up the copy of Philip Carlton's typed suicide letter. It hit her again now – that weird mixture of high language with basic errors that just couldn't be typos. She highlighted them all on the iPad.

Dear Joyce and David,

It is with great regret I am writing these sad words. By the time you read this, I will be gone to my eternal rest, sadly. Of late, things have become more and more difficult. My health is failing, I no longer seem to have any purpose in the life and I feel it is time for me to make my exit. I am not doing this lightly. I have given it much thoughts. To those who have loved me and who I have loved, I would like say sorry, from the bottom of my heart. Joyce, you have been a good sister to me; David, you have been honoured brother to me. I can no longer face the darkening days and have decided that I must not burden the rest of the world anymore with my declining health.

Please forgive me.

With all love,

Philip

THE WONKY USE of articles hinted at the sort of mistakes, say, a Slavonic or Asian language speaker might make. Even a Turkish speaker. 'In the life' could be a Romance language speaker's gaffe. And the tenses and the idioms weren't quite right either. How could a scholar like Carlton make such mistakes? It didn't make any sense. She read the note again. Maybe somebody else had typed the note. Or composed it. But someone who could write such high-register sentences would hardly go on to make such basic errors, would they? And there was nothing to indicate a second person with Carlton in the portacabin. Anna Crowley hadn't found anything on the site security cameras either.

Lucy pulled up the site plan and marked in all the possible entry points. There were dozens of them. She x'd the possible CCTV blind spots and sent the image on to Anna Crowley to check in the morning.

She turned back to the suicide note again.

It wasn't exactly 'Google Mistranslate' but it wasn't the work of a fluent speaker either. And it was a bit wordy for a suicide note. It was like someone had downloaded phrases from a few different suicide notes – so one particular note couldn't be traced as the original? – and doctored it badly. But that still didn't explain the errors. Maybe they were deliberate. Was that possible? It was a bit like copying a few lines of Beethoven and adding in a few bars of your favourite jig.

The length of the note was about right, though. Suicide notes tended to be around one hundred and fifty words. The general tone was par for the course, too. Apologetic and contrite.

The mess was at the micro level. That odd collocation: *honoured brother*. Sounded like something from a bargain-basement dubbing of a kung fu film.

She tapped Peter Brosnahan's phone number.

Brosnahan's heavy Cork accent came over the phone. 'Lucy, what can I do for you?'

'Forensics come back with anything new?'

'The DNA results aren't in yet. And the fingerprints on the desk, on the materials, on the note he left and on the keyboard are all Philip Carlton's. Apparently, he was very fussy about anyone touching his sacred space. It's clean as a whistle.'

'Thanks. See you in the morning in Boynebridge. Conference at nine.' Lucy knocked off the phone and went into the kitchen. Her mother was storing the plates in the cupboard. Silently. Which meant she had something to say.

'That child needs some friends.' Her mother looked straight at her.

Lucy paused a moment. 'Well, she goes to the playgroup a couple of times a week. It's holiday time.'

'And are you still bringing her to see Gerhard in Hamburg?' Her mother's tone changed to something a little harder now.

Lucy looked away. 'It's being sorted out, *Maman*. Ok?'

'Good. It will be good for Saoirse. You lost your father. She shouldn't lose hers.' Her mother closed the cupboard.

'I know. Now, I have to go out and check on Chantal.' Lucy was half-regretting that she had agreed to bring Saoirse to Hamburg at all now. It had all seemed so simple at Christmas, when she and Gerhard had spoken about it. She would leave Saoirse for a week or two with him in Hamburg. Father-daughter bonding sort of stuff. It would be a break for her, too, and Saoirse would get to see Germany and her father and have a bit of fun. Now it suddenly seemed a bit harder to deal with. The separation. The sort of thing that scared her more than death itself: being cut off from one you loved and the fear that the separation might suddenly be final. The curse that Cairo had put on the tail end of her childhood.

THE STABLE DOOR WAS BOLTED. Lucy could hear Polly, the old golden retriever, nosing about. She opened the door to the big stable where the dog slept. Polly loped over to her and nuzzled into her leg.

'Little treat, Polly.' Lucy pulled a chewstick from her pocket and watched the ancient teeth bite into it. She checked the bowl was full of water and stood up.

'Night, night, Polly.' She made her way to Chantal's stable. The three-year-old shuddered as she ran her hand along its flanks, staring at her with its big bright eyes. 'Good girl. We'll go out at the weekend. I promise. Just myself, yourself and Saoirse.'

She pulled out a couple of sugar cubes from her pocket and watched the horse nibble them. She was about to go back into the house when the phone buzzed. The voice at the other end was high end, with rounded vowels, studded with little glottal stops like a goldfish gasping for breath.

'Is that Detective O'Hara?'

'Speaking.' Lucy waited for the voice to continue.

'This is David Carlton. I believe you wanted to interview me?' The voice was less than warm. Less than lukewarm even.

'More like a brief chat.' She should watch her words now. This fellow seemed more awake than his sister. Or, at least, not as stoned.

'Sounds very sociable. You do realise we've just been bereaved?'

Lucy caught her breath. 'And I'm very sorry for your recent loss, Mr Carlton. I didn't mean any —'

'Yes, well. Poor old Philip. Very fond of the sauce, of course.' David Carlton's voice sounded almost casual.

'Well, we'll have to wait for the pathology results. I thought we might meet up in Dublin.'

'Well, let me call you tomorrow, Detective, when I've spoken with my sister, Joyce.'

'Thank you. Once again, let me say —' The phone knocked off. It was all so short, so snotty. Lucy crossed back into the house, musing on the ways of the Carlton clan.

In the Arkenses' house in the hills of North Wicklow, David Carlton left down his phone and looked across the glass coffee table at Jeremy Arkens. 'That O'Hara woman sounds a bit full of herself.'

Jeremy Arkens smiled graciously. 'Her father was a senior

diplomat, according to Superintendent McHugh. Speaks five languages, apparently.'

'Well, let's hope she's more civilised in the other four.' David Carlton popped a pretzel in his mouth and smiled.

The Arkenses' house was North Wicklow channelling Southern California. It was built on a rocky promontory thirty miles south of Dublin city and based on a 1950s design from an American catalogue. It had twin car ports underneath, and the living space commanded an unbroken view through enormous plate-glass windows of the Sugarloaf Mountain.

Jeremy Arkens topped up David Carlton's wine glass. 'So, what did she say exactly?'

David Carlton popped another pretzel in his mouth. 'Not a lot. I agreed to meet in the city for a chat.'

'A chat? How nice.' Jeremy Arkens's laugh filled the room. He was a tall, thin man in his late sixties. An attempt at casual dressing meant he looked like an overdressed tailor's dummy from the 1950s. He glanced over at his wife. She suddenly remembered she had to check the coq au vin in the new Samsung oven.

Jeremy Arkens waited until her footsteps had died away. 'You need to keep me up to speed on things.' Jeremy Arkens stared hard at David Carlton.

David Carlton frowned. 'What does that mean in plain English, Jeremy?'

'Well, I mean, this is a very sad and serious situation, David. It's very hard on yourself and Joyce. Hmmm...'

David Carlton hated that *hmmm*. It was the sort of supercilious sound Jeremy Arkens brought along with him to family gatherings. David Carlton raised the glass of wine to his lips and took a sip. Jeremy Arkens looked right through him.

'I know this O'Hara woman sets your teeth on edge, but we have to cooperate. Not least of all because of your family's good name.'

David Carlton frowned suddenly. 'You know, I still can't believe that Philip would take his own life. It seems so out of character.' David Carlton stared into his glass of wine.

'But we have to face that unpalatable fact. That note he left...' Jeremy Arkens reached over and patted the younger man's shoulder. David Carlton stiffened suddenly.

'There's something you should know.'

'Oh?' Jeremy Arkens didn't like the tone now. It betokened conversations and confabs he wasn't party too. Secrets.

David Carlton looked away as he spoke. 'That Saunders woman phoned me just after Philip's death, wherever she got my number.'

'I'm sorry?' Jeremy Arkens smiled softly.

'You know who I bloody well mean! That Saunders woman who had the child for Philip.' David Carlton's red face looked across at Jeremy Arkens.

'Ah...' Jeremy Arkens kept his ear cocked for his wife's footsteps. 'And...?'

David Carlton paused a moment. 'She said she had information for the authorities.'

'What sort of information?' Jeremy Arkens seemed puzzled.

David Carlton looked straight at him. 'Something to do with some dirty dealings in the past. I didn't think anything of it at the time.'

'And have you mentioned this to the O'Hara woman?'

David Carlton shrugged his shoulders. 'No. I mean, if Violet Saunders had information, why didn't she tell someone before Philip died? I thought I would mention it to you first.'

'Good idea. Listen, best keep it under wraps for the moment. If the papers get wind of this, they could make mischief.'

David Carlton nodded silently.

. . .

SHEILA ARKENS CALLED them in to supper as night was finally settling in around the hills and dales of North Wicklow. Jeremy Arkens watched the plump scion of the Carlton family amble towards the kitchen, and frowned. He slipped out to the annex to pick up a bottle of Rioja and switched on the shortwave radio in the corner and pulled the door after him and locked it gently.

The conversation was short and to the point. The Collector's voice was even. 'So Ms Saunders is now the fly in the ointment, so to speak. I will have to arrange an intervention before she decides to speak.'

'An intervention? How do you mean?' Jeremy Arkens spoke in a whisper.

'Our Lithuanian friend will know what to do.'

'I don't know what you mean?'

'Better that you don't. Now, good night to you. We have profited from David Carlton's chatter. Let's continue to do so.'

'Thank you, too.' Jeremy Arkens didn't quite know what he was thanking the Collector for. It was like the way passengers thanked drivers when they got off buses in Dublin. It just seemed the right thing to do somehow, strangely.

He knocked off the radio and made his way back into the kitchen, where David Carlton was already sitting at the long table, ready for the feast.

An intervention. A curious name. It sounded like something Californian families did with big boozers. He vaguely remembered having seen something like that on TV. Ambush them and read them the Riot Act. He hoped it didn't mean what he thought it meant.

And for a moment, for just one bright moment, he felt a strange nameless pity for Violet Saunders.

6

LUCY GOT TO THE CHILDMINDER'S ON THE SOUTH BEACH IN Skerries just before nine. The big white house was buzzing with the noise of small children playing. A baby was crying beneath the chatter of the toddlers and waddlers. Lucy could see a cluster of mothers in the front room and made a mental note not to get stuck in a round of baby prattle. She scanned the house as she rang the doorbell. It was a big comfortable-looking house looking out over the sea, snapped up for buttons in the middle of the recession.

There were a couple of other mothers in the back room, watching their children playing in the garden with the younger childminders. Lucy nodded at them but said nothing, having nothing much to say at that time of the morning. It was a habit she knew she had imbibed wholesale from her father.

Kitty, the owner, came over to them and stooped down. 'Hello, Saoirse! We'll be going to the beach later, by the way.'

'Great. I've packed her a lunch. My mother will pick her up around five.'

Saoirse smiled up at Kitty. '*Mémé* will be late. We all know that, don't we, *Maman*? *Mémé's* clock has twenty-five hours.'

'Right. Well, let's wait and see how she does today.' Lucy smiled and gave Saoirse a hug.

She didn't go straight to the Boynebridge station, but made a detour to the Boyne Valley instead to check the CCTV cameras again. At the entrance, she called one of the younger local garda. 'Tadhg, I'm going for a little walk around.'

She took out the iPad. The cameras were easy to locate. Easy enough for an intruder to spot and dodge, too. She walked the length of the field. The dig was partly covered over with a couple of tarpaulins. The digging equipment had all been stored away in the portacabins. The whole place felt strangely eerie without the presence of the young archaeology students. Morbid even. She walked the circuit of the field, stopping a few times to get her bearings.

She was about to get into the car when she spotted a camera fixed to a pole near the second portacabin. The camera wasn't in the layout. It seemed a pretty useless angle anyway. She slipped on a pair of plastic overshoes and called out to the young guard.

'I need to drop back into the big portacabin for a minute.'

All was as it had been, minus the presence of the late Philip Carlton, the whiskey bottle and the syringe. She crossed to the desk and checked the security camera layout on the corkboard. There was no sign of the extra camera. Why was that, now? Maybe it had just been missed by McHugh. Outside, she took a shot of the camera on its forlorn pole.

BACK AT THE station in Boynebridge, McHugh had his backside up on a desk in the incident room. He looked faintly pleased with himself.

Moyra Killanin was finishing her overview and looking over those ancient spectacles of hers. 'Professor Carlton took an overdose of insulin. The evidence seems to be clear enough.

The consequences certainly are. It can't have been an easy end, though we don't need to broadcast that fact, of course.'

McHugh grunted to himself. 'And where do you stand on all this, Detective O'Hara?' McHugh was baiting her now. Inviting her to help him shine in front of her own team.

Lucy paused a moment. 'I don't buy it, sir.'

'And what precisely do you have difficulty purchasing?' McHugh glanced around him, anticipating support, but no one moved.

Lucy paused to clear her throat. 'The whole suicide theory. The note in particular.'

McHugh waved his hand at the room. 'Forensics have shown Professor Carlton's prints on the letter, the printer, the computer, the keyboard.'

Lucy drew a deep breath. 'I mean the note itself, Superintendent. The language. The lexis, the syntax, the whole style.'

'And you've already done an analysis of this, I suppose?' McHugh gave her the side-eye. Lucy imagined he had picked that little habit up from too much TV.

'I have. But I want to run it by a senior forensic linguist for a second opinion.'

McHugh suddenly looked peeved. 'I see...'

Sullivan waded in, out of the blue. 'A forced suicide is not an impossibility, Superintendent.' Sullivan kept his eyes on McHugh, avoiding her gaze.

McHugh's eyes moved from one face to the next. 'Well, Detective Sullivan, I haven't come across one instance in my thirty years of service.'

McHugh turned back to Lucy. 'Your prelim report by this evening.'

'Yes, sir.'

McHugh was out the door before they realised it. Moyra Killanin made her excuses to them and headed off slowly, making sure not to be caught in his wake.

Lucy turned to Anna Crowley. 'There's an extra camera on the site not on our diagram. You and Dennis go down and check it out. Gerry, you and Peter can start formally interviewing the students from the site. I'll take Ms Delaney myself just in case there was something funny going on between her and the late prof. Right?'

She was about to take Sullivan to one side when he and Brosnahan disappeared. Why had Sullivan been so eager to support her against McHugh? When they were gone, she wondered for a moment: was Brosnahan privy to something she wasn't now? No: she was overthinking now.

Lucy turned back to Dennis and Anna Crowley. 'Check everything. CCTV, random witnesses, just in case. Petrol station forecourt footage, shop footage. Everything within the agreed radius.'

DEIRDRE DELANEY, the blonde student from the dig, was waiting for her in the interview room. All nail polish and eyeliner, with just the faintest shadow of a smirk on her lips.

Lucy pulled up a chair. 'This is not a formal interview, by the way.'

'Alrighty.' Deirdre Delaney leaned back in the chair sunnily.

'You were close to Professor Carlton, Deirdre?'

Deirdre Delaney gave her a thousand-yard stare now. 'We used to just chat. He was a brilliant scholar.' The voice grew a little shakier now.

Lucy tapped the table with her pen. 'I'm sure. So, what did you chat about?'

'Just this and that, you know. Look, do I need a solicitor?' The eyes narrowed.

'No. You're not being formally questioned.' Lucy smiled. Guile more than guilt. Maybe just a young woman keeping an elderly, semi-alcoholic academic company in his latter years.

But in return for what, exactly? Nobody did anything for nothing these days. Maybe they never did...

Deirdre Delaney perked up. 'Professor Carlton helped me write up my thesis.' The wide-eyed innocent smile was back.

Lucy looked straight at her. 'Does that mean he rewrote parts of it?'

'I didn't say that, Detective O'Hara. He guided me. That's all. Guided me.'

'Cool the jets now. Tell me, what sort of form was Professor Carlton in over the last few weeks?'

Lucy listened carefully now. Too many fancy Latin-French words meant it was too formal for the heart, dishonest and calculating. Stumpy little Anglo-Saxon words were always more truthful when the ire was raised: *Love, live, hate, eat, sleep, shit, fuck, die.*

And *lie...*

'He was a little down, I think. He mentioned enemies. Old ones.'

Lucy's ears pricked up. 'What sort of enemies? Can you be more specific?'

'He wouldn't say. When I tried to ask him more, he just shut up.' Deirdre Delaney's voice was softer now. Either she was being sincere or faking it well.

Lucy fixed her in her gaze. 'And did you bring up the subject again?'

'No. I thought, if he wants to take it any further, he will. By the way...' Lucy caught the change of tone. That little touch of hardness was back in the voice again now.

'Yes?'

'You're not going to make a big issue of him helping me with my thesis, are you?' The eyes opened wide.

Lucy closed the notebook in front of her slowly. 'Not my business. Look, I think we'll leave it at that, for the moment. If you need to add anything, contact me.'

The blonde head nodded.

Lucy made a note to get Anna Crowley to do a bit of digging. Never know what a random social media trawl might reveal.

LUCY TOOK the coast road home to the Black Hills. The bumpy coastal road always reminded her of the one south of Waterford, where her father's crowd came from. Her earliest memories had been down there, before all the travelling and the uprooting.

She pulled up at Bettystown, near the strand. The sun was still high in the sky and the beach was full of families. She looked north towards Boynebridge and the mouth of the Boyne and suddenly thought: Bateman happened only thirty miles inland from here.

Trevor Bateman, nutjob son of landed gentry, with several chips on his shoulders, had abducted his toddler son and hidden out in friends' houses for six months. When they finally tracked him down to a cottage down a back road, there was a standoff. Lucy was brought into the negotiation team by Reese on the basis of her qualifications and specialist training. The situation dragged on in the little cottage for three tense summer days. Days of dead heat and speculation. Days when, a dozen times, it seemed that Trevor Bateman had seen reason and was going to hand himself in.

Then, when they least expected it, when it seemed like they were on the last stretch, something suddenly soured in Trevor Bateman's voice on the phone.

He made to scarper back in from the porch with the child ('He's going for the shotgun!'). Trevor Bateman hadn't managed to reach the shotgun behind the door and do what she thought he was going to do because Lucy made a run for the house and opened fire with her pistol from the garden gate. *Central body mass... reasonable force...* the words still rang out in her memory. Not quite UK shoot-to-kill Kratos antiterrorist protocol, but the result was the same anyway.

She could still see Trevor Bateman lying on the porch, twitching in his death spasms. Hear that terrible gurgling breathing as he drowned in his own bright red blood. The shouts behind her.

'Get the child! Get the child!' She swept the little boy up in her arms, covered his eyes and ran back to the garda cordon as fast as she could, just in case a backup whacko was going to appear out of the blue with the shotgun.

Trevor Bateman died in the air ambulance before he got to hospital.

But she had saved a life the child's. Little Robert... But you can't prove a negative. A what-might-have-happened. Reese understood that much, but the poison pens and the trolls persisted in persecuting her.

She got back in the car and flicked on BBC Arabic to smother the images insinuating themselves in among her thoughts. Some old lady was rambling on about her childhood in a village in the Nile delta. She smiled at the woman's earthy tone. Suddenly, she was out the other side and Bateman had been airbrushed away again, waiting to pop up another time, like a scream heard on a dark night.

WHEN HER MOTHER retired for the night in the Black Hills, Lucy went over the suicide note again. The odd syntax. The strange vocabulary and stilted phraseology. A beeping sound in the kitchen suddenly brought her back to the world around her. Her mother had thrown in coloured items with the whites. She smiled at the new range of pink T-shirts. She unloaded the washing into the plastic basket, then went out to the yard.

In the warm semi-darkness of the stable yard, she was alone

with her thoughts again. She started hanging up the washing in the warm evening air. Suddenly it hit her: one language bleeding into another. Maybe that was it. What if Philip Carlton hadn't composed the suicide note himself? What if it had been dictated to him by someone for whom English was a second or even a third language? If not, why all those grammar mistakes, then? Had the bad English of his attacker just bled into the text he was writing because Carlton was in such a mental state? Or was there something else?

Maybe Philip Carlton was trying to hint at the fact that he had written the letter under duress.

She straightened up suddenly. That was it: someone had put together the letter for the killer, the killer had dictated it, and Philip Carlton had typed it out and studded it with the killer's own speech errors.

'I get it, Professor Carlton. I get it now.' She suddenly felt as though the dead archaeologist were talking to her from beyond the grave. Giving her a nod.

She took the phone out of her pocket and walked back in with the empty wash basket. In the sitting room she made the call. Professor Martin Schliemann of Kiel University came on the phone from the north of Germany, a smoke-choked, laughing voice.

'Lucy, nice to hear you again! How are things with you?' He sounded like he had had a few.

'All good here. I'm travelling over to Hamburg in a few days, actually.' Lucy ran her hand through her hair as she pulled her thoughts together.

'Great. So we can meet up then.' The voice was warm and welcoming. Fatherly, almost.

'Actually, I'm bringing Saoirse over to see her father. To see Gerhard.' There was a nervous little laugh in her voice. She knew that foxy old Schliemann would spot it for what it was: the pain of the past smothered in a self-conscious chuckle.

'I think that's a very good idea.' There was a pause. 'Something else on your mind?' Schliemann coughed slightly at the other end of the line.

'There is, as it happens. I have a suicide note typed up by a native English speaker. A professor found dead on an archaeological site a few days ago. The thing is, I don't believe he wrote it.'

Schliemann was all ears now. She heard a glass clink in the background. 'And what makes you think that, Dr O'Hara?'

'It's all wrong, linguistically speaking. I'd like you to look at it, if you could. Cold.' She held her breath. She needed this second opinion now, before McHugh could shoot her thesis down. Needed to feel Schliemann had her back, from a distance.

'OK. How soon do you need a comment?'

'Yesterday. I'm under pressure here.' She took a deep breath.

'I'll get back to you by midnight, latest, with a first opinion.'

Lucy breathed a soft sigh of relief.

SHE WAS WATCHING a documentary about migration from post-Communist Eastern Europe when the phone rang. Schliemann's voice was steady. 'Well... in my opinion, your text was either written by a non-native speaker, or else it's a double bluff.'

'What do you mean?' She reached for the glass of wine on the table and took a sip.

Schliemann continued slowly. 'Someone pretending they're not a native speaker. What's the exact provenance of the letter?'

'This academic was alone on an archaeological dig late at night and died of an overdose of prescribed insulin. No witnesses and no CCTV suggesting anyone else was involved. Just initial forensics, bloods and the suicide note, so far. But I think it should be ratcheted up to a murder investigation before the momentum is lost. Or evidence.'

She sat back on the sofa. Schliemann wouldn't be goaded into anything. He would take his own sweet time before making a pronouncement.

'I see where you're coming from. Won't you need more than this to prove a crime took place?' The voice was steady and clear. Behind it lay years of aid to law enforcement in a time when forensic linguistics was in its infancy.

She braced herself to ask the question now. 'So, why leave in these mistakes? He was a high-ranking academic, after all.' Lucy bit her lip.

'Maybe to show the world it was dictated to him under duress?'

She tried not to get too excited, but it was hard to hide it in her voice. 'Yes, that's what I was thinking too.' She took another sip of wine. 'Ok. Well, see you in a few weeks, or so.'

'Ring me if you need anything else. *Auf Wiederhören, Frau Doktor O'Hara!*'

Lucy knocked off the phone.

SHE MADE one last phone call before sleep. It was the hardest one – to Gerhard. She heard a woman's voice in the background. Was this the new squeeze or just a bird of passage? What did she care anyway? She took a deep breath. 'Hi, Gerhard. Listen, I want to firm up the arrangements for Saoirse's visit.'

'Sure. Look, if you want, you can stay too, Lucy, you're welcome. You know that.' The voice was smooth as silk. Gerhard didn't flap, more was the pity.

'Thanks, but I'm really tied up with a new case here. Can you still fly back to Dublin with her the week after?'

'Of course. I'm free for the summer.'

They exchanged a few more sundry pleasantries. Her voice didn't miss a beat as the conversation wound down. She made sure of that. But it wasn't because of Gerhard. That was long dead, she hoped. It was just that she would now have to steel herself for being separated from her daughter for the longest time since Saoirse's birth.

The first wound reopened again then, out of the blue. Cairo: the stopped watch, the smile on the lips, the ancient overhead fan vainly churning the scorching air. She threw back the last of the wine and stood up before memory drew her down that blind alleyway again.

Then she headed for the stairs and the sanctuary of sleep.

7

THE PHONE RANG ON THE BEDSIDE LOCKER. LUCY OPENED HER eyes groggily to the sunlight streaming into the room. She could hear Saoirse and her mother down in the kitchen chatting. She squinted at the caller ID. It was a brief call to confirm their meeting later. Did David Carlton not understand the concept of unsociable hours?

She showered, threw on her clothes and headed downstairs to breakfast with her mother and Saoirse, wondering what sort of creature she would find in David Carlton. She would read the file Reese had sent her when she got to the city.

She headed off for Dublin a short while later, into the mid-morning traffic.

The car radio was full of a shooting on the northside. Just some Darren or Wayne or Deane who had got into what the reports loved to call 'an altercation'. Nothing ever 'happened' in news reports of crime anymore. It was always 'it was alleged' and 'it was reported'. Very like a version of that strange Turkish tense she had once studied in linguistics: the past dubitative.

Dublin had its own perma-underclass now, like most cities. The Northern row had died down and only raised its head occasionally. And even then, it often had a criminal element. But the heroin and the cocaine and the crack circuses were here forever. Like a boil on the ass – you couldn't sit on it, and you couldn't ignore it either.

The radio cut in on her thoughts again. 'First reports say that the shooting involved a local drug debt...' Moyra Killanin would be there in all her forensic finery. It would be an open-and-shut case, standard-issue slaughter. Not even sad anymore, just pathetic.

The phone rang as Lucy exited the port tunnel. 'Anna here. That camera at the dig was set up last summer when the new Boyne site was first discovered.'

'Why there? Isn't it a very odd place?' Lucy glanced in the mirror at the traffic behind her.

'Wide-angle camera for general site security. The porta-cabins weren't there then.'

Lucy overtook the car in front of her and swung back into lane. 'Could it still be running, do you think?'

'That's what we're checking. By the way, Peter is talking to the hotel staff, and Dennis is with the security men. Superin-tendent McHugh has given us a few uniforms to do other bits and pieces.'

Lucy felt the rush of air as an articulated truck overtook her. 'Good. Nothing about an official incident room yet?'

Anna's voice dropped a little. 'No. But we've just found out that your Deirdre Delaney was with Professor Carlton the evening he died.'

Lucy's eyes opened wide. 'What? She didn't mention that to me, now, the little wagon.'

'It's all on CCTV, when she arrives and leaves.'

'I'll soften her cough for her. OK. Send me on the CCTV clip. Talk later.' Lucy knocked off the phone.

· · ·

David Carlton and his husband were staying at the Merrion just behind government buildings. Lucy found a parking space in Merrion Square and checked her file again. David Carlton had been living in the South of France for the last five years. He was involved in some sort of antique sourcing business in France. He had shares in a few Irish and British companies. Nothing out of the ordinary.

She waited in the lobby until David Carlton appeared. Lucy ran her eyes over him. Late fifties and a little gone to flesh. David Carlton hadn't missed too many meals.

'Let's go up to my room. My husband, Michel, is there, by the way. Is that a problem?' David Carlton took her by the arm graciously.

Lucy stopped a moment. 'Why would that be a problem, Mr Carlton?'

'For some people it would be, you know. My sister, for example. Would you like something sent up – tea, coffee or something stronger?'

'Tea is fine.'

Michel was standing in the middle of the room when they arrived in. Lucy noted the Mediterranean complexion and the take-me-as-you-find-me attitude.

Michel bowed in Lucy's direction. 'I will go down to the garden and give you two some space. Ok?'

'Thank you.' The door closed gently behind Michel.

David Carlton sat down on the sofa. 'Now, Detective O'Hara... what do you need to know?'

Lucy took out a notebook and left it down on the coffee table in front of her. She moved the vase of flowers aside and left her phone in its place. That was the foreplay over and done with. 'Tell me about your brother. Did he have any particular worries? Or enemies?'

'We all have worries. It's the human condition, isn't it, after all? But enemies? An archaeologist digging up four-thousand-year-old graves? I hardly think so.' David Carlton smiled pleasantly.

Lucy opened the notebook. 'I heard rumours of possible threats.'

David Carlton frowned. 'From whom, pray tell? This is all news to me.'

'Like I say, just rumours.' Lucy flicked to another page in the notebook, watching David Carlton's eyes following hers. 'So, how was your relationship with Philip in general, then?'

David Carlton reached for a serviette on the coffee table and wiped his lips. 'We didn't really have one. Philip was more like a fussy father than a real brother. And, of course, Mam and Dad died a long time ago.'

Mam and Dad. Lucy smiled.

There was a knock on the door. Room service arrived with coffee and tea on a little trolley. David Carlton poured elegantly and bit into a fancy biscuit. 'I wish I could tell you more, Detective. I really do.'

'I understand. By the way, you and your sister, Joyce, are the beneficiaries of Philip's estate. Do I have that right?' Lucy took a sip of tea and watched for any reaction.

'Yes. Philip's late ex-wife she died a few years ago and signed away her claim, and they had no children. I'm financially independent. Few more shekels wouldn't go astray, of course.'

'I'm sure.'

There was a little toing and froing after that, but Lucy couldn't get any purchase on anything David Carlton said. She decided to get to the point. Bluntly, for effect.

'Why do you think your brother took his own life, Mr Carlton?'

The biscuit chewing suddenly stopped now. David Carlton seemed momentarily thrown. He looked away from her. 'He was ill, I suppose. Maybe he was depressed.'

'Yes, I suppose that's possible.' Lucy watched the eyes carefully.

David Carlton left down his coffee cup and looked straight at Lucy now. 'And you? What do you think?' There was that suave tone slipping back into the voice again. The smarm of an upscale rug merchant.

Lucy shifted uneasily. 'I haven't come to any final conclusion yet.'

David Carlton was suddenly awake now. 'Which means you don't really accept what they're saying on the radio, then?'

Lucy spoke again, slowly and carefully. 'It may well have been an accidental overdose. Especially if your brother had been drinking and was confused.'

'Confused? Really, most of the human race, myself included, are constantly confused and we don't, willy-nilly, consider checking out.'

David Carlton suddenly excused himself to go to the bathroom. She heard the tap running as he splashed his face. Was he crying? She wasn't sure. The Carltons wouldn't do public sniffling, anyway.

Lucy crossed over slowly to the window and looked down into the garden. Michel was standing over by a pergola, smoking a cigarette without a care in the world.

When David Carlton came back into the room, Lucy gave him her contact card. He glanced at it and looked back at her. His voice was softer now. There was a strange sincerity in it too. The smarm had slipped away like spring snow: he had been crying. 'Do you think someone could have killed my brother, Detective O'Hara?'

Lucy didn't flinch. 'Do you, Mr Carlton?'

David Carlton's eyes narrowed. 'I know you have suspicions. Those questions you asked me about enemies aren't exactly random queries, are they? You're following a line of enquiry that's not in the papers.'

Lucy winced. 'Maybe. Look, let's just call it a day, for the moment.'

Lucy took up her phone and bag, and David Carlton saw her to the door silently. When it closed behind her, she lingered a moment. Through the door, she heard David Carlton speak on the phone, and cocked her ear to listen.

His voice was high and edgy. She strained to hear. 'Jeremy? David here. This detective woman seems to think that someone might have killed Philip. Tell me that's not possible!'

There were footsteps behind her. Lucy turned around to see Michel approaching her with a soft, syrupy smile on his lips.

'Goodbye, Detective O'Hara.'

Lucy smiled and made her way to the lift, feeling the eyes on her back all the way.

IN THE CAR, she called Anna Crowley. 'What time was Deirdre Delaney with Carlton?'

'After work till about eight.'

Lucy's voice jumped up a notch. 'Is Gerry Sullivan there?'

Sullivan came on the phone.

'Gerry, I need a check on Deirdre Delaney's bank account to see if there's anything of interest.'

'That isn't legal, strictly speaking.'

Lucy snapped at him, 'Neither is concealing evidence in a potential murder inquiry, strictly speaking.'

'Did you say potential murder enquiry?' Sullivan's voice was all soft now.

'You heard me.' Lucy knocked off the phone and waited quietly for Sullivan to phone her back.

8

LUCY KILLED AN HOUR WALKING AROUND DUBLIN CITY CENTRE, ON the south side.

The north side was just too grim these days. The streets along the red tram line were strewn with the homeless, the drug-addled, psychiatric cases with no beds or care, and a new addition: East European street-dwellers, scarpering out of the UK before the Brexit axe fell and their welfare payments vapourised. You could spot them in the crowds from a hundred metres against the wind. Pairs of hard-looking men, covering one another's backs, like soldiers on foot patrol, scouring the streets for food, money and chemical comfort.

Lucy picked up a paper and went into a coffee shop off Grafton Street. She scanned the suicide note on the iPad again. It still stank.

Her phone buzzed. It was Sullivan. 'Your Ms Delaney has been getting regular infusions of moolah into her account over the past year.'

'So what's your best guess?' She drew a couple of overlapping circles in the notebook. A little Venn diagram with Deirdre Delaney at the centre.

Sullivan gave a chuckle. 'Well, who am I to cast asparagus, but maybe the good professor was paying for services rendered.'

Lucy took a deep breath. 'Well, he wasn't in great physical condition. Every rooster has to stop crowing some time.' Lucy shaded in the overlap between two circles in the notebook.

'Paying for her company, then. Old men like that type of thing.'

'Do they, indeed, Detective Sullivan?'

Sullivan sounded a little too chipper. 'Sure. Old women have their children and grandchildren for company before they die.'

'I'll try to remember that when I'm old and grey.' Lucy knocked off the phone and dug out the young woman's number.

DEIRDRE DELANEY SOUNDED VERY subdued when Lucy phoned. 'Deirdre, new information has come to light, and I need a little clarification.'

'I don't understand?' There was an edge in her voice. Lucy could hear her going into another room and the door closing.

'I believe you were with Professor Carlton the night before he died.' She mustn't feed her lines. Let her wriggle a little.

There was silence at the other end for a moment. 'I must have forgotten.'

'Don't worry. It's all on CCTV.' Lucy saw the blonde hair in her mind now. The tearful face at the dig, crying in public.

'We were just talking, Detective. That's all.'

Lucy spoke super softly now. 'And the money going into your account every month?'

'What? You have no right to search my accounts!' The voice was suddenly hissy-fit-Valley-girl with a bit of bog thrown in.

'You have two choices, pet. We can meet today and clarify things. Or...' Lucy didn't need to finish the sentence.

Deirdre Delaney's voice sounded panicky now. 'Kilkenny. There's this pub I sometimes go to there... the Clarion, up near the castle.'

'Fine. Say an hour and a half? Now, you be straight with me and nobody else will have to get involved. Right?' Lucy slipped the phone back into her bag and made her way out onto the street.

KILKENNY WAS awash with tourists from more sensible economies, all dressed practically for the undependable weather. Lucy made her way through the throng up the parade, past the food stalls and the pot-bellied castle towers. Deirdre Delaney was sitting in the back of the Clarion, sipping an over-priced orange juice. It was mid-afternoon and the lunch crowd had gone.

Lucy pulled up her chair and leaned across the table. 'Ok. Tell me about the money.'

Deirdre Delaney glanced about her. 'Professor Carlton helped me out. That's all.'

'But how did you help him out? That's the real question, isn't it?' Lucy angled her head slightly and smiled sweetly.

There was a little sniffle. 'I kept him company. There was nothing physical involved.'

Lucy glanced down at her notebook and watched Deirdre Delaney's eyes tracking her nervously. 'All sounds very Florence Nightingale to me.'

The younger woman threw her head back suddenly. 'Would you like to check my knickers for DNA, Detective O'Hara?'

Lucy smiled at the raised snout. 'I could have the Criminal Assets Bureau check them for you. They're always keen to investigate mystery money. Especially money connected with a sudden death. Would you like that?'

The bullshit threat worked. The almond eyes widened suddenly and a sniffle came into the voice. 'Myself and Professor Carlton just got on well together.'

Lucy smiled. 'And he paid you? How sweet.'

'Why do you have to be such a... bitch?' Deirdre Delaney was crying now. *Good call, Lucy. Keep her sniffling.*

'I just hope you're telling me the truth, Deirdre, for your own sake. Now...' Lucy glanced at her watch. It was time to get back on the road.

'What?' Deirdre Delaney's voice was a lot calmer now.

'Anything else you can tell me about those threats you mentioned before?' Lucy waited and watched. The almond eyes looked uneasy now.

'Professor Carlton told me about this online forum where he posted stuff.'

'What sort of stuff? What sort of forum?' Lucy took up her notebook and flipped to the page with the Venn diagram.

Deirdre Delaney ran her finger along the table as she spoke. 'It was a forum for scholars and collectors. He posted stuff about wrongdoing in the past.'

'What sort of wrongdoing?' Lucy took a sip of her Coke and watched the body language. This was real, alright.

'He wouldn't say. But he seemed to be worried about it. Really worried.'

'OK. I'll have that checked out.' Lucy let her voice transpose slowly into a kinder key. She closed the notebook. 'So, tell me, when do you submit your thesis?'

The eyes were wary again. 'End of summer. I'm tidying it up now.'

'OK, so let's leave it at that for the moment.'

Deirdre Delaney took up her shoulder bag and stood up slowly. Lucy watched her walk off through the crowd, then phoned Anna Crowley again. 'There's this online forum Carlton used. He may have crossed someone on it. Dig it out from Carlton's computer records.'

'Got it.'

Lucy threw back her Coke and headed back out into the tourist traffic. She picked up the car on John Street and headed back towards Dublin. She reached the outskirts of Dublin just in time to get snarled up in the M50 teatime traffic north.

She spent the rest of the evening with Saoirse, watching a Disney movie about princesses and flying carpets.

'I think I'm getting too old for princesses, *Maman*.' Saoirse turned away from the TV screen, knocked off the movie and passed her mother the silver-backed hairbrush with the rabbit motif.

'Why do you say that?' Lucy smiled at the frowning little face. Lucy took the brush to start doing her hair before bed.

'The stories are too simple for me now.'

'Oh, really? You've suddenly got very sophisticated, have you?'

The little face broke into a smile. 'Anyway, most of those princesses are pretty stupid. Even *Mémé* is smarter than them.'

'Watch out, young lady. That's my mother you're talking about!'

Saoirse looked at her through the tangles of blonde hair. 'Well, my mother is smarter than your mother. *Ça va sans dire. Vale?*'

Lucy looked into the blue eyes, then pinched her nose. 'Well, what can I say? No point in rejecting praise, even if it is wrapped in an insult.' She grabbed Saoirse and held her tight and they started roaring laughing together.

THE LAST MOVEMENT of the Pastoral always stirred something in him. A certain sense of peace after the storm. Of a deeper peace, more ethereal peace. Which, of course, was what it was meant to do, after all.

It was late afternoon when the Collector set off for the woods. The sun would still be out till nine or ten. He finished cleaning the .22 and placed the cleaning rod and the cloths back into the box. No need for a heavier rifle, like a 22.250 or a .230. Blow a rabbit to kingdom come with it. It wasn't as if he was shooting deer or even foxes. Rabbits, pigeon and rodents were enough. Foxes got a free pass, of course. He couldn't stand shotguns, though. Uncouth. And, anyway, you could hear them at a great distance, even in the wilds of West Cork, not like the short, whiplash sound of a .22 round.

He took the right path, heading for the ancient woodlands, crossing the dry bed of the stream, and walked on towards the old mine. A sound made him stop all of a sudden. He raised the rifle to his shoulder. Mustn't be too hasty. A bullet could hit a branch or twig en route and deflect it. You had to be very careful, especially with a telescopic sight. When you long-focused, you could easily hit things in the middle distance. Maybe there was a moral in that. Never ignore the middle distance. Those things that come between you and the target. A clean, clever shot was what was needed.

Crack! The .22 spat once.

There was a flutter of wings and the pigeon fell to the forest floor. He would try to take another one before he went home. That would do nicely in a casserole. The Irish were too grand to eat pigeon now, of course. But the French. Well, the French would eat anything that moved. And some things that didn't, as well. The French – didn't Arkens tell him that the O'Hara detective woman had a French mother? Maybe that accounted for her feistiness.

He had just reached the firebreak when the phone buzzed. Once. Then twice. That would be Arkens.

He took his time getting back to the house. Arkens could

wait. The man was getting a little jumpier every day. Not a good thing. Not a good thing at all. Half an hour later, he made his way down to the bunker. In the side room, the shortwave radio blinked into life.

He put on the headphones, listened carefully, then responded slowly, 'Yes, Mr Arkens. I do see.'

Jeremy Arkens sounded more nervous than usual. 'This O'Hara woman seems to have her suspicions, according to David Carlton anyway. And now he's getting suspicious himself.'

The Collector spoke softly, trying to calm the listener down. 'And does this detective woman really believe Professor Carlton's death may not have been suicide?'

'I'm sure of it. David Carlton was clear about it. He felt she might be holding back some special information or evidence, like this Violet Saunders. One thing is for sure, her nose is up. And so is David Carlton's.'

The Collector was silent for a moment, considering things. 'Well, that puts a new complexion on things. Now, listen carefully to what I have to say.'

'I'm listening.' Jeremy Arkens sounded relieved.

'First of all, keep David Carlton onside. We need to know which way the wind is blowing, at all times. As for our Lithuanian friend...'

'Yes?' Jeremy Arkens's high-pitched voice sounded higher than normal now.

The Collector's words were soothing. Gentle, almost. 'I might have to have a word with him about Detective O'Hara too. But first things first.'

Jeremy Arkens sounded puzzled. 'I don't understand?'

'Ms Violet Saunders... I'll put the Lithuanian on notice.'

· · ·

WHEN HE HAD FINISHED, the Collector switched off the receiver and stood up slowly. For the first time in a long time, he didn't stop to gaze at the Genesis of St Fergal. Instead he continued up the stairs to the sitting room to think in silence.

About what he knew and what he didn't know. But, most of all, about the spaces in between.

The middle distance...

9

THE SALLOW-SKINNED SECURITY MAN WITH THE CREW CUT leaned forward to look at the picture Peter Brosnahan had shoved in front of him. 'OK, Pavel, let's go over it again. You finished at what time?'

'I am finish my shift at six, like every day, sir.'

Brosnahan's voice was friendly but authoritative, like someone calming a nervous puppy. Or someone who could drop-kick you through a plate-glass window if he took the notion. 'Anything else strange happen that week?'

Pavel frowned. 'Just the woman that visit in afternoon. Then big fight with professor in portacabin.'

'And could you understand anything, Pavel?'

The middle-aged Polish man threw his hands up again. 'Only when she say there's gonna be trouble. Big trouble.'

Brosnahan leaned closer to him and dropped his voice. 'But she didn't say what sort of trouble?'

The other man shrugged his shoulders. 'I don't hear it. I'm busy with student fall in dig. Taxi bring him in hospital.'

Brosnahan pushed a photo of Deirdre Delaney across the

table. 'And you never saw this young student, Deirdre Delaney, the blonde girl, with him?'

'Never I am see her with him. Maybe night-time and I not there. This other woman, she was different woman. More older than this one. More bigger, too.'

Brosnahan pushed another print across the table. 'And you're sure this is the car the woman was in?'

The other man squinted at the picture. 'Very sure.'

Brosnahan tapped the photo with his index finger. 'We have no number on the CCTV. Do you have any idea of the number?'

'No. Red Golf is all what I remember.'

Brosnahan gathered up the photos and slipped them back in the folder. 'And the woman? What did she look like?'

'Red jacket. She is maybe forty or fifty. Not fat, not thin. With black handbag. No more I remember.'

Brosnahan smiled and stood up. 'Good. Well, thank you, Pavel. You've been a big help.'

'No bother, sir.'

Brosnahan smiled at the localism. Lucy would love that. Add it to her collection.

BROSNAHAN CAME STRAIGHT OVER to Lucy in the incident room, carrying his interview notes. He left them down on the desk in front of her.

She looked up at him. 'Anything new?'

Brosnahan shrugged his shoulders. 'He told me the woman he saw drove a VW Golf. No reg, unfortunately. He didn't give much of a description of the woman either.'

Lucy stood up slowly. 'OK. Listen, I need to take a trip to the dig. I want you to come with me.'

She walked down to the back desks, to the two uniformed garda working the phones. She spoke to the younger man. 'All peripheral witnesses sorted and sifted?'

'We're putting the statements together and cross-checking with the analysis software.'

Lucy nodded at him. 'Good. Let me know when you've got the file ready.'

She called up to Anna, 'We'll be about an hour or so, Anna.'

BROSNAHAN DROVE, his eyes scanning 360 as he drove along. This was army training, Lucy knew situational awareness. It was a hard habit to kill. She was always slightly amused by the ex-army men she met on the force. They all seemed to retain a slight snootiness towards their garda colleagues like they were part of a real world the men in navy blue would never know. It had its uses too, she knew. It made Brosnahan less clubbable. Less vulnerable to the likes of McHugh. He could tell them all quietly where to go, and the army would take him back in a heartbeat.

Off the main road, the weekend traffic suddenly thinned out as the car nosed southwards for the bend in the Boyne. They pulled in just before the gate and walked back up the road to the far end of the third portacabin. There was a broad view of the Boyne from there.

Lucy turned to Brosnahan. 'OK. You were an army Ranger once. Give me a dig out here.'

Brosnahan turned to her slowly and smiled. 'Few years ago now.'

Lucy pointed to the sweep of the river below them. 'Say you're a mean hombre coming here to kill someone. It's after midnight. Which way would you come?'

Brosnahan scanned the panorama stealthily, from right to left. He turned back to her. 'I'd approach from the river. But not near here.'

'Why not?' Lucy glanced around at the patchwork of fields.

Brosnahan pointed over to his left. 'There are houses on the far side and a farmhouse this side. It's just too exposed.'

'A boat, then?' Lucy nodded down towards the river.

'That's over the top and asking for complications. No, I'd cross further back, then walk along the bank. No farmhouses down there.' Brosnahan nodded his head towards the river as if to confirm his own words to himself.

Lucy took out the map in the plastic folder. She ran her finger over the surface. 'We're here, Peter. So, where exactly?'

'The interpretative centre, maybe. I think there's a bridge up there.' Brosnahan pointed to a location on the map.

Lucy took out her phone and called Anna Crowley. She could hear McHugh in the background barking orders.

'Anna, check the security footage from the interpretative centre, especially at the bridge, and any of the other cameras nearby.'

Anna Crowley's voice dropped a couple of notches. 'Actually, I was just about to ring you, Lucy. We've tracked down the CCTV company, and the line from that odd CCTV camera is still active. They think they may have some footage.'

'Excellent. Stay on it.'

They walked slowly back towards the car. Brosnahan suddenly stopped. 'But he wouldn't have left here on foot. That would be pushing it.'

Lucy turned to Brosnahan. 'OK. So what then?'

Brosnahan opened the car door slowly. 'Somebody must have picked him up on a back road.'

'Maybe. Let's get back to base.' Lucy sat into the car beside him and started scanning the map again. The car pulled out onto the road for Boynebridge.

.   .   .

MᴄHᴜɢʜ ᴡᴀꜱ ᴅᴏᴡɴ with the uniforms, sitting on the edge of a desk, when they arrived back; but he hardly registered her presence. Lucy crossed over to Anna. 'Show me.'

Anna Crowley swung the screen about. The image was from a reflective surface – a window. Lucy kept an eye on McHugh over her shoulder. Anna's fingers tapped the screen. The image of a man in a jacket with a cap pulled down over his face appeared in the window of the portacabin as a reflection.

Lucy nodded at her. 'Freeze it, frame it and get it enhanced, then send it to me. Time?'

'The readout says 1.15 a.m. on the morning Philip Carlton was found.'

Lucy scanned the image on the screen again. 'No one pays social calls at 1.15 a.m. Good work.'

Lᴜᴄʏ ꜱʟɪᴘᴘᴇᴅ ᴅᴏᴡɴ to the canteen and called the childminder. She would pick Saoirse up around four and take the boat out and get a break from it all. Her phone beeped.

She opened the link. The image was a lot clearer now. The man in the video clip was wearing a peaked cap with a little badge on it and a light summer jacket. There was something military in the bearing, she thought now. That was worth noting.

Could this be the one who had dictated the suicide note to Philip Carlton? He looked professional, alright. Not the sort of half-megabyte dork they used to settle cocaine overdrafts in Dublin, anyway.

Lucy walked slowly back up the stairs. She could hear McHugh talking with Sullivan just inside the door. She opened the door slowly. Both men turned towards her at the same time.

She nodded over at Anna and stretched out her hand. 'Do you have that print?'

Lucy passed the print to McHugh. 'This is an image from a

camera near Philip Carlton's portacabin at 1.15 on the morning Carlton died. It's just in.'

McHugh's eyes narrowed. He scrutinised the image carefully. 'And you're saying what exactly, Detective O'Hara?' McHugh had that tone in his voice.

Lucy kept her eyes on the photo. 'I think the suicide note may be connected to this man, sir.'

McHugh looked up at Lucy. His voice suddenly seemed less sure now. The smartass tone was gone. 'So, why no fingerprints? Why no DNA?'

Lucy smiled politely. 'Yet...'

Gerry Sullivan was standing downstream of McHugh. 'With all due respect, Superintendent McHugh...'

McHugh looked over at Sullivan curiously. 'Yes, Detective Sullivan?'

Sullivan studiously avoided Lucy's gaze. 'This may be adding up to something more complex. It's early days yet, of course.' The little genuflection in the voice tickled Lucy.

McHugh glanced around him. 'I don't know... it's possible, I suppose.'

Lucy glanced over at Sullivan, but he still avoided her gaze. Why was he sticking his neck out? He must believe what he was saying. Or suspect more than he was saying.

McHugh checked his watch. 'OK. Might be worth checking out. You can keep me posted on it. Now, I have a meeting with Superintendent Reese in Harcourt Square.'

McHugh strode out of the room.

Anna Crowley was suddenly at Lucy's side. She glanced back at the uniformed guards to make sure they were out of earshot. 'There's something else I've managed to dig up. I didn't want to overdo it with Superintendent McHugh here and box him into a corner.'

'Right. Let's see what you've got.'

Lucy followed Anna back to the computer. Anna passed her

a set of headphones. 'It's the cloud backup from the voice app on Carlton's phone. There's just a few seconds. Listen...'

A voice came over the headphones. A thin, reedy, hard voice. Lucy moved closer to the computer. Then she started smiling. 'This is gold. Solid twenty-four-karat gold! First picture, now sound...'

10

ANNA CROWLEY CLICKED THE MOUSE AND THE AUDIO FILE KICKED in again. There were a couple of indistinct grunts, then a heavily accented voice spoke. 'Good evening. Professor Carlton...' The audio was clear, too. Except for the muffled bit at the beginning, it was very clear.

'Play it back one more time.' Lucy closed her eyes and cocked her head to one side. This was English as a second or even third language, laid over a Slavonic or Baltic language, by the general accent.

But she thought she heard something else when she listened again, was that really possible? A hint of Cockney?

She decided to keep it simple for the moment and stick with what she felt sure of.

She looked at Anna. 'OK. Get a copy timestamped and scrubbed up. The original is forensic evidence now. And send me a copy.'

She made a mental note to send the audio file on to Schliemann for a second opinion. Schliemann's ears would reveal a lot.

Sullivan came over to them. He looked like he had something on his mind. He glanced between the two of them. 'Like to head out for lunch?'

'This on your tab, Detective Sullivan?'

Sullivan smiled sleekly. '*Mais oui, madame.*'

Lucy winced. 'On your tab be it, then. And drop the dodgy French accent. *D'accord?*'

THE ROSEMARY WAS CROWDED with tourists and locals noshing at the cut-price carvery. They found a quiet corner over by a window. Sullivan stood up slowly. 'Drink?'

'Just a Coke. No ice.' Sullivan returned with a Coke and a whiskey for himself.

Lucy nodded at the glass. 'This the Harcourt Square lunchtime tipple, then?'

'A whiskey at midday helps me think.' Sullivan smiled at her. Then he opened his phone to show an image of a red VW Golf with a clear registration.

Lucy looked closely at the photo. 'Let me guess, that's the car the woman who visited Carlton was driving?'

'Young Dennis tracked it down, but we have no idea where it is at the moment. It's a rental from Dublin airport. The woman's name is Violet Saunders.'

The waitress appeared. They ordered and watched her melt back into the mob.

Lucy turned back to Sullivan. 'So, what do we know about this Violet Saunders?'

'Not much, really. She's a British passport holder, but Irish. She lives in London and has one adult child. A daughter.' Sullivan took out a couple of printed photos from an envelope.

'Any record in Britland?' Lucy ran her eye over the photos. Woman in her fifties. Smart looking, wearing glasses and a

choker with a little charm on it. She looked a little like a Pres-
byterian minister's daughter on day release. From the nine-
teenth century.

'Brits have got nothing on her. Maybe we should do a
deeper dig on Ms Saunders.'

'That's my feeling too.' Lucy nodded.

'When all is said and done, she was one of the last people to
phone Philip Carlton before he died. There were three phone
calls made to his phone that night. Your Deirdre Delaney and a
second call before midnight. That was this Violet Saunders.
And a mysterious phone call – possibly our man on the CCTV,
maybe making sure Carlton was still in the portacabin.'

Lucy took up the photos and scanned them again. 'So, you
think that her ladyship here may be involved in some way?'

'Might be.'

Lucy turned to Sullivan and looked straight at him. 'Tell me
something, Gerry, why are you really up here? Who wound you
up and set you off?'

Sullivan pursed his lips. But there was no smile now, just a
little frown that told her she wasn't going to hear anything she
didn't already know.

'I told you. I'm here to assist in...'

'Yes, I know. Second-level case management, analysis of
evidence and statements, special tasking. Is that your best and
final offer?'

Sullivan looked for a moment like he was going to say
something. Then he seemed to think better of it. 'I can't go
beyond my brief.'

'Which is?'

'Second-level...'

Lucy eyed the approaching waitress and lowered her voice.
'Case management, etc. I know. Have to go back to Reese,
will I?'

Sullivan half-shrugged his shoulders. 'Come on. Let's eat.'

The waitress arrived with the tray. Sullivan smiled and took a sip of his Black Bush. Lucy turned to her food, wondering once more about what the man beside her was really up to. And when she would be let in on the game.

11

IT WAS JUST BEFORE MIDNIGHT. THE STARLIT COUNTRY ROAD WAS deserted save for the odd soul trying to avoid the breathalyser on the main roads.

Lukas Petraskas felt uncomfortable, hunched down in the back of the Skoda. He sat up from time to time to get his bearings, but mostly he stayed low. It was the wisest thing to do, he knew. Two men tailgating a woman's car would have been spotted and noted. He kept an eye on the GPS map on the phone as they passed the Louth border into Meath.

Pity it had come to this. Tracking the woman's car and phone should have been enough. But when he monitored the phone calls to her daughter and realised that she was thinking of talking, just like the stupid professor, what could they do? He had reported the conversations back to Arkens, the middleman, and the old man at the end of the line had made his decision, wherever he was.

He sat up in the back seat for a moment. 'Where she is going now?' Lukas's voice was hoarse. His shoulder was cramping from lying down.

Adam Bielski glanced around him to look at Lukas. 'Back to B and B, maybe.'

'You're sure is right woman?' Lukas's voice was testy now. This was all getting a bit messy. Why did she have to open her big mouth? And the daughter was involved, too. How much did *she* know? He put the question out of his mind and tried to concentrate on the job in hand.

The young Polish driver nodded. 'Same car she get from airport when we follow first time.'

The Skoda swung right onto a narrow road. The woman in the Golf was probably following a GPS herself, Lukas realised. Taking a route back to the B and B that avoided the main roads. Lukas looked at the GPS map again. Soon the woman would be back on the main road.

'Next crossroads. You drive front her and stop. OK?' He felt the car accelerate on the quiet country road.

'There she is. Now!'

There was a screech of brakes as the Skoda slewed across the road, blocking the other car. Lukas Petraskas threw open the car door, grabbed the backpack and sprinted back to the Golf. He ignored the startled eyes of the woman at the wheel. Her hand was over her mouth now. She glanced over her shoulder and tried to put the car into reverse. Lukas pulled the back door open and jumped in.

'Drive and I will not do nothing.' Lukas's voice was suddenly soft. It was a voice he used for debt collecting on the East coast of Spain.

'Please don't hurt me.'

'You do what I say, I do nothing.' He crouched down in the back seat to hide himself. The Golf pulled out and passed the Skoda, easing its way along by the ditch.

Lukas glanced at the map. 'Now, right. Next right.'

The woman glanced in the mirror but couldn't see the author of the voice. Lukas shouted at her, 'Now, right this time.

Now!' He felt the car sway as it turned down a small boreen off the main road. The woman's pathetic voice started up again.

'What do you want from me? Please...' The woman glanced in the mirror, but she couldn't see his face. Lukas banged the driver's seat with his fist. 'Now, you stop here.'

The woman pulled the car in to the left and the car jerked to a halt. Lukas ran his hand over the backpack.

They were in the middle of nowhere. In the rear-view mirror, Lukas could see the woman weighing up the odds. Maybe she was thinking of making a run for it across the fields. Or beating him off until she reached the main road again.

'Close the engine now.'

The woman turned the engine off.

'Give me key!'

She pulled the key out of the ignition and passed it back to the man crouching down behind her seat.

'Please don't hurt me!' The woman's voice sounded pathetic and weak now. He saw her looking in the mirror. The eyes were full of fear.

Good...

12

Lukas Petraskas took a deep breath and shouted at the woman again. 'Handbag!'

The woman's hand was shaking. She reached down to the floor and passed the handbag to the man in the back seat. He made a big show of going through the handbag, opening the purse and counting the money out loud.

Lukas stared at the woman. 'This all money?'

The woman's whole body was shaking now. 'And my cards. You can take the cards too.' The woman put her hand to her mouth nervously and stammered, 'I won't tell the police. It's only money.'

Lukas looked into the mirror. He made a big show of checking her cards, too. Then he took a quick look at the passport and threw it to one side as if he wasn't interested. It was her, alright. He was sure of it.

He nodded at the woman and passed her the key. 'OK. Turn on engine now.'

The woman turned on the engine. He knew he had convinced her that everything would be alright now.

Lukas followed the woman's eyes in the mirror. She was staring straight ahead through the windscreen. Praying maybe. Then Lukas Petraskas moved, when she least expected it.

Moved with the speed of a striking snake. Spetznatz style.

He whipped the cord from his sleeve, reached forward, slipped it around the woman's neck and pulled it taut. There was a high, squealing sound, like an animal being garrotted. The woman's foot stabbed at the accelerator for a moment, then jerked to one side. The clutch roared and the car jumped forward. She was fighting to get her fingers under the cord now. But it was no use. Lukas's sinewy hands were much stronger than hers. He felt the woman spasm in her death throes for a few moments, almost like an orgasm, he thought.

He released the cord for a moment, then tightened it again.

It was over now.

Lukas Petraskas leaned forward and turned off the engine and then the lights. Then he started to unpack the backpack. He left everything out on the back seat carefully. The plastic petrol container, the explosives, the detonator and the sugar. He set the timer for six minutes. Time enough to get across the fields. He connected up the detonator to the explosives carefully. He set the timer and checked the circuit with the bulb.

He was out the door and into the nearby field in a flash. He could see the Polish guy's car on the GPS. There were just two more fields to cross. He arrived at the crossroads breathless, jumped into the back seat, crouched down and shouted at Adam Bielski, 'Go! Go!'

They had just reached the corner when the car went up with a terrifying roar. Lukas could see the flames across the fields to his left.

Adam Bielski turned to him sharply. 'What you put in that, Lukas?'

'All what I need. No fingerprints, no nothing.' Lukas

Petraskas turned back to the GPS map to guide them through the back roads, southwards towards the city of Dublin.

And the body of the late Violet Saunders began to turn to carbonized bone on the back roads of County Meath.

13

LUCY WATCHED SAOIRSE THROUGH THE KITCHEN WINDOW, playing with the dog beside the old horse trough. Another few days and she would be leaving her over to Gerhard in Hamburg. The hard lesson of leave-taking: as soon as we meet, we begin to part. But that was life. Mothers, children, partners. Yourself, even. Hardly get to know yourself and you're gone.

The radio news broke in on her thoughts.

Reports are coming in of the body of a woman found in a burnt-out car, outside the Naul, near the Meath-Dublin border. First reports indicate...

The phone rang and she put it on speaker. Brosnahan's broad tones filled the kitchen. 'Lucy. Peter here. Have you heard the news?'

'The woman's body in the Naul, you mean?' Lucy wiped her hands on the tea towel and threw it to one side.

'We think it's Violet Saunders. The woman who visited Carlton. Same car.'

Lucy knocked off the radio. 'Where are you now, Peter?'

'Boynebridge.'

'I'm going to head down to the Naul now. Meet me there.'

Lucy tapped the window and made a sign for Saoirse to get her jacket. She slipped upstairs, strapped on her shoulder holster and jacket, and glanced at herself in the mirror for a moment. She touched up her lips with a little balm and took a deep breath. A dead woman in a burnt-out car. Someone was playing hardball now. No doubt about it.

Ten minutes later, they were out on the road to Rush, just down the coast. Her mother was waiting for them at the door of the bungalow. Lucy gave Saoirse a hug. 'She's had her breakfast. I'll phone you as soon as I get a chance.'

Lucy's mother smiled at Saoirse. 'Come on, *ma fifille.*'

Lucy waited until the door closed behind them. She drove back northwards and crossed the motorway after Man of War. The garda cars appeared as soon as she hit the main street in the Naul.

She pulled up behind the forensics van just outside the town. There was a tent set up in the middle of the road, just behind the van. What was left of the car would be in there, safe from prying photographers and drones. She could see an army bomb squad truck in the field off the road, but there was no sign of Moyra Killanin.

Inside the tent, a couple of technical bureau people were busy photographing the car, which looked like it had been hit by a cruise missile.

Brosnahan was at the door of the tent. 'This is like the North thirty years ago, Lucy.'

'How so?' Lucy turned away from the burnt-out wreckage for a moment.

'Petrol canister with sugar in it. Works like napalm. And we've just found a phone.' Brosnahan took an evidence bag out of this knapsack.

'In that mess?' Lucy's eyes fixed on the remains of Violet Saunders in the driver's seat.

'It was thrown in the ditch. We have a trace on it already. It's her daughter's phone from London. Jenny Saunders. The Brits are on to it.'

'And when did all this happen?' Lucy turned away from the burnt-out car, suddenly feeling unwell. Then the moment passed. 'Come on, let's stand outside, Peter.' They walked back out onto the road.

Brosnahan slipped the phone back into the bag. 'About 1 a.m. First on the scene was a night deliveryman. Saw nothing or no one.'

Lucy spotted Sullivan standing over by the gate beside the bomb squad truck. Her eyes followed his bulky frame as he chatted to one of the army men. There was a clear sense of seniority in his stance. 'When did our good friend Mr Sullivan get here?' Lucy kept her eyes on Sullivan.

Brosnahan smiled softly. 'Just seemed to appear out of nowhere.'

Lucy turned back to Brosnahan. 'That's his MO, alright. Where's young Dennis, by the way?'

'Doing the rounds in the Naul. Random check. Sullivan sent him around.' Brosnahan was chuckling now.

'Did he, now? Any idea which way the bad boys headed?' Lucy took out her phone and took a couple of shots of the scene.

Brosnahan pointed to his left, over the fields. 'We think the Oldtown road.'

Lucy glanced at the photos on the phone. 'So, a five-mile perimeter, Peter. You and Dennis. Never know what you might pick up in the first hour or two.'

'Someone said they heard a car just before the explosion. A diesel car with a biggish engine.'

Lucy slipped the phone back into her jacket and smiled at Brosnahan. 'OK. That's a start. We might be able to match it with CCTV. Call me if you and Dennis get anything.'

. . .

BROSNAHAN HEADED off up the road and got into his car. Lucy waited until he had pulled away, then made her way over to the gate. Sullivan watched her approach.

Lucy nodded back towards the tent. 'You beat me to it. Why the bomb squad?'

Sullivan glanced at the bomb disposal technician. 'They thought it might be a come-on bomb. Second bomb waiting.'

Lucy turned to the man in the bomb suit. 'What's your read on this?'

'This is a pro job. Just enough explosive to make a big boom with the petrol. Like a fuel air bomb.'

Sullivan butted in. 'Possibly the same killer as Carlton.'

Lucy looked over her sunglasses. 'Oh, so you think that Carlton was murdered now? What led you to that conclusion?' Lucy kept her eyes firmly on Sullivan, but it was clear that he was more accustomed to asking questions and getting answers.

Sullivan waited until the bomb disposal man headed back to the truck; then he spoke. 'Maybe Violet Saunders said something, or just knew something. She was the mother of Philip Carlton's child, too. There's that.'

Lucy's jaw dropped. 'You what? When did you plan on telling me this?' She could feel her spleen rising now.

Sullivan glanced around him uneasily. 'Let's chill here.'

Lucy suddenly pushed Sullivan back. 'Don't ever, ever tell me to chill! *Capiche?*'

Sullivan raised his hands slightly in an attitude of surrender. 'I didn't mean it that way.'

'Yes, you bloody well did. Now, what else are you holding back from me?' Lucy saw Sullivan look past her shoulder. She could hear heavy footsteps behind her, but she ignored them.

There was a cough at her shoulder. She turned slowly to see Reese standing in full regalia. He stretched his hand out to her and she shook it. 'Good to see you, Lucy.'

Lucy squeezed out a smile. 'Mutual. Now, how about a little

colour and texture here?' Lucy looked between the two of them. 'Come on, lads! I'm beginning to look like the gobshite here.'

Reese grimaced and glanced over at Sullivan. 'All I can say is that it has to do with dealings from a long time ago.'

'I'm fighting in fog here. It's not fair, and you know that.' She could feel Sullivan biting his lip beside her and saw Reese giving him the nod to keep his beak buttoned.

'It won't affect the immediate investigation here into Philip Carlton's death.'

'Like fun it won't. How can it not affect it?' Lucy felt her voice rise again.

Reese took off his superintendent's cap and ran his finger around the headband. 'We're going to bring you in on the background here soonest.' Reese glanced over at Sullivan.

Lucy took a deep breath. 'Well, that's very thoughtful of you. Sharing information pertinent to the ongoing investigation of two murders.'

'Trust me on this.'

'Why, exactly?' She could see that Reese was getting exasperated now. She was beginning to wonder, for the first time now, whether he was under a bigger thumb himself.

Reese slipped his hat back on. 'Just give me a few more hours to get a couple of monkeys off my back. Political ones.'

Lucy nodded. 'Define "a few more hours", please.' She glanced from one to the other.

'I'll contact you this evening. Now, I suggest you and Gerry head back to Boynebridge and put together as much as you can on both cases.'

Lucy took a deep breath. 'And will there be an incident room for this?'

'In Boynebridge. The same incident room for Carlton. It's all official now.' Reese made ready to leave.

Lucy gave a little cough. 'Just one more thing, gentlemen. For the record.'

Reese regarded her warily. 'Yes?'

Lucy lowered her voice. 'You two knew all along this Violet Saunders had a child with Philip Carlton. Right?'

Reese nodded slowly. 'We did.'

'And that it might have some bearing on his death?'

Reese nodded. 'This we didn't know. We still don't know, in fact. But we can say that this poor woman's death is connected. That's not stretching it.'

Lucy nodded back towards the tent with the bombed-out car. 'OK. So, from now on I want to play with a full deck of cards.'

Reese nodded again and headed off towards the bomb squad truck.

SULLIVAN LOOKED OVER AT LUCY. 'I don't have my car with me.'

'So I'm forced to enjoy your company all the way back to Boynebridge, am I?'

Lucy's phone rang.

Dennis Sheehan's soft Kerry voice came over the speaker. 'Got something here. Petrol station on the Oldtown Road.'

'Right. We'll be there in five.'

DENNIS WAS STANDING on the forecourt of the garage when they pulled up. He looked like that young chef she saw on television about to launch into a homily on carbonara for slow learners. She could see the owner of the petrol station inside, chatting to Brosnahan.

Dennis opened his phone for Lucy. 'This is from the CCTV monitor.' The clip showed a large green Skoda passing the forecourt just before, tailgating Violet Saunders's Golf.

'Got a number?' Lucy looked around the forecourt.

'Yes. The Skoda was stolen in Dublin. We'll find it burnt out, no doubt.'

Lucy jabbed her finger at the screen. 'There! Stop!' She pointed at the blurred figure in the passenger seat that popped up for a second and then disappeared. 'Send it to Anna. One of these boyos could be our old friend from Boynebridge.'

LUCY AND SULLIVAN got into the car and headed north for Boynebridge. It was all she could do not to start snapping at Sullivan. As they passed out onto the motorway, Sullivan turned to her like he was reading her thoughts. 'You will be brought in on this. Reese has told you that.'

'But you can't tell me anything now?' Lucy glanced across at Sullivan.

Sullivan looked at her. 'I'm under starter's orders too, you know.'

'Oh, right. You work for a higher power and all that crap.' Lucy gritted her teeth.

'This is serious stuff here, Lucy. We're dealing with the sweepings of Eastern Europe here. This lot would make a midnight snack of most of our own scumbags.'

'You don't say? Look, I know what a bomb does. I'm personally familiar with the effects. Very personally.'

Lucy turned back to the road. The northbound traffic was building up. She slipped in behind a big articulated truck and thought again of the carbonised body back in the tent. It reminded her of photos she had once seen in a history book of the first Iraq war. The Basra Road. Trucks incinerated with their drivers inside them. Death grinning in the sun.

Lucy turned on the radio. It was playing a mawkish version of 'She Moves Through The Fair'. High-cholesterol Celtic kitsch. It was just the sort of saccharine stuff she hated.

She turned it up and started humming along, deliberately off key. At least it was annoying Sullivan.

THE COLLECTOR STOOD stock-still on the headland. He held the binoculars firmly and focused on the three figures. A man and a woman and a small child were down on the beach. On his beach, that was. How did they get there? Maybe crossed by the cave when the tide went out. Let them   if they got cut off, he couldn't risk talking to them. They didn't look like the stupid type, though. The woman had spotted something now. Realised they would soon be cut off. She wouldn't take a chance, not with her child. Nature...

He watched them turn around and make their way back towards the cove. Then he started back for the house.

He wiped his shoes on the doormat and switched on the coffee machine. He sent one beep and then two beeps on the phone then sat in the sitting room to listen to a podcast about fly fishing in Scotland. While he was doing so, he dusted the coffee table and the mantelpiece. Just how did dust get into so many places? It wasn't as if he were in the middle of a city. He made his way down to the bunker. In the radio room, he watched the dials kick into life. Then the spiky little voice came over the radio.

'Good morning, Mr Arkens.' Christ, that man was getting so tiresome.

'This O'Hara woman seems absolutely convinced that Philip Carlton was murdered.' Jeremy Arkens's voice was almost like a squeal now.

The Collector took a slow sip of his coffee. 'Really? And David Carlton is sure about that?'

'One hundred per cent. She was on the phone to him. And he's got very suspicious himself now.'

The Collector left down his coffee cup and thought a

moment. Then he spoke softly into the microphone. 'Nature will take its course.'

Jeremy Arkens took a deep breath at the far end of the line. 'I don't understand?'

'You don't need to. And remember, stay close to David Carlton, like I said before. All the Carltons are great talkers. I have plans for Ms O'Hara and our Lithuanian friend.'

The Collector knocked off the radio and crossed into the adjoining room, where he set to dusting the glass cases with the little silver crucifixes.

14

PETER BROSNAHAN AND DENNIS HAD ALREADY GONE, AND THE uniforms were winding down for the day. It was a soft summer's evening with not a cloud in the sky. Lucy had nailed the last rivet into the Carlton case prelim overview. Now all she wanted to do was get home.

Five minutes later, she was on the motorway heading south to Skerries. She played the audio recording of Philip Carlton's midnight caller in the car again. 'Good evening, Professor Carlton...' Then she caught that something else again: a sort of meaningful mumbling that she had initially thought was just grunting. Maybe some expletive. From what? Polish? Russian? Latvian? Lithuanian?

She hoped it would be enough for Schliemann to go on.

If there was anything else, he would find it. The suicide note seemed to point to a Slavonic or Baltic language speaker. But the audio was the icing on the cake. Schliemann had access to the same software and databases as she had. But it was his razor-sharp ears she was counting on. Ears that could crunch audio data the way someone with perfect pitch could plot a melody spatially. This was the scholar, she reminded herself, who had nailed a murderer near Hamburg, locating his home patch to within a twenty-kilometre radius from a scratchy old audio tape.

She couldn't wait any longer. Lucy hit the speed dial, and Schliemann's voice came on. 'Lucy, I've got news for you.'

'Sounds good. Go ahead.'

Schliemann paused. 'I scrubbed up the audio, and there are a couple of extra *tokens* in another language used before your friend speaks directly to your Philip Carlton.'

'Right. I thought first of all they were just sort of grunts.'

'No. He mumbled something under his breath. Maybe some sort of phatic phrases. It's not English or Russian either, as you said. And not Polish.'

'So?'

'Well, one of my Polish colleagues thinks it may be Lithuanian. We've got a young Lithuanian postgrad connected to the department. He'll be back from leave in a couple of days, and I'll scrub the audio up a bit more and let him listen. I'll phone you back later this evening with my synopsis so far. But the definitive statement on the early bit will have to come from our Lithuanian postgrad.'

'Excellent. Now, just to recap on the letter...' Lucy switched lanes and made for the Balbriggan exit.

SAOIRSE WAS FEEDING Chantal in the stable with her mother when she pulled into the yard. She could hear their voices in the fading light. Saoirse came running round the corner. Lucy swept her up in her arms and carried her into the house.

Lucy sat her down at the kitchen table and listened to the day's doings as she unloaded the dishwasher. 'How was the beach?'

'We played football, but *Mémé* wouldn't let me in the water.'

Saoirse pulled out a couple of seashells from the pocket of her jeans.

'Well, *Mémé* knows the sea well.'

'It's a different sea to her sea, *Maman*. She doesn't know our sea that well. *Mémé* doesn't even sail or swim.'

'Well...' Lucy watched her mother make her way in from the stables.

She turned back to Saoirse. 'Right, pyjamas on and I'll be in, in five minutes.'

Her mother ran her hands under the tap and wiped them on the little floral apron. 'I'm going to open a bottle of nice Bordeaux, Lisette.'

'Pour me a glass and I'll be there in a minute.' Lucy crossed into the bedroom and sat in on the bed beside Saoirse. It was the Giant's Causeway story.

When she had finished, Saoirse looked up at her with her little pouty face. 'Is this a true story?'

Lucy smiled. 'All stories have some truth in them, pet.'

'Even lies?' The little fairy face looked up at her.

'Sometimes there's more truth when people are telling lies, but they don't realise it. Now, lights out.' Lucy switched off the bedside lamp kissed her daughter on the nose. Her phone buzzed. Missed call from Schliemann in Germany.

She called to her mother from the door of the living room. 'I'll be in, in a moment.' Then she crossed to the study and pulled the door closed behind her.

Schliemann's smooth voice came on the phone. 'It all seems to point to a native Lithuanian speaker of English as, at least, a third language. Probably Lithuanian, Russian and then English. He would know some Polish too, probably. Fiftyish, I would say.'

'Any peculiarities?' Lucy picked up the pencil and pad to take notes.

Schliemann's voice was clear. 'I would say his primary

English lexis was acquired in London, in a working-class community. You may have picked up on a couple of those working-class London tokens yourself.'

'I did, but I didn't want to prejudice your analysis. So, possibly Lithuanian, fifties, London life experience. Anything else?' Lucy bit into the end of the pencil. It was the *anything else* that often counted.

Schliemann paused a moment to think. 'Oh, and a Russian speaker, like I say. But that goes without saying. His age alone would tell you that. So he was military trained, probably. The British police might even have something on him if he's a gun for hire. You should send them the images and the audio file. When you're in Kiel, you can meet with my Lithuanian postgrad. He may have more.'

'Right, that's good enough for a start. I'll see you in a few days in Kiel, Martin.' Lucy knocked off the phone and sat into the living room with her mother, who was knitting a scarf for Saoirse.

'It's cold here, Lucy, even in the summer.' But Lucy wasn't listening. She was reading a text from Reese.

Harcourt square. 9 AM. NBCI access only meeting.

So she was being let into the inner circle, in NBCI. Reese had cleared the way now that he could show her skills were needed. Violet Saunders's death had changed everything. She was out of quarantine now. Philip Carlton's death had knocked whatever they had been investigating before completely off course. Her mother coughed. '*Ca va*, Lucy?'

'*Ca va*.' But her mother went on glancing at her over her reading glasses, from time to time, as she sipped her lukewarm Bordeaux.

15

LUCY LEFT THE CAR IN SURGEONS AND WALKED UP TO THE GARDA headquarters in Harcourt Square from Stephen's Green. Sullivan was waiting for her in the lobby. On the third floor, he led her into a small conference room. Reese was sitting there with another NBCI clone. Same high-end suit. Brains, brawn and braggadocio.

Reese stood up slowly. 'Lucy, this is Jim Daly. He's head of a new task force on gangs.' There was no mention of rank.

'Nice to meet you.'

'You too. Gangs? Which ones?' Lucy glanced around at the others.

Jim Daly spoke. 'East Europeans and Baltic. There are overlaps with our own, too.'

'That's what the EU's all about, isn't it? Free movement of people, goods and scumbags. And our man?' Lucy glanced at Reese then turned back to Daly.

'We think your man is a floater. The name is Lukas Petraskas. The Brits did a cold stop about five years ago in King's Cross, at the Eurostar terminal. It was a general antiterrorist operation check, but they came across our friend here. No terrorist connection, but they found dodgy papers on him.'

'So why didn't they bring him in?'

'Word came from above to let him go, because they thought he might be part of a bigger picture, and they wanted the Spanish to track him at the other end. They think this chap belongs to a little vipers' nest near Alicante, on the East coast of Spain. But the Spanish had nothing solid on him. Bottom feeder, apparently.'

Reese smiled. 'Thank you, Jim.' Lucy grinned to herself. Now, the bullshit was out of the way. Jim Daly nodded at Lucy and headed back to his own burrow.

Reese waved her to a seat. 'What you're going to read here, stops here. It doesn't form part of the current investigations. It might in the future, though.' Reese looked straight at her.

'And does Superintendent McHugh know about this?' Lucy made her voice sound as innocent as she could.

Reese glanced over at Sullivan. 'Actually, Superintendent McHugh has been moved sideways to a new section.'

'Oh. May I ask where?'

Reese didn't miss a beat. 'Sligo. There's an emerging situation over there.'

So McHugh's usefulness was over now. Shagged out into the wilds of Gallia Transalpina, Or west of the Shannon.

Reese continued. 'So now you have been appointed senior investigating officer. That is, unless you have any particular objection.'

Lucy swallowed hard. 'No. And thank you, George. I appreciate that.'

Sullivan reached for the box file lying beside the percolator. 'These files are all off-line, which is a new security protocol.'

Sullivan and Reese stood up as one. Reese pointed at the box files 'We'll be back in an hour or so. You can ask us all the questions you like then.'

The door clunked closed behind them. Lucy took out the first file and read the abstract.

Historical Crimes Assessment Unit: Antiquities Subsection.

Derry Carlton and Associates.

She read the first line. Derry Carlton, the baby of the Carlton flock, long gone to his eternal reward.

This file relates to the ongoing investigation into the activities of Mr Derry Carlton, of Windgap, Dublin, and the matter of the suspected illegal disposal and exportation of antiquities, in particular those considered to be of importance to the national archaeological record.

She read on carefully. There were names and places and dates now. No wonder there had been pressure from above not to stir up the mud. Derry Carlton's name appeared and reappeared like a will-o'-the-wisp, yet there was no evidence of any attempt at impending prosecution. What was clear was that antiquities, including treasure trove and manuscripts, had been passed on for profit without let or hindrance.

But to whom? This part was unclear. The principals were all named, but the end users seemed to have gotten a free pass. Now, why would that be? Were they too exalted or protected to be named in such files?

Lucy had the feeling that she was just at the beginning of something. And she was sure too, that Reese and Sullivan had been ploughing through the same cold-case material until Philip Carlton's murder, and now Violet Saunders's murder had blown the whole thing open.

She closed over one of the files and sat back in the chair. This was the sort of stuff that got people maimed or killed. She began to understand, for the first time now, that her own name might end up on a bullet if she pushed on with her investigations.

There was a knock on the door. Sullivan came into the

room silently. He nodded at the files. 'Do you see why we were so reticent about all this?'

Lucy nodded. 'I do. But where does it go from here?'

Sullivan sat down across the table from her. 'That's what we're going to discuss now. And this stays with the three of us.'

The door opened behind Sullivan, and Reese walked in. 'Right, let's start from the beginning here. Back in the glory days of Derry Carlton and his cronies.'

IT WAS a grungy old Volvo estate, badly maintained and in desperate need of a wash. How could a detective drive around in such a piece of rubbish? Had she no shame? Still, it meant Lukas Petraskas had no trouble finding it in the covered car park off St Stephen's Green.

The tracker he had planted a couple of days before worked perfectly too. It was easy enough to get around the alarm, too. He opened the driver's door and popped the bonnet. The covered car park was quiet enough, because the second floor was full and all the traffic was going straight to the top floors. He peered into the engine and tugged at a few wires. It all looked straightforward enough. He knew his way around Volvos, and he had used a similar device a couple of years earlier, in the south of France. It took him just ten minutes to put the driveshaft unit in place, rig it to the mercury tilt switch, and to do the work on the brake fluid reservoir.

He slipped the tools back into the satchel, slammed the bonnet shut and locked the car again. Then he pulled the cap down tightly over his forehead, so that the security cameras wouldn't catch him, and headed for the staircase.

Out on St Stephen's Green, Lukas Petraskas slipped in among the crowd getting off the Green Luas from South Dublin, and vanished into the warm Dublin day.

16

Lucy opened the stable door slowly. Chantal was stamping her feet and whinnying. Lucy turned back to Saoirse. 'Never, ever go near her when she's like that, Saoirse. OK?'

'Why, *Maman*? Is she having a *little off day*, like *Mémé* has sometimes?'

Lucy smiled. 'It means something's wrong with her.' The horse shuddered. Lucy rubbed her flanks gently. Maybe a fever. Could happen, even in summer.

She patted the horse on the forehead and spoke softly to her. The big intelligent eyes. '*Tranquille*, Chantal.' She would phone the vet later in the morning. Probably nothing at all.

Saoirse was skipping around the yard when she came out of the stable. Lucy watched her absentmindedly, thinking back to the files she had read in Harcourt Square. The information on the late Derry Carlton was pretty damning. But what was even more damning was that the files had led practically nowhere in that investigation. The Carltons were too connected to be touched, and no newspaper would have dared print anything in those days. And now? She wasn't sure. The investigation was officially a murder investigation now, and the papers would make the connection with Violet Sanders in jig time.

She must focus on recalibrating the murder investigations. Try to track down the man with the peaked cap in the porta-cabin video. It was hardly credible that such a creature had a personal beef with the Carltons, was it? Possible but unlikely. Unless money was involved. Hardly drugs. Hardly sex, either, mind you. But then, you never could tell.

In the house, she sorted out her briefcase and sent a message to Brosnahan: full meeting at nine for upgrade of investigation. Then she packed a couple of tarts into Saoirse's backpack for a treat. No point in putting in a bottle of wine for her mother. She would already have sacked that supermarket in Swords on her weekly raid.

The Volvo was sluggish and kicked up when she turned the ignition. It needed to be serviced and the brakes felt soft too. Funny the way a car goes to sleep fine and wakes up sick. Just like a horse. Or a human. She turned the car around in the yard and glanced over her shoulder. 'Seatbelt on, Saoirse.'

She waited until she heard the click, then turned out onto the road. The car got stuck behind a big red tractor. When the tractor finally pulled into the left, she swept on by for the junction.

A minute later, she turned onto the coast road. She could see a line of cars coming from the right, heading northwards towards Balbriggan. There was a big red tour bus at the head of the line.

That was when she got the first inkling that something was wrong. Really wrong.

The steering felt stiff and the brakes suddenly started acting up. There was a roar from the engine, like a jet about to stall. It was like everything had jammed. Brakes, clutch, accelerator. She was flying along the coast road at a rate of knots now. She was going to collide with the bus coming towards her. *Get off the road, Lucy! Get off the road! Now!*

She heard herself shouting at the child. 'Saoirse! Hold on! Hold on!'

The car was rolling with the camber of the road towards the big red tourist bus now. She dragged the steering wheel to the left to get down off the coast road. There was a screech of wheels as the car careered around the bend almost on two wheels. Then it charged down the slope towards the incoming tide. The brakes were dead; the accelerator had locked some way.

She shouted at Saoirse again. 'Hold on! Hold on tight!'

'Maman! Maman!'

All of a sudden, her peripheral vision slipped away. Everything to the left and right disappeared. She was in a long grey tunnel, fighting to stop inside it before they hit the water. She couldn't hear Saoirse now. Only her own thoughts bouncing around in her head.

One shot... focus, Lucy... focus...

The car slammed into the sea with a wallop, and an enormous wave rose in front of them. Suddenly the car flipped over onto its roof, and she was thrown against the windscreen. A wild screech came from the back seat.

'Maman! Maman!'

She couldn't get into the back seat. Would have to push her way outside against the force of the water and grab Saoirse from the back.

They were alive, at least. They had survived the traffic on the road and the race into the sea. But she was strapped into the car with Saoirse, upside down now.

But now the sea was preparing to drown them both now, in just a few inches of salt water.

17

'Just hold on, Saoirse!'

The seat harness cut into her, and the water was seeping in through the door of the old Volvo. She could hear Saoirse's screams now. There were only seconds to spare now. She started struggling with her seatbelt, tearing at it.

Free yourself first. Focus on that, then Saoirse.

She shifted herself this way and that to take the strain off the seatbelt. Ignoring the screaming coming from the back seat.

The seat buckle suddenly gave way, and Lucy fell upside down onto the car ceiling in a heap, her face down in the water. Every bone in her body seemed to ache now. She lifted her head slowly and looked into the back. Saoirse's head was just over the water. Just about.

There was a sudden inrush of water as she tried to right herself. She could feel a surge of energy through her body. The passenger door was suddenly thrown open and hands were dragging her out and pulling her to her feet. A middle-aged man and a woman. She heard herself shouting at them.

'My daughter!'

Lucy waded through the water to the back of the car and fumbled with the hatchback lock.

There was a clunking sound as the hatch door finally opened. Lucy pushed her way into the car, struggling to reach the buckle on Saoirse's seat.

'It's OK, honey. I've got you.'

Her fingers pressed once, twice, three times. On the fourth attempt, the buckle gave. She dragged Saoirse over the back seat.

'Hold your breath, Saoirse!'

And then, suddenly, she had the child swaddled in her arms and she was walking back up to the beach with the couple on either side of her.

The man called to the woman, 'I'll phone the ambulance. Get the blanket and the flask of coffee.'

Lucy looked back over her shoulder at the upturned car and the water lapping over it and the couple of gulls that were wheeling about above it.

THE HOSPITAL in Boynebridge was settling down for the evening. Lights were dimming in the wards. Saoirse was sitting up in the bed, smiling. Lucy's mother was beside her, chatting in soft, sibilant French. There were teddy bears and sweets. A young Filipino nurse came in and checked Saoirse's temperature and refreshed the drip.

The nurse looked at Saoirse. 'That's a nice teddy bear. Do you have a name for it?'

'Not yet. I'll think of one in my dreams tonight.'

Lucy looked into Saoirse's blue eyes without saying anything, but she could see the shock buried there. The same glazed eyes you saw in war children. The stubborn shutting out of the unfathomable world. That was what Saoirse needed now: home, dog, mother, grandmother and sleep and food and teddy bears and quiet. Then back into the noisy playgroup as soon as possible.

Lucy mustn't pass her panic on by word, thought or deed, though. She would fake it. Fool herself and the child. Lucy turned to her mother. 'Can you manage for a few minutes? I need to drop into the station.'

'Go on. She's OK.'

Lucy leaned over and kissed Saoirse. 'I'll be back in half an hour, *ma petite*. OK?' The child hardly looked up at her as she pulled at the teddy bear's nose. Good.

On the way out, she slipped into one of the bathrooms. There was no one else there, thankfully. The last thing she needed was to explain herself to some stranger. To be counselled by some kind-hearted woman. The terror had to be vented alone. She sat in the cubicle for a few minutes, rocking back and forth, sobbing to herself. Shaking with upset until the moment had passed. Then she washed her face in the handbasin and dried her eyes and spoke sternly to herself in the mirror.

'It never happened, *Lisette*. It never happened. *D'accord?*'

Then she took a couple of deep breaths and walked out of the hospital towards the taxi.

18

BOYNEBRIDGE WAS STRANGELY QUIET AS LUCY WALKED ALONG THE late-night corridor. Mid-week. The only sound was a radio crackling in one of the side rooms. Lucy nodded at the late-shift uniforms as she passed. She saw it in their eyes: you winged it. She took a deep breath and slipped up the stairs.

They were all waiting for her in the incident room. Anna, Brosnahan, Dennis. Sullivan gave her a hug when she came in the door. 'Everybody OK?'

Lucy swallowed hard and steeled herself. 'Fine. Fine. They're keeping Saoirse in overnight.' She suddenly felt wrong-footed by the closeness.

'And what about yourself? You must still be in shock.' Brosnahan's voice was soft.

'I'm fine, Peter. Fine...' Lucy took a deep breath and glanced around at the faces.

She felt it welling up in her now. The *what-ifs* and the awful images were still in her head. Saoirse's white-faced gasps as she dragged her out of the car. Her pale little face, her limp body. Then, another voice speaking to her from somewhere else:

It didn't happen. It never happened. Push on through, Lucy. Ten minutes. Then back up to the hospital. Push on through. Hold the line.

She looked from face to face again and winced. 'First of all, thank you for all your well wishes. We're all OK, like I said. Now...'

She cleared her throat. 'Philip Carlton's death is now a murder investigation, as you all know. The truth is, it has been one all along. As you know, too, I am replacing Superintendent McHugh as SIO.'

She caught a sardonic smile on Sullivan's lips but put no pass on it.

'What about Violet Saunders?' Brosnahan's voice cut through the room.

'This is the incident room for both investigations. It's not so much economics as common sense. We'll have extra detective power and uniforms from tomorrow morning. Tomorrow, we recalibrate. I'm going to leave it at that for tonight. Thanks, everyone.'

Sullivan walked over to her. 'Quick word with you offside?'

'Make it quick. I want to get back up to the hospital.'

They descended the backstairs. Sullivan pointed to a door and stepped inside. He took out an evidence bag from his briefcase with a shiny little gizmo inside. 'This was attached to the driveshaft of your car. It overrides the driver's input from the pedals and...'

Lucy looked at the little object in the plastic bag. 'The driver loses control.'

'In a word. It's not in the average toerag's toolkit, either.' Sullivan passed the plastic bag over to her.

Lucy stared at the little device through the clear plastic. She was trying hard not to let her voice betray the fear creeping up on her again. 'But how do you get it to work at the right time?'

Sullivan pulled out another evidence bag and held it up.

'Mercury tilt switch and timer. Provos used this type of thing during the Great Patriotic War up North and in the UK. The current is set to switch on at a certain time. Then, when the car tilts up or down over a certain angle, say twenty degrees, the mercury makes contact, the current runs and the unit is activated. In your case, the driveshaft controller was the part that was knocked out of whack. The guy who did this bled your brakes a little too, as backup. A perfect storm. And your car was pretty ancient. It wouldn't have been hard to fiddle with the mechanics.'

'That all sounds pretty sophisticated.'

Sullivan tapped the little device with his index finger. 'This is the sweet spot between criminality and paramilitary. One lot learns from the other.' Sullivan snapped the case shut. 'We want to put a military-grade alarm system in your house, by the way. Orders from Harcourt Square.'

'Is this all really necessary?' Lucy stared hard at the floor.

Sullivan's voice dropped to a whisper. 'These fuckers are for real. And you need to keep your personal weapon with you at all times now. That's straight from Reese.'

SULLIVAN DROPPED her back to the hospital up on the hill. They hardly spoke along the way. The shock was starting to set in now that the immediate threat was over, Lucy knew. All she wanted to do now was hug Saoirse and never let her go again.

Darkness had descended on the hill over Boynebridge now, and the hospital was bedding down for the night. Lucy turned to Sullivan as the car pulled up outside. 'Nine a.m. start tomorrow, Gerry.'

Sullivan leaned across and opened the door for her. 'Fine. Anything you need, just call.'

'Thanks.' Lucy walked away swiftly into the hospital without turning back, despite the odd twinge she felt as she reached the doors. When she was inside in the corridor, she looked back through the window as Sullivan got into the car. For a moment, she wanted to walk back out. Say something. Anything. Then the car did a 180 and disappeared into the night.

19

THE SUMMER SUN WAS STREAMING THROUGH THE CORRIDOR
windows in the Boynebridge station. Lucy locked the shiny new
Volvo with the remote control key and skipped up the steps,
balancing a skinny latte and a bunch of files in her hands. She
kneed open the door of the incident room. Brosnahan was at
the back of the room, talking to a couple of seconded
detectives.

She nodded to Sullivan to join her. 'You and Peter are on the
East European and Baltic trawl. Even a gun for hire needs a bed
every now and then.'

Lucy crossed over to Anna's desk. 'And keep track of the
Delaney girl.'

She phoned Reese from her desk. 'George, I need to see
Philip Carlton's diaries, letters and any other relative material.
The stuff that's in the family home.'

'Right. Any particular line?' Reese sounded surprised.

Lucy glanced through her diary as she spoke. 'Well, Deirdre
Delaney reported a personal threat to Carlton. Might be something in his personal papers.'

'Fair enough.'

'I'm meeting David Carlton this afternoon to update him on the investigation, so I can sort it out through him.'

Reese dropped his voice. 'Light touch there. OK? Even dead Carltons can sting. And remember, that material you read in Harcourt Square isn't relevant until...'

'Until it's relevant? I get it.' She drew a circle around David Carlton's name. She hoped he wouldn't bring the partner with him.

SHE ARRIVED at Howth just before three. The Summit Inn was bustling with tourists. A couple of Germans were at the next table, microanalysing the menu. Bavarian dialect, heavy on the vowels. She earwigged unconsciously as she nosed her way through the *Irish Times*. The headline article stitched the Boyne Valley murder and Violet Saunders's murder together seamlessly.

David Carlton swanned in a few minutes later in a light summer suit and straw hat. Michel wasn't with him, thankfully.

He smiled over at Lucy, then ordered a gin and tonic and proceeded to sip it with gusto. 'So, any fresh news for me?'

'Let's take a walk outside.' Lucy nodded at the Germans beside her.

'Just let me finish my tipple first.' David Carlton slurped back his gin in jig time. 'Now, Detective O'Hara.'

They crossed into the field at the back of the car park overlooking the maw of Dublin Bay. David Carlton began pointing out this and that to her, as though he were talking to a little child on a day out. The lighthouse, the power station stacks, the Sugarloaf behind Dun Laoghaire, in north Wicklow.

Lucy looked around to make sure they were alone. A young couple with two small children were sitting on the grass, picnicking. Lucy turned back to David Carlton. 'I'll get straight to the point.'

'Please do.' David Carlton brushed a piece of dried grass from his fawn trousers.

'We believe now that your brother Philip's death was actually a forced suicide.'

'What?' David Carlton threw his hands up in the air. 'How can you force someone to commit suicide? Isn't that a contradiction in terms?'

Lucy walked on a little, to put some distance between them and the family. 'You make them take an overdose of their own prescription drug.'

David Carlton's puffy face looked like it was going to explode. 'And what, threaten to kill someone if they don't kill themselves?'

'Like I said. Philip's death may have been a forced suicide. And a parallel investigation has started into the murder of a woman, Violet Saunders, who had a relationship with your brother Philip many years ago, as I'm sure you know.' Lucy glanced over David Carlton's shoulder at the little family. It all looked so innocent.

David Carlton suddenly exploded. 'That bitch! And her daughter, whatever her name is, Jackie or Jenny. I knew she would come back to haunt him sooner or later.'

'Maybe we should keep our voices down a little, Mr Carlton.' She was glad now she had got them to leave the pub. Lucy started walking on.

David Carlton followed her, quieter now. 'Look, maybe Philip didn't have enough blood to run his brain and his John Thomas at the same time. But he wasn't a criminal.'

Lucy smiled. 'So?'

'Well, Philip impregnated this Saunders woman, and that grown-up child, Jenny, started to harass Philip some time ago.'

Lucy looked past David Carlton's shoulder at the young couple and their children. She kept her eyes on them as she spoke. 'And do you have any proof of this?'

'My sister Joyce does. A couple of letters and emails recently forwarded to her by Philip. I think it was really a cry for...'

'For help?' Lucy angled her head.

'For money, Detective. Don't be so naive! Philip helped the girl and her mother when she was a child. Made a full and final settlement with her mother when she was small. And now that little gold-digger is coming back for more, years later!' David Carlton started walking away slowly. She caught up with him again.

'Mr Carlton... David.'

David Carlton turned around slowly. The anger had settled down to a sort of sullenness now.

'Do you think Jenny Saunders was blackmailing Philip, then? Who would care about an illegitimate child born almost thirty years ago?'

David Carlton gave a Gallic shrug of the shoulders. 'I have no idea. Philip always liked young women students, you know. He had a bit of a god complex.'

Lucy bit her lip. 'You do know that he had a close friendship with a young woman on the Boyne site too?' She watched David Carlton's eyes open wide again.

'Oh, Jesus wept! Another one? Have you any more uplifting news for me?' David Carlton looked close to vexed tears.

'I'm obliged to share these matters with you. It's not very pleasant for me either.' Lucy glanced at her watch. 'Look, I have to get going. I just wanted to update you off the phone.'

They walked slowly back towards the Summit Inn. Lucy drove back down the hill to the Dart station near Howth Harbour.

David Carlton turned to her as they pulled into the station. 'Detective O'Hara, forgive me. This was just more upsetting news. I will help you all I can, of course.' There was a sincerity in the voice now that she hadn't heard before. 'Who do you think might have killed Philip? And why? What was to be gained?'

David Carlton's eyes clouded over again. 'I still can't believe that anyone would actually want to kill Philip. The only enemies he had were academic ones, with one leg in the grave. And he didn't have any dodgy debts that I know of. It doesn't make sense.'

'I understand. We're looking at a few lines of enquiry, but it's early days.'

'Of course.' The eyes cleared. David Carlton pulled himself together and smiled awkwardly. 'Well, if there's anything I can help you with...'

'There is, actually. I'll need access to your late brother's diaries and notes. The type of material that's off-line, in Windgap.'

'Done. I'll sort it out with Joyce.'

Lucy waited until David Carlton had entered the station; then she pulled out slowly into the traffic.

ON THE WAY back north to Boynebridge, she called Anna. 'See if the Brits have any soft information on Jenny Saunders. David Carlton thinks she might have been demanding money from Philip. Nothing new on Deirdre Delaney?'

'No, but I'm keeping an eye on her social media profile.'

She pictured Deirdre Delaney again. A princess minus a pony. Unfortunately, bank statements didn't have a column with reasons for lodgement like guilt and bribery and love. More's the pity.

She put on a French station on the radio to fast-rinse her thoughts. A man with a southern French accent was banging on about wild dogs. It was gloriously irrelevant and soothing. Then she hit the accelerator and quietly savoured the pickup as the new Volvo kicked up a gear.

20

A LIGHT DRIZZLE HAD SOFTENED THE DRY EARTH ALONG THE banks of the Boyne. It was a relief from the un-Celtic annoyance of constant sun. Lucy stepped out of the car and looked about her. A couple of security men were walking the site and chatting. She recognised Pavlov, the one Brosnahan had questioned a few days earlier.

In the portacabin, she ran her finger over the computer screen. The hard drive had already been downloaded, and Anna Crowley had finished going through it. She would have it all bagged up and stored this evening. On a stone-in-the-shoe sort of feeling, she gave Deirdre Delaney in Carlow a buzz, but the phone rang out. She just needed to know more about the young woman's relationship with the late professor. Sometimes, asking exactly the same question in a different location threw up something unexpected.

She sat into Philip Carlton's swivel chair and pictured him throwing back a whiskey as he spoke into the voice app. That half-Brit patois of his, an accent that had cachet long before the new mid-Atlantic drawl did for it, in the posher banlieues, south of Stephen's Green. She smiled softly to herself. Life is change; language is life; language is change.

She turned around to the whiteboard and ran her finger over the shiny surface. Then she doodled a makey-uppy Celtic design on the board with the red marker. The sort of thing you found on the Neolithic stones in the Boyne Valley. She wrote a couple of words underneath it.

Tempus fugit

She erased it all slowly with the whiteboard eraser. But she could still see a trace of her drawing on the board. And no one would have written on the whiteboard after Carlton's death but her.

So, what if?

She pulled out her phone. 'Dennis, little job for you. Get onto forensics and see if it's possible that erased writing on a whiteboard can be retrieved.'

'Professor Carlton's writing, you mean, I suppose?' Dennis's soft voice always amused her. Could sell snow to Eskimos with it.

'Yes. He was the last one to write on the whiteboard in the portacabin.' Lucy ran her gaze around the room again. There wasn't much to go on. An unclear video and audio. Clutching at straws. One more straw wouldn't go amiss.

She headed back out.

THE INCIDENT ROOM was almost empty. Only Anna Crowley and a couple of uniformed guards were still there. Anna pointed at her screen. 'I've done a trawl of social media sites for Jenny Saunders.'

'Show...' Lucy moved closer to the screen.

A raven-haired girl with sallow skin filled the computer screen. Jenny Saunders standing outside a pub with a pint in her hand. Jenny Saunders singing in a pub. Jenny shouting into the camera about British politics. Anna looked up at Lucy. 'Bit teenagey, for a twenty-eight-year-old woman.'

'Has she a job?'

'No visible means of support and a GBH charge that was dropped last year. Watch this...'

There was a video clip of Jenny Saunders singing in an Amy Winehouse nightclub competition to backing tracks. Then a kerfuffle down in the audience when some guy slagged her singing. They watched Jenny Saunders sling down the microphone, jump into the crowd and start pummelling the poor prole into the floor.

Lucy gave a little laugh. 'Ms Saunders doesn't really do critiquing, does she?'

'No. She's giving the Brits a lot of grief, too, about releasing her mother's body.'

Lucy herself straightened up. 'Stall them if they contact us. OK?'

Her phone rang. It was Dennis. 'Forensics says it might be possible to retrieve something that has been erased from a whiteboard. They stressed *might be*.'

'OK. Put in an official tech request.'

Lucy looked back at the photos of Jenny Saunders on the computer. No visible means of support. It was a hard thing to swing in modern West London. There were no squats left to squat in.

Was it really possible that Jenny Saunders was also leveraging money from Carlton? An angry and neglected daughter. What would she have to threaten Carlton with, though? No one would give a toss about her illegitimate status. Half the world was born out of wedlock these days. The others would end up

as children of divorced parents anyway. And what was behind
those dark, whacky eyes? Not just her mother's death. Some
earlier slight, maybe. When bad things happened to women
when they were young, it often came out at critical points. She
didn't have to learn that from a shrink's bible.

'Dig a bit more, Anna. And Deirdre Delaney too – don't
forget her. She's just dissed me, the little miss.'

'Oh, dear. Naughty Miss Delaney.'

THE COLLECTOR POINTED an age-freckled finger at the block of
cheese on the farmers' market stall. 'That one, if you please.'

'Sir?' The young hippy with the flaxen beard and blue eyes
beamed back at him. He spoke in German-accented English.

The Collector pointed at a large wheel of cheese. 'Two
hundred grams of that one, please. And five hundred grams of
the one behind it.'

The young hippy smiled. 'Clooneen, medium soft. You will
really love this one, sir. We all do. Very much.' It sounded like
the little hippy was talking about a human, not a hunk of
cheese.

'Yes, yes.' Christ, all these faux Gaelic names for a bit of
overpriced faux Roquefort.

The Collector didn't usually do local shopping. He was used
to bringing all the extras down from Dublin. He carried no
traceable device when he travelled. Kept his phone switched off
and never used a satnav. Those things that had presaged the
death of the age of chivalry, in his view, had also presaged the
death of privacy. He had no need of Google Maps either. The
landscape of West Cork, with its hills and valleys and redoubts,
was as familiar to him as the streets of Dublin.

The system was simple: from his Dublin door to his West
Cork door in a little over four hours.

The Collector slipped the cheese into his satchel. He spoke little to anyone. Shop assistants, petrol attendants or stall keepers. If anyone had been asked, they might – just might – remember an elderly gentleman with a high-end accent. British blow-in, perhaps. They wouldn't have spotted the clear glass in his spectacles. Or queried the tweed hat pulled down over his face against the cold wind, which also helped to conceal his features.

Back in the house, he set to making a salad with the blue cheese, supplemented with a couple of slices of wholemeal bread. That night, he would be back in Dublin. He would arrive in Dublin in the dark. His neighbours in the city, in the other detached houses with high hedges and walls, would assume that he had been on one of his foreign jaunts. He gave them no cause to intrude. He was as anonymous in south Dublin as he was in West Cork.

In West Cork, in among the bulrushes and the damp fields, he was thought to be a rich foreign widower who wanted to be left alone to mourn amid his money. Nothing had disturbed his tranquillity over the years until Philip Carlton started babbling on the wretched internet. Nothing, that is, except the O'Hara woman, in North Dublin, who seemed hell-bent on causing further chaos. A chaos that could undo all he had built up over the years.

Everything.

He cut a slice of blue cheese with the cheese knife and popped it in his mouth. Then he paused a moment as he digested it, and bit into a slice of brown bread. He closed his eyes and tried to picture the scene on the beach in North Dublin. How close he had come to eliminating the nuisance. What had gone wrong? A mixture of serendipity and smarts.

'*Touché,* Madame O'Hara! But next time we will use the direct method.' He reached across the table and picked up a box of .22 cartridges. He took one of the shiny cylinders out of the box and tapped the conical point with his index finger.

'Cartridge, powder, projectile, propulsion and...'

The Collector slipped the round back into the box and stood up slowly. As he cleared away the table, he admitted to himself, grudgingly, that the detective woman had form. But the next time, serendipity and smarts wouldn't be enough.

Lucy O'Hara tried Deirdre Delaney's phone again. This time, she picked up. 'You're a very hard girl to reach, Deirdre.'

There was whispering in the background. Deirdre Delaney sounded like she was in the company of a boyfriend.

Lucy assumed she was on speaker, so she made the most of it. 'Anything new to share about Professor Carlton's murder?' Whoever was listening on speaker would now be fully awake: the word *murder* wasn't a commonplace of chit-chat. A boyfriend would freeze.

'I would tell you if I remembered anything, wouldn't I?' Deirdre Delaney's voice sounded nervous.

'Yes, I suppose you would. OK. Look, I'll check in with you again, in a few days.'

Leave her be now, Lucy. Unlikely that she was squeezing money out of Carlton with threats. No. Sullivan was probably right: an elderly man paying for bright young company. He would only be taking his dosh with him to the grave anyway. Why not splurge it on spoiling a young postgrad student on the way to the box?

Jenny Saunders was another story altogether, though, Lucy sensed. Emotionally bruised, like a bull elephant about to make a second charge, maybe. She glanced at the images of Jenny Saunders that Anna had sent to her phone. A clip of Jenny squatting in the street with a bottle of wine beside her. The caption underneath read:

Que sera, sera. If it's meant to happen, it's meant to happen.

So what would her motivation be? Maybe Jenny Saunders really was just getting back at Philip Carlton, Papa, for ignoring her?

The phone rang. It was David Carlton. 'Good afternoon. My sister Joyce says she is happy to allow you to go through Philip's study.'

'Excellent. I'll phone her later.' Lucy flipped open her diary.

'And the arrangements for Philip's remains? People will be coming from abroad.' David Carlton had that tone again. That slightly stifled sense of entitlement.

'The body will be released this evening.'

'Good. Joyce is expecting your call.'

'Thank you.' Lucy smiled to herself at the grandeur of the voice.

It was just after six when Lucy hit the motorway south. She was looking forward to getting in the door and switching off. Putting on some music and having a quiet glass of wine. Her mother would head home to her own house further down the coast, in Rush, for the night.

She had hardly put the pedal to the floor when Anna Crowley rang from the station in Boynebridge. 'We have a serious situation here.'

Lucy frowned. 'What? Where?'

'Here. Jenny Saunders. She's f'ing and blinding down in the day room.'

Lucy turned up the volume on the car speaker. 'What's she doing there?'

'She must have flown over from London. Screaming blue bloody murder about why won't we let her see her mother's body. She's a heartbeat away from being arrested, so she is.'

Lucy glanced over her shoulder at the traffic and switched on the flashers. 'Ten minutes, Anna. Just give me ten.'

'That's probably all we've got before she hits someone again.'

'I'm there.' Lucy put the pedal to the floor and headed for the next exit.

21

THE SUMMER SQUALL THE PREVIOUS NIGHT HAD SOURED THE VIEW
of the Sugarloaf Mountain.

Jeremy Arkens felt like he was peering through a steamed-
up bathroom window. The whole house was shrouded in mist.
The visitor would arrive that day, and he would hand him over
the expenses, in cash, as agreed. There would be no electronic
trace anywhere. It would be under cover of darkness, because
even the North Wicklow mists wouldn't be enough cover
during the day.

He spent the afternoon in the annex at the back of the
house. An annex that couldn't be seen from the road, only from
the hill behind the house.

Sheila Arkens kept out of the way that day. She had a lunch
appointment with a couple of other women in Dublin city.
Lunch in the Trocadero, followed by (just one) glass of wine
afterwards, in the back bar of the Shelbourne. When she got
home early in the evening, her husband was prowling around
like a hunted animal.

She left her handbag on the hall stand. 'When is this
gentleman due?'

'Shortly. No phone contact.' Jeremy Arkens thought of the visitor. Hoped it would all be over soon.

'So you're supposed to sit here like a hen on a griddle waiting for this man?' Sheila Arkens's rural roots slipped out of her mouth whenever she was vexed.

'That's the arrangement.'

'Well, I'll be upstairs in the front room.' Sheila Arkens disappeared upstairs.

Jeremy Arkens slipped back out to the annex, opened up one of the glass cases and began polishing a little silver cross. A cross said to have belonged to St Fergal. A companion piece to the Genesis of St Fergal secured many years before.

There was a tap on the window.

He turned around to see a figure at the far side of the glass, but the figure couldn't see him. The face at the window was long and pinched. A nineteenth-century phrenologist would have had a lot of fun with the flattened skull, he thought, and the square head. Jeremy Arkens tapped back in response. The face disappeared. A chill stole over Jeremy Arkens's body now. This felt dangerous.

This was dangerous.

He opened the side door to the annex. The man was even grimmer in the flesh than through the smoked glass. He beckoned to the stranger.

'Come in.'

No name was used. Not that this sort of individual was going to give one anyway. He looked like the sort of footpad who would cut your throat for tuppence. And change sides with the wind too, of course. He closed the door behind the stranger, fearful now. Conscious, for the first time, of his own jerky breathing. He led him into the downstairs dining room. Sheila Arkens wouldn't appear. But she would have seen the visitor arrive on the security app on her iPhone. She wouldn't be privy to the conversation either. She had nothing to bring to

the discussion besides demands for more funds for their lukewarm marriage bed.

The stranger sat down on the sofa and ran his finger absentmindedly over a brass coaster on the coffee table. Jeremy
Arkens leaned over him. 'Coffee or tea?'

'Just you bring water. Just water.'

It was clear that the word 'please' wasn't going to form part
of their colloquy. When he returned with the glass, the man
was standing in front of the window, staring out through the
mists. 'Lot rain here!'

'Yes. Quite a lot. Mountains, of course. High precipitation.'
Maybe they didn't do mountains in Lithuania, Jeremy Arkens
thought.

He left the glass of water down on the coffee table. Arkens
assumed his visitor was armed. The concept of remorse would
be laughable to such a thug. True, Jeremy Arkens had had
distant dealings with rough customers over the years. With
smugglers and thieves and con men of one sort or another. But
it had always been at a distance.

He watched the man sip the water. How did you get to be
like that? Was it family experiences? Genetics? War? Did it even
matter?

The stranger looked up at Jeremy Arkens. 'You have money
for me?'

'Yes. Of course. The sum we agreed, with our mutual friend,
for expenses.' Arkens passed over the large envelope. He
watched the stranger count the money slowly. Thousands.
Serious money. Not that a few thousand here and there would
count if the whole operation went down.

Darkness had now descended upon the house. Arkens tried
not to show his nerves to the stranger, but such people, he reckoned, could sniff out fear like a dog. A panther stalking a
gazelle near a watering hole. Or did panthers do that? Jeremy

Arkens wasn't sure, but he felt he should check it later, for some reason.

He just wanted the stranger to go now. To set everything back to zero. Wasn't that what this had been all about anyway?

The stranger stood up suddenly. 'I go now.'

'Right, so. I'll let you out.' One hardly said 'thanks' to such individuals. Maybe there was a website with etiquette for such encounters. How to express gratitude to a killer. Jeremy Arkens smiled secretly at his own morbid joke.

He just hoped the whole problem had been dealt with now. That nothing more would be heard of it all. As soon as the door closed behind the visitor, he called up the stairs to his wife, feeling, in an odd sort of way, a little more manly now than he had felt half an hour before.

LUKAS PETRASKAS HEARD the door of the annex click shut behind him. The Arkens guy was nervous, alright. Another idiot without discipline, like all the Irish and the British. He looked back at the annex again and thought of the wealth inside it. Probably easy enough to get into. Not his sort of job though. Might pass it on to someone else, as a favour. He slipped the envelope in his bag and made off up the hill for the trees. When he reached the hillock above Jeremy Arkens's house, he paused a moment to check his bearings.

He slipped down by the far side of the hillock to a tall tree at the edge of the field. He kept himself pressed in against the tree until he heard a car approaching. The car pulled up near the tree and flashed its lights. He slipped over the fence and into the passenger seat and turned to the Pole. 'Go home on mountain road. Now, go!'

The Pole put the car in gear and they carried on along the damp Wicklow roads towards the suburbs of Dublin city.

. . .

SHEILA ARKENS APPEARED in the sitting room. 'Well?'

'Well, what?' He suddenly felt a little cheeky now. He had dealt with a very rough person and come out of it unscathed.

'Is everything OK?' Sheila Arkens looked over her reading glasses.

He knew his wife didn't really want to know. That was their deal. They had a couple of shots of Napoleon brandy together (Hennessy gave Sheila Arkens heartburn). Then Sheila Arkens retired for the night. She had a pressing engagement the following day. A lunch in Belfast and a meeting with her choral society that evening in Bray. You had to watch your health. Wealth wasn't everything, she told herself.

As his wife slept, Jeremy Arkens hoped, once again, that that was an end of it. He didn't cop the photos the stranger had taken when he was in the kitchen and outside the house. Or the private collector's catalogue he had slipped into his bag either. And he certainly didn't spot the listening device Lukas Petraskas had planted on one of the legs of the dining room table.

Because he was too busy being happy and basking in the warm buzz of the brandy.

22

LUCY COULD HEAR SCREAMING ALONG THE LONG CORRIDOR OF Boynebridge station and the sound of a woman's voice with a London accent. 'Don't touch me again, you mingers!'

Anna Crowley met her at the foot of the stairs. 'She's in the second interview room.'

Lucy frowned. 'Sullivan and Brosie around?'

'Gone. Dennis is on his way back in. Two men and two women guards in there with her now. She's wrecking the joint.'

'Right. Stay upstairs. I'll call you if I need you.' Lucy heard the sound of a chair slapping off a wall. Then a table being dragged across the floor. Whatever else about Jenny Saunders, she certainly had plenty of energy to burn. Another scream rent the air.

'Touch me again and I'll do you!' The London accent was even stronger now.

Lucy reached the room. She took off her jacket and hung it on the door opposite. She opened the door of the interview room slowly. The table was over by the far wall. A broken-backed chair lay in the corner. Two women garda had Jenny Saunders in an armlock. The two men stood to the side, keeping well clear of the woman-on-woman action. Jenny Saunders looked heavier than in the photographs and clips on YouTube.

Lucy shouted, 'Knock it off!'

Everyone froze.

'Who the fuck are you?' Jenny Saunders glared at Lucy.

Lucy ignored Jenny Saunders's question. 'I want everyone to leave.'

The men looked at one another, delighted to be off the hook. The two women still held onto Jenny Saunders.

Lucy looked at them again. 'You can all leave now, I said.'

'She'll do a runner.' The taller of the two women nodded at the door.

'She won't get past me. I can guarantee you that.' Lucy turned to face Jenny Saunders. Her voice dropped a couple of notches. 'This isn't going to bring your mother back, Ms Saunders, unfortunately.'

'My mother was murdered and those bitches won't even let me see her body!'

Lucy dragged the table back into the centre of the floor. It stood between her and the three women now. Lucy eyed all the officers. 'Everyone out, please.'

Jenny Saunders started reaching for one of the chairs again.

Lucy raised her voice. 'You want information, Jenny, I've got it. I'm the senior investigating officer on your mother's case.'

'Well, you're not doing very much senior investigating, are you? Tell these mingers to let me go.'

Lucy nodded at the women. They released their grip slowly on Jenny Saunders. Jenny Saunders moved back against the wall until she was almost in the corner.

Lucy opened the door and the officers started filing out like Brown's cows. One of the men turned to her at the door and half-whispered to her, 'Are you sure this is safe?'

'Safer for me than for her. She's all mouth and no knickers.'
Lucy glanced back over her shoulder at Jenny Saunders.

'We'll wait outside anyway.' The last of the officers left the
room.

'If you like.' Lucy closed the door over. She crossed to the
table and sat down slowly. She ran her finger along the edge of
the table and was silent for a moment. She spoke without
looking up at the younger woman. 'Now, the way I see it,
Jennifer, either I leave and they lock you up until you cool
down or...'

'You wouldn't dare lay a finger on me!' Jenny Saunders
gritted her teeth.

'You've already assaulted two women police officers. A court
wouldn't find against me. Or...'

'Or what?' Jenny Saunders stared hard at her.

Lucy waved at the chair beside her. 'Or we can sit down and
discuss your late mother. Violet... Come on. Sit down. Tea or
coffee?'

'Are you for real?' Jenny Saunders's voice slowed down.

Lucy stood up, walked to the door and opened it. One of the
men was standing at the wall opposite. 'Tea for two, if you don't
mind, gentlemen.'

'What?'

'Canteen is still open, if you hurry.' Lucy crossed back to the
table and sat down. She looked over at the woman in the corner
and stretched out her hand to her.

'Come on, Jenny. The sooner we get started, the better for
both of us. I have my own daughter to get home to. Where are
you staying?'

Jenny Saunders drew herself up to her full height. Lucy
could see the dark eyes now. Pretty face. Smart. With an edge of
anger under the torment of sudden, violent bereavement. Too
much for even a balanced person to process.

Jenny Saunders suddenly spoke. 'B and B near the hospital... why won't they let me see my mum?'

'It's not so simple, Jenny, unfortunately.'

'She's my mother. It's very simple!'

'Come on...' Lucy nodded at her and pointed to the chair again.

Jenny Saunders moved slowly towards the table and sat down awkwardly on the chair. There was silence for a moment. Then she spoke, slowly at first. 'Did my mum die quickly?'

'It was instantaneous. I can promise you that.' Lucy pulled in her own chair.

'Why can't I see her?' The voice was plaintive now. Pathetic, even.

Jenny Saunders turned towards the wall for a moment, like she was sussing out something with herself. Then she turned back slowly. 'It's bad, isn't it?'

'It would be very hard to see, Jenny. And I've seen a lot. But I can get you a counsellor tomorrow morning, Jenny. Whatever you decide, I'll abide by. I promise.'

Jenny Saunders straightened up. 'Is my mum's body still here in Boynebridge?'

'No. It had to be brought to Dublin because we don't have the resources here.'

There was a knock on the door. The door opened and Dennis appeared in with a tray of tea and biscuits. 'Everything alright?'

'We're fine, Dennis. Look, get onto Mary Fegan and arrange an emergency bereavement session for Ms Saunders here. Priority.' Lucy pushed a cup in Jenny Saunders's direction. The door closed over.

Lucy turned back to Jenny. 'Jenny?'

'What?' Jenny Saunders looked at Lucy.

'I lost my father violently when I was fourteen. Never had a chance to say goodbye, either.'

'It's not the same. Mum will never get to see my babies now, Detective. It's not the same.' Jenny Saunders began to cry now, big tears streaming down her face. Lucy came over to the other side of the table and knelt down beside her. She stroked her hair. For a few minutes, there were no words at all between them, just the sound of sobbing.

Lucy leaned across to her. 'I can't bring her back for you, Jenny. But I can help.'

'I want her buried in London. So I can visit her every day.'

There was the sound of a siren out on the street. Friday night fever. Kebab shop rows and drunken stags baiting one another. Lucy waited until the crying had subsided. 'I need to ask you something important.'

'What?' Jenny Saunders spoke through hot tears.

Lucy put her hand on Jenny Saunders's hand. 'You were in touch by email and letter with your father over the past couple of months, according to the Carltons. Why was that?'

The angry tear-stained eyes looked up at her. 'I just wanted him to talk to me. To listen to me.'

'Why? You hadn't met since you were a child.'

'Because of what Mum told me about all the threats he had got.'

Lucy's eyes narrowed. 'Threats? From whom?'

'They were anonymous. I wanted to scare him into meeting me by saying I would reveal he was my father. Sure, I wanted to meet him and be recognised. But, most of all...'

'Yes?' Lucy looked into the other woman's eyes.

'I wanted him to stop posting on that internet site. He ignored my phone calls, so I wrote to him and emailed him, and he ignored all that too. And now he's dead. And Mum's dead.'

'So your letters and emails had nothing to do with money?'

'No! I just wanted to save him. And now they're both gone.'

Jenny Saunders buried her head in her hands and started sobbing again.

IT WAS another hour before she left Jenny Saunders. She went back up to the incident room. Dennis was at his computer.

'Thanks for sorting out the counsellor.'

Dennis smiled a toothy smile. 'Sound. I got something from the whiteboard, by the way.'

'Show...'

'They do this scanning thing. Same technology they use for looking under old paintings.'

Lucy took the sheaf of printouts from him. She could see the words she had written. Then some of Carlton's own writing. Numbers. Dates. And then, down in the bottom right-hand corner, a word in capitals and underlined. Lucy read two words in Gothic script.

Der Sammler

'What's that when it's at home?' Dennis cocked his head quizzically.

'It's German. It means the Collector.'

'Is it someone's name?'

Lucy ran her eye over the printout again. 'I suppose it's some sort of professional handle or even an academic nickname. Whoever it is, his name was important enough for Philip Carlton to write it on the whiteboard. Do you notice anything about the writing?'

Lucy traced out the letters on the sheet of paper. 'It's more like a scrawl than proper writing.'

'Maybe Professor Carlton was drunk.' Dennis smiled over at her.

Lucy shook her head. 'Stoned, I'd say.'

'Stoned?'

'A legal high. I'd say he wrote the suicide note first, at gunpoint, then injected himself. When the killer had left, he wrote these two words on the whiteboard. He was probably out of his head, too, and just about to lapse into unconsciousness. See the way the letters trail off? And there's another big question, of course. Who erased the words?'

'I think I might have the answer to that.'

'Which is, Dennis?'

Dennis grinned sheepishly. 'Well, for pig iron, I took a couple of samples and swabs around the area of the writing.'

'Did you, now? And?'

'There are some fibres on the whiteboard that match Professor Carlton's ancient tweed jacket. Looks like he might have leaned against the whiteboard after he had written the words and rubbed them off himself accidentally before staggering outside. I think.'

Lucy smiled. 'Well done, young man! That makes sense. I can see that. OK.' Lucy glanced at her watch. 'I'm going to drop Jenny Saunders up to the B and B. Right, see you a.m.'

'Good night.'

Lucy made her way down the back stairs. A drunk was being brought in the front door. Friday night's first casualty. She would be going to Windgap the following day, to Joyce Carlton. A bunch of flowers was in order. She would talk to Jenny Saunders after that and see if there was anything she should know.

IT WAS dark when she got home to the house in the Black Hills. She pulled into the yard, turned off the engine and just sat there for a moment, listening to the clink clank of the car engine cooling down. She tried not to think of Violet Saunders and her last horrible moments. The terror and the knowing that death was coming.

She phoned Jenny Saunders's number and left a message.
Jenny, this is Lucy O'Hara. Have a good rest. You have my number. Talk in the morning.

Then she went into the house, where her mother was baking bread for the morning and her daughter was sleeping soundly beside a big bear called Waldo.

And she was quietly thankful...

23

WINDGAP WAS LODGED IN A RUS-IN-URBE SETTING IN OLD Foxrock. Houses built by the well-heeled fleeing the city when the railway from Dublin was built, over a hundred years before. There were long driveways and manicured lawns and even the odd gate lodge. It wasn't hard to find the Carltons' home – it was just a stone's throw from Samuel Beckett's old crib.

Lucy pulled up at the gates and rang the bell. An ancient golden retriever came loping down the avenue towards the gate.

'Hello, fellow!' *He smells my dog from me. I know a dog who knows a dog who knows another dog...*

A figure approached from the distance down the gravel path. Joyce Carlton presented a morose, matronly profile as she walked down the gravelled avenue. When she reached the gates, the dog started barking, making a half-hearted show of guarding the grounds.

'Good boy, Cato.' Cato. It couldn't be Jack or Spot, of course.

Joyce Carlton suddenly started smiling, like Lucy was the surprise guest at a boring party. 'I could have opened the gates from the house. Still, a little fresh air doesn't do any harm.'

They shook hands formally. Joyce Carlton's grip was firm. She sat in beside Lucy in the car and they drove up to the house.

Windgap was an eight-bedroomed house standing on an acre and a quarter of land, according to Joyce Carlton. It was set in a hollow with a view of precisely nowhere, which was its main attraction. It couldn't be seen and no one was visible very much from its ancient windows either because of the fences and trees flanking the front and back gardens. There was no two-way trouble from neighbours and no gratuitous socialising.

Joyce Carlton brought Lucy around to the back door. 'It was a working farm in our father's time. All the farmland was sold off long ago. Father was a builder and dealer and a business-man. Not at all scholarly, like poor Philip and Derry.'

Lucy glanced at the stables and outhouses. 'This must take a lot of maintenance and upkeep?'

'Well, we were left well provided for. I moved back in here after my divorce, then Derry died, and myself and Philip split up the house between us.'

'I see.' Lucy followed her around to the kitchen.

Joyce Carlton opened the back door. 'Myself and Philip had separate floors, but we shared the big kitchen and the drawing room. Philip was very self-contained, you see. He was only in the real world half the time, I think.'

'And the other half?' Lucy smiled sweetly.

'Somewhere between 2,000 BC and the coming of the Normans. He was happier with BC than AD. Tea or coffee, Detective?'

'Coffee will be fine.'

Joyce Carlton nodded sagely. 'The best Colombian Arabica. Father taught us all about coffee before it was ever heard of here. You go on into the drawing room and I'll follow you.'

Lucy walked off ahead up the dark corridor for the front of the house.

.   .   .

THE DRAWING ROOM walls were covered in prints and lith-
ographs, and the walls were painted in clinically depressing
heritage colours. It was like Joyce Carlton had been preparing
for death all her life. A much-mauled baby grand stood in one
corner of the great room, and a series of framed photographs
had been placed on it. The centrepiece showed the Carltons *en
famille*. With the mother and father and the six ducklings, three
boys and three girls, all ranged around them on the front
doorsteps.

Joyce Carlton appeared in, bearing a silver tray. Lucy
pointed at the picture. 'Beautiful photograph.'

'Yes, indeed. Taken on the front steps of the house. There
are only two of us left now, to my sorrow.' Joyce Carlton left
down the tray and poured coffee from a silver percolator. 'I'm
told you want to see Philip's private papers?'

Lucy nodded. 'The circumstances of your brother's death
seem somewhat odd. We want to see if I can find any suggestion of potential enemies.'

Joyce Carlton was silent for a moment. 'I understand from
my brother that there is a suggestion of...'

'Forced suicide. That's one current line of enquiry.'

Joyce Carlton looked suddenly frail. The chirpiness had
disappeared as though the words themselves had just brought
home the reality to her. Joyce Carlton stared into space for a
few moments, and her breathing suddenly sounded heavier.
For a moment, Lucy wondered if she was taking a turn.

Lucy stood up slowly. 'Would you like me to get you a glass
of water?'

Joyce Carlton looked over at Lucy as though she was trying
to fathom something that was beyond both of them. Then a
little tear appeared in her eye. Lucy said nothing for a moment.

She made her way out to the kitchen and filled a glass from

the tap. When she came back into the room, Joyce Carlton was smiling again. This was clearly the Carlton way of doing things. File under forget until such time as things could be quietly digested later, anaconda-like.

Lucy passed the glass of water to the other woman. Joyce Carlton pointed at the prints on the wall. 'My father gathered them from all sorts of places. India, China, Japan. He travelled in the timber business. Mahogany and that sort of thing.'

There was a noise out in the corridor. A petite, older woman stuck her head in through the door. 'I've finished up, so I have, Ms Carlton.'

'Fine, Betty. I'll see you next Wednesday, then.'

The little woman nodded at Lucy and disappeared. Joyce Carlton turned back to Lucy. 'That's Mrs Egan. She does for me twice a week. She's almost as old as the house, but a great cleaner and a great cook.'

'You mentioned the circumstances of Philip's death?' There was a sharpness in the eyes now. Joyce Carlton had pulled herself back together.

'We think he may have had enemies. Maybe old ones.'

'The only enemy Philip had, Detective, was whiskey, as he got older.' Joyce Carlton thought for a moment. 'You don't think the mother of his child could have been involved in all this, do you?' Joyce Carlton looked at Lucy anxiously.

Lucy frowned. 'We have no idea. That's why I want to go through Philip's papers. My team is already working on emails and phone records.'

'Philip was scrupulous about notes and diaries. You'll find a lot of material.'

Lucy smiled graciously. 'I'd like to do an overview today and come back for a more detailed trawl, if that's alright.'

'Of course.' Joyce Carlton stood up stiffly and led the way back through the house. She stopped at a large oak door and pointed to the motif over it.

Lasciate ogne speranza, voi ch'intrate

'Philip's little Dante in-joke.' Joyce Carlton opened the great oak door to show an enormous room with a window in the side of the house, giving onto a vegetable garden.

'Philip was a good gardener. No time for flowers, though. Now, Detective O'Hara, over on the right wall, you have the academic books and reference books. On the back wall, you have Philip's diaries and notebooks and various files. Opposite the window, you can see his music collection.'

Lucy ran her eyes over the titles. 'Lots of Mozart, I see. No Beethoven?'

'Top shelf, Beethoven. Beethoven was above everybody else, you see. He used to say the Mozart symphonies were like music written by a software engineer coated in sugar. Except for the Great Mass, that is. But Beethoven was brains and brawn and heart. Philip used a ruder phrase, of course. Bit like himself, I suppose, old Ludwig. Now, I'll leave you to it. Call me if you need me. We're having dinner at around five-ish, myself and David. We'd be happy if you joined us.'

The door of the study closed over behind Joyce Carlton. Lucy walked over to the back wall and pulled out a page-a-day diary dated 1998, to start the ball rolling. She sat behind the desk and ran her hand over the baize surface. She opened the diary. It was all written in elegant, schoolboy copperplate from the fifties.

There were lots of appointments. Words and phrases here and there in Latin and Greek, German and French and a couple of Gaelic words too, in the old script. She could get what that was about: making sure that prying eyes (like her own) would have a hard time sorting through Philip Carlton's personal entanglements if the diaries ever fell into the wrong hands. There were names like 'Maria Jose' and 'Cynthia' and 'Niamh' (with no surnames) all written in Greek letters, with phone numbers and times beside them. On balance, Lucy decided these names were probably not relevant. Too far in the past and too ephemeral. There were sums of money scribbled on pages and, latterly, email addresses. The amounts of money hardly seemed significant though and, anyway, would anyone be so foolish as to detail dodgy money in a desk diary?

Philip Carlton had even added drawings from sites and drawings of artefacts here and there. The line drawings revealed a meticulous mind under the boozy bonhomie Philip Carlton had concocted for his occasional television appearances.

It was when she opened the third diary and skimmed through its pages that she came across two simple words, from 28 August 1998, that jolted her awake,

Der Sammler

She flicked through the diary. The word was repeated at least ten times. It was the same name Philip Carlton had written on the whiteboard just before he died.

This was someone of importance in Philip Carlton's life. There was no doubt about that now. Certainly, more important than the transient young women whose names were enshrouded in Greek letters. But the name had nothing else added to it. There was no additional information like place or ID or phone numbers. Was it some German contact? A scholar of some sort? (It was a man, anyway, unless the masculine title was a double bluff.) She was as wise when she closed the diaries, a couple of hours later, as she was when she opened the first one.

IT WAS ABOUT four in the afternoon when she decided to call it a day in Windgap. There had been more coffee and cake that

Mrs Egan had baked. She was finishing up her notes when she heard voices out in the corridor.

The door opened and David Carlton's enormous head peered in, with its shock of wiry hair. 'Detective O'Hara! Well met!' The eyes tracked around the room.

Lucy looked up from a sheaf of notes. 'Just getting an overview of things.'

David Carlton's eyes lit on the diaries on the desk in front of her. 'Anything of interest?'

'I have a list of names that keep popping up. Maybe yourself and your sister might have a moment to go through them with me?'

David Carlton smiled. 'Of course. I'd say a lot of them have gone to their eternal rest by this stage, though.'

LUCY SAT into the dining room with David Carlton and his sister. Over dinner, they whittled the list of names down to six possible long-term acquaintances. Lucy left down her cutlery and looked between brother and sister. 'By the way, the name *'Der Sammler.'* Does that German name mean anything to you?'

'Should it?' David Carlton looked genuinely puzzled.

'It's a name I came across in a couple of documents of Philip's.'

Lucy looked over at Joyce Carlton, but she just shrugged her shoulders. 'Sounds awfully like one of those boys' club handles academics like to use. Doesn't ring any bells, though.'

'Fair enough.' Lucy reached for her briefcase. 'I think I'd better get going before the traffic starts up.'

David Carlton stood up. 'I'll see you to the door.'

Lucy followed him back through the long, morose corridor to the back door. She nodded at the stables at the far side of the yard. 'Do you still keep horses?'

'Not anymore, I'm afraid. Everything is winding down here, I'm afraid. Even poor old Joyce back there.'

Lucy glanced around her. 'I'm sorry?'

'Don't put too much store by her memory of things, distant or recent. Joyce's memory is getting a bit wonky, I'm afraid. I'll take a ride down the gate with you, if that's OK? The walk back will stretch the legs a bit.'

The car crawled slowly down the gravel path. When they pulled up at the gate, Lucy turned to David Carlton. 'Superintendent Reese and myself would like to attend your brother's funeral as a mark of respect.'

'We'll see you there, then. And thank you for all your help, by the way. Myself and my sister really do appreciate your diligence.'

The gates opened. David Carlton stepped out of the car and waved her a vague goodbye. Then he carried on back up the gravel path at a tidy trot.

24

REESE WAS STANDING IN FULL REGALIA AT THE CAR PARK IN Killiney Catholic Church, a picture of probity and poise all rolled up into one stern figure. Lucy realised again, as she strode towards him, why she trusted him so much. It was that certain obstinate duty-before-uniform idea that spoke to her; she wondered, once again, where it had sprung from. The Bateman fiasco had brought it out in her, big time, and Reese had backed her because he read it in her, too: speaking truth to sleeveens and charlatans.

They shook hands.

Lucy cast her eye over the solid stone walls. 'They hid this church well when they built it, George.'

Reese grinned at her. 'Different times. No one gives a beggar's curse about religion these days. Even my own crowd scarcely know their Bible anymore. I don't know which is worse, too much religion or none.'

Lucy cast her eye over the crowd. The great and the good and the not-so-good were all well represented. There was a clatter of academics over by the church door, huddling together for comfort like jumpy starlings. Half of them looked like likely candidates for the big box themselves. She recognised a portly barrister from the land tribunals grown fat on other people's wrongdoings, and wondered silently whether there was a mathematical formula for converting legal fees into kilos of human flesh. RTE had a camera there, and TV3 too. She reminded herself silently to steer clear of all lenses as much as possible. The last thing she needed was her mug on a screen.

As they trooped slowly into the church, Reese whispered to her, 'Let's stay downstream, with the sinners, Lucy. We're well matched: a Church of Ireland heretic and a renegade Roman Catholic.'

David and Joyce Carlton walked behind the coffin as it was wheeled up the aisle on the little trolley. She caught sight of Michel stage left, in the midsection with that suave smirk of his. A small group sang hymns on the altar. First a Gaelic song, then a Latin hymn and, finally, something by Handel, according to the service pamphlet.

David Carlton said a few well-burnished, plummy words. He gazed out serenely over the congregation calmly as he spoke. 'My brother Philip was, to use a common TransAtlanticism, the go-to guy for Ireland two thousand BC. That's no mean feat, especially in this internet-saturated age.'

As the coffin was carried back along the aisle a while later, the quartet on the far side of the altar played a selection of slow Irish airs. Michel caught her eye from the far side of the aisle and gave a little bow. When the cortege reached the porch, it halted suddenly and they heard shouting. A woman's voice, loud and London. Reese and Lucy looked at one another. The shouting suddenly grew louder.

Lucy turned to Reese. 'That's Jenny Saunders.'

Lucy made her way slowly down the aisle to where the coffin was swaying on the shoulders of the pall-bearers. The crowd were getting uneasy now. She pushed her way through the throng to where she could see Jenny Saunders at the head of the little cortege.

Behind her, she could hear David Carlton. 'What's she doing here?'

Lucy turned around slowly and took his arm. 'I can sort this out. I've already dealt with her in the station. Please...' David Carlton flushed like a baby with chronic constipation. Lucy pushed her way on ahead until she reached the head of the procession in the porch. 'Jenny... Jenny.'

Jenny Saunders looked at Lucy through a veil of angry tears. She looked like she hadn't slept in an age. 'This is my father they're burying. I have a right to be here!'

Lucy took Jenny Saunders by the hand. 'Of course you do. Now, come on, let's walk together.'

She led Jenny Saunders slowly out of the church and stood with her near the hearse. Reese kept his distance from them as the coffin was loaded into the hearse. Lucy put her arm around the younger woman's shoulders. 'Do you want to go to the burial? You don't have to, you know.'

Jenny Saunders nodded.

'Come on, then. We can go together in my car.'

DEANSGRANGE CEMETERY WAS chilly for a summer's day. A snippy little breeze cut across the well-tended resting places of the dead. Lucy stood with Jenny Saunders down from the grave. Just as the coffin was lowered into the earth, Joyce Carlton crossed over slowly to them. She stretched out her hand and offered Jenny Saunders a crimson rose from the bunch she was holding. Jenny Saunders blinked and sniffled through her tears. Then both women crossed to the open grave and dropped their flowers onto the coffin.

Reese came up behind her. 'I'm away now. It might do no harm to mingle at the funeral baked meats after.'

Lucy nodded.

THE AFTERS WERE in Killiney Castle. The academics were huddled in one corner like naughty children. The legal whodunits were canoodling with one another in another corner. Lucy passed from one little knot of mourners to the next, with Jenny Saunders in tow, like a nobody's child. The remnant of the Carlton clan, brother and sister, were standing over by the big fireplace with another couple. When there was a break in the crowd, Lucy crossed over to the fireplace, leaving Jenny Saunders listening to an old lady wittering on about 'the vegan conspiracy'.

David Carlton was full of red wine and bonhomie. 'Ah, there you are!' The face relaxed into an inane sort of smile. 'Thank you for defusing that situation in the church. It could have been very unpleasant for us all.'

'You're welcome.' Lucy regarded the awkward-looking couple beside David Carlton quietly.

David Carlton beamed benevolently. 'These are two old friends of the family, by the way – Jeremy and Sheila Arkens.'

'Pleased to meet you.' There was a creeping Jesus look about the man, Lucy thought. And his better half didn't look like much to write home about either. What was it her father used to say? *As God made them, he matched them.*

Jeremy Arkens piped up in a squeaky voice. 'We were just saying we are missing a few souls today. Father Mullins, the biblical scholar, an old friend of Philip's. He's at some conference and couldn't make it back. And, of course, the professor. Old Professor Rohan.' Lucy recognised the names from Joyce Carlton's list from the Antiquities files in Harcourt Square.

Jenny Saunders was suddenly back at her side. David

Carlton smiled awkwardly over at his brother's daughter. He seemed to be trying to say something but couldn't quite find a smooth enough formula. The Arkenses nodded over at Jenny Saunders serenely. It was starting to feel awkward now.

Lucy signalled to Jenny Saunders, then turned back to the little group. 'I have to get home, Jenny, I'm afraid. I'll be in touch over the next few days.'

Jeremy Arkens piped up. 'Nice meeting you, Detective O'Hara.' Jeremy Arkens sounded altogether too sweet to be wholesome.

'Mutual.' Arkens. Yes, she knew that name was in Philip Carlton's diaries too. All over them, in fact. She glanced between the two Arkenses.

'Perhaps you would have time for a little chat? You might be able to fill me in on some background details.'

'I'd be delighted to. Anything I can do to help.' Jeremy Arkens pulled out a business card from his breast pocket and passed it to Lucy.

'I'll be in touch so.'

'We look forward to that.' Jeremy Arkens smiled sweetly.

Joyce Carlton walked with them to the lobby. She took Jenny by the arm. 'Jenny, why don't we meet up when everything has settled down again.'

Jenny Saunders nodded but said nothing.

Lucy and Jenny walked down the steps into the car park. Jenny Saunders turned to Lucy. 'Can you drop me back to the new B and B? It's in Donnybrook. I've decided to stay in Dublin until the arrangements have been sorted out.'

'And what about the other business?' Lucy waited for the reply.

Jenny Saunders looked away. 'I've decided not to see my mum's remains. I don't want to remember her that way.'

They got into the car silently. Lucy turned on the engine

and looked across at Jenny Saunders. 'I think that's a wise decision.'

They pulled out of the hotel and headed south for the city.

THE SEA WAS smooth as glass as the wooden-hulled Mermaid moved languorously across the water. Even when they rounded the Rockabill lighthouse, out onto the open water, there was scarcely a breath of wind. She gave Saoirse the tiller when they finally turned back for the harbour. It took an age to reach Skerries, though, with the wind down.

Lucy's mother picked them up, and they drove back to her house near the south beach, in Rush. Reese phoned just as they were sitting down to supper. She took the call in the sitting room, away from ears.

Reese sounded upbeat. 'All OK?'

'All fine. I dropped Jenny back to her B and B and we had a little chat about things.'

Reese's voice softened. 'Good. By the way, how did Windgap go the other day, Lucy? I didn't get a chance to ask you at the funeral.'

'Nothing really stood out in the diaries. I want to go back for another bite, though.' Lucy wondered what Reese was really phoning for.

Reese coughed that special cough of his. The one he reserved for state occasions and indirect commands. 'Right. By the way, I hear you're tasking Gerry Sullivan with the East European end of things. Can you spare someone to work with him?'

Reese sounded like he already knew the answer.

Lucy did herself the dignity of pausing for a moment. She thought about what Reese was really looking for. 'I suppose Peter Brosnahan would be a good match, don't you think?'

'Good idea. Be in touch.' Reese signed off warmly. He had

got what he wanted and they both pretended it was Lucy's big idea.

Lucy went back into the sitting room. Her mother was pouring a 'not-too-bad Bordeaux' into cut-glass goblets. She sat down in front of Saoirse and opened up the chessboard.

Half an hour later, she was in check.

25

BROSNAHAN MET UP WITH SULLIVAN AT A TOURIST HOTEL JUST off the Naas Road, and they had coffee in the bar. Sullivan took a sip of his coffee and grimaced. 'They really boiled the bollox out of that coffee.'

He pushed the cup to one side and started laying out the day. 'There are two locations in Dublin and one outside Portlaoise we have to look at. The first is a tanning salon in the city centre that's really a glorified knocking shop. We drop in from time to time because it helps us catch bigger fish.'

Brosnahan took a sip of coffee. 'Where's the other Dublin one?'

Sullivan nodded over his shoulder. 'It's a garage near here with a dodgy Lithuanian connection. We can drop in on the way out of town.'

Brosnahan followed him silently to the car.

THE TANNING CENTRE was five minutes from O'Connell Street. They parked downstream and walked around the block to an old building with a Chinese restaurant and a laundrette on the ground floor.

A couple of local apaches were hanging around outside. Sullivan rang the intercom and glanced over his shoulder. 'Shallow end of the local gene pool.'

A man's voice spoke in broken English. 'We open three in afternoon. You come back then.'

Sullivan smiled across at Brosnahan. 'Garda detective unit. Open up, please.' Footsteps clattered down the stairs, and a tall man with a shaven head opened the door with a smaller man behind him. Sullivan and Brosnahan flashed their IDs.

The taller man spoke. 'You new garda? Where is Tom?'

Sullivan walked straight in past him. 'Tom's busy at the moment. And you're Jakub, right?'

'Yes. There is problem?' The taller man glanced around at his friend.

Sullivan smiled an alligator smile. 'Let's hope not, Jakub, old stock. Now, let's go upstairs to your little boudoir.' The two men looked at one another and started back up the stairs slowly. Sullivan and Brosnahan followed them. In the salon on the first floor, a half a dozen tanning beds were scattered around the room.

Sullivan nodded to Brosnahan to have a scout around, then turned to the taller man. They walked into the smaller room and sat facing one another across the desk. Sullivan left his phone down on the desk in front of him. 'No sign of any strangers coming or going, Jakub?'

'Nobody special. If special, I tell Tom. Just myself and Majik here, and the two women, in the evening.'

Sullivan smiled sourly all of a sudden. 'And Tom tells me you haven't given him anything in a long time.'

'I...'

'You need to work a bit harder for me here now. We're looking for a Lithuanian bad boy, passing through. Possibly based in Spain. This fellow is a professional. Probably military trained, in his forties or fifties. Maybe a local Polish guy with him. Someone might have noticed something or heard something. It's a small island.'

'Yes, very small island.'

'So I need you to ask around for me.' Sullivan tapped the table. 'Everyone you know. Understand? Oh, I forgot to tell you...'

Jakub's eyes narrowed, but he said nothing.

'Tom tells me your situation will be reviewed in a few weeks. And, of course, we'll be in touch with the Polish authorities. Do you like living here?'

Jakub nodded. 'Yes. Very much.'

Sullivan smiled and stood. 'Better than the kip you came out of near the Russian border, eh? We all have to help one another in this life.'

'Of course. I understand, Detective...'

'Sullivan. Gerry Sullivan. And you won't find me on Google, so don't bother.'

Jakub called over to his companion, 'Majik, go get coffee for men.'

Sullivan closed up the ledger he was pretending to look at and stood up. 'No, thanks, my friend. Now, if you hear anything...'

The taller man stood up and shook Sullivan's hand. 'I will ask everywhere.'

'Of course you will. Sound man.'

Sullivan smiled and called to Brosnahan, 'Come on. Saddle up.' They headed back down the stairs.

BROSNAHAN TURNED to Sullivan as they walked back to the car. 'You weren't very polite to that nice brothel-keeper back there.'

'He wants to keep his whorehouse and his kids in that

South Dublin school and service his wife's credit cards, he needs to get off his hole and show willing.'

'So, what's the story there anyway?'

'The little fellow is the arse-wiper. The older guy, Jakub, was human resources guy for a gang back in the old country. He was told by the authorities, unofficially of course, to fuck off to London or Dublin or get locked up. Paddyland must have been the best option.'

Brosnahan stopped for a moment. 'So why did we visit him, exactly?'

Sullivan laughed. 'It gets the word out in the jungle that there's a price for not telling us. And he may actually come up with something specific if he thinks he's on a short leash.'

Sullivan zapped the car and they got in.

THEY DROVE out of the city by the Liffey and turned in west by the Grand Canal. At the edge of the Naas Road, on the outskirts of the city, they crossed into the Robinhood industrial estate.

Sullivan pointed to a large warehouse. 'This place does spurious parts for spuriouser customers. It's run by a couple of Ukrainian hard-asses who wouldn't piss on you to put you out. They get a lot of passers-through, though. It's like the dodgy watering hole in a small town that helps us keep tabs on the local lowlifes.'

'Not really going to win PC cop of the year any time soon, are you?'

'Pond scum is pond scum, whether it's local or imported.' Sullivan swung in off the access road and pulled up outside the warehouse. 'This looks shut up. You hang on here and I'll go 'round the back.'

Sullivan slipped around the building and peeped in through the office window. There were papers thrown here and there and piled-up post. He came back around and climbed into the car beside Brosnahan.

'No sign of life. Right, next stop the bog of Allen.'

THEY REACHED Portlaoise on the motorway in under an hour. The car dismantlers was outside the town in a failed start-up industrial estate.

Sullivan turned to Brosnahan. 'They provide genuine stolen spare parts and make serious brass. They're worth more to us alive than dead. Not literally, of course. God forbid!'

'Right.'

Sullivan pulled up in front of the open doors. He stood out onto the greasy tarmac and stretched himself ostentatiously. The young mechanic standing at the oil pump regarded him warily. Brosnahan could see this was going to be difficult.

The mechanic called over to Sullivan, 'Can I help?'

Sullivan showed his ID.

Sullivan turned around to Brosnahan. 'Peter, go into the office and wait for me there. I'll follow you in.'

The mechanic threw the oil rag down onto the ground. 'No go in there! Private!' Sullivan ignored him. The mechanic pulled out a mobile phone and started shouting into it.

Brosnahan made his way into the office. There was no one in there and no sound but the radio chatting away to itself. He could see and hear Sullivan shouting at the other mechanic. 'Where's your boss man?'

'You go! Now!' Sullivan walked past him to a couple of cars under tarps. He pulled back one to reveal a newish Merc.

Through the window, Brosnahan saw the mechanic go for a wheel brace. Sullivan was onto him like a terrier with a rat. 'Drop that fuckin' thing now!' Sullivan pinned the mechanic to the bonnet. The wheel brace clanged off the floor.

Brosnahan came out of the office and walked towards them

slowly, but was clear that Sullivan was on top of things. 'Where's your boss man?'

Sullivan turned around to the sound of an engine. An ancient Pajero jeep swung into the yard and screeched to a halt beside Sullivan's car. An older man stepped out of the car.

He looked between Sullivan and Brosnahan. 'Sorry for this! He doesn't understand. He's new.'

Sullivan kicked the wheel brace across the floor. 'He'll understand if he tries that move again, Viktor, so he will.'

Viktor began shouting at the mechanic. The other man stood up slowly, glowering. Sullivan and Brosnahan followed Viktor back into the office and sat down at the desk.

Viktor followed them in and kept an eye on the other mechanic through the window. 'Is this something special?'

Sullivan threw a still from the Boyne Valley CCTV camera down on the table. 'It's about two murders and an attempted murder. We're looking for this cowboy. Possibly a Lithuanian involved and one other, could be Pole, Russian, Ukrainian, we don't know. But this guy is a Litvak.'

Viktor opened out his hands. 'I heard it on the news. I'm sorry. I know nothing.'

Brosnahan weighed in now. 'This isn't happy-ending girls trucked in from some kip in Kiev, Viktor. This is murder. Understand?'

Viktor glanced over at Brosnahan and spoke slowly. 'Look, I have to drop by to someone. I'll be passing the motorway hotel after. Understand?'

Sullivan nodded. 'Got you.'

Sullivan pulled the door after them. The mechanic bowed his head as they passed like a vengeful dog. They swung into the car park of the hotel at the edge of the motorway and pulled up at the far side of a large van, where they were invisible.

Half an hour later, Viktor's car drew up beside them. Viktor rolled down the window and looked straight ahead of him as he spoke. 'Here's what I hear. Some Lithuanian with a Polish or Russian passport. He come out of nowhere. I don't know his connection here.'

Sullivan frowned. 'And what else? You're not helping your-self here.'

Viktor lowered his voice. 'This old explosives come from someone who is not living here. From a mine, long time ago, I hear this. Maybe just, you know, talking.'

'But not paramilitary? You sure?'

'I sure. Not paramilitary. Hundred per cent.'

Brosnahan leaned across Sullivan. 'What sort was his accent?'

'I hear maybe like little English, maybe. Not sure.' Viktor shrugged his shoulders.

Brosnahan continued on. 'London accent?'

Viktor looked over at the two of them. 'I don't know this. Then he was gone. That's all what I hear. I hear more, I tell you.'

Sullivan smiled graciously. 'Too right you will, old chum, or you'll be on the first Ryanair back to Warsaw.'

Viktor smiled gently and turned on his engine.

They waited until he had driven away, and then headed back to the motorway. Sullivan put his foot to the floor. Then he hit Lucy's name on the speed dial.

Two days after Philip Carlton's funeral, Lucy took the road back south to the foothills of the Wicklow Mountains. It was time to cosy up to Jeremy Arkens and his wife and see what could be seen. The voice on the phone had been smooth as honey. Jeremy Arkens would be delighted to assist her in her very important work. At her convenience.

Lucy brought Anna and Dennis with her to make a few visits. At the exit from the N11, in North Wicklow, they turned up into the hills, for Roundwood. Lucy pulled in at the Round-wood Inn.

'I'll pick you up in, say, an hour, Anna, after myself and Dennis finish with these two.'

Anna Crowley disappeared into the pub. A few minutes later, they rounded a corner in the windy road, and Jeremy Arkens's house appeared, as if from nowhere. They drove over the cow bars and pulled up in front of the house.

Jeremy Arkens was standing in the door to greet them, all hail-fellow-well-met. 'Ah, Detective O'Hara. And...?'

Dennis smiled softly. 'Detective Sheehan. Dennis.'

'Welcome. I've just put on the coffee.'

They followed Jeremy Arkens into the house. The whole house was flooded with light. Dennis walked over to the window. 'That's a magnificent view you have here.'

'Yes. You couldn't buy it. Back in a moment with coffee and bikkies.' Jeremy Arkens disappeared into the kitchen.

Dennis turned back to Lucy. 'Is that the Sugarloaf in the distance?'

'Think so. Like Mr Arkens says, you couldn't buy this view. Unless you have the money, that is.' There was a cough behind them. Sheila Arkens, in twin set and choker, was standing there. She came forward and shook Lucy's hand. 'Detective O'Hara. And this young gentleman is?'

'Sheehan. Detective Dennis Sheehan.'

Sheila Arkens beamed. 'Gosh, you look far too young to be a detective! In my day, they were all stout fellows with big guns inside their jackets and thick Kerry accents.'

Dennis summoned up a smile. 'Well, the guns are smaller, and we're younger now. But I'm from Kerry.'

'And more power to you! That's what I say.' Sheila Arkens raised her voice. 'Jeremy, is that coffee ready?'

They sat down at a great glass coffee table with an inset Hill of Tara design. Lucy pointed at the prints on the far walls. 'These remind me of the ones in the Carltons.'

'Well spotted! Old Mr Carlton and Jeremy's father were bosom buddies, you know. They both collected artefacts on their travels. That's how Jeremy acquired his own taste, such as it is.'

Jeremy Arkens appeared in with a tray and left it down on the glass table.

Sheila Arkens glanced at Lucy and Dennis. 'Let me pour, darling. Jeremy has a habit of splashing tea and coffee onto the parquet.'

Jeremy Arkens winced silently. Lucy made a big production

of taking a notebook from her handbag. 'I'd like to run through a couple of these names Joyce Carlton mentioned.'

'Of course.'

Lucy scanned the list. 'Tim McDonagh?'

Sheila Arkens clanged her spoon on the coffee cup. 'In a home, I'm afraid. Great scholar in his day, of course. Now he hardly knows the day of the week, poor creature.'

Lucy moved further down the list. 'Dermot O'Leary?'

Sheila Arkens looked almost wistful now. 'He's been stateside for twenty years. Michigan, I think. Well retired now.'

'And Andrew O'Neill?'

Sheila Arkens seemed triumphant. Not a single name had passed muster yet. 'Ah, yes. The O'Neill brothers. Both passed away, over the last year. One died, then the other followed him into the grave, as it were. Quality people. Joyce's list is a little out of date, if you don't mind my saying so. Quite a lot of Philip's contemporaries have passed.'

Lucy took a sip of coffee. 'Professor Carlton had relationships with a number of his postgrads over the years, I believe.'

Sheila Arkens put her hand to her mouth as though to stifle a little laugh. 'Relationships? Oh, dear! Philip would never have divulged that type of information to us, Detective.'

'I see.'

'Is there anyone else you need help with?' Sheila Arkens angled her head elegantly.

'Well, not really, since most of these names are no longer with us.'

Jeremy Arkens suddenly piped up. 'It's quite scary, isn't it?' Jeremy Arkens didn't look that scared, Lucy thought to herself. More like personally annoyed by the idea.

Lucy ran her finger down the list. 'Just Professor Rohan left.'

Sheila Arkens perked up. 'Ah, dear old Professor Rohan! When you meet him, you'll just want to mind him. He's really an old dote.'

'I'm sure.' Lucy smiled.

'The oldest of our diminishing circle, you might say. Apparently, he was in England and couldn't get back for the funeral, Detective. I think there's a secret girlfriend there. Is 'girlfriend' even the right name for someone so old, Jeremy?' Sheila Arkens turned to her husband in a show of solicitousness.

'I think 'boyfriend' would probably be closer.' Jeremy Arkens seemed glad to be asked for an opinion and started to chuckle at his own joke.

Lucy looked back at the list again. 'I just have a landline number for him.'

Sheila Arkens started giggling. 'That's because he's the only being on this island who doesn't have a mobile phone. He reads Greek, Latin, Sanskrit and a couple of common or garden European languages, but can't master a smartphone! Can you credit that?'

Sheila Arkens was laughing out loud now. She sounded like she had been at the gin early.

Lucy looked up and smiled. 'Actually, I tried to phone the professor's number earlier. No answer. Never mind, I can try to see him another day.'

Jeremy Arkens topped up his coffee cup. 'Will that be all?'

Lucy closed over her notebook. 'For the moment, I think. And thank you both for your time.'

Jeremy Arkens looked like he was about to wag his tail now. He glanced over at his wife as though seeking affirmation. 'Would you like to have a quick look at my little collection before you go?'

Sheila Arkens gave another gin giggle. 'Jeremy is very proud of his collection. Everyone gets dragged in there.'

Lucy and Dennis followed Jeremy Arkens into the annex. He threw a switch and all the little glass cases lit up. Lucy walked about, looking at the collection as her host chatted away.

'This is an Irish relic from St Gallen, in Switzerland. As you know, we brought culture to Europe hundreds of years ago.'

'Delighted to hear that. I think the culture might be coming the other way these days.' Lucy pointed at the little bog oak crosses. 'And these here?'

'These are famine crosses. Hard to imagine the hardship people suffered.' Jeremy Arkens put on a sad clown's face.

'Indeed.' Lucy nodded at Dennis. Time to go.

Suddenly Jeremy Arkens waded in. 'Your area of expertise is linguistics, I believe? Very unusual for a garda.'

'Forensic linguistics, actually.' Lucy smiled sweetly.

'We must all watch our mouths then, eh? Anything you say may be taken down, and all that. One day, it will be anything you think, hmmm?' Jeremy Arkens laughed pleasantly at his own little joke.

'Well, we should really get going, like I said.' Lucy shook hands with Jeremy Arkens.

'Fine. Remember, if you need to contact us, feel free to.'

If I need to contact you again, Lucy thought, *you'll be the last to hear about it.* But she said nothing and hooshed Dennis ahead of her.

JEREMY ARKENS SAW them to the door. From the car, they could see Sheila Arkens watching them from the big wide window. Dennis spoke through the side of his mouth. 'Bit of a shyster, that fellow, if you don't mind my saying so. Butter wouldn't melt in his mouth.'

Lucy swung out onto the road, heading downhill for the motorway. 'He's a businessman. They're all wheeler-dealers. They could run rings around the scholars.'

Dennis looked across at her. 'All that palaver about crosses. I'd say the silver means more to him than the bog oak, somehow.'

Lucy eased along the ditch to avoid a car coming up the hill.
'That's very unkind of you,. Remember, we brought culture to
Europe.'

'What? Kerrygold and Guinness and Baileys? Sure, this is
the best country in Ireland!'

Lucy chuckled. 'Right! Right! Are you getting all cynical on
me, Detective Sheehan?'

Dennis gave a little laugh. 'Just saying, like. That fella would
sell sand to the Arabs and snow to the Eskimos, so he would.'

Lucy dropped the car down in gear as they made their way
up the hill for Roundwood.

ANNA WAS HUNCHED over her laptop in the Roundwood Inn
when they arrived. They had coffee together and then headed
back down from the hills for the N11. As they turned north,
back towards the city, Lucy leaned back over the driver's seat.
'Dennis, I'm dropping you at Bray station, and you can take the
train straight back to Boynebridge.'

'Sound.' Dennis looked relieved.

Lucy looked across at Anna. 'We have another little call to
make.'

'Where to?'

'Professor Rohan's house.'

Dennis piped up from the back. 'I thought you were going
to leave it for another day?'

Lucy smiled in the mirror. 'Oh, dear! Did I mislead the
Arkens? Whoops!'

They dropped Dennis at the station and carried on towards
Foxrock, not far from the Carlton household. Edenmore was
another house hidden in its own shadows, just like the Carlton
pile at Windgap. Lucy had already phoned ahead, but she was
careful to knock off the phone just as it was picked up at the
other end.

So, there was someone in at Edenmore. The last (and oldest) man standing of the Carlton circle, apparently. She reckoned he had to have some read on the Carltons, past and present.

Memories of a family that were mostly below ground now.

—————

27

THE GATES OF EDENMORE WERE OPEN, SO LUCY DROVE STRAIGHT in. She pulled up beside a dry water feature in the front garden and a tatty-looking nymph with her right arm lopped off.

'This is old Professor Rohan's little gaff. I thought two women calling would work better than myself and Dennis.'

They got out of the car and crossed to the big red door. The bell didn't seem to work, so Lucy hammered on the door. There was still no answer. She peeped in through the window, but there was no sign of life. They heard a shuffling sound to their left.

An elderly man dressed in an ancient sports jacket and cavalry twill trousers came around the corner with a pair of secateurs in his hand, beaming. 'Can I help you two ladies?'

Lucy stepped forward. 'Professor Rohan?'

'Emeritus professor, strictly speaking. And even that was aeons ago.' The old eyes looked out at Lucy kindly.

'I'm Detective Lucy O'Hara and this is Detective Anna Crowley. I'm the senior investigating officer on Philip Carlton's case. May we come in?'

'Good gosh! Detectives! Of course!'

Professor Rohan opened the door into a gloomy-looking hallway and an ancient tiled floor from a bygone age. Even the bric-a-brac in the hall looked from another era: an ancient clothes stand and mirror, an umbrella stand and a mahogany weather barometer complemented the gloom of the dark walls.

He shepherded them into the sitting room, dragging his right leg a little. He leaned on the door jamb and smiled at them. 'Touch of arthritis in my leg, I'm afraid. Happens to the best of us, I suppose.'

The sitting room was just as gloomy as the hallway. 'Take a seat, ladies.'

Lucy's eyes took in the photographs on the wall. They were all of the same woman, in different poses. The professor caught her gaze. 'That's my late wife, Sybil. We weren't blessed with children, unfortunately. I sometimes talk to her, you know.'

Lucy smiled kindly. 'I understand.' The place looked like a mausoleum.

The old face smiled at them. 'Can I interest you ladies in tea?'

'No, thanks, Professor. We have just been with the Arkens, and we're going through a shortlist of people who knew Philip Carlton.'

Professor Rohan nodded. 'I understand. I felt so bad at not being able to attend the funeral.'

Lucy nodded. 'Of course. Are you retired a long time?'

'Ages and ages. On health grounds. Then Sybil fell ill. She only lasted a year after we returned to Ireland, poor thing.'

'That's very sad.'

Professor Rohan suddenly seemed distracted. 'Do you know what I'm going to tell you?'

'No?' Lucy and Anna glanced at one another.

Professor Rohan dropped his voice to a hush. He put his finger to his lips as though trying to recall some knotty detail.

'Some days, I'm not really sure I'm alive at all. That I'm in the world at all, so to speak. Is that strange?'

Lucy smiled a tidy smile and kept her eyes on his eyes. 'Well, we all get a bit like that sometimes.'

Professor Rohan looked thoughtful. 'Of course, when you go back to Ancient Greece, they were already wrestling with that sort of metaphysical problem. And do you know why?'

Lucy glanced back at the list in her hand. 'I can't say I've given it much thought.'

'Well, they had the leisure and money to think about it all. Everyone else had to work and jolly well get on with it, you see.'

'I suppose.' Lucy opened up her bag and took out the notebook.

Professor Rohan glanced at the notebook, then turned back to Lucy. 'Still, you're not here to be bored with ancient Greece, are you?'

Lucy smiled. 'You knew the Carltons very well, I hear?' Lucy ran her eyes over the names crossed off her list. Her guess seemed correct: Professor Rohan was probably the last one standing.

'Oh, yes. The two girls, Olwyn and Helen, who died tragically. Then Derry and Philip and Joyce and David. Philip was the one I was friendliest with, of course. Overlap, you see. Not in age, of course. You see, I was a historian-linguist, a classics scholar, and he was a historian-archaeologist, a dealer in dead things and people, as someone said somewhere. He would have made a poor classics scholar, though.'

Lucy glanced around at the photos of the Carltons on the wall. 'I see. And were you aware of any enemies Philip Carlton might have had?'

'Enemies? Can't imagine poor Philip had any real enemies.' Professor Rohan seemed puzzled by the question.

Anna coughed and excused herself. 'Would you mind if I got a glass of water?'

Professor Rohan started to stand up. 'Let me fetch you a glass.'

Anna smiled. 'No, you carry on. I don't want to interrupt you. The kitchen is this way, Professor Rohan, is it?'

'Straight ahead, steady as she goes. The glasses are in the cupboard.' The professor turned back to Lucy.

'Where were we? I tend to lose the thread sometimes.'

Lucy glanced over her list again. The one name she deliberately kept off her list. The most important name of all, maybe. 'The late Derry Carlton... were you close to him, Professor?'

Professor Rohan pursed his lips in a diffident sort of way. 'Can't say I was, really. Almost never saw him, in fact. He was a little too young. The afterthought of the family, don't you see. No, Philip was my main contact with the family. The others I saw up and down, of course.'

Lucy made a point of writing down a few disconnected words. She caught the old man's eyes tracking her hand. 'And were you in contact with the Carltons much over the last while?'

Professor Rohan paused a moment. 'With Philip, mostly. Not Joyce or David. And even with Philip, not so much. We met occasionally for lunch, in Dublin. We always ate in the Shelbourne. Old style.'

Lucy looked up from her notebook. 'So when was the last time yourself and Philip met?'

Professor Rohan looked away into the distance. 'Let me see, now? It was Easter. Yes, Holy Week. On Holy Thursday. I had saddle of lamb and Philip had steak, well done, as always.'

Lucy heard Anna turning on the tap in the kitchen and the clink of glasses. 'And you talked about?'

The old man perked up. 'The new discoveries in the Boyne Valley, of course! I hadn't seen Philip so happy in a long time. There was this henge they discovered. The hot summer revealed quite a lot of things – in the UK, too. Quite extraordinary.'

Lucy moved close to the old man. 'Do you know if he was worried about anything in particular?' The eyes looked suddenly tired to her now. She could imagine how upsetting the whole thing was, at his age.

'Can't say I noticed anything odd.' Professor Rohan looked like he was drifting away now.

Anna came back in with her glass of water. She left it down on the ancient coffee table with a little napkin underneath.

'I hope that wasn't too chaotic in there.' The old man smiled kindly.

Anna Crowley took a sip of water. 'Not at all. You keep a very tidy house, Professor.'

'Everything in its place. That was one of Sybil's old saws.' He turned back to Lucy.

'No. I can't say I noticed anything odd about Philip. He had put on more weight, of course. Too fond of his tipple. Still, I find it impossible to believe that anyone...' Professor Rohan caught his breath. It was almost as if his words were failing him.

'Yes?' Lucy waited.

'That anyone might have done him harm. Who would want to do such a thing?' The voice seemed distressed now. Lucy imagined that Attic Greece was probably more real to Professor Rohan than the road outside his house.

Lucy closed up her notebook. 'That's what we're trying to tie down. Look, we'll leave you in peace for the moment. You've been a great help to us. I tried the phone earlier, but it disconnected.'

'Ah, so that was you ringing, then? Blessed thing never seems to work when you want it to.' They stood up to go. At the hall stand, Anna paused to settle her hair in the mirror.

'Red hair, Detective. You're a true Celt.'

'Yes, I suppose I am.' Anna Crowley shook the old, age-freckled hand.

AT THE DOOR, he waved to them. By the time they reached the road, the big door had closed over. Lucy glanced in the mirror to make sure it was shut. 'Well? What's your take on all that?'

'Gay old gentleman, I'd say. The companion in the UK is probably some other jolly gentleman. I can see them sitting on a park bench, comparing notes on Homer.'

Lucy laughed. 'How old?'

'Early to mid-eighties? It's hard to tell. He's very well preserved. He wasn't pissing it up against the wall for years, if you'll pardon my expression, like his protégé, Philip Carlton, of course. And the kitchen...'

Lucy looked across at her. 'What?'

Anna laughed. 'Spotless. It looked more like a stage set than a house.'

Lucy thought for a moment. 'I was hoping he might help me with the more distant past. With Derry Carlton's days. He doesn't seem to have much to do with the young brat. He did seem a little nervous when I brought up the subject, though. Maybe he's afraid something will happen to him too.'

'Maybe.'

'Like I say, he didn't seem to know much about Derry Carlton, anyway, Anna.' Lucy pulled up at the T-junction and checked the road.

'Really? That's very odd.' Anna Crowley sounded puzzled.

'What?' Lucy looked over at her.

'Well, there's a fairly big photo – a very old one – of him and Derry Carlton and someone else, taken, I would say, on holiday somewhere. It all looks very cosy.'

Lucy swung out onto the main road. 'Where?'

Anna looked over at her. 'Inside the pantry door. You can't see it from outside.'

Lucy laughed. 'You devil you! You were snooping on him.'

Anna shrugged her shoulders and smiled. 'I couldn't find the glasses, so I had a little look about.' Anna was laughing now.

'Because you thought the glasses might be in the pantry?'

Anna Crowley shrugged her shoulder again. 'It's strange, don't you think?'

Lucy looked across at Anna. 'What, that the glasses weren't in the pantry? Are you serious?'

'No. That he was so eager to deny Derry Carlton.'

Lucy said nothing. Then she turned to Anna. 'You didn't, by any chance...'

Anna Crowley glanced back over her shoulder at the road disappearing behind them and started laughing. 'I did, of course. Just for the record.' She pulled out her phone and passed it to Lucy, who glanced at it quickly and passed it back.

Lucy smiled. 'Maybe fear, like I say. Or just the forgetfulness of an old man.'

'Who can probably still quote you slabs of Homer?' Anna stared down at the image on the phone of Professor Rohan, Derry Carlton and the unknown man with the thin face and the petulant look.

'Right...' Lucy turned right onto the main road.

SHE PICKED up Saoirse on the way back to the Black Hills. Her mother had prepared a little travelling bag of goodies for Saoirse, for the German trip. At the door, she whispered to Lucy, 'It will be fine. Really. The hardest part is leaving.'

When Saoirse was in bed, she spoke with Brosnahan, who would deputise for her while she was away in Hamburg for the two days. 'Just keep everything ticking over. Phone me any time. OK?'

She didn't sleep much that night, even when she checked on Saoirse for the last time and tucked her in. It was that kind of night. And when she woke, at dawn, the dread of leaving her daughter out of her sight for the next few weeks brought her close to tears.

But she played it down, and by the time her mother dropped her at the airport, she had come to some sort of vague ease with the whole idea.

28

SHE, LUCY O'HARA, WAS GOING BACK TO GERMANY.

Not that she hadn't been back many times before. But this time, it was different. This time, she would be leaving her child there and flying back on her own. It wasn't the Germany she had known, for a few years, as a schoolchild, though, not even the one of her doctoral years. That was the Germany she thought she could live in long-term. Build a university career in. Raise a child in.

Until the past caught up with her and the 'slip' happened, as her mother liked to call it.

The nervous breakdown that nature deferred, after Cairo, until conditions were right. Until she was well enough to get sick. When all the psychobabble was over, it was nothing more than the profound, existential sadness of the realisation that she would never see her father anymore.

Not this side of the grave anyway.

WHEN THEY ARRIVED IN HAMBURG, they wandered around the Altstadt, looking at the quaint little shops, then took a taxi to the apartment, in Eppendorf, a quiet, well-mannered, tranquil part of Hamburg.

Gerhard was his usual neatly trimmed self. The face had grown a bit fuller, but the jet-black hair was as it was. And the piercing blue eyes hadn't dulled. He carried Saoirse and her suitcase up the three flights of stairs. The apartment had changed a little, Lucy could see. She sensed the spoor of a woman about it, though. Maybe not a live-in, but a regular all the same.

They sat out on the balcony together, looking out at the well-mannered dark trees and the manicured bushes. Lucy could hear the sound of children playing quietly in the nearby playground. No, this could never have been hers, even with the best will in the world. Because something inside her just wouldn't let it be, no matter how hard she tried.

Some people float down the river; some people swim against the current. Lucy Divonne O'Hara knew she would never be a floater.

'What will you two do for the week?' Lucy tried to avoid looking at his eyes. It still made her uncomfortable.

Gerhard smiled at her. 'A typical German holiday; in other words, doing stuff. We'll go on the river and go to the zoo. Maybe take the train to the coast...'

Her phone buzzed. It was Sullivan.

'Sorry, I have to take this.' She crossed into the main bedroom. There was the presence of a woman here, alright. A scent of attar of roses. The way the room was arranged. But more: a certain energy that was impossible to mask.

Sullivan's voice broke in on her thoughts. 'Hi, Lucy. Just a catch-up. We're carrying on with the East European trawl and keeping an eye on Jenny Saunders.'

'Good. Anything else come up?'

Sullivan gave a little cough at the other end of the line. 'Actually, there is. Reese is worried.'

'I'm sorry? About what?'

'He feels that this character isn't done with you. He's ordered the new alarm system to be installed tomorrow, before you arrive back.'

Lucy glanced over her shoulder to make sure no one was listening. 'You don't think this is all a bit over the top?'

'Who knows? And I'm to pick you up at the airport and drop you home. The system will be installed by then.'

'So be it. I'll send you on my flight details. Anything important, phone me right away. Talk tomorrow.'

Lucy crossed back out to the balcony. She would have to leave Gerhard soon, before it got too cosy. 'Listen, I have to go up to Kiel to see Schliemann. I should get going.' Gerhard gave her a little peck on the cheek.

She stooped down to kiss Saoirse. 'See you in seven sleeps, love. I'll phone you this evening.' She held up her fingers.

'I'm eight, *Maman*. I think I can count to seven without using my fingers!'

She hugged Saoirse and stood up slowly.

Gerhard looked at her. 'She'll be fine.'

Lucy nodded. At the door downstairs, she paused a moment to gather herself. Then she walked out into the bright Hamburg day, still trying to stem the tears springing to her eyes.

She could smell the North Sea as soon as she got out of the train in Kiel. This was Hanseatic Germany. The old Germany that had traded with Scandinavia, the Baltic Coast, England, and further afield a thousand years earlier, before there was a Germany at all. Well-heeled burghers doing business across half a dozen seas. And now in charge of Europe.

Schliemann was waiting for her in his office in the university. He still hadn't managed to work out how to use a razor. He looked over his glasses and smiled at her.

'Dr O'Hara! Lovely to see you!' Schliemann stood up from his desk and shook her hand. He might have been a cousin of Philip Carlton's. There was the same calculated chaos on the desk and the same indifference to personal dress.

'Detective O'Hara to you, Martin.' She gave him a hug, laughing.

'Come on! Let's grab a coffee.'

They headed off to the lecturers' common room. After she had been introduced to a few people, they sat over in a corner. Schliemann sat back in the armchair. 'So, your daughter is with Gerhard for the week. She'll have a great time.'

Lucy swallowed hard. 'It wasn't easy. Not easy at all.'

'You're doing the right thing. Even if she decides not to visit Germany in the future, at least the decision will be made from her side.'

'I know.' Lucy left down her coffee and watched Schliemann open up the plastic folder he was carrying.

'Now, about this document. I haven't changed my opinion about this man. Lithuanian, London English in the mix, Russian speaker. By the way, that Lithuanian postgrad I mentioned, he thinks he has something extra.'

'Oh?' Lucy took another sip of coffee.

'Something at the beginning of your audio. It's a bit of a giveaway, it seems.' Schliemann glanced at his watch. 'He'll be in the audio lab now. We can catch him there. He'll explain.'

Lucy smiled. 'Good. Every little helps.'

'What's your position with the police in Ireland now?' Schliemann passed her a couple of pages of notes with audio graphs.

'Unofficial probation, you might say. You remember Superintendent Reese, the one who spoke up for me at the tribunal? Well, he appointed me as SIO on this case.' Lucy bit into a biscuit and glanced over the notes Schliemann had handed her.

Schliemann pointed to the transcription on the top sheet. 'So, how is it all going?'

Lucy flicked through the printed sheets. 'We still have to find this guy, Martin.'

Schliemann leaned forward. 'He'll slip up somewhere, Lucy. Always happens.'

'I'd like it to happen before he kills anyone else. Myself and my daughter included.' Lucy passed back the sheets.

SHE FOLLOWED Schliemann along the maze of corridors to a stairs leading down to the basement of the building. The audio lab was located at the far end of a corridor. Schliemann nodded at a man standing in front of a wave analysis display on a screen.

The man turned 'round slowly and came over to them.

Schliemann turned to Lucy. 'Matis, this is Dr Lucy O'Hara. You've been going through her material.'

Matis shook her hand. 'Pleased to meet you. Let me show you what I've got from your audio, Dr O'Hara.'

They passed into another soundproofed room with banks of speakers around the walls. Matis pulled up a file on the computer. 'I've scrubbed it up, though it was actually quite clear as it was.'

The audio file played. There was something like a grunting or a curse at the beginning of the clip now. Then the killer's voice speaking in broken English and Philip Carlton's nervous responses.

Lucy turned to Matis. 'So, the transcription in the file is exactly what we're hearing?'

'Yes. He's saying the equivalent of "here we go... let's get it over with" in Lithuanian... It's like he's psyching himself up. Then he breaks into English.'

'And the accent?' Lucy glanced around at Schliemann, who was smiling politely.

Matis pointed to part of the graph on the screen. 'The accent is Kaunas, working class, with just a trace of Russian.' Matis reached over and played the audio file again.

Lucy pointed at the display on the computer screen. 'And the phraseology?'

'Just common or garden Lithuanian phrases. The accent and stress patterns are the thing. It's as distinct as the infill *schwa* you have in working-class English in Dublin... *filem* for film.'

Lucy looked around at Schliemann. 'If his background is urban Kaunas, he's likely to be in a police database, or even an army one, wouldn't you say?'

Matis spoke again. 'Or maybe a Russian one. That's what I say in my report, actually, Dr O'Hara.'

Lucy stretched out her hand. 'Thank you very much, Matis. Much appreciated.'

'For nothing.' Matis knocked off the clip and they headed off.

THEY TOOK a walk to the lake, at the far side of the campus. Schliemann took out one of his thin little cigars and started puffing on it. 'You know this case may be your comeback.'

Lucy kept her eye on the lake as she spoke. 'Or my end.'

'You're not a college academic or a civil service police-woman, of course.'

Lucy came to a halt and turned around to look at Schliemann. 'Sometimes I don't know what I am.'

Schliemann pulled on his little cigar. 'You're a strange

mixture of academic and practical. Applied linguistics. Applied with a gun, that is.'

'I sound like Annie Oakley with a PhD.' Lucy walked on ahead of Schliemann, then turned back slowly to him.

Schliemann smiled at her. 'You're your father's daughter. Alan O'Hara had to be out on the streets, meeting people and seeing things.'

'That's what got him killed, Martin. Meeting people and seeing things.'

Schliemann frowned. 'You can't hide from the world. It'll just come and get you in the cave, anyway.'

Lucy glanced at her watch. 'I suppose. Look, I think I'll head back to Hamburg. I haven't even checked in at the hotel yet.'

They turned around and started walking slowly back to the main campus.

LUCY COULD FEEL the energy of Hamburg as soon as she stepped off the train. She felt it pull her out of the slough that was starting, now that she had 'handed over' Saoirse, like some bizarre hostage exchange.

Later in the evening, she took a walk and went for a quick drink at a flashy bar. She took her time walking back to the hotel. The pain had died down now, and she slept better than expected. Though when she woke, at about three in the morning, she knew she had been there again.

In Cairo...

In the Akhenaten Cafe.

She could see her father sitting bolt upright in the wicker chair with that same smile on his face. The ancient Seiko watch on his wrist had stopped at 3.30 exactly... the time the points switched suddenly and her life was shuttled onto another line.

Forever...

29

It was the end of August, and Cairo was hotter than hell.

She had just turned fourteen, and Cairo was to be her father's last foreign posting for the moment. They would be returning to Dublin at the end of the school year, and she would finish her secondary schooling there. London, Paris, Madrid, Berlin, Cairo. She could segue between four European languages fluently now, and, thanks to an Egyptian nanny and schoolfriends, handle herself well in the middle-class and the working-class registers of Cairene Arabic.

Her father's work at the embassy was supplemented by meetings, formal and informal. Sometimes Alan O'Hara had to fly to London or Paris or Brussels for high-level meetings. On other occasions, the meetings were local. The meeting that day was informal and social.

The Cafe Akhenaten was about half a kilometre from Tahrir Square, in the downtown area. Haunt of artists, hangers-on, political debaters and likeminded entities. Her father sometimes went there to meet up with an old chum, Mr Desouky, a senior Egyptian diplomat he had known from the Berlin days. They played backgammon, talked politics in low voices, and drank a lot of coffee. She wouldn't normally have asked to be at such a meeting. But that day, after being stuck back in the apartment in Dokki all morning, she begged to be let out. Most of her friends were in Alexandria or abroad. And there was no question of her being let to walk the streets of Cairo on her own – even in Dokki – as the daughter of a senior foreign diplomat. And, besides, she and her mother were having one of those weeks when each side got on the other's nerves.

They took a taxi to the chaos of Tahrir and walked from there. The sidewalks were swamped with people. Here and there, on the street corners, beggars recited verses from the Quran. Inside the Cafe Akhenaten, all was cool and relaxed. A couple of ancient fans beat over their heads, but it was the air-conditioning units that provided a real reprieve from the boiling streets.

The waiter led them to a table beside the patisserie display. He stood silently waiting for their order.

'Lucy...?' Her father's soft voice sounded in her ear.

Lucy pointed at the patisserie display case. 'Orange juice and one of those raspberry tarts, please.'

'And for me, a coffee, *Mazbut*...' They watched the waiter disappear into the crowd.

Mr Desouky was late arriving because there was some protest somewhere. Her father was in good form. The couple of weeks in Ireland and France had been a real break for him. By the end of the school year, their new life would start, back in Dublin.

'Will you miss Cairo?' Her father's voice was gentle.

'A lot. My friends. And my Egyptian Nana and the way she says *Lucy, b'hibbak! I love you!*'

'Right.' Alan O'Hara's eyes swept the room for a sign of his friend; then he turned back to Lucy.

'Yes. And all those places we visited. Karnak, Abu Simbel, the pyramids, the oasis. The Nile...'

'No one ever gets used to moving. I think it will be good for you though. Home. The same place. Familiar faces.'

Mr Desouky appeared and bowed politely to them. Lucy regarded the soft skin of his face. What her mother called 'an Alexandrian patrician face' and her father said was an old Greek face. His perfect, bone-china English and flawless French. When he spoke in 'high Arabic', she felt it was like listening to grammar set to music.

'*Wie geht's, Fraulein* O'Hara?'

'*Ça va bien, Monsieur* Desouky.'

She excused herself and crossed to a little table over by the window. This was the usual drill when her father was meeting someone. She saw the waiter arrive with the backgammon board for the two men; then she took out the magazine from her handbag. There was something in it about protecting your skin from the sun. After the meeting with Mr Desouky, her father would take her for a walk up Imad al Din Street to 26th of July, to the stalls and the shops and the street-sellers. The women in peasant dresses and the men in galabiyyahs and the smiles of the children. She loved all that, especially since she could chat with them now in colloquial Arabic. Wasn't that what language was for, anyway?

Touching other people.

She smiled over at her father and Mr Desouky and turned back to her magazine.

It was as she stood up to go to the bathroom a few minutes later that she saw him: the stranger.

He was standing awkwardly by the open door, wearing a dark blue suit and an uneasy smile. It was the sort of heavy suit no one wore in a Cairo summer. There was something not right about his eyes, too. The way they flitted from side to side. And the awkwardness of the man's walk, too, like he wasn't used to being in places like the Akhenaten. So what was he doing here, then?

She looked across the floor at her father, but he was engrossed in the game. She wanted to say something, but she wasn't quite sure what. Her father turned towards her slowly and she called his name. But the gurgling of the air-conditioning unit above her head smothered her voice.

The word was lost.

All of a sudden, the man in the dark blue suit caught her eye again. He was smiling at her now. A smile that she couldn't quite decode. That didn't feel right somehow. She wanted to cross over to her father and say something. But what? Maybe he would think she was being silly. No, she would go into the bathroom and splash her face with water and freshen up.

She turned back towards the door. The man had disappeared. Maybe left the cafe. Good. Why had she been so silly?

Inside the bathroom, she splashed cool water on her face, taking care not to let it touch her lips, like her mother always said. A woman appeared behind her and began touching up her lipstick in the mirror. She smiled at Lucy.

The next thing she remembered was the scorching wind.

It wasn't like the hot wind coming in off the desert at the oasis they had visited the previous year. Not like the hot air channelling up between the tall buildings near Tahrir. No. It was more like she imagined the scorching wind from a jet engine, if you were unwise enough to stand behind it. Then that feeling in her stomach like someone had just kicked her there. She doubled up and keeled over. Then nothing.

Only blackness.

She woke in a cloud of dirt and dust. The lipstick woman was lying beside her, sobbing like a wounded animal, with half her face torn away. Lucy stood up slowly, holding the hand basin as she looked at herself in the shattered glass of the mirror. Her bloodshot eyes. The face caked in dust. She thought she was going to go unconscious again. She had to get out.

She pushed herself through the remnant of the door. She could hear terrible screaming now. Crying. Heard a voice calling out in Arabic for a father.

'*Baba! Faynak! Baba!*'

She cast about to look for the source, then slowly realised that it was her own voice she was listening to. Pleading with the world to return her father to her. She passed through the tangle of broken bodies and shattered furniture and glass. She spotted an arm cast aside on the floor like the arm of a mannequin. The table over on the left, near the patisserie stall. That was where they were.

The dust began to clear now, and she could hear sirens in the distance. One of those dark little Nubian policemen in the black uniforms was shouting in the doorway. She saw the big shards of glass from the patisserie counter. Then the dust cleared a bit more and she saw Mr Desouky. That fawn summer suit he was wearing. His neck was in an unnatural position. Her father had to be somewhere near, didn't he?

'*Baba! Faynak! Baba!*' The words just wouldn't come in any other language.

And then she saw him. Exactly where she had last seen him. He was sitting bolt upright in that old wicker chair. Maybe that had protected him from the blast. Maybe.

'*Baba!*'

Her eyesight was flickering now like someone pulling a cable on a computer screen. She trampled over the broken glass, kicked pieces of wood out of the way. Alan O'Hara was sitting up in the chair with a little trickle of blood running down the side of his mouth. His eyes were still open. He seemed to be about to say something.

But Alan O'Hara said nothing at all.

He just kept on staring at her.

And then she started to slip away again. The blackness came back. And when she finally woke in a ward in a big hospital, two months later, when the pressure on her brain had relented, it was her mother she saw before her.

'Lucy...'

'Baba... Fayn Baba!'

'Lucy... *Baba est mort...*'

And then her mother started crying, too. And they cried together. And the smell of burning and the feel of the heat on her body was back again as she struggled to speak to her father across the floor of the Cafe Akhenaten.

The lost word...

30

SHE FLEW BACK TO DUBLIN FROM HAMBURG THROUGH THE TAIL
end of a summer storm. It looked liked Armageddon over
North Dublin as the plane finally dipped below the low cloud
cover. Even the cabin crew looked whey-faced as they rode in
over Dublin Bay. When the plane slapped down on the tarmac,
there was a round of applause.

Sullivan was waiting for her at arrivals. 'Nice to see you
again.'

'Mutual, I'm sure. Now, let's hit the road.'

The rain cleared as they pulled out of the airport for North
Dublin. Sullivan glanced across at her. 'Quick drink?'

'OK. Just the one, now.'

The Blue Bar in Skerries harbour was crowded, but they
managed to find a table at the back. Sullivan came back with
two brandies. 'Got some more info on that fellow's possible
provenance.'

Lucy took a sip of brandy. 'Provenance? Are we talking
about Impressionist paintings here?'

They clinked glasses and Sullivan spoke. 'Anyway, the

explosives in Violet Saunders car were mining explosives. Apparently, if they don't use all the batch of explosives during a mining operation, the rest is usually burnt off. They've traced them by the chemical composition, apparently it wasn't the regular type of stuff, back to a batch stolen from a mine in the midlands a few years ago. But we have no real leads to anyone so far. Myself and Peter have shaken a few trees here and there. East Europeans, mostly. Nothing so far.'

Lucy took another sip and looked straight at Sullivan. 'Why did this latchico go for Violet Saunders?'

Sullivan frowned. 'Maybe afraid she might spill the beans. Or his boss thought that.'

'And why go for me?'

Sullivan took a sip of brandy. 'You must be getting close to something.'

'If I am, I haven't noticed it.' Lucy took a couple of nuts from the little bowl on the table and bit hard into them. She didn't look at Sullivan as she spoke. 'You don't think the Carltons themselves are involved, do you?'

Sullivan shrugged his shoulders. 'Who knows? Families, like lovers, don't fight fair. Listen, here are the alarm fobs to the new alarm system in your house.' Sullivan pulled out a couple of coloured key fobs, and Lucy slipped them into her bag.

THEY LEFT the bar and drove slowly through the drizzle for the Black Hills, just up off the coast road to Balbriggan. To the higgledy-piggledy scattering of houses along a winding stretch that she now called home. She glanced back over her shoulder as they rounded the big bend in the road. She could see the lights of Skerries harbour down from them. She must get out in the Mermaid soonest and ground herself again, with the wind and the waves and the salt sea air.

As they pulled into the yard, Sullivan pressed one of the

fobs and the house lit up like a Christmas tree. 'It's a one-stop fob. You set the alarm on and off with the second recessed button, or on the panel in the house or from your phone. That's the panic button. Then the cavalry will come, hopefully.'

Lucy ran her finger over the device. 'Like a coffee before you hit the road? And I mean just a coffee.'

Sullivan followed her into the house and sat into the living room. She could hear him talking on the phone to Reese from the kitchen. She came back in with a tray. 'Ideologically correct vegan bites, from Hamburg. No animals killed in the production, only vegetables killed.'

Sullivan took a sip of coffee and looked across at Lucy. 'Reese will be in Boynebridge first thing for a review. Violet Saunders's remains won't be repatriated for another week.'

'So Jenny Saunders will be with us a bit longer. Maybe it's just as well.'

Sullivan nodded at the photos on the wall. 'That your father?'

Lucy pointed at the photo. 'When we lived in Paris. The one beside it is my mam, the month before Dad was killed in Cairo. It was taken at the Gezirah Club. It was a very swanky, last-days-of-the-Raj sort of place. And you? What's your situation? Am I allowed to ask?'

'One marriage that ended in a divorce that died of terminal boredom. No children and no big row. Fade to black. Not much else to tell.' Sullivan's eye caught another photograph.

Lucy nodded at the photo. 'That's Gerhard. Saoirse's father.'

'Ah...'

Lucy gazed over at the photograph. 'We were polar opposites. And I was still too disconnected, ten years after Dad's death, I suppose. Anyway...' Lucy turned back to Sullivan.

Sullivan took a sip of coffee and glanced at his watch. He stood up slowly. 'Look, give me a bell if you need anything.'

Lucy watched Sullivan get into the car from the back door.

She felt a momentary jolt when his car pulled out onto the road. Then she went back and poured herself a glass of wine to dissolve the feeling before it could grow too strong.

She threw back the glass of wine and headed out into the yard.

THE YARD WAS DARK, but she could still see the rain glistening on the ground under the security lamp. Chantal had been fed and watered by the neighbour. In the stable, she rubbed her down and spoke softly to her. The big, sad horse eyes looked out at her. They seemed to say: *Why did you leave me?* She passed the creature a couple of sugar cubes and started to make her way out of the stable for the house. It was only then that she noticed it.

The dog that didn't bark.

That didn't whimper even. She called out Polly's name once, twice, three times. Maybe Mr Synott, the neighbour who had looked after Chantal, had brought her back up to his house. She would phone when she got back to the house.

The house...

Lucy suddenly froze and reached for her pistol, but it was back in the house, in the bedside locker.

She opened the stable half-door slowly and glanced around. Maybe someone had been watching the house while she was away. Then waited for the perfect moment, when she had just arrived back and before she had got used to arming the system.

And was alone. All alone.

She would have to get to the far side of the stable and make a run across the front yard to get back in, find the fob and get the gun.

The drizzle had cleared now. In the distance, she could hear a car driving up through the Black Hills towards Ardgillan Castle. She was steeling herself to make a run for it when she heard it. A heavy breathing sound, in the dark at the far side of the stables, facing the back door of the house. Like someone had been running and was catching his breath.

He had waited until Sullivan left.

She slipped back into Chantal's stable. She must do something random. Anything. Catch him unawares. She took out another sugar cube for the horse; then she started turning Chantal around slowly, hearing the hooves ring out on the concrete floor.

Lucy whispered to the horse, 'Now, girl, let's go for a little walk.'

In the darkness, a form flitted across the front of the stable door. He was almost on top of her now. She guided the horse to the half-door.

It was now or never.

She kicked the half-door open and smacked the horse on the flank.

Chantal lurched out through the door into the yard, and she ran out beside the horse, without looking back, cutting right with the horse running behind her now. Expecting any minute to feel the thunk of a bullet in her back, she burst in through the door, grabbed the fob from the coffee table and raced for the stairs, pressing the red button as she ran.

The house lights started flashing now.

She made for the stairs. Fucksticks! She had forgotten to close the backyard door after her. She lunged for the stairs, stumbled and suddenly felt something dragging at her ankle. A terrible pain shot through her leg. She swung round in one smooth movement to see a balaclavaed face bearing down on her and the glint of a knife in the hall light. Where had he come out of?

'Get the fuck off me!'

The arm swung and the knife swished in the air, striking the wall. She drew back her leg like a spring and struck out, with her heel catching the madman in the groin. He screamed a curse and fell back against the door jamb. The knife clanged onto the stone floor. She leaped up the stairs and heard the feet thudding after her. She made the bedroom door just in time, slammed it behind her and grabbed the pistol from the bedside locker.

In a flash, she racked the Glock, hoping the sound would carry and tell the stranger that there was one in the breech. Where was the other button on the fob? Her finger felt for the recess.

A piercing shrill cut through the air as the alarm kicked in.

She dropped to the floor at the far side of the bed and shouted, 'I'll blow your fucking head off if you come in!'

She fired once, without thinking, hearing the bullet strike the door near the brass handle.

She leaned against the bed and steadied the pistol in her hands. She mustn't waste rounds. She visualised a rectangle with a man's figure in it and started to take aim.

She could hear a siren in the distance now. She took a deep breath. If she could just hold out for the next couple of minutes. She heard footsteps retreating down the stairs. A bluff, maybe. A ruse to get her to stand up and reveal her position in the darkened room. Nine shots left. Have to push the envelope.

She sighted the mid-panel of the door.

Thwack! Thwack! Thwack!

Three shots placed across the door frame in the centre. Whoever was coming to help from outside would hear the shots too, and arrive faster, and the retreating footsteps would reconsider, caught between herself now and the sirens.

Maybe.

She heard a heavy engine screeching to a halt in the yard. Voices were shouting commands now. She must stay where she was. No point being shot by your own. She heard the back door being thrown open and more shouts.

'Armed garda! Detective O'Hara, are you there?'

Lucy refocused the gun away from the door now. 'I'm in the back bedroom. Alone. I'm OK. I'm armed.'

The footsteps were coming up the stairs now.

Two figures in helmets and flak jackets, carrying HKs, barrelled in through the door and swept the room. The lights from their helmets blinded her momentarily. She left the Glock down slowly on the bed.

'We're clearing the house. Just stay where you are for the moment. Who fired those shots?'

'My gun. Four rounds.'

WHEN THE ALL-CLEAR was called a few minutes later, she followed the men down the stairs and out into the yard. Sullivan was already there, and the yard was full now with ERU and local garda. The team in their helmets and flak jackets were positioned at the corners of the yard, and a local car was blocking the exit.

Sullivan crossed over to her. 'What happened exactly?' Sullivan leaned forward and looked into her eyes.

'He must have watched the alarm system being installed and realised he had a very small window to get to me. What about the dog?' Lucy looked around the yard at the armed men.

Sullivan nodded towards the stables. 'Stone cold. Probably killed much earlier.'

The senior officer came over and took off his helmet. 'We've been asked to do local surveillance for the night. I'd say the likelihood he'll try again tonight is low. But you never know.'

Sullivan looked at her. 'I can stay if you like. Just for the night.'

'Give me a minute. Don't crowd me.' Lucy walked back towards the house and scanned the yard. Then she nodded over to Sullivan.

AN HOUR LATER, the ERU unit pulled out of the yard. The local sergeant went through the protocol with her, and Reese spoke with her on the phone. When the cars had all left, she sat into the sitting room with Sullivan and opened the bottle of wine she had brought back from Hamburg.

Sullivan poured two glasses. 'That was a close one. You just nicked a draw there.'

'They must really feel we're onto something, whoever they are.' Lucy put her fingers to her lips and picked up the phone. Gerhard's voice came on the line in Hamburg.

'Hi, Gerhard. Just ringing to say I'm back home, safe and sound. I didn't get a chance earlier.'

Gerhard's voice was strangely soft, like he knew that something was up. 'Good. Saoirse is fast asleep. I'd better not wake her.'

Lucy took a sip of wine and glanced over at Sullivan. 'No, no. Listen, I have something to ask you. How would it be if Saoirse stayed another week with you?'

'No problem.' Gerhard's voice suddenly changed. 'Is everything OK over there?'

'Everything's fine. Look, Gerhard, I'll ring again tomorrow and explain more. Give Saoirse a kiss for me.' She knocked off the phone and turned back to Sullivan.

'Your bed is in the front, Mr Sullivan. My mother's room.' She clinked glasses with him.

Sullivan tapped the sofa. 'I'd prefer to sleep on the couch, Lucy. I'd feel more relaxed.'

'Suit yourself. Come on. Let's kill this bottle. I need to sleep.'

Lucy poured for them. In front of her, on the coffee table, the gun lay with its safety catch on. It irked her to admit it, but she suddenly felt safer with Sullivan around. It was the sort of feeling that always led to problems. Start depending on a man, it ends badly. Hamburg, Dublin, Cairo.

She finished her glass of wine and smiled at him. *'Bonne nuit.'*

'And to you too, Detective O'Hara.'

She made her way slowly up the stairs. Alone, confused, distracted, alive. She ran her finger over the bullet holes in the bedroom door, climbed into bed, fully clothed, and fell into a deep sleep, secretly happy that the stranger down on the couch was the first line of defence.

LUKAS PETRASKAS KNEW how this worked.

The special unit would comb the area, tasked from above by the helicopter he could now hear whoomping loudly above his head in the dark. They would work their way up the roads and back roads in tandem with the whirlybird, cross-referencing with one another. Maybe they had an antiterrorist unit out in the fields.

But he knew what worked.

And his twofold fallback plan would see him through the night.

He lay quite still in the attic space of the deserted house and pulled the aluminium foil sheet over his body just in case they were using heat sensors. Even still, they wouldn't have time to search every house in this Black Hills area. Within an hour or two, they would have come to the conclusion that he had escaped the net. And in the morning, the little furniture delivery van would pull in off the road and pick him up.

He had been so close! If he hadn't stumbled on the stairs, he would have ended it there and then. Where had the detective woman learned this stuff? She was too fit and focused to be a regular detective. Not that it mattered now. He had failed again, and it stuck in his craw.

He smiled sourly to himself and cursed silently in Russian.

'Well done again, bitch!'

31

THE COLLECTOR LEFT DUBLIN JUST AS DARKNESS WAS FALLING.

When he reached the city limits, he slipped a CD into the player. Beethoven's Third, the first movement, wound its way in among his thoughts, slowly ensnaring them in a mash of melancholy. At the exit for Kilkenny, he took the M9 south, a roundabout way to go to Cork. He was quite aware that, by varying his route and adding an hour to it, he was also giving himself time to muse over things.

He stopped only once, leaving the motorway to join the N25 south, just outside Waterford, where he drank coffee from a flask and ate a salad and tuna sandwich. He didn't stop again until the car was riding in over the hills near the house. The sand track at the last stretch of the laneway to the house hadn't been disturbed. A low-tech border device used by countries around the world. He saw a couple of animal prints here and there, in the glare of the car headlights. He would scan the security footage the next day, just in case. He parked the car in the garage and went straight into the house. Unpack the provisions in the morning.

The air in the house seemed stale now, from his absence.

He must freshen up the place when he got up. He foostered about a bit in the kitchen, clearing away this and that, to wind down from the long drive. He poured himself a glass of whiskey before turning on BBC world service to listen to a couple of items about the Democratic Republic of Congo (more killing) and Afghanistan (more killing, too). The truth was, he knew, he could hide from his own thoughts as easily with words as with music. But good whiskey masked a lot, at that time of night. And it put him straight to sleep.

When he woke, it was as if the decision had already been made for him. Arkens must be monitored much more closely. He felt just a momentary twinge of unease. Then, as though talking to an invisible stranger in the room, he spoke softly.

'*Carthago delenda est...*'

It was a line from Livy (out of Cato), one of his favourite authors. *Carthage must be destroyed*. There was a sweet finality to the phrase even if, as he well knew, the phrase was a historical misquotation. Historical misquotations, like misquotations from songs and movies, often said a lot more than true quotations.

Ask any movie buff.

Despite going to sleep so late, the Collector still woke with the sun. It was an old habit. There was a lot to do. When he had hauled the provisions in and freshened up the house, he descended to the bunker. He marvelled, yet again, at the symmetry of its construction. Not for the first time, he thought of the corridors and rooms crammed with equipment fifty years before. Radios and monitors and primitive computers. Everything that would have been needed for a retreat if the Cold War had suddenly turned hot. The long storeroom would have held enough supplies of canned and preserved foodstuffs to last for months on end. These assets were all long gone now, of course.

The rooms and corridors were filled with his own collection now.

He checked again, as he did on a weekly basis, those systems put in place, long ago, if secret materials and documents had to be destroyed before the advancing Soviet forces the incendiary devices in the various rooms. He checked the pressure valves on the system that would flood the bunker when the fire system had incinerated everything. All it would take would be the press of a big red button, and a tidal wave of destruction would obliterate everything in the bunker.

There was only one thing in the world he was sure of now: no one was going to take him or his collection.

But what was bothering him most of all was that the Lithuanian had failed again. What was the use in hiring an illiterate thug if he couldn't deliver? He had been assured that this was the man for the job. Never met him, of course. That was Arkens's bailiwick. Maybe even assassins needed a quality control system. He would just have to live with the wretched woman for the moment, until, if and when, the opportunity presented itself.

In the afternoon, when he had catnapped to catch up on the sleep missed during the night, he took out the .22. He cleaned it thoroughly and set off for the little forest by the headland. Near the firebreak, he took out a rabbit sitting out staring into the hot sun like a ditzy hippy. He would have it at the weekend, in a stew. Satisfied with the day's doings, he made his way slowly back to the house.

And later that evening, he contacted the thug he was now so grudgingly dependent on, to make sure he was keeping tabs on Jeremy Arkens in his palace in the Wicklow Mountains.

32

THE SUN WAS HIGH IN THE SUMMER SKY AS LUCY DROVE DOWN the snaking road from the Black Hills. She scarcely took in the panorama of Skerries harbour at the big bend in the road. She had breakfasted semi-silently with Sullivan, and he had gone on ahead to meet up with Reese in Boynebridge.

An hour later, the three of them were hunched over a bunch of printouts in one of the interview rooms.

Reese nodded at the files on the table. 'This is the complete record of Philip Carlton's financial dealings over the years. The files you looked at in Harcourt Square related almost totally to Derry Carlton, of course.'

'And?' Lucy glanced from one to the other.

Sullivan flicked through the pages. 'The payments suddenly stop when the child is about six.'

Lucy scanned through the printouts. 'Well, I knew from David Carlton that he stopped paying way back. By agreement, it seems. So, what are we saying here?'

Sullivan looked at Lucy. 'There must be a really good reason. In those days, it would have been a big scandal for someone in Philip Carlton's position to have fathered a child with a postgrad. And another thing...'

Sullivan slipped the sheets of paper back into the bundle. 'Anna found CCTV of Philip Carlton and Violet Saunders in a hotel, in Boynebridge. The Blue Rose. They must have met a number of times before the fatal night.'

Reese turned to Lucy. 'By the way, what about the Windgap material? Any more joy there?'

Lucy grimaced. 'Nothing you might call menacing. Anna has already trawled the emails. There's nothing much there either.'

Reese sighed. 'Well, people tend not to make death threats by email, sadly.'

Lucy pointed at the pile of papers. 'But there's no actual record of any wrongdoing on Philip Carlton's part?'

'None that we know of. Even academics like Philip Carlton have to get their hands a little dirty every now and then. Ask the British Museum and the Louvre how they got half their collections. That doesn't mean they're criminals.'

'So, back to square one? Is that what we're looking at here?' Lucy looked over at Reese.

Reese looked at Sullivan and then back to her. 'Well, not exactly entirely.'

Lucy sat back in her seat. 'Don't keep me in suspense, George.'

Reese sat on the edge of the table. 'There was another investigation, around the same time as the original garda investigation.'

'A parallel investigation, you mean? And why was that, now?' Lucy kept her eyes fixed on Reese.

Reese paused a moment. 'There was some suggestion of paramilitary money laundering, so an ad hoc team, military intelligence and a deep detective unit were let off the leash.'

Lucy left down the file in her hand slowly. 'And this investigation... did it have a handle?'

'The Kilowatt Investigation.'

'And, any material?'

'Yes. But the thing is, the thirty-year cabinet papers' rule applies.'

Lucy smiled. 'Tell me another one. For a start, they're not cabinet papers.'

Sullivan pulled up a chair and sat down facing her. 'No, but they are, technically speaking, army intel files. So the Official Secrets Act etc....'

'There's also a Freedom of Information Act.'

'We've tried all that, covertly. We've been gnawing away at this for a couple of months.' Sullivan looked over at Reese and turned back to her. 'But there may be one other option.'

'Which is what?' Lucy took up her phone and read the message from Anna: CCTV of Carlton and Violet Saunders in hotel ready to view.

'We have made the case, officially, to the DPP's office and the attorney general, that these documents might be central to a current double-murder investigation. The attorney general will reply in a week. And then we might know the name of the man at the top.'

'Sounds like the last drink saloon, boys.' Lucy smiled and closed up her notebook.

Reese stood up slowly. 'When we started on this as a cold case, last year, it was because Philip Carlton contacted Harcourt Square, and Gerry was to meet him and discuss his situation. We only got to know about the forum stuff when Professor Carlton was dead. We still don't know whose toes he walked on. The Kilowatt Files may tell us this.'

Lucy nodded to Sullivan and they both headed upstairs to the incident room.

· · ·

LUCY CROSSED over to Anna's desk. 'Run those clips.'

They watched the footage of Philip Carlton and Violet Saunders arriving at the hotel together. Then one of them eating in the hotel restaurant – too far from the camera to be of any use.

Anna pointed at the screen. 'The detail on the one at the rear of the hotel is good enough for lip-sync analysis. Watch...'

This one was crystal clear, alright. There was no audio, but the lip movements were clear. Lucy clicked the mouse and froze the frame. 'Right, get on to Theresa Downes in technical. Make it urgent. I want to nobble Miss Saunders this afternoon now. We need to have a little catch-up, anyway.'

LUCY SPENT the next couple of hours going back through Philip Carlton's accounts. She phoned Theresa Downes in the early afternoon. 'Have you had a chance to look at it, Theresa?'

'I'm sending you a transcript. Ninety-percent-plus accuracy.'

Lucy bit on the end of the pen. 'And?'

Theresa Downes chuckled at the other end. 'The killer line, if you pardon the expression, is the same in all the software readings. It confirms my own lip-sync reading.'

Lucy bit harder on the end of the pen. 'Which is what?'

'Violet Saunders says to Philip Carlton: *Your life is in danger, Philip. We've been told to tell you that your life is in danger.*'

Lucy paused a moment. 'Told by whom? And who does *we* refer to?'

'She doesn't say, unfortunately. Look, I'll send on everything now. Any questions, ring me back.'

'Thanks, Theresa. You're a star.' Lucy knocked off the phone and thought for a moment. Then she phoned Jenny Saunders.

'Hello?' Jenny Saunders sounded sleepy and snarky, like she had just got out of bed. Or got back into it.

'I need to speak to you, Jenny. Soonest.' Lucy waited for her words to bite.

The voice at the other end had suddenly woken up now. 'Is something wrong?'

Lucy's voice was honey smooth. 'It's just regulations, Jenny. I have to keep you officially updated. When are you in?'

'I'll be here in the B and B from four.'

'Good. I'll catch you around five. OK?'

Lucy printed out the transcript and ran a yellow highlighter over the relevant bits. It was time for the metal to meet the road.

SHE HAD JUST PASSED the Peace Bridge on the motorway outside Boynebridge, going south, when Joyce Carlton rang. 'Detective O'Hara?'

'Ms Carlton. How are you?'

'I'm fine, actually. Considering. The thing is, I've come across a little collection of Philip's letters yesterday. I thought you might like to go through them.'

Come across. Lucy smiled at the euphemism. Like coming across a strange receipt when you were going through your spouse's trousers. 'Personal letters?'

Joyce Carlton's voice sounded tired. 'Personal and professional, I would say. There's no need for David to know about this, by the way. He always makes things so complicated.' Joyce Carlton sounded breathless.

'I understand.'

Joyce Carlton's voice grew a little croaky. 'We're having a memorial ceremony in the house for Philip around eight tonight. David is in London with his companion. I could give you the letters then. I just don't want to make a song and dance of it.'

'Of course. I'll see you at about eight, then.'

Lucy knocked off the phone and focused on the large truck that was overtaking her. What could possibly be in a collection of random letters? Random clues. The sort of stuff that happenstance lay along the way for the wise to find. Dates, numbers, locations.

Names even.

But, of course, you usually didn't know what you were looking for until you found it, in life and love.

And death...

33

LUCAS PETRASKAS GLANCED AROUND AT HIS SURROUNDINGS AND rubbed his eyes.

The barn was clean and dry, true. The little room he had been sleeping in for the past number of days wasn't that bad, either. It had been used to hide Polish workers dodging revenue a few years before. There was even an electric cable connected up to a domestic supply on the remote farm. Every now and then, a tractor rolled by along the far road. But the land itself and the barn hadn't been worked in an age.

He glanced at his phone to check that the recordings of the Arkenses' conversations had been sent on to the old man at the other end of the line. He gave a satisfied grunt. At least this much was going right. Even he could figure out where Jeremy Arkens was in his mind: scared.

He stripped the pistol and laid the components out on the biscuit tin lid. He wiped the slide with the rag and ran his eye along its length. This was good Austrian engineering.

When would the call come? It was an awkward communication system, but a smart one. A shortwave radio connecting to an app on his phone. It would be almost impossible to tap into. The signal in the barn probably wasn't that good though. Too much metal. He glanced at his watch. Should be getting a call around now.

He clambered down from the loft and stretched himself. Then, like every morning, he did a ten-minute series of exercises to get the system going. Stretches, push-ups, planks. He took the last of the bagel out of his pocket and finished it off. Then he slipped around the back of the barn, keeping an eye on the road nearby. He could see across the fields to the farm near the hill. Just an elderly couple there. There was a series of deserted cottages over on the left. Old estate cottages, in ruins now. Death, emigration, sickness. Who knows? Long gone anyway.

He took out the phone and opened up the photo file to look at it again. Jenny Saunders's face smiled out at him. The raven dark hair. The blue eyes. That quirky smile.

He glanced at his watch. It was just gone eleven. He moved back in towards the barn and lit up. Drew hard on the cigarette and thought again: *When are they going to call me home?* There was no way he could ship out without permission from Spain. If he turned up with the job half done, that would be the end of him. The odds were shortening though. CCTV, phone tracing, DNA, fingerprints. Even a random witness who might identify him.

The longer you stayed in the field, the shorter the odds.

The phone buzzed as the app opened. The same voice spoke to him, as always. Bit of an arrogant tone to it, he always thought. It sounded like one of those Russian officers who were always lording it over you in the army.

Lukas Petraskas didn't say a word. He just listened. It was the same old message. He wanted to curse at the voice. But the suave voice on the phone had higher connections, with men as hard as himself. Harder. You would need a platoon of soldiers to protect yourself if you crossed those sons of bitches.

The old man's voice was crystal clear, not like that snivelling excuse for a man he had collected the cash from in his mountain palace, the Arkens fellow. 'You stay where you are for the moment, sir. Are we clear? Just make sure to record all Mr Arkens's conversations.'

He grunted a yes and fixed his eyes on the image of Jenny Saunders on the phone. *Like a piece of that, all the same.* He knocked off the phone and stubbed out the cigarette. Then he picked up the cigarette butt and slipped it back into the packet. Basic military etiquette: don't shit on your own doorstep.

He took a deep breath and glanced around him. All clear. Then he went back into the barn and climbed back up into the loft. Ten p.m. tonight. The Pole would be calling around ten. Irregular hours. More food, cigarettes and a couple of magazines.

And more bloody waiting...

34

LUCY PULLED UP OUTSIDE THE B AND B IN DONNYBROOK AND looked up at the lace-curtained windows. It was an old-style mews in a back lane off a very expensive Dublin 4 street. She turned off the engine and stood out of the car. It was late afternoon. Plenty of time to sort out Ms Saunders before heading out to the memorial service in Windgap.

Jenny Saunders appeared out a few minutes later, with a leather shoulder bag and a well-rehearsed pout.

Lucy sat into the car and threw the door open and Jenny Saunders sat in. 'We need to talk about some things, Jenny.'

'What sort of things?' Jenny Saunders stared suspiciously at Lucy.

Lucy smiled sweetly at her. 'Like how much you really knew about the threats to your father.'

Jenny Saunders began to open the car door. Lucy reached across and pulled the door shut. 'I could have you arrested for withholding information.'

'Are you mad?' The Estuary accent ratcheted up a few notches now.

'Mad as hell. Got it in one.' The dark eyes flashed. Lucy

swung the car around slowly and headed for Sandymount. She parked near the Martello tower and turned off the engine.

She waited a moment and then turned to Jenny Saunders. 'Let's walk and talk.'

They walked slowly towards the Irishtown end of the strand, cutting right in the direction of the Pigeon House. The walkway wasn't clogged up with health nuts and dog walkers just yet, so they had it almost to themselves. It beat bitching in a car or in a cafe, Lucy reckoned. They were alone by the time they reached the bend in the strand.

Lucy turned to Jenny. 'Your mother met your father in Boynebridge a few times before he died. Don't bother disputing that. We have it all on CCTV.'

Jenny Saunders nodded. 'They met in a hotel, in Boynebridge, a few times. Then the last time, on the dig.'

Lucy stopped walking and looked into the dark, troubled eyes. 'You knew about the threats to your father. Right? And about these meetings between your mother and father?'

'Yes.'

Lucy fixed the younger woman in her gaze. 'So why didn't you tell us about the meetings?'

The big eyes looked at Lucy. There was the sheen of truth in them now. 'Because... because I felt guilty about what happened.'

Lucy sighed. 'You don't think that information outweighed your feelings? Could have helped us earlier?'

Jenny Saunders nodded. 'I was afraid, too... guilty and afraid.'

Lucy paused a moment. 'You thought, if you shut your mouth, it would all go away?'

The big eyes looked out at Lucy. 'If my old dad had shut his mouth, he would still be here.'

'Right. Right. So how did the whole thing start? Now, be straight with me.'

Jenny Saunders nodded and then spoke slowly. 'Mum got these phone calls at all hours of the day, telling her to tell Dad to shut his big mouth.'

Lucy listened carefully now for the tone of the telling. 'And did your mother know what it was all about?'

'Yes. But she wouldn't tell me. She said if I knew, that I would be in danger, too.'

Lucy took the younger woman by the arm. Jenny jerked back a moment with a vexed look on her face. 'And did you yourself get a phone call from anyone?'

Jenny Saunders was suddenly silent. She pulled her arm away and walked on ahead of Lucy. Lucy caught up with her and grabbed her arm again. 'Did you get a phone call? I need to know. It won't put you in any more danger than you are now. Tell me, please.'

Jenny Saunders turned back to Lucy slowly. 'Yes. I got a phone call, too. Just the one.'

'Go on.'

Jenny Saunders looked away from Lucy as she spoke. 'It was after Mum had this big row with Dad at the site. I think it was that morning or the next, at about three or four in the morning, my phone rang. This foreign voice with a bit of a Cockney accent told me to tell my dad to shut up. If my mum couldn't, I had to.'

Lucy made Jenny Saunders look at her. 'You're sure it was a Cockney accent, Jenny?'

Jenny Saunders nodded. 'Foreign and Cockney, like the way my mum's Irish accent was mixed with an English one. Only his was like German or East European, maybe.'

'What did you say to this voice?'

'I said I can't make my father shut up. I should have tried harder, I know!' Jenny Saunders suddenly put her head in her hands.

Lucy held her close and waited a moment. 'You have no idea at all what it was all about, Jenny?'

Jenny Saunders spoke through sobs. 'About something, years ago, when I was a child. That's what my mum said.'

Jenny Saunders looked up into Lucy's eyes. They waited until a woman with a little toy dog had passed. Lucy raised Jenny's chin to look straight at her. 'And that's all you know?'

Jenny Saunders nodded a yes. The path was quiet again.

Lucy took Jenny by the arm. 'Let's start walking back. Listen, you may be in danger. Whoever is behind this may think you know something.'

'Can't you tell them I know nothing?'

Lucy took Jenny's hand. 'We don't know who they are. And even if we did, why would they believe us? Maybe you would be safer back in London.'

'I'm not leaving Dublin until my mum's body has been released, Detective.'

THEY TURNED BACK for Sandymount Strand. Lucy waited until they were back inside the car again; then she turned to Jenny. 'There's another thing I'm curious about, Jenny. Your father stopped paying support when you were still small.'

'Yes. I know that.' Jenny Saunders wiped her tears with a paper tissue and sniffled a little.

'Oh. And did your mother ever explain it?'

'Dad bought this flat for us in Camden Town, in place of support. I didn't hear about that until years later, of course.'

'And whose name is that flat registered in?' Lucy turned on the engine.

'My mum's name. It's my flat now, I suppose.'

The traffic had picked up now. They crawled back slowly to the B and B, through the thickening traffic. Lucy pulled up by the kerb. She watched Jenny Saunders make her way into the B and B.

SHE WAITED until the light went on in a first-floor room; then she phoned Anna. 'I need you to check Violet Saunders's flat in London, title deeds and the rest. See if there's a lien on the flat, or any loans or other interested parties. And one more thing...'

'Yes?'

'I need an eye kept on Jenny Saunders, for her own safety. Get onto Reese and see what he can do.'

Lucy pulled out slowly into the evening traffic.

SHE TOOK her time driving on to Windgap. She drove on to the Forty Foot, at Sandycove. The bathing place was full of men and women braving the swell. She sat down on the stone bench to watch the comings and goings. An elderly woman made her way gingerly down the stone steps. Lucy watched her slip smoothly into the water and move out into the deep. She waited until the woman swam back to the steps, smiled at her silently as she passed, then rose and made for the car and the memorial service in Foxrock.

The whole idea seemed just a little bit yellowpack Quaker to Lucy, according to Joyce Carlton's description anyway. A memorial session in Windgap, with everyone sitting around in a circle, sharing their gilded memories of Philip Carlton. Almost spooky, in fact. Never know what you might see or hear, of course. But Joyce Carlton had a sack of letters waiting for her.

She was almost in Foxrock when Anna called back. 'Hi. Reese will discuss Jenny Saunders with you tomorrow morning. And the London flat...'

'Yes?'

There was a clickety clack of the keyboard at the other end.
'Bought outright in 1999.'

'Interesting. How much?'

There was more clicking of the keyboard at the other end of the line. 'Eighty thousand pounds. Worth north of Eight hundred thousand pounds in today's money.'

'OK. Well, he hardly pulled that off on an academic's salary, not with all his other expenses. There's something not right here, as my mother says, in her fancy *Froglais*. Get onto the Criminal Assets Bureau bucks and let them set their software spiders on it.'

'And you're looking for what exactly?'

Lucy thought a moment before speaking. 'Where did Philip Carlton get such an amount of money? Digging up ancient Ireland can't have been all that lucrative.'

'OK. Got it.'

'I'm off to the memorial session in Joyce Carlton's. I'll have the phone off for a while.' Lucy swung onto Torquay Road and prepared herself for another encounter with Joyce Carlton.

THE MEMORIAL SERVICE was already in progress when she arrived. She could hear murmuring behind the closed curtains and hoped there wasn't going to be too much hocus-pocus with candles and essential oils and mantras, thank Christ. The only mantra she felt she needed regularly was the slapping of cold waves on the wooden planks of the dinghy beyond Skerries harbour.

A young, fair-haired woman with a red rose in her hair opened the door. 'Yes?'

Lucy smiled at her. 'I'm Detective O'Hara.'

'Aunt Joyce is expecting you. I'm Caroline, her niece.'

Lucy was led into the dining room. The furniture had been pushed back against the walls, and twenty or more people were sitting around in a big circle. A table had been set in the middle of the group with a portrait of Philip Carlton, a burning red candle and a trowel of what she took to be Boyne Valley earth in it. Most of the group seemed to be in their sixties or seventies. She took a chair at the edge of the circle.

Joyce Carlton nodded over at her. 'This is Detective O'Hara. She has been of great assistance to both myself and David over the past few weeks.'

There were warm nods all around.

Joyce Carlton turned back to the little cabal. 'Professor Dunleavy, if you would like to finish off the evening.' Lucy spotted Jeremy Arkens in the low light for the first time now. The yellow, saturnine smile. There was no sign of his other half, though.

Professor Dunleavy rose to his feet slowly, put on his reading glasses and started reading.

'It was on that warm summer's night, in Mycenae, among the relics of ancient Greece, that Philip and I first got in touch with the *genius loci* of a place. And I'm glad to say that, forty years later, Philip shone a light on the same *genius loci* at the settlements at the Boyne Valley. It is fitting that he passed into the land of his forefathers in the place to which he gave so much, and which gave him so much in return.'

There was a shifting of chairs. Joyce Carlton stood up to announce refreshments in the conservatory. Jeremy Arkens made a beeline for Lucy. 'Nice to see you again.'

'Thank you. I don't see your wife?'

Jeremy Arkens smiled a cuddly, creepy sort of smile. 'She finds this sort of thing morbid. Anyway, better get out to the conservatory before the choicest nibbles are gone. Hmm?' She watched Jeremy Arkens make his way through the crowd.

Joyce Carlton came over to her. 'Let's go through the old scullery. Keep it to yourself. I can do without any stuff and nonsense from David and his so-called husband.' Lucy smiled and followed Joyce Carlton out into the scullery.

'It must have been a very beautiful evening.'

'Oh, yes, it certainly was. My niece, Caroline, is a little treasure, mind you. Like a daughter to me. The child I never had.'

The child I never had. Odd choice of words. They seemed a bit too weepy for Joyce Carlton.

Joyce Carlton opened up the press under the sink and pulled out a little jute sack.

Lucy took the sack in her hands. 'I'll return the letters as soon as I've gone through them.'

Joyce Carlton waved towards the conservatory. 'That's fine. Will you join us for refreshments?'

'I should be getting home. I met up with Jenny Saunders earlier, by the way.'

'Ah. I asked her to contact me when things settle down. She is family, after all. Now, I'll leave you to let yourself out.' Joyce Carlton disappeared.

Lucy slipped out into the yard and popped the boot of the car. She had just closed it over when she heard a noise behind her. Jeremy Arkens was standing smoking a cigarette, leaving a sour sting of the saltpetre was on the evening air.

'You're not joining us?' His eyes fixed on the boot of the car.

'No. Duty calls.'

'Always duty. Hmm?'

Lucy smiled and slipped into the car. When she glanced over her shoulder before pulling away, Jeremy Arkens had already disappeared back into the house, like a true middleman. The sort, she reckoned, who would have flogged relics of the saints in the plague times of the Middle Ages.

And she just couldn't dispel the idea from her head, all the way back home.

A middleman...

35

DENNIS WAS STANDING OVER BY THE BACK DOOR OF THE STATION, chatting with a young woman garda. He had that cheeky, boy-chef look on his face. He straightened up suddenly when he saw Lucy, and she waited for him to join her. 'Bring that sack in the boot upstairs, Dennis. Everyone on board?'

'Detective Sullivan is back in that lock-up garage in Robin-hood with forensics. Detective Brosnahan has just arrived in.'

Lucy watched Dennis heave the sack over his shoulder and headed into the station. She phoned Gerhard. Saoirse answered the phone. 'How are things, pet?'

She could hear Saoirse inject a little sob into her voice just to make her feel good. It sounded cute. 'It's great. But I miss you, *Maman*. Tell *Mémé* I miss her too.'

'I will. Well, we'll have a long catch-up tonight, love. Let me have a word with your dad.'

Gerhard came on the line. Calm, cool, collected Gerhard. 'Hi.'

'Hi. Listen, it's a big help having Saoirse over there, for the moment.'

Gerhard's voice was soft and calm. 'I understand.'

Lucy took a deep breath. 'I'll ring tonight, so I can explain a bit more then.'

'OK. *Bis später,* Lucy.'

SHE HEADED INTO THE STATION. A couple of uniforms were working away at the back of the incident room. She had a word with them and then went back to the others. Dennis and Brosnahan had arranged a little island of tables in the middle of the room. The jute sack with the letters was placed in the centre.

'Anna, divvy up the letters between us. On each letter and envelope write a number in pencil. I'll keep track of the sequence.' They pulled up chairs and sat down.

Lucy continued. 'Anything odd, circle it in pencil and make a note of it beside your list. We don't know what we're looking for until we find it. Right, Anna, letter number one...'

The letters to Philip Carlton were varied. Some were from his former wife, some from foreign academic correspondents, and some from casual and not-so-casual acquaintances. There were several gushing letters from women friends (postgrad students?). No wonder Joyce Carlton didn't want her brother reading them. Almost all were typed, thankfully. Lucy dealt with the few in French and German.

Gerry Sullivan strolled in an hour later. He gave Lucy that look, the one that said 'let's get offside.'

'OK, everyone, take a break for twenty minutes.' Lucy followed down the stairs with Sullivan and out into the car park.

Sullivan glanced around him as he spoke. 'Forensics have finished in the Robinhood property. No prints and DNA clean, so far. We just missed them.'

Lucy nodded. 'So be it. What about the explosives?'

Sullivan perked up a bit. 'That chap Viktor, we talked to down in Portlaoise, was right about the explosives. They were lifted from a mine in Laois years ago. We tracked them down by chemical composition to a stolen batch of Frangex. Old '70s stuff. Viktor didn't know the exact details. Just something he heard on the wind, as they say. Someone knew the location, though. Someone not local, it seems. And not paramilitary.'

'Come on. Let's head back to the bunkhouse.'

IT WAS noon by the time all the letters had been speed-read. Sullivan stood up and walked over to the whiteboard to make notes. Lucy suspected that Sullivan's Kerry ancestors had probably all been local schoolteachers. Autodidacts, used to standing in front of noisy classes. He hadn't picked up that sense of his own grandeur in the guards, anyway.

The notes on the letters came thick and fast. There were items that could be cross-referenced   local and foreign names, unusual locations, romantic attachments.

Sullivan had almost filled the whiteboard when Dennis Sheehan spoke. 'I've found a pattern in a couple of these letters.'

Lucy looked over at Dennis. 'What, exactly?'

'In thirty-two and ninety-six. The words "Der Sammler" are repeated. The letters are signed off with that name.'

Anna Crowley held up a letter. 'So have I. In number sixty-three.'

'Show me.' Lucy took the letters. On the end of each one, the German words were handwritten in old Gothic script. 'What about the sources of the letters?'

Dennis shook his head. 'None of them have addresses or dates, and the envelopes are missing.'

'So, both the writer and the receiver must believe these are important, then. OK, after lunch, you can all check up on the names and locations Gerry has written on the whiteboard. See you back at the ranch at two. Gerry... lunch?'

'Sure.'

Lucy tapped her watch. 'In five.'

THEY WERE in the car park of the Oasis boutique bar when Lucy's phone rang. Dennis sounded a little breathless. 'We've matched up one of those "Der Sammler" letters with an empty envelope.'

Lucy was suddenly awake now. 'And?'

'It matches the paper in a letter sent to Philip Carlton by his younger brother Derry.'

'So maybe this "Der Sammler" was Derry Carlton all along? I suppose he was a bit of a collector. Collector of other people's property, that is.'

Dennis sounded pleased with himself at the other end. 'Looks a bit like that.'

'Can't ask him, of course, Dennis, can we?'

Dennis sounded puzzled at the other end. 'Why is that?'

'Well, he's dead, isn't he? Very. And quite a long time. Unless you have some special technique for talking to the faithful departed.'

'Ah...'

'Never mind. Thanks. See you after lunch.'

She knocked off the phone and turned to Sullivan. Then they got out of the car and headed into the desert of bad taste that was the Oasis.

36

It was just before noon when Lucy turned into Foxrock from the main road. She had been out in the Mermaid that morning and could still smell the salt on her skin. It felt like a sort of barrier against the wear and tear of the day. Joyce Carlton was waiting for her on the doorstep. The gummy golden retriever beside her barked half-heartedly as she approached the door.

She could hear Mrs Egan pottering about somewhere in the house. 'I've got those letters in the boot.'

Joyce Carlton smiled. 'Were they a help at all?'

Lucy nodded. 'Yes. They were. Sometimes you find a piece of a puzzle and then...'

Joyce Carlton patted the dog on the head. 'What? You realise it belongs to a different puzzle?'

Lucy smiled. 'Yes. You might say that.'

A man's voice called from upstairs. Lucy recognised the voice of David Carlton and glanced over at Joyce Carlton.

Joyce Carlton whispered to Lucy, 'Leave those letters in the boot for the moment. You can drop them back another day.'

Lucy nodded. 'I was wondering if I could have another look around Philip's study?'

Joyce Carlton brightened up. 'Of course.'

Lucy heard footsteps upstairs. David Carlton came down the stairs slowly.

'Detective O'Hara! We'll really have to start charging you high-season rates!'

Lucy shook his hand. 'I've come back for a second look through the files.'

'Right! So, come with me to the casbah!'

She followed David Carlton down the long corridor to the study. She saw at once that some things were missing. The statuette of Minerva was gone from over the marble fireplace and the series of Celtic motif drawings on the wall had disappeared, leaving three bare patches in their place.

She looked over her shoulder. 'I'm fine now. I can find my way 'round.'

'Good. And you'll join us for lunch? It's *salmon en croûte*. Mrs Egan and I have an arrangement: I pronounce it perfectly and she cooks it perfectly! She calls it *Salmon on Kraut*. Sounds a bit like fish served on some poor German.'

Lucy smiled politely. 'A rose by any other name...'

'Salmon on Kraut it is, then – *à bientôt!*'

Lucy closed the door behind David Carlton. She started working her way through the filing cabinet, then the appointment diaries. She could see that someone had been at them since she had last looked through them. The little chit of paper she had left between 1989 and 1990 was missing. David Carlton? Joyce Carlton? Or a third party?

She took a few photos here and there as she progressed. She turned to the diary relating to the year Jenny Saunders was born, but there was no mention of the event. She moved on to the year the flat was purchased in London, but there was nothing there either. She had just reached 2010 when the dinner gong sounded.

Mrs Egan's curly head appeared in the door. 'Dinner will be ready in five minutes, so it will. You do like salmon, I hope?'

'Love it, actually.'

Mrs Egan looked pleased. 'And a glass of good red wine to go with it won't do any harm either.'

Lucy made her way into the dining room. David and Joyce Carlton were already there.

David Carlton stood up. 'Red or white?'

'Red. Half glass, please. I'm driving later.'

David Carlton poured. 'Of course. Which part of France is your mother from?'

'The southwest. Near Bordeaux. Vineyard land.'

David Carlton raised his glass to her. 'But your father was Irish, of course.'

'Very. Waterford.'

Joyce Carlton turned to Lucy. 'So, any new lines of enquiry?'

'None. We just need to catch our main man.'

David Carlton took a sip of wine and sat back in his chair. 'Indeed. And you still stand by the forced suicide theory?'

'All the evidence seems to point that way. By the way, I notice the study has been tidied up a bit.'

Joyce Carlton suddenly perked up. 'Well, as executor, I'm allowed to dispose of the less valuable assets from the estate. I've offered certain pieces to people who would appreciate them.'

'The Minerva?'

'That went to dear old Professor Rohan.'

Professor Rohan: Lucy made a note to call the old gentleman and arrange another visit. She wasn't sure that he mightn't be a target himself now. It would stand to reason – as the 'last standing man' of the circle, he was bound to know things no one else did. She would ring him that evening and arrange to drop around.

'David plumped for some of the paintings and drawings. The ones over there, by the armchair.' Lucy glanced over at the little collection stacked against the armchair.

'Myself and Michel are keen amateur collectors.'

When lunch had finished, Joyce Carlton suggested having dessert out in the back garden. Lucy let them go ahead of her and walked over to the little stack of framed drawings and paintings by the armchair. There was a watercolour of Howth – a signed oil painting by Carlton *père* – done some fifty or sixty years before. The three framed images of Celtic icons caught her eye then. The first one was of a fish inlaid with ornate lettering, the second was an image of a dog, tricked out in bright reds and greens, and the third one was a simple drawing of a bird, with minimal decoration.

She lifted the frame out to look at it more closely. In the bottom right hand corner, she could see the artist's signature.

Der Sammler

A voice called out to her from the corridor. 'Aren't you joining us in the garden?' David Carlton came into the dining room and glanced at the painting. Lucy turned to him.

'Do you mind my asking... the signature... that name "Der Sammler"?'

David Carlton shrugged his shoulders. 'Ah, that name again. Sorry, can't help you there, I'm afraid. It's one of Dad's old paintings. Someone gave it to him as a gift. Must be the pen name of some artist he knew.'

'Just curious.'

Lucy followed David Carlton out into the garden, where they joined Joyce Carlton for a feast of fresh soft fruits and cream.

37

EDENMORE WAS AS SILENT AS THE GRAVE. THERE WASN'T SO MUCH as a bird twittering in the bushes at the front of Professor Rohan's morose house.

Lucy walked around to the side of the house. She opened the gate to the back garden slowly, and there he was – standing on the lower rungs of a stepladder, snipping away at a box hedge. He suddenly looked quite frail to Lucy, with his spindly legs and wren-boned wrists. She spoke softly so as not to startle him.

'Professor Rohan...'

The old face turned around slowly to her. *A little deaf, too.* 'Detective O'Hara!'

She could see he was glad to see her. Maybe she was the only visitor he'd had all week. The thought suddenly saddened her a little. Lucy smiled up at the old man. 'Don't you think it's a bit dangerous up there?'

'My father was in the RAF during the war. I'm just cutting a common or garden box hedge.'

She helped him down off the ladder and took the clippers from him. He dusted himself off and limped towards the table in the middle of the garden. 'I'll be back in the shake of a lamb's tail with a nice pot of tea for us.'

She took a walk around the garden and had a look at the raised flower beds and the little vegetable garden. There was a little ornamental pond in the corner of the garden.

A couple of plump Chinese carp were swimming about in the clear water. She watched them absentmindedly for a few minutes until a voice called across the garden, 'Tea for two and two for tea!'

She crossed over to the table and helped unload the tray and the bone china tea set and the little silver sugar bowl. Lucy lifted up the teapot. 'Let me pour.'

'If you insist. I'm a tea first man, by the way.'

Lucy set a teacup down in front of the elderly man. 'I drink it black from my time in Egypt.'

'Is that so? I imagine Egypt must have made a great impression on you.'

Lucy sat down and took up her cup. 'It did. We visited a lot of sites and I had a wonderful Egyptian nanny, Khadija. She was like another mother to me. And then there was the street life, of course.'

Professor Rohan took a sip of tea. 'Your father would be very proud of your achievements, I imagine. Mr Arkens told me that he passed away in Cairo. That must have been a great loss, of course.'

Lucy nodded. 'It was. A great loss. To all of us.' She took out a notebook with a drawing of the extended Carlton family tree. They spoke about the Carlton sisters first. Then the talk turned casually to Derry Carlton. She could see a certain change come over the old professor now. A sort of weary wistfulness seemed to enter his voice.

Professor Rohan stared down into his cup of tea as he stirred it. 'Ah, Derry. The apple of his mother's eye and the scourge of her heart too, sadly.'

Lucy glanced down at the family tree in her notebook. 'How so?'

'Women, drink, and a complete spendthrift, I'm afraid. Very clever man – possibly even smarter than his two older brothers – but he put it to bad use, unfortunately.'

The old man looked away from Lucy as though he were listening to prompts offstage. 'It's all so far in the past, Detective. All the trouble Derry got himself into.'

Lucy drew closer. 'What sort of trouble?'

'Well, associating with bad sorts. He dealt in antiques and fine art, as you know. But he dealt with the greyer area of the market too, if you see my meaning.'

Lucy poured herself another cup of tea slowly. 'And do you have any details?'

The eyes dimmed a little now. 'Just rumours, from long ago. But rumours from people who were in the know, you might say.'

'And do you think his brothers knew about all this?' Lucy glanced down at the diagram in her notebook again.

'In some minor way, maybe. Philip and David were always straight as a die and busy with their own lives. Six children in a family, bound to be one black sheep, don't you think?'

'I suppose.'

Professor Rohan frowned. It was clear he had something on his mind that he was weighing up. 'There were rumours, as I say, over the years...'

'Yes?' Lucy smiled sweetly.

'Rumours that people in high positions in the banks hid the proceeds of unorthodox transactions in accounts with false names. By the by, you said on the phone you had something to show me?'

'I do. Do you mind if we go inside?' Lucy stood up and started loading up the tray.

'Of course. Let me do the washing up first. I'll bring you into my study.'

She followed him back into the house. The kitchen was just as Anna Crowley had described it. There wasn't a thing out of place, from the ancient Kenwood Chef food mixer with the shiny chrome to the tea caddies and pots and pans.

The study was much as she had imagined it would be. Dark wood, book-lined walls and a large desk piled with even more books. The bookshelves were crammed with Greek and Latin texts. Over the mantelpiece, her eye caught a black-and-white photo of Philip Carlton and the professor taken at least thirty years before.

Lucy set her briefcase down on the desk and took out three photocopied letters from it.

'Do you see, Professor Carlton? The same signature on these three letters to Philip Carlton. "Der Sammler. The Collector." I came across it on a painting in Windgap, too. Does it mean anything to you?'

'Nothing at all. Perhaps someone's *nom de plume,* or even a little in-joke between scholars.'

Lucy slipped the sheets back into her briefcase. 'I see. Well, it was worth asking.'

Professor Rohan seemed a little disappointed on her behalf. 'I can do a little further checking, if you like. Ask a few people.'

Lucy snapped the briefcase shut. 'That would be very helpful. Thank you. Oh, by the way, there was just one more thing...'

'Yes?' The old eyes looked out at her, eager to please.

Lucy took out her phone and opened up the image file. The photograph Anna had copied opened up. Professor Rohan leaned over and looked at the image.

'Ah! That's the same photograph I have hanging in the kitchen! Where did you come across it, might I ask?'

Lucy selected a suitable lie from her stock. 'I found it among a collection of photos in Philip Carlton's study.'

Professor Rohan peered at the photo. 'Gosh, that's a long, long time ago! Derry Carlton could only have been in his early twenties.'

'And the other man?' Lucy tapped the man in the middle of the photo, the one with the tartan cap who looked like a research physicist on day release into the real world.

'Not the foggiest. I can't even remember where that photo was taken. The shrubs in the background look like Windgap, mind you.'

Lucy knocked off the phone and smiled. 'Just wondering.'

Professor Rohan saw her to the door a few minutes later. For the first time now, she really began to fear for him, the way she did for Jenny Saunders. Began to think that maybe he knew too much about the past, and that he too might be a target. As the last man standing, he must know much more than many other people.

It was at times like this that the original sin of omission came crawling back to her like a wounded, vengeful dog: what if she had acted on her instincts that day, in the Cafe Akhenaten in Cairo? What if she had signalled her suspicions to her father in some way?

He would probably still be alive.

But for the lost word... the word of warning she'd failed to deliver. That she should have given. That might have saved her father's life. The Akhenaten Cafe...

And it had become her life's mission, she knew: hunting for the lost words and bringing them to light, that others might live.

To save her father, over and over again.

.   .   .

FOR A MOMENT, as she drove back along, she was going to phone back to Edenmore with its gloomy rooms, but then she put the idea out of her head. She would talk to Reese again about the business with Derry Carlton and about the old professor's position. Could a dead man's wrongdoings really have something to do with all this?

Could two people really be dead for dirty financial deeds done years before?

It was a question she would ask again and again in the coming days. But that was the problem with asking yourself awkward questions.

You never seemed to get a straight answer.

38

VIOLET SAUNDERS'S FUNERAL SERVICE WAS ON A MUGGY FRIDAY morning in Mount Jerome, a Victorian chapel and cemetery. Cremation made the most sense, Lucy realised grimly, even if the body had been pre-cremated, in reality. There was hardly much point in burying a body that was hardly there anyway.

The mourners just about filled the first couple of pews in Mount Jerome chapel. Joyce Carlton sat with Jenny Saunders, but there was no sign of David Carlton. Reese appeared in with Anna Crowley. A cousin appeared out of the woodwork, from Wicklow, and took his place beside them. There were two women co-workers of Violet Saunders, over from the British Library Service. The Arkenses appeared in just as the service started. Sheila Arkens was wearing a floral hat that wouldn't have looked out of place at the Dublin Horse Show.

Jeremy Arkens had a fine face for a funeral, she thought.

There was no sign of old Professor Rohan. Maybe he felt a bit too close to the grave for another outing. Lucy turned to Reese and whispered, 'I'm worried about old Professor Rohan.'

'What way?' Reese glanced over his shoulder at the empty pews.

'I feel he could be a target because of what he isn't telling us. At least we know Jenny Saunders isn't privy to too much info.'

Reese nodded quietly but said nothing.

One of Violet Saunders's colleagues, a small, plump woman with a north-of-England accent, said a few words. There was no mention of Violet Saunders's violent death at all. Joyce Carlton put her arm around Jenny Saunders's shoulder as the coffin was committed to the flames.

Outside the chapel, Joyce Carlton raised her voice above the chatter. 'You are all invited back to the Shelbourne for food and refreshments.'

LUCY DROVE JENNY SAUNDERS, Joyce Carlton and the two English ladies to the Shelbourne. Reese and Anna headed off back to Boynebridge. Just as they sat down to eat in the Shelbourne, Sullivan rang to report in.

She slipped out to the bathroom to take the call. 'Listen, I want you to do a bit more rooting around about the late Derry Carlton. Old Professor Rohan hinted at some extra knowledge of serious crooked dealings in the past.'

'This we know already. You saw the files in Harcourt Square. You don't think Professor Rohan might be putting you off the scent, do you?'

Lucy was silent for a moment. 'How do you mean?'

Sullivan gave a little chuckle. 'Well, covering for one dead man with another dead man. Philip Carlton was his protégé, remember. It would reflect badly on himself, too, besides anything else. He probably venerates the Carltons.'

'Maybe. He mentioned something about hidden bank accounts owned by Derry Carlton. Could be some dodgy dormant account somewhere that might turn up something. Never know.'

'Worth a try, Lucy. I'll get on to it first thing tomorrow.'

She rejoined the crowd. Jenny Saunders was tucking into the gin big time now. The Arkenses didn't come to the meal. The Wicklow cousin, a widowed farmer, on a day off the farm, turned out to be chattier than expected. When the two English women headed off to their hotel in Parnell Square and the farmer weighed anchor, she was left with Joyce Carlton and Jenny.

Joyce Carlton whispered quietly to Lucy that she would 'make sure Madame gets home in one piece.'

Lucy smiled. It was time to leave off. Leave Jenny and her late father's sister to it. 'Thank you.'

Half an hour later, she was cruising north for the Black Hills on the M50.

39

LUCY TROTTED THE HORSE DOWN ONTO BARNAGEERA BEACH AND felt the creature juke gently as the sunlight hit its eyes.

The sun was well up now, and the sea was washed with a gentle early morning light from the east. It was just herself and the soft thrumming sound of Chantal's hooves on the wet sand. It had been a hard night. It was the first night Saoirse's absence had really got to her. She could have doused the flames in one of the town bars, or even in the city. But, instead, she chose to tack into the wind. To pass the evening hours at the piano and pottering about in the stables and the sheds.

Because she knew that, somehow or other, she had to walk through the fire alone.

At one stage, in the early hours of the morning, she woke realising dimly she had seen her father walking down a dusty, sun-drenched street in Cairo. The sound of the muezzin's call-to-prayer was in the background, and she could feel the choking dust of the Egyptian streets. Her father wasn't speaking to her, though. He was just there, walking beside her. Keeping her company maybe, because Saoirse was away.

And then she'd turned back for sleep, realising that she

was, in some new way, between two worlds now. The lost world of her father and the new, bright world of her daughter, who was already moving away from her, out into life.

When she woke a second time, just before dawn, she knew that she had travelled somewhere she had never been before. And she wasn't sure what she thought of this new land at all.

Sullivan was waiting for her in the lobby of NBCI in Harcourt Square. He was on his own patch. He had a bit of a face on him, but she ignored it. 'Come on, Gerry. Let's get on with it.'

He left her at the door of a small room on the second floor and said he would be back shortly. Reese was waiting in the room with another detective. Half a dozen box files were placed in the middle of the table. Reese tapped one of the box files. 'These are the Kilowatt Files, from the Phoenix Park archives. They were finally released to us last night, and we've spent since then going through them. But all of them have been redacted, sadly.'

Lucy smiled. 'You mean censored. Right?'

Reese affected a weary sigh. 'Whatever you like to call it. The same rules apply as before. No photographs. Are we clear? Thank you, Dermot.'

The other detective left. Sullivan arrived in after him and took a seat beside Reese and looked across the table at Lucy. 'Here's the thing...'

'Go on.'

Sullivan glanced over at Reese and turned back to Lucy. 'This stuff contains the names of politicians going back to the seventies, eighties and nineties. It's dynamite. Some are dead, of course.'

Lucy gave a sour little laugh. 'Lucky for them.'

Sullivan continued. 'But some are not, Lucy, and the descendants of the dead ones are still above ground. This might have had a lot to do with the resistance to letting us see them.'

Lucy pointed at the files. 'Well, *quelle surprise*, gentlemen. I'm missing the point you're making.'

Sullivan leaned across the table. 'Well, we're not going to skew this murder investigation and be stymied by an injunction if someone hears about this.'

Lucy looked at Reese. 'Which means what, in plain English?'

'Let's just focus on anything relevant to the murders of Philip Carlton and Violet Saunders.'

Reese stood up and disappeared out the door.

AFTER READING through a few pages with blanked-out names, Lucy looked over at Sullivan, at the far side of the long table. 'So, how were these blanks to be filled in? With some sort of overlay?'

'Yes. Like the sort of thing you use to mass-correct school tests. Old school high tech. A sort of key.'

Lucy set the sheet of paper down on the table. 'So, who might have this... key?'

Sullivan threw up his hands in mock despair. 'Keys, actually. Search me.'

'I would, Gerry, if I thought it would make any difference. How about searching Jeremy Arkens's property?'

Sullivan angled his head. 'On what grounds, specifically?'

'On the grounds of attempting to pervert the course of justice by being an aggravating little bollox.'

Sullivan gave a tidy little laugh. 'Classy. Real classy.'

IT WAS ABOUT five in the evening when they finished the last file.

Lucy closed up her notebook slowly. 'It's all been so well redacted with those blank spaces that only Derry Carlton and Jeremy Arkens gets a real look in. We've got a lot of stuff about the black market in antiquities, that's for sure. Long time ago though. The safely dead and the safely dumb. No mention of Top Cat, whoever he or she might be.'

'I know. It's all old stuff. Not much of a paper trail and no cyber trail at all. Old God's time, I'm afraid.'

Lucy flicked through a couple of typed pages. 'Look, thanks for trying, Gerry. I mean it. At least we know how close he was, businesswise, to Derry Carlton.'

'Sure.' Sullivan smiled awkwardly.

LUCY MADE her way down to the lobby. When she sat in the car, a few minutes later, she glanced at the photos she had taken secretly with her phone. She read the title of the first one aloud to herself.

Special Unit Report: Kilowatt/File 3

Her eyes focused on the name 'Jeremy Arkens,' and she thought for a moment. Then she rang Jeremy Arkens's number. Jeremy Arkens sounded like he didn't have a care in the world. 'Detective O'Hara, what can I do for you?'

'I'd like to meet up, Mr Arkens, soonest. I need a little bit of clarification, you might say.'

'Clarification?' The voice was smooth as honey.

'About your relationship with the late Derry Carlton, for example.'

There was a little sigh at the other end of the line. 'Alas, poor Derry. Infamous son of a famous father, you might say. An old story. Well, we'll be down in Vincent Mayhew's Estate, in Wexford, for the next few days. Old Norman territory, you know. I have a little bit of business there.'

'That's no problem, Mr Arkens. I could drop down there.'

'Alright, then, I'll send you on the location and we can arrange something.'

She rang through to the incident room in Boynebridge. 'Anna, just pass on a message to Dennis to meet me at Bray station tomorrow at ten a.m. We're going for a little trip down the coast.'

'Will do. Anything else?'

Lucy glanced at the Kilowatt file page again. 'Tell him ears only. I'm sure he'd like to be in on a bit of mystery. Young lad like him.'

'Got you.'

Lucy knocked off the phone and dug out the location of Vincent Mayhew's ancestral home, in Wexford, on Google Maps.

40

BEING INVISIBLE CAME EASY TO LUKAS PETRASKAS. HE COULD SIT silently for hours on end, just thinking to himself. It came from nights of forced marches and hiding out silently on manoeuvres with only your own thoughts for company.

It was just the chirping of the birds that got under his skin.

More than once, he wanted to take out one of the greasy-looking starlings with his handgun. Then he drove the idea from his head and settled down to the tedium of the day, in the old hay loft. A car passed by on the road outside as he sat there at the table, in the little cabin. But there was no need to worry about it. Even the light bulb was invisible outside the barn.

He played back the latest recording of Jeremy Arkens's voice.

The instructions from the old man on the phone were clear: record every word on the voice-activated device and send it on daily.

Lukas couldn't exactly understand everything on the recordings, true, but he understood enough, he reckoned, to get where Jeremy Arkens's jumpy mind was at. Sometimes, the voice-activated device even caught Jeremy Arkens talking to himself, in the enormous house with the huge glass windows. Over and over again, Lukas Petraskas heard the same words, in the same monotone. He began to wonder if Jeremy Arkens was starting to have some sort of breakdown.

'Why? Why is this all happening to me?'

But now, he had some new information for the old man at the other end of the line: Jeremy Arkens was going down to stay in some big house in Wexford for a couple of days.

Something about valuing the collection of some guy called Mayhew. Collection of what? Maybe more silver and crosses and furniture. He would be out of contact with Arkens for a few days. Pity he hadn't bugged the car as well, but that would have been a little harder. Anyway, he would pass on the info to the old man, as instructed.

Reference upwards.

He pressed 'send' and the recordings went winging their way to the Collector.

He glanced at his watch. It would be sunset in another hour or so. He would take a little walk in the dark then, down to the edge of the farm. Just to get out and stretch his legs and his mind. No one would spot him. He was sure of that much. His military training really stood to him in this sort of situation, he figured. Invisibility. The Pole would arrive around eleven, as promised, with provisions. Food, cigarettes and a bottle of Polish vodka.

The only good thing to come out of that God's curse of a country, in his opinion.

41

THE WALL AROUND THE MAYHEW ESTATE RAN FOR MILES. THEY seemed to have driven through most of Wexford to get there. Dennis checked the GPS again and turned to Lucy. 'Those were the old gates back there, Lucy. The new ones are coming up.'

There was a sudden curve in the long estate wall. Open gates and a cute little lodge house rose up in front of them. Two lichen-smothered, brazen stone eagles looked down on them from the ancient pillars.

Lucy nodded towards the gates. 'Just drive straight in. They're expecting us.'

They drove slowly up the beech-lined avenue to the early-nineteenth-century pile at the far end. A couple of fussy-looking peacocks wandering about the front lawn looked at them disdainfully as the car crunched to a halt on the gravel. One half of the double doors opened and an elderly gentleman descended the steps, leaning on a walking stick. They got out of the car and approached him.

The elderly man smiled at them. 'Good morning. I'm Vincent Mayhew. And you are?'

'I'm Detective Lucy O'Hara and this is Detective Dennis Sheehan.'

'Very nice to meet you both, I'm sure. I'm not used to having detectives around here. Mind you, during the troubles, we got the odd visit from the guards. I keep a couple of shotguns and a rifle in the house, you see. All legal, of course.'

'Of course.' Lucy made her way up the steps with Dennis behind her.

'Jeremy and his wife are waiting in the back garden. Mr Arkens is down to value some of my late wife's antiques. They overnighted last night. Great company, actually. Gets quite lonely here sometimes. Let's cut through the house.'

They followed Vincent Mayhew into the mansion. There was a smell of beeswax as soon as they entered. They could see ancient mahogany and the odd bit of silver and ivory. A suspicious-looking ginger cat glared at them when they crossed through the big scullery.

'Damn cat thinks she owns the place since my wife passed. I sometimes wonder if her soul isn't in the wretched thing.'

Jeremy and Sheila Arkens were sitting at a white wrought-iron table in the garden. Jeremy Arkens looked spry enough, but his wife seemed to have aged ten years in as many days.

Vincent Mayhew leaned forward on his walking stick. 'Tea? Coffee?'

'Tea will do fine for both of us.'

'I'll get the girl to drop it out to you.' *The girl.*

They sat down with the Arkenses. Jeremy Arkens spoke first. 'Let's get straight to the point, Detective O'Hara. We are both in fear for our lives now.'

Sheila Arkens chipped in, 'In fear for our lives from these people, like Jeremy says.' Lucy saw Jeremy Arkens give his wife an agreed-story sort of look, but said nothing.

The 'girl', a young, fair-haired woman, appeared out with a tray of tea and biscuits and set everything out carefully on the wrought-iron table. She spoke with a strong local accent. Summer job. There weren't too many 'girls' around who wanted to skivvy full-time anymore. When she had finished pouring the tea, her mobile rang. She stood to one side to answer it. Lucy's ears cocked up when she heard her switch into what sounded like Polish. Her voice had a high tone to it. This was probably her mother ringing to check up on her.

The 'girl' turned to Lucy. 'I've left extra milk, so I have. Are you alright, now?'

Lucy smiled. Good local Hiberno-English untouched by her Slavic mother tongue. Two software programs running in parallel. 'We're fine, thanks.'

Lucy waited until she had made her way back into the house, then turned to Dennis.

'Detective Sheehan, would you show Mr and Ms Arkens the copies of those pages, please?' Dennis took out the iPad and tapped an icon.

Lucy pointed to the iPad. 'You're a very popular character in the Kilowatt files, Mr Arkens.'

Jeremy Arkens shrugged his shoulders. 'All stuff and nonsense. Unfounded speculation from years ago.'

Lucy could see the brain working out the cost-benefit analysis. Trading off self-incriminating information for a *get out of jail* card.

Or a *get out of grave* card, more like.

Jeremy Arkens's voice, when he finally spoke again, had an edge to it. 'We might be able to come to some arrangement.'

Lucy glanced over at Sheila Arkens. Sheila Arkens was playing her part by keeping her mouth closed, as she had learned over the years. 'Are you saying you could help us with the investigation into the murders of Philip Carlton and Violet Saunders?'

'As per what you have on that tablet thingme there.' Jeremy Arkens waved an imperious digit at the iPad.

Lucy sat back in the wrought-iron chair. 'You mean you could bring us up to date?'

Jeremy Arkens nodded slowly. 'On condition of immunity from prosecution.'

'I beg your pardon?'

'You heard me. Immunity from prosecution.'

Lucy smiled. 'You know well that I'd have to reference that upwards.'

Jeremy Arkens leaned forward. 'You do that, then. And, by the way, the Kilowatt file keys... I can get them for you.'

Lucy didn't blink. 'I see. And just how did the Kilowatt keys come into your possession?'

Jeremy Arkens smiled serenely and shrugged his shoulders. 'All so long ago now. Hard to recall. Mists of time and all of that.'

Jeremy Arkens turned away from her and started to top up his wife's tea. He didn't turn back to her, but started chatting to his wife as though Lucy weren't there. Then, just as she was about to leave, he turned around to her slowly.

'Immunity. That's the key to the keys, you might say.'

Lucy caught something in the eyes just then. The tiniest smidgen of real fear buried deeply beneath the smarm and the smugness. 'Well, as the song says, you have to know when to hold them and when to fold them.'

Jeremy Arkens frowned. 'Are you threatening me, Detective O'Hara?' The tone was arch. Impudent, almost.

'No. But a lot of other people are. You want cover, it costs. You may fool your wife with your patter, but you don't fool me. I can see through bullshit in five languages. And I'm working on a sixth.'

There was anger in Jeremy Arkens's eyes now. The sullen anger of the card sharp finally cornered by his own cleverness

Lucy smiled sweetly and made her way across the back lawn to where Dennis was standing chatting to Vincent

Mayhew. She didn't look back again until they were driving towards the gate lodge, past the snooty peacocks.

LUCY DROPPED Dennis at Bray station, gave Joyce Carlton a quick ring and then carried on alone for Windgap. It was dark when she drove up the long driveway, and there was scarcely a light on in the house. Joyce Carlton opened the door, and she followed her into the drawing room.

David Carlton was seated at a low table, going through a portfolio of some sort. A bottle of red wine stood in front of him on the coffee table. They shook hands.

David Carlton pointed to the copy of the *Irish Times* on the table and a headline that read *Carlton Investigation Inconclusive*. 'How are the mighty Carltons fallen, eh! Very Old Testament, if I might say so. The newspapers just can't get enough of us.'

Joyce Carlton turned to Lucy. 'Surely you have enough information at this stage to charge someone, Detective O'Hara?'

'That's why I've dropped in today, actually. I didn't want to get into it on the phone. We think we may be getting closer to identifying the culprits. That means they may react violently. I'm legally and morally obliged to issue you with a threat-to-life advisory.'

David Carlton threw up his hands. 'Oh, splendid! So now we have to stay penned up inside until these hoodlums are caught.'

Joyce Carlton stood up slowly. She suddenly seemed very tired. Whatever row had taken place before Lucy arrived had clearly worn her out. 'I haven't been feeling too well today. I think I'll just have an early night. David will see you out when you're leaving.'

'Actually, I think I should be making tracks too.' Lucy reached for her handbag.

David Carlton beamed at Lucy smarmily. 'Do tarry a little. Why the unseemly haste?'

Joyce Carlton disappeared out the door. She saw something odd insinuate its way into David Carlton's features, as if the wine had loosened his tongue as soon as his sister left. 'Jeremy Arkens knows where this all started. He has chapter and verse on this, from years ago.'

David Carlton's face looked boozy and boorish now. He had the face of a middle-aged brat about to snap at an uppity waitress.

'I understand.' Lucy watched the eyes dim then flicker to life again.

'No, you don't. You don't understand a damn thing! But I know it all goes back to that spineless lizard in his mansion in the Wicklow mountains.' David Carlton suddenly started laughing for no reason. He swayed in the armchair and leaned over towards Lucy.

'How silly of me! Of course, all lizards have spines! What I meant was... metaphorically, of course...'

'A metaphorical lizard, Mr Carlton?'

'Indeed. Jeremy Arkens is a metaphorical lizard.' The voice wasn't so much snarky now as bitter.

Lucy took out her phone from her handbag. 'Maybe you could help me with something?'

The boozy eyes focused on Lucy. 'At your service!'

Lucy pulled up the photo of Professor Rohan, Derry Carlton and the stranger. She pointed at the unknown figure between them.

David Carlton straightened up in his armchair. 'That's Jeremy Arkens, of course. The old spineless reptile, metaphorically speaking.'

'Ah...' She peered at the picture more closely now. Yes, it was Arkens alright. She should have spotted it before. The smarmy, supercilious smile. The suave demeanour.

'Oh, yes. Jeremy knows names. But then, the old chap...
Professor Rohan...'

'Yes?' Lucy smiled encouragingly.

'Professor Rohan must know more than everyone else. He's
the longest on the planet. Longest one with a spine anyway.'
David Carlton started chuckling to himself again.

Lucy froze. 'So, do you think Professor Rohan might be in
danger?'

David Carlton paused and squinted at her. 'That could very
well be, Detective. Myself and Joyce, well, we're second line, so
to speak. Backline in the band, you might say. But Jeremy
Arkens. And old Professor Rohan...'

Lucy leaned closer to David Carlton. The woozy eyes tried
to focus on hers. 'You don't think Professor Rohan is actually
afraid of Mr Arkens, do you?'

David Carlton gave a little laugh.

David Carlton's eyes closed suddenly, and he slumped back
into the big armchair. The glass fell from his hand onto the
deep carpet. Lucy reached over and picked it up. She sat down
a moment just to make sure David Carlton was alright.

Her eye fell on the copy of the *Irish Times* and she picked it
up. Underneath it, she saw a photo lying face down on the
table. She read the half-obscured date on the back. 1950 something. A young woman in her late teens. She peered closer at
the photo and suddenly sat back in surprise. The figure in the
photo on the table was definitely Jeremy Arkens. But who was
the young woman?

On instinct, Lucy took a shot of the photo, without a flash.
David Carlton's eyes opened slowly at the click of the phone
camera, but he didn't seem to take in what she was doing.

Lucy slipped the phone back into her bag and stood up
slowly. She considered the drunken head lolling against the
wing of the ancient armchair for a moment; then she gathered
up her things. She didn't call up to Joyce Carlton as she left. Just

pulled the door gently to and drove back slowly down the avenue.

WHEN SHE REACHED the Black Hills an hour later, she heard the horse neighing in the stable. She got out of the car in the sharp light of the security light and went around to the back of the barn.

And in the dark of the warm summer night, she whispered her fears to the not-so-dumb animal.

42

THERE WASN'T A HINT OF THE SUMMER SUNLIGHT OUTSIDE, IN THE Collector's bunker. The only sound to be heard was the gentle hiss of air as a fresh page of the Genesis of St Fergal presented itself to the Collector's eyes.

Dixitque Abram: Domine Deus, quid dabis mihi?

He read slowly, savouring the sibilant sounds of the Latin. Behind him, the air-purification motor kicked in. Good German engineering. Metal, technology, machines, back to the Middle Ages and even further. He intoned the rest of the scripture to the background of the thrumming motor; then, when he had finished, he stood up, turned away from the glass case and left the chair back against the wall. He crossed himself and made his way out of the bunker up into the house, threw back a cup of coffee and headed out into God's clear, bright air.

THE EARTH WAS WARM NOW. A couple of weeks of strong sun had changed everything. The Collector marvelled again at the ways of the planet on which he lived. How it responded to each season with equanimity. Drawing in its horns in winter,

seasoning the world in colour in spring. He crossed over by the
firebreak and stood in against a tree. There was a rustle of
leaves to his left. He pulled in tighter against the tree and raised
the rifle to his shoulder. Through the scope, he beheld a young
fox tipping along through the little glade, the head sweeping
this way and that for any threats. He tracked the beautiful creature for a few moments until it loped off towards a clearing.
Then he lowered the rifle and smiled softly to himself.

Some creatures deserved to live; others deserved to die.

He continued his walk all the way to the headland, where
he sat for a while, scanning the sea with his binoculars.
Watching a large tanker make its way towards the Atlantic.
When he arrived back at the house, over an hour later, he
stored the rifle away and put the box of rounds back in the
drawer in the bureau.

Then he stretched himself out on the ancient chaise longue
in the study and catnapped until the clock on the wall struck
three. When he woke, he realised he had overslept. He made
his way into the kitchen and began preparing the day's main
meal – a hotpot of beef and veg that would last three days. He
ate just as the distant bells of a church sounded six. Then he sat
back into the sitting room and turned on the TV to catch the
tail end of the news. His phone beeped three times. He stirred
himself slowly and stood up from the sofa, then made his way
down to the bunker.

A couple of minutes later the voice of the Lithuanian came
on. 'I have send you new recording from this Arkens guy.'

'Excellent. And was there something else?'

'Yes. You tell me contact you if something special.'

'And?'

The Lithuanian spoke slowly. 'Well, this Arkens guy, he
meet this O'Hara detective woman before two days in Wexford,
where he stay with friend. I think they are do deal.' The

Lithuanian's accent was thicker than the sole of a boot. The Collector struggled to make out his exact words.

'What kind of deal?' The Lithuanian was annoying him now. Why didn't he just come out and say it?

'He is say something to his wife about keys he have in house. He will give this keys to the detective woman. All is on recording from Arkens house I am send you. About this keys.'

'Alright. I'll listen to it and get back to you if necessary. Thank you kindly.'

'For nothing.' The Lithuanian's voice sounded almost polite for a moment. In a gruff sort of way.

The Collector knocked off the radio and made his way back up the stairs to the house. He sat down on the sofa again and connected his phone up to the stereo system by Bluetooth. Then he sat back and listened to Jeremy Arkens's conversation with his wife over what they were planning with the 'detective woman.'

Jeremy Arkens's intent was very clear to the Collector now. This was betrayal, nothing short of it. He had been given enough leash, and he had abused the chance.

THE COLLECTOR HELD out until eight o'clock that evening. Then he went down into the bunker and turned on the shortwave radio. A few minutes later, the Lithuanian's voice filled his headphones. He kept the chatter brief. And clear.

'Deal with our friend in Wicklow now. Immediately.'

'And his woman?'

'Her too. They are both in this together. Immediately.' The Collector switched off the radio and sat there for a while trying to get his temper down to an acceptable level. When he felt easy in himself again, he ascended to the house and crossed into the study. There, he picked up the .22 and attached the silencer to the muzzle. He filled the clip from the box of rounds and made his way out to the sea side of the house.

Then, as the sun began to decline in the west, he slammed six .22 rounds into an entirely innocent beech tree standing about fifty yards from the house.

SHEILA ARKENS WATCHED from a back-bedroom window as her husband fired up the ancient barbecue of breeze blocks and iron grating that had been the scene of so many summer get-togethers in the good old days. She watched as the flames rose from the kerosene poured over the papers and notebooks.

Her husband threw a heap of old CDs and computer disks on the pile. She could smell the pungent plastic from where she stood, embittering the pure Wicklow air. Jeremy Arkens turned momentarily and peered at her through the smoke, as though she were a stranger witnessing some primitive ritual he was involved in.

He waved at her, for some reason he didn't quite understand himself.

Then Jeremy Arkens poked the blaze with a long stick and watched a heap of letters burst into flame. On top of the flames, he placed a pile of printed material and a couple of box files with the title 'Acquisitions' written on them. The files burst into flame immediately, and he stood back, watching until the fire had devoured them. He waited until all had turned to ash; then he stooped down to pick up the final box file. He read the title on the side panel again.

Kilowatt File: Keys 1, 2, 3, 4, 5, 6

He set it to one side and went back to stoking the fire up.

He lingered a while, toying with the long poker to make sure everything had been consumed; then he made his way back into the house by the annex. In a drawer under one of the glass cases with crucifixes, he placed the files he had saved with the Kilowatt keys.

Then he made his way into the living room, where his wife was settling down with a copy of *Country Living*. She turned to him as he approached.

'Everything gone?'

Jeremy Arkens smiled at his wife. 'All gone up in smoke. Except what we have to keep. I left the keys in one of the drawers under the glass cabinet with the wooden crosses.'

'Why are you telling me this, Jeremy?'

'Just in case something happens to me.'

Then he walked over to the great window to look out on the majesty of the Sugarloaf and congratulated himself on his own astuteness.

43

THIS WAS IT, THEN – FINALLY. THE LAST NIGHT LUKAS PETRASKAS would have to stay in this Godforsaken hay barn. With the sound of field mice scampering about and the dawn chorus of starlings and rooks. There was just one more job to do, and then he would be gone, never to darken anyone's door in this damp little country again.

Adam Bielski, the young Pole, picked him up just before dawn. They drove cross country, along narrow roads and lanes on the way to Dublin. Then, avoiding the motorway and the feeder roads, they slipped into the Robinhood industrial estate by the rear entrance. It was early Saturday morning. A tradesman's van wouldn't arouse much suspicion at that time of the morning.

The rifle was hidden where they had been told, in a little compartment in the inspection pit. It would be picked up later at another location. That was the Pole's problem, anyway. Lukas would be well out of the country by that time.

The Pole climbed out of the pit with the rifle in its hardcase. Lukas laid it out on an old abandoned workbench and examined it. He nodded at the Pole to keep lookout from the side window. An M4 with an optical sight. It wasn't an Accuracy International or a Barrett, but it would do the job alright. And it had already been zeroed and checked. There was no way he could do that himself, in open country, even with a silencer. This would be a two-shot job. A shoot-and-scoot operation.

Like in the first siege of Grozny, in Chechnya, when Lukas Petraskas had received his real blooding. How many of his comrades had fallen during that operation? And then there was the return match, a few years later. All sniper detail. The real stuff.

This was child's play in comparison. The only problem was getting in and out. He familiarised himself with the rifle and put it to his shoulder to locate the centre of gravity. Then he took out the map from his jacket and pinpointed the location and the access and escape roads.

The Pole called to him from the door. 'People arriving at the other building. Come on, Lukas!'

Lukas Petraskas ran his hand along the stock of the gun and felt the smoothness of the composite material. He sniffed the cold steel of the barrel, then he placed the rifle back in its case.

'Let's go.'

They pulled out of the yard and headed out of Robinhood for the Wicklow Mountains. It was only when they reached the foothills, near Bohernabreena, that he realised he had left the map on the workbench. Bloody Pole! If he hadn't been fussing like an old woman!

But he had memorised the roads. Had been there before anyway. And it was just early morning, after all. No problem with light.

He turned to the Pole and smiled. 'Right. I will guide you from here.'

'No map?'

'No map.'

'We can use Google.'

Lukas Petraskas laughed a hard laugh. 'Screw Google! Use brain!' Then he cursed loudly in Russian and pointed to a right turn on the road ahead of him.

44

GERRY SULLIVAN FELT THE PHONE VIBRATE IN HIS JACKET POCKET
as he arrived at the pickup spot opposite the Phoenix Park gate.
He didn't recognise the number, but he knew the voice. It was
the bigger guy from the tanning shop.

'Well, Jakub, my good friend?'

'I get story about couple of guys in and out of this place in
Robinhood, off Naas Road.'

Sullivan was suddenly awake now. 'I know the gaff. Go on.'
He watched Brosnahan crossing the road, coming from Garda
headquarters inside Phoenix Park. He beeped at him. When he
got into the car, Sullivan put his finger to his lips. 'Why do you
think they were there, Jakub?'

Jakub's growly voice broke in again. 'Maybe they are pick up
something. Half hour ago.'

Sullivan's voice suddenly jumped an octave. 'Why the fuck
didn't you phone me then?'

'Only I am hear this now. This is all. If more, I phone you.'

'Right. Right. OK. Thanks.' Sullivan knocked off the phone
and looked over at Brosnahan. 'Odd couple spotted at that

place we visited off the Naas Road. We'll head there now. You carrying?'

Brosnahan patted his jacket. 'I wouldn't feel dressed without it.'

Sullivan smiled, and they pulled off down Infirmary Road for the M50.

SULLIVAN DROVE into the Robinhood industrial estate and pulled up at a printing works behind the lock-up. While he hid the car in among the customers' cars, Brosnahan slipped inside and talked to the staff. A couple of minutes later, they were upstairs looking out through the blinds at the entrance to the Ukrainian car fitters.

Sullivan phoned Lucy. 'Some suspicious activity at the Robinhood site.'

'Where are you?'

'Right here.'

There was a pause at the other end of the line. Lucy's voice came back on the phone. 'Just hang fire till I get there. They might come back.'

LUCY PULLED into the site a half an hour later and parked in front of the print works. 'You and Peter go 'round the back, I'll go in the front.'

Lucy began walking around the lock-up. The floor was full of empty oil tins and abandoned hand tools. Sullivan scoured the lockers in the office and the storeroom. Brosnahan knelt down beside the inspection pit. 'Fresh shoeprints here.'

Brosnahan walked down the steps into the car inspection pit in the middle of the floor and glanced over to the side. He pulled out a pair of plastic gloves from his pocket and looked up at Lucy. 'The tool locker door has been left open.'

'Right. Let's leave it to forensics. Peter, yourself and Gerry set up a stake-out tonight. Just in case.'

Brosnhaan began going through the bric-a-brac cast aside. 'All sorts of rubbish here. Empty cans of beer, cigarette packets, gloves, a map.'

'Map?' Lucy came forward.

Brosnahan picked up an AA map and passed it to Lucy. She pulled out her plastic gloves and flicked through it. There were markings on various pages and a couple of words in Cyrillic.

Lucy ran her finger over the letters. 'Could be drug drops. Addresses. Anything. What do you think?'

'Might be our guys. Peter thinks they were down in that pit picking up something.'

Lucy glanced at her watch. 'OK. I'll talk to you both later.'

REESE WAS WAITING for her in a hotel near Heuston Station for a quiet, off-base catch-up. She was just passing the Phoenix Park gates when it hit her: the map. She pulled into the side with her flashers on and called Sullivan. 'You still in Robinhood?'

'Yes. Forensics are here. What can I do you for?'

'Grab that AA map on the worktop and find the quadrant south of Enniskerry.'

'Got it. Ah...'

Lucy jerked back. 'What?'

Sullivan's tone was high. 'There's a mark on a location near Roundwood and the letter *A* in Cyrillic writing.'

Lucy laughed. 'I didn't realise you know Russian, Detective O'Sullivan.'

Sullivan ran his finger over the map again. 'You mustn't have read my file properly, then.'

'Whatever. Look, that must be the Arkenses' house near Roundwood. Get an ERU call out and get on the road.'

'What about forensics?'

'Leave Peter there. I'll see you at the Arkenses'. Christ, I hope we're in time.'

'You don't think...?'

'You're right: I didn't think. That's the problem.' Lucy swung the Volvo around and headed back along the Liffey towards Islandbridge and the M50.

LUKAS PETRASKAS CROSSED over by the old farmhouse and hid in behind the derelict stables. Then he slipped up the hill he had used the first time he visited the Arkens household.

He had just breasted the hill when the sound of loud conversation came to his ears. For a moment, he didn't believe his luck: the two idiots were sitting out in the little grass patch behind the annex, at the back of the house, dining *al fresco*. He could almost smell the coffee and croissants from his position in the trees. It was clear that the Arkenses were at ease and at one with the world.

Like two people who had just won the lotto.

Of life.

Sheila Arkens was dressed in a bright yellow dress with a straw sun hat. Through the trees, he could see the glint of her jewellery. He zeroed in on the table in front of them. Sheila Arkens took out her sunglasses and sat staring into the face of the sun like a bewildered bunny rabbit.

She poured coffee for her husband then dropped a couple of cubes of sugar into his cup. There was no point in dilly-dallying about looking for the perfect shot, Lukas thought. A mid-body hit at this range would be fatal to people of their age. No one would hear the shots, and there would be no Swiss air ambulance to get them off the mountain. Still, better to go for the head. He could get in another couple if the light breeze caused problems.

Sheila Arkens stood up slowly. She looked like she had

forgotten something in the house. Lukas Petraskas waited until she had gone into the house; then he settled down for the first shot. Jeremy Arkens's silk-smooth skin and lank hair filled the rifle scope. Lukas adjusted the setting slightly for windage and distance and factored in the fall, because he was shooting downwards. He would try to get Jeremy Arkens before his wife came back out.

One... two... three...

There was a little kick from the rifle. Across the river, at the breakfast table, an 8M3 round, specially developed during the First Chechen War, severed Jeremy Arkens's relationship with the known world around him. He jerked backwards, decapitated by the hollow point with the little dimple in the tip, onto the warm grass.

Sheila Arkens reappeared and looked around, momentarily puzzled. Lukas Petraskas let her walk as far as the table. Far enough for her to spot her late husband reposing in the patch of grass the Husqvarna robot mower had trimmed just that morning.

But not far enough for her to scream and attract unwanted attention from the surrounding hills. Or babble into the phone she had just dropped from her right hand.

The second kill shot struck home.

Lukas laid the rifle on the ground, slipped down the hill and into the annex. The papers were in a little cabinet under one of the glass cases. He had learned that through the bugging device.

He took care, when he was burning the Kilowatt file keys, to make sure that everything was destroyed. It was all done in ten minutes. He glanced down at Sheila Arkens's slowly cooling corpse as he passed, considering for a moment the glittering bracelet on her wrist. Then he shook his head sadly and slipped back up the hill, retrieved the M4 and rendezvoused with the Pole at the old cattle shed.

When they reached the Blessington Lakes a short while later, Adam Bielski dumped the rifle and case, as instructed, inside an abandoned shed at the Kilbride side.

Then they swung back west to cross to the far side of Naas, where Lukas Petraskas climbed into the back of a commercial van that would carry him to Belfast, where he would slip across to the UK and, from there, back to Spain.

45

THE WICKLOW MOUNTAINS WERE DRENCHED IN A DEEP MIST, AND the Arkens residence was smothered in low cloud. Lucy stood aside to let the tall man in the white forensics suit pass, and looked down at the late Jeremy Arkens and his wife on the floor of the white forensics tent.

Sullivan stooped and came into the tent. 'The collection inside will be moved this afternoon. Nothing stolen, by the way.'

Lucy nodded at the site. 'Two birds with one stone, though. And, by all accounts, a bonfire of files. That's our Kilowatt keys gone, I assume.'

The forensics officer turned around to them. 'All clean as a whistle. This fellow was wearing forensic footwear and the rest, I'd say.'

Lucy angled her head. 'And the shots?'

The forensics officer nodded towards the hill behind the house. 'Probably came from up there. Two head shots with hollow-point rounds. This wasn't Dekko or Anto on the razzle after a skinful of pints.'

Lucy nodded at the hill behind the house. 'Anything up in the trees?'

'We'll do a fine-comb search, but, like I say, this boy is a pro.'

Sullivan grunted. 'Well, the pro left a map behind earlier on.'

Lucy grimaced. 'Which we sussed too late, unfortunately.'

The forensics officer pointed towards the annex. 'There's something you might like to see inside, Detective O'Hara.'

They followed him back into the annex, sidestepping the markers on the ground. He walked them over to a little table in the corner of the annex and pointed to a damaged radio receiver. Sullivan ran his gloved hand over the radio. 'A short-wave radio would be a very smart way of avoiding surveillance. The technical team will have a look at it.'

Lucy turned back to the forensics officer slowly. 'Do you really think this might be something?'

The forensics officer nodded. 'He did his killing, burnt those files and banjaxed the shortwave radio. A time-on-target operation.'

Lucy and Sullivan made their way up to the little glade of trees where the shots had been fired from. Sullivan pointed down towards the house and the little strip of grass with the forensics tent. 'Jeremy Arkens was having breakfast. Our friend took him out while he was alone. We know by the splatter pattern.'

'And what then?'

Sullivan glanced around him. 'He took Sheila Arkens out; then he was free to search the house. And he knew what he was looking for and where.'

Lucy frowned. 'So, serious inside information, then? How?'

Sullivan reached into his pocket and drew out a plastic evidence bag. 'The sitting room was bugged. For how long, we don't know yet.'

Lucy crouched down and scoured the patch of grass under her feet. 'Come on. Let's head back to Boynebridge. I need to sit the team down again and have a pow-wow.'

Sullivan slipped the evidence bag back into his pocket, and they started to make their way back down the hill again, towards the little white tent.

46

THE SOUTH BEACH IN SKERRIES WAS EMPTY AT SUNRISE THE NEXT morning. Only an elderly man and a little bitty dog were out walking in the clear salt air. At the Red Island end, she paused to catch her breath; then Lucy jogged back to where she had parked the Volvo.

Standing in the shower half an hour later, she considered the situation again: five people dead and the newspapers screaming for explanations. Every know-all troll from here to Timbuktu was throwing in his halfpence worth, like they knew anything. All they needed was to see her name mentioned, and the Bateman shooting would be back in the news again. She could even write the headline: *Disgraced Detective Heads New Murder Investigation*.

The couple of stories planted by Sullivan's newspaper and radio contacts had borne fruit though: the general consensus was that some sort of protection racket had been uncovered. There was no mention of any long-term involvement of the Carlton clan.

Fake news was sometimes good news. The faker, the better.

She put on BBC Arabic on the radio in the shower. There

were more riots in Cairo and more disturbances in Iraq and Syria. A Syrian refugee was talking about his lost home in Idlib and the members of his family who had been killed. She barely heard the phone ring over the sound of the water and the radio.

She slipped out of the shower and grabbed the phone from the bedside locker. 'Anna here. We've just had a call from monitoring. Professor Rohan got a phone call in the earlier hours of the morning. It sounded very like our Lithuanian friend.'

Lucy grabbed the bath towel. 'And?'

'Here, I'll play it back to you.'

Lucy sat in the armchair with the bath towel wrapped around her. The harsh voice of Lukas Petraskas filled the room.

'Just a small message. One professor, he is already die because he not shut his mouth. Silence, it is gold, Professor. That is all.'

Lucy towelled her hair as she spoke. 'Right. Send that recording to Schliemann in Kiel. Where's Gerry Sullivan?'

'He's in Phoenix Park with the radio technicians.'

Lucy stood up and stretched. 'Tell him I'm off to Edenmore, Professor Rohan's house, and to be on standby.'

THE TRAFFIC WAS at rush-hour levels by the time she finally got onto the M50 south. On the way to Edenmore, Lucy caught a French programme about colonisation in Africa. It almost sounded nostalgic. She smiled and thought of one of her father's lines: *Only the British do postcolonial guilt, Lucy. The French just get nostalgic about their rejected civilising mission.*

Lucy pulled off the M50 at the Sandyford exit and headed for Foxrock through Torquay Road. In her head, she could hear Professor Rohan's squeaky voice. He had sounded shaky on the line a few days before, alright. She pictured him lying in bed at night, in fear for his life after such a phone call. Was she feeling some sort of strange filial sense of duty now? Saving an older man when she couldn't even save her own father?

. . .

PROFESSOR ROHAN WAS DRESSED in a matching suit and tie. Matching the nineteen fifties.

He pottered about in the kitchen, then resurfaced with tea and biscuits. He sat facing Lucy on the couch. 'My friend across the water has invited me to stay with him until all this bother is over.'

'That's a good idea.' Lucy smiled sweetly. Sullivan was probably right: an old gentleman friend. She pictured them poring over Greek texts together and fussing over picky points of grammar and syntax.

'It's all got a bit too much, at the moment.'

'Is there any particular thing bothering you, Professor?'

'No. Nothing special. I just thought it would be a break.' The old eyes clouded over. For a moment, she thought he was going to come out with it. But there was no point in mentioning it herself and having to admit to the phone tap.

'Well, we hope to have things tied up very soon, Professor. The final push.'

'The final push. Gosh! That sounds like Montgomery in North Africa. Like a pincer movement on a battlefield.'

Lucy poured herself another drop of tea. 'Yes, you could say that, I suppose.'

Professor Rohan brightened up again. 'The Greeks used a phalanx system. The Hoplite warriors, you know.'

'I see...'

Professor Rohan started chuckling now. 'Oh, dear! I'm starting to bore you again!'

'Not at all. Are you absolutely sure everything is alright?'

'Absolutely. As soon as I get to the far side, I shall take a train to Birmingham, and my friend will pick me up there.'

'Do you want to leave us a contact address?'

'I...'

The old man blanched. She realised she had put her foot in it. Lucy smiled gently. 'Never mind. The main thing is that you will be off the island, so to speak, for the next while.'

'On another island...'

Lucy stood up slowly. The ancient eyes gazed up at her with a new sort of pleading now. For a moment, she wanted to say something, but then she let it go. He would be out of harm's way for the next while. That was the main thing.

Professor Rohan saw her to the door. For a moment, as Lucy stood on the doorstep, she thought she saw just a little flicker of fear in the rheumy old eyes. She shook his hand. '*Bon voyage.*'

'I think it's more *au revoir,* Detective. I was a war baby, remember? *We'll meet again* and all of that.'

It was after dark when Lucy got back to the house in the Black Hills. She had a chat with Saoirse on the phone and spoke with Gerhard for longer than she had intended. Then she sat into the sitting room and went over the session notes from the station.

Out in the farmyard, she fed Chantal and cleared out the rubbish in the other stable. She glanced about her in the dark, suddenly uneasy, and felt for the fob in the top pocket of her jacket. She could feel the gun pressing against her chest. Lightning could strike twice, that was the thing.

But she would be prepared this time. *Si vis pacem para bellum... if you want peace, prepare for war.* Or words to that effect.

In the house, she opened a bottle of Rioja and sat down at the baby grand in the corner of the room. Her hands found the first sombre chords of the *Moonlight Sonata* on the Yamaha. She closed her eyes now, feeling the touch of the dark melody. She stopped playing after a few bars and thought: *This is my life now, such as it is. I am a mother and a daughter and a semi-orphan, with a boat, a piano, a horse, a Glock 17 and a dead, much-loved dog. Is it really such a bad life? And do I really want to drag a man back into it and shake the equilibrium?*

She pictured Sullivan hosing down the yard outside and smiled to herself.

Maybe yes.

Maybe no. Can't plan your life away, either...

When she had finished playing, she lay back on the sofa and waded into the illustrated diary of a nineteenth-century French lady traveller in Indochina that she had left aside the day of Philip Carlton's murder. She found herself quietly vocalising the elegant French prose. It had a strangely soporific effect on her. So much so that, after a few minutes, she gave in to fatigue and nodded off.

She woke an hour later, to the ticking of the clock on the mantelpiece. She picked up the book from where it had fallen on the floor and left the bottle of wine back in the kitchen.

When she woke again from her second sleep, a few hours later, like a traveller pulling into a silent railway station at night, she realised what had been bothering her now. It was as clear as clear could be: the late Jeremy Arkens had once had some hold over the old man, over Professor Rohan. But whoever had terminated the Arkenses had now, clearly, decided to warn Professor Rohan about following the Arkenses' path.

The plummy, chummy face of David Carlton was suddenly in her mind again. And she wondered what arcane department of her subconscious brain had thrown up that image.

47

THE PRESS CONFERENCE WAS IN BOYNEBRIDGE AT ELEVEN O'CLOCK that morning. Three TV crews, including Sky, were lined up in the car park, and national and local journos were hanging out of the rafters. The orders from Reese were to stay well away until the all-clear was given. A stray camera shot could do a lot of collateral damage.

Reese's avuncular manner would keep the bloodhounds off the track and let the investigation team focus their energies on putting an end to the killing.

Lucy was east of Lambay Island in the Mermaid, killing time before heading up to Boynebridge, when something welled up inside her. She leaned back on the tiller and thought: *How did I not spot this before?* She answered her own question almost at once: *Because you didn't want to see it, Lucy.*

She pulled up the photo she had copied as David Carlton booze-snoozed in Windgap. The eyes of the young woman said it all. There was something slightly at odds with the world in those glassy eyes. Something more than a little vexed, too. And what Lucy had taken for a smile smeared across the young woman's lips was anything but, she saw now. It was more like resignation.

Bitter resignation.

Her eyes tracked down to the woman's right hand laid over the slightly swollen stomach. It was like one of those ancient, untold stories. Young man and pregnant young woman, unmarried. The man was Jeremy Arkens, alright   David Carlton had confirmed that.

But who was the woman?

Maybe the photo had been the source of the unpleasantness that night in Windgap   not the newspaper coverage of the Carltons. All that venom about Jeremy Arkens from David Carlton. And then that strange atmosphere between himself and Joyce Carlton. It would explain a lot. She stared hard at the photo of Jeremy Arkens and the young woman, willing them to speak, over the years.

By the time she was putting into harbour a short while later, she couldn't hold back anymore. She phoned Anna. 'I need a little legwork.'

'Fire away...'

Lucy paused a moment. 'How far can you go back into someone's personal and medical files, legally?'

'A long way. What do you need to know exactly?'

'Birth, marriage and death records, etc.'

'Well, those are public records anyway, as you know. Am I hunting for anything in particular? Off-piste, like?'

Lucy thought for a moment. 'You are. Here it is...' Her voice dropped to a whisper, even though there was a stretch of water between her and the nearest listener.

'This is just between us, Anna. Clear?'

'Clear.'

She turned the tiller and the wind filled the foresail. She watched an older trawler chug its way out of the harbour and a couple of young men checking the nets on the deck. When she brought the boat in, she phoned her mother. *Keep to the schedule. No point fretting like a brooding hen. If there is something there, Anna will find it.*

Lucy's mother was cooking ratatouille for them. She prepared the vegetables while her mother scoured the ancient Le Creuset.

Her mother glanced sideways at her. *'Ca va?'*

'Oui. Ca va, Maman. I had a few hard days over Saoirse, but it's settled down.'

Her mother laid her hand on her shoulder. 'She will be home soon.'

'I know. I'm going to phone Gerhard this evening and sort things out.'

Her mother gave the pot a wipe with the tea cloth, then looked across at her. 'So you think this Carlton business is finished?'

'Hopefully.'

Her mother suddenly snapped, 'Attention! Don't cut the peppers like that! That is the wrong way, Lucy!'

Sometimes it was good to be chided. Being chided meant someone cared enough about you to get annoyed. Sniping mothers, cantankerous fathers, hectoring daughters. How many children were growing up with no one to care enough about them to get angry?

They ate out in the back garden as the light began to fade from the day. Her mother had just started clearing up when the phone rang.

'Anna here. I think I might have what you're after.'

Lucy stood up and walked to the end of the garden. 'Good. Can't talk, but I'm listening.'

'I've checked and double-checked. Dates and locations and medical references. A bit off-piste, but not exactly against regulations. Made a few phone calls, too, to make sure.'

'Just give me the gold.'

Her mother appeared out in the garden with dessert. Lucy listened carefully to the phone, but said nothing. Her mother looked down at her. *'Que-est ce que c'est?'*

'Rien, Maman.'

But it wasn't nothing. And when she had started into the raspberry coulis, she began to think about how she would play her new hand.

Out in the Carlton crib, in Windgap.

But first she had to meet Sullivan in Phoenix Park with the techies.

PHOENIX PARK WAS DESERTED but for a few walkers strolling in the half-light of the park lamps. She turned into the great courtyard and parked. Sullivan was waiting for her with a young audio technician. 'This is Terry, the man who's done all the work on the ham radio.'

Lucy stretched out her hand. Terry had that pale, IT-bunker look about him. A life squashed between zeros and ones. In the basement, he led them over to a computer screen surrounded by stacks of audio equipment. He tapped on the screen. 'Our suspicion is that the radio was broadcasting to other radios in a closed network. Maybe to only three or four people.'

'Do we know who he was broadcasting to?'

Terry shook his head slowly. 'Unfortunately, no. And furthermore, we believe a shortwave radio app was also being used by at least some of the listeners.'

Lucy glanced over at Sullivan. 'Traceable?'

'Again, no. Not easily. We're going to broadcast on the frequency the radio was using, in the hope that someone will pick up the signal and respond.'

'On a real shortwave radio?' Lucy glanced around at the array of equipment.

'Yes. Then we just might be able to triangulate. Maybe.'

Lucy shook the technician's hand. 'Well, thanks for all this. Every bit helps.' Lucy turned to Sullivan. 'Come on.'

OUT IN THE COURTYARD, Sullivan took her aside. Lucy nodded back at the building they had just left. 'This is a long shot. Anyway... see you back at base.'

She pulled slowly out of Phoenix Park, down the hill and out along Parkgate Street for the M50 south.

For Windgap.

48

THE TOOTHLESS OLD RETRIEVER GREETED HER WARILY AT THE door of Windgap. Joyce Carlton hooshed the creature back inside. Lucy watched the dog weaving its way back up the steps. 'I've brought back those letters, Ms Carlton.'

'Come in.'

Lucy wiped her feet on the mat and followed Joyce Carlton into the sitting room.

'Something to drink, Detective?'

'Just a cup of tea, thanks.'

She scanned the family photographs again when Joyce Carlton was in the kitchen. The paterfamilias standing with the other man – could it be Jeremy Arkens's father? There was a certain resemblance in the face – on some sun-drenched beach. Then a photo of all of the Carlton children together. She started doing the maths again as she stood there. The names and dates. Anna Crowley wouldn't mess up on something like that.

Joyce Carlton came back into the room with a tray and left it down on the coffee table. 'You take it black?'

'Yes, thanks.'

Joyce Carlton regarded her uneasily. 'I believe you had something you wanted to discuss with me? It all sounds very mysterious.'

'Not mysterious. Just life. We can discuss it now in peace.'

Joyce Carlton looked puzzled. 'How do you mean?'

Lucy paused for a moment. She looked straight into the dark eyes of the woman in front of her. 'Now that your son, David, has gone back to France, like I say.'

There was a silence. Joyce Carlton's teaspoon clanged off the side of the cup. She didn't look up at all as she spoke. 'My son, Detective O'Hara?' Joyce Carlton kept her eyes fixed on the willow-pattern cup.

Lucy nodded at the portrait of David Carlton on the piano. This was the presumptive close. Every amateur salesman's trick-up-the-sleeve. *Which would you prefer – the red shoes or the black ones? If you just pass me over your credit card, I'll sort out the rest.*

'David must have been a beautiful baby, Joyce?'

Joyce Carlton's eyes dimmed slightly. This was the moment now. Lucy had to stay strong and not let faintheartedness make her falter. Joyce Carlton lifted her head slowly and looked over at the primary school photograph of David Carlton. 'They took him away from me on the second day, you know.'

'That must have been very hard.'

Joyce Carlton's voice lightened a little. 'Oh, yes. I was still in shock from the birth. The birth was very hard. I cried all day, like a bereaved person. I was bereaved, in a way.'

Lucy kept her voice soft and steady. 'Where was that?'

Joyce Carlton closed her eyes for a moment. 'A private care home, in the south of England, in Berkshire. Quite a few Irish girls from good families had their babies there. All very discreet. Yes, they took him away from me. My David...'

'And then?' Lucy tried to keep a gentle tone in her voice. Gentle but insistent.

'I came back here, to Windgap. Flying was very select in those days, of course. You would have been spotted on the Holyhead boat, you see. The story was, I was in boarding school in England, and home for the holidays.'

Lucy took a sip of coffee. 'I see.'

Joyce Carlton gave a strange little laugh of recollection. 'My mother went away and came back with the baby, with David, a few weeks later, like he was her own. Just the way they did in the poorer families, in Dublin.'

Lucy took a sip of tea. 'Really? And no one knew a thing?'

Joyce Carlton smiled at Lucy. 'It fooled no one, I'm sure now. But people didn't want to know, you see. They didn't want to believe anything else.'

'Believe what?'

'That my mother wasn't David's mother. So I played the big sister. I was only seventeen when Jeremy Arkens got me pregnant, you see.'

Lucy left down her coffee cup slowly. 'And Jeremy Arkens? Maybe there's something you'd like to share about him? Something that might help us all.'

Joyce Carlton suddenly stiffened. The eyes glazed over a little now. 'Let's not speak of the dead. Jeremy was the father of my child, for better or for worse. There will always be some strange connection there.'

'Of course.'

Joyce Carlton started laughing lightly. 'So, now, my David has a wife! A man wife! How the world has changed! He's very good to me, actually. David, I mean. I'm still a sort of big sister to him more than a mother.'

It was like Joyce Carlton was coming out of a trance or a séance. The eyes focused closely on Lucy now, and she reached over to take her hand.

'Murder must be paid for. Philip was the one who

supported me when I was carrying David. Didn't treat me like a leper.'

Lucy squeezed the older woman's hand tightly. 'Our man is out there. But we just haven't identified him just yet.'

Joyce Carlton smiled sweetly. 'So how are you going to get to him, then, if it's no harm to ask? You can hardly look for someone you don't know.'

'We may have to flush him out.'

Lucy looked over at the photographs again. Her eyes fixed on the one of Philip Carlton in his doctoral robes, in Oxford. The supremely confident grin. The edge of irony in the eyes.

Joyce Carlton looked over at Lucy. 'Flush him out? But you don't even know where he is, my dear!'

Lucy took a sip of tea. 'That's why I may need your help. It's a big ask, and it could be... well, dangerous.'

Joyce Carlton's eyes focused fast on Lucy now. The dreamy look had been replaced by a new toughness. 'If it will help to catch Philip's killers, of course.'

SHE MET Sullivan in a sports bar in the main street in Swords. A bunch of young fellows at the counter were gaping up at a mega screen over their heads. Lucy found herself wishing, for the umpteenth time, for one big football game that would get it all over and done with.

The match. A match to end all matches.

Sullivan leaned across the table to her. 'And how do you expect Reese to react to this plan?'

Lucy sat back a minute and thought. 'I expect him to kick up blue bloody murder.'

'So, how will you get him to agree to it, then?'

Lucy glanced over at the young fellows sitting at the bar. They were high-fiving one another now. She realised, once more, that she just didn't get the whole team thing. Couldn't even abide team sports in school. She turned back to Sullivan. 'I'm going to make him an offer he can refuse. But at his peril.'

Sullivan smiled. 'I see. May I know what that is?'

'You may, Detective Sullivan. And you may phone it in to Reese right away.'

Sullivan smiled his conspiratorial smile and glanced at his watch. 'So, I'm the sandbag, then?'

'More like the jam in the sandwich, as Reese would put it.' Lucy turned back to the group at the bar. Someone had scored, and they seemed suddenly downhearted about it. The wrong people, obviously.

Sullivan nodded at the screen. 'That was a Spurs goal.'

Lucy swung round to Sullivan. 'It's all the one bloody goal, Gerry, as far as I can see. I didn't know you followed football?'

'I don't. But I have a pair of ears.' Sullivan clinked glasses and took out his phone. Lucy nodded at him, and Sullivan slipped out of the bar to make the phone call.

49

LUCY HEARD THE BIG GRUMBLY DIESEL ENGINE OF THE TOYOTA pulling into the farmyard. She put the phone to her ear again. 'Saoirse, love, there's someone at the door. I'll phone you back in a bit.'

The car ground to a halt outside. She waited until the knock came, then walked slowly to the door. Reese was dressed like a creamery manager about to make a speech to the local farmers. He smiled at her and gave her a peck on the cheek. 'Just dropping by.'

'I'm sure, George. Come on in. Little tipple?'

Reese smiled. 'Glass of red would take the pain of existence away for a while.'

'Well, thank God for that.'

They sat into the sitting room. Reese was in a different mode now. She had seen this before. That steeliness was in the eyes. Cruise control had been knocked off, and he was pulling rank on her now, even out of uniform.

Reese took a little sip of wine. 'Grand drop of wine that.'

'OK, you can drop the rustic charm. You're not here to discuss the merits of my mother's French wine.'

Reese left down his glass slowly. 'Indeed. Reports have reached my ears that you want to prepare some sort of sting. Would that be the right word for it, I wonder?'

'Sounds a bit chi-chi for south Dublin. Look, we both want the same thing. This killer. Or he will kill again.'

Reese took a sip of wine and sat back in the armchair. 'And just how can you know this? All indications are that he has been stood down.'

'Because I realise that David Carlton, according to his mother, Joyce, anyway...'

Reese looked quizzically at her. 'His mother?'

'His mother, George. And, please, don't tell me you didn't know that years ago.' Lucy angled her head and watched Reese squirm just a little.

She nodded and poured herself another drop of wine. 'And I know, furthermore, that you were hobbled during the first investigation, by our unelected elites who were beholden to Derry Carlton and his middleman, Jeremy Arkens. Right up to the big guy behind this, whoever he is. The one who seems to be called "Der Sammler".'

Reese stared ahead of him and said nothing.

'So why did you hand over the keys to the Kilowatt files all those years ago? What was in it for you?'

Reese stood up slowly and began walking around the room. He crossed to the piano and touched a couple of keys. 'Lovely tone on that piano.'

'George... please. You threw me a lifeline; now I'm throwing you one.'

Reese turned around to face her. 'As you know, Joyce Carlton was made pregnant by Jeremy Arkens when she was eighteen or nineteen.'

'Seventeen, actually. But you're a man. Big bellies are academic for you. Go on.'

Reese took a deep breath and continued, 'They managed to

cover it up, and the boy – David – was segued into the family. But someone had a hold on Jeremy Arkens because of it.'

Lucy bit her lip. 'I'm missing something here. Little colour and texture, please.'

'Well, Derry Carlton, the little blackguard, blackmailed Jeremy Arkens into fencing archaeological artefacts for collectors with deep pockets. And he pulled the same trick years later when Violet Saunders was made pregnant by Philip, her thesis supervisor. When we dug deep into this, we were shot down.'

Lucy raised her voice. 'By whom?'

Reese spun around. 'Oh, come on, for Christ's sake! You couldn't piss crooked in those days, or you'd be done for libel, or some part-time paramilitary would put a bullet in you on a dark night.'

'You still haven't answered my question... the Kilowatt keys?'

Reese took a deep breath. 'I was prevailed upon to pass them over.'

Lucy angled her head. 'Prevailed upon. By whom?'

'By the lead investigators, who had named this man they called "Der Sammler" confidentially. They have all since gone to their graves with that name still hidden.'

'And did the newspapers not get a hold of anything?'

Reese started laughing loudly now. Bitterly. 'The Irish newspapers were terrified to cross church or state. Now they're all full of piss and wind about the past now, when it's safe to go back in the water. They're all great fellows, blowing hard about the bad old days when they weren't to be seen for the dust.'

Lucy coughed to clear her throat. 'And the other names?'

'The only names I was allowed to know were those of Derry Carlton and Jeremy Arkens.'

'So you still don't know who is at the top of the tree?'

Reese shook his head slowly. 'An old, wounded lion. There's big money behind these bullets and bombs.'

Lucy took a sip of wine and swilled it around in her mouth. 'So you started up the cold-case investigation because of what? Revenge? Guilt?'

Reese smiled curiously. 'Even Protestants believe in a little penance every now and then. We just don't believe in going into wooden boxes with a man in a black dress to do it.'

'Go on.' Lucy poured herself another drop.

'Well, myself and Gerry Sullivan were considering reactivating this cold case when Philip Carlton contacted Harcourt Square. Like I told you earlier, we knew nothing about Philip Carlton and his chat room. If we had, we would have warned him.'

There was a beep on her phone. Lucy glanced at the message from Joyce Carlton and then turned back to Reese. 'So you think we should back down a second time?'

Reese sat down at the piano and started playing a couple of notes. 'They tried to kill you and your daughter. If anything goes wrong with this scheme you're planning...'

'Joyce Carlton is in fear for her son's life.'

Reese stopped tapping at the piano suddenly. 'Because you have put the fear of God in her, Lucy!'

'Not true! These guys won't stop. Especially when they realise David Carlton and Professor Rohan may still be carrying old information.'

Reese looked at her thoughtfully now. 'And how do you know David Carlton and Professor Rohan have all this information?'

Lucy sat up straight and stared hard at Reese. 'Because when Carlton was sizzled, a couple of days ago, out in Windgap, the only thing that stopped him telling me even more was the drunken coma he fell into. Now...'

'Yes?'

Lucy raised her finger and pointed it straight at Reese. 'We've come to a dead end with the Kilowatt keys gone.'

Reese started laughing. 'And so I'm to sanction you using Joyce Carlton as a tethered goat?'

Lucy leaned forward into Reese's face. 'Do you think I want to do this? I'll be back in the target zone, too. Myself and Saoirse.'

Reese didn't speak for a moment. Then he started up slowly. 'This is way off-book. Off every book I know.'

'Maybe it's about time you went off-book, then.'

When Reese turned back to the piano again, Lucy reached for her phone and sent the text message. Then she put the phone on speaker through the stereo Bluetooth and waited for the callback. It wasn't long coming.

The loud ringing of the phone through the stereo shattered the silence. Reese looked up at her suspiciously. Lucy hit the receive button on the phone.

Joyce Carlton's calm voice filled the room, in stereo. 'I know you're there, George Reese. So don't try to hide from me.'

Reese turned around slowly and grinned ruefully at Lucy. 'Yes, Joyce. I'm here, with your new best friend.'

Joyce Carlton paused for effect at the other end of the line. 'I'm doing this for David and Philip. Philip, who you and yours let down all those years ago. Are you listening, Superintendent Reese?'

Reese turned round from the piano and took a deep breath. 'And you're really willing to put yourself in harm's way with this mad scheme, Joyce?'

'They're coming for us anyway. Why not meet the scoundrels at the crossroads of our choosing?'

'That's a very colourful turn of phrase for such a dangerous venture. Did Detective O'Hara coach you on that one?'

'Don't patronise me, George Reese! Philip tried to do the right thing, in the end, George. You must do the same now.'

Lucy hung back and just continued staring into space. The space between Reese and Joyce Carlton.

Reese gave that little sigh. 'I need to go and think about this.'

'Then think, George. And come back with the right answer. The only answer.' The phone clicked off in Windgap.

Reese stood up suddenly and looked at Lucy. 'We'll talk later.'

LUCY WATCHED the car pull out of the farmyard, then went back inside and sat at the piano. Her fingers found the opening bars of *Für Elise*. She was back in Berlin once more. Piano lessons with Frau Steinmann in her cramped little pre-World War flat in Charlottenburg. The old, gnarled fingers and the crotchety voice. '*Immer langsam, Kind! Doucement!*'

She continued playing until the phone rang almost an hour later.

Reese's voice was very subdued. 'OK. Deal. Let's just hope we're not signing up for Bateman two.'

When she fell into bed a while later, there was little sleep. Just a string of random thoughts and scenes swirling around inside her head. Paris, London, Berlin, Cairo.

Bateman...

Like a faint radio signal from an unknown galaxy that just wouldn't fade away.

50

THE INCIDENT ROOM IN BOYNEBRIDGE SOUNDED LIKE A CROWDED pub, from the far side of the glass door. Reese was drawing big circles on the whiteboard and various voices were calling out details to him. Beside the whiteboard, Lucy could see a couple of e-fits of the Lithuanian and his driver.

Reese turned to her. 'You can take over now.'

Lucy stood in the centre of the floor. 'Right. On the Lithuanian front... Anna, please.'

Anna Crowley stood up. 'We have a patchy video, and a good voice recording, but no prints or DNA. And the Brits are convinced he's the guy they pulled over on a cold stop a couple of years ago.'

'Background?' Reese's voice was clear as a bell.

'If it's him, he was born in Kaunas, Lithuania, and is in his early fifties. Russian army, regular then Spetznaz specialist. Sniping and counter-insurgency, that sort of thing. Two terms in Chechnya. In the mid-nineties, after the second Chechnya campaign, he cut loose and moved to Western Europe. General enforcer and occasional hit man. Sellable, transferable skills, you might say.'

Reese grimaced. 'It's still general enough. It could apply to a lot of people.'

Anna looked up from her notes. 'The Spanish say he once offered to rape and garrotte a detective's wife, in a choice of three languages, Spanish, Russian or Lithuanian. They suspect he provides cover and transport for East European high rollers coming and going from Spain. A go-fer with a gun.'

Lucy pointed at the whiteboard, at one of the circles Reese had drawn. 'The driver or the assistant, we think, may be Polish.'

Dennis stood up. 'Late twenties. We have a good shot of him from forecourt CCTV on the morning of Violet Saunders's murder.'

Reese nodded. 'Good. So, he may be local or localish, and we might strike lucky there. Push on with that.'

Lucy pointed to another one of the circles Reese had drawn on the whiteboard. 'The Carltons, Gerry.'

Sullivan stood up. 'David Carlton's clean enough. Sharp businessman who was dragged unwittingly into his brother's business years before.'

Lucy looked at Sullivan. 'Could he be a target?'

Sullivan demurred. 'Hard to say. We don't know who's making the snowballs here.'

Lucy turned back to the group. 'OK, Anna, collate all the online stuff. Dennis, slip back down to the dig and do one last recce of the portacabin. Fresh eyes might see something we've missed. Gerry, get back onto the East European end again and get that fuzzy image of the possibly Polish driver out there. Everyone else, uniformed gardai and detectives, I'll be tasking you further after lunch. And thank you again for all your help, individually and collectively.'

Lucy crossed over to Reese and sat on the side of the desk. 'We're ready to roll on all fronts. We're going to try the short-wave radio lure first.'

'Our gent is hardly likely to fall for Nigerian prince scams. Still...' Reese didn't finish the sentence.

'I know. But we're out to catch these guys and this is the first step. It's not just for the optics.' Lucy picked up the phone and dialled Phoenix Park.

Reese raised his voice. 'But how will you know this "Sammler" character has received the message on the radio, if he doesn't reply?'

Lucy paused a moment. 'We won't. And that's why we have to use this online forum to double down on the message. We'll definitely know he's been on there.'

Lucy's phone rang. The techie from the Phoenix Park was on the line. 'We're good to go, Detective O'Hara. The radio message is on a loop, ready to start playing.' She knocked off the phone and crossed over to Sullivan, who was talking with Brosnahan by the whiteboard. She stood in front of them and smiled gently.

'Gentlemen, start your engines...'

51

THE COLLECTOR HAD BEEN UP SINCE SIX IN THE MORNING, AND IT
was now just after eight. Something brought him back down to
the bunker, though. Maybe some sudden need to touch the
crosses, the ancient weaponry, the bog oak carvings.

The Genesis of St Fergal...

He flicked on the switch, and the huge chamber was
flooded with light. He crossed over to the glass case with the
Latin manuscript. He had already read the daily portion. He
did a little tour of the bunker then. The sort of thing he
normally did once a month or so, tidying, rearranging, dusting.
Then he went into the room with the two golden torcs, passing
on to the room with the collection of medieval daggers and
swords, which had once served as a food store with Cold War
rations in great big tins.

He considered his lifetime's work for a moment. A lifetime
of caring for the past. The past that the modern world outside
just couldn't get rid of fast enough.

He had respect for the generations. That was the thing.

For their toil. For the sanctity of their ways.

For this reason, he had toiled so hard himself, slowly spiriting away the spoils he saw before him now. And if they tried to take it from him? If they tried to break up the collection and scatter it around the world, through the grubby hands of dealers like the late Mr Jeremy Arkens?

He would take it all with him in a final fire and a final flood. Fire and water.

Very biblical. Sodom and Gomorrah, followed by the Deluge.

HE CROSSED into the room with the shortwave radio, switched it on and sat into the chair.

There would be no more contact with Mr Arkens now. And the Lithuanian was back where he had come from, his work done. On a whim, he put on the headphones and turned the dial idly. He was sitting there, just meditating on the events of the past weeks, when, out of the blue, he heard a voice.

For one shocking moment, he thought he was listening to the voice of the dead man. But this was a different voice. A strong, forthright voice. Not the carping, querulous tone of the late Jeremy Arkens. For an instant he was going to reply to the call. A sort of reflex action.

'This is BX 2351 calling. Come in. I have a message for *Der Sammler*, in connection with the late Professor Philip Carlton, sent by Ms Joyce Carlton. It contains material written by Professor Carlton himself. This is BX 2351 calling. Come in... I have...'

He closed his eyes and listened carefully. A come-on – that's what it was. Somehow or other, they had managed to retrieve Arkens's old radio and decode the frequency he used. The Lithuanian mustn't have destroyed the radio completely. He smiled to himself. Did they think he was a complete idiot?

He took off the headphones slowly and switched off the

radio, watching the light fade in the diodes. Then he stood up slowly and made his way to the door.

Back on the ground floor, he opened the patio doors and knelt down to open the innocuous little box set into the wall at his feet. The green button and the big red button under the Perspex safety cover. He pressed the green button and heard, far below his feet, the soft moaning of the system running through its paces. Then he knocked off the switch and closed the cover over the buttons.

They would not take him.

Or the collection.

Ars longa, vita brevis.

He secretly wondered if, when the time came, he would actually be able to do it. To press the red button and consign the collection to eternity. He stood up and looked around him. His eyes fell on the little copse to his right.

That was the way they would probably come, if they came.

But it would all be too late. He smiled to himself softly and went indoors. Then he turned on the big Stanley oven and started chopping up vegetables for the goulash he had been promising himself all week.

He left down the knife a short while later and glanced at the clock. It was just gone 9 a.m. There was no point in delaying any further. He had made up his mind now. He couldn't take the chance that the radio message was a bluff. Perhaps Carlton really had left letters or notes behind detailing everything.

No, it was time to act now. To nip the nuisance in the bud: Joyce Carlton.

He took out the notebook from the kitchen drawer and typed in the Spanish phone number for the dead drop. Then he wrote the brief message and pressed 'send'. A moment later, a message pinged back: *received*.

Then he picked up the knife and continued chopping the carrots.

52

THE BAR IN ALICANTE WAS CROWDED AND IT WAS JUST MIDDAY. The remnants of the club above the bar were finishing off the night in high style.

The *thump, thump, thump* of the dumb disco music was really getting on Lukas Petraskas's nerves now. It was his first job back on the beat. He glanced over at the baby Russian oligarch with the Syrian woman. He had been partying hard all night, right into the morning, and looked ready to drop. A movement at his shoulder startled him. He turned and saw a young Spanish man staring at him. '*Para usted.*'

The young man slipped him a piece of paper. Lucas opened it in the palm of his hand and glanced at the message in Russian.

You must return to Dublin. Contact me immediately.

Shit! He thought the whole thing had been put to bed. Now he had to climb back into the ring again. All because of the drug debt he had reneged on the year before after his private coke deal fell through. But it was the same choice as a month ago: get it over and done with or face a bullet in the neck himself.

He glanced over at the Russian, who was starting to slump over the table now. Then he pulled up the shortwave radio app on his phone and pressed it. That snooty old voice came over the phone again.

'Good evening, sir. I'm sorry that you have to be called back.'

Lukas glanced to either side of him to make sure he wasn't being overheard. 'Just tell me what is job?'

'Just get back immediately. Today. When you are back, I will send you exact information. I am sending you a link.'

He knocked off the phone and looked across the bar.

The Russian had finally slumped over the table. Good. He pulled up the image of the beautiful house in South Dublin on Google Maps from the link and read the name on the pillar: Windgap. *Right.* He pulled up a travel app then and grabbed the last seat on an afternoon flight out of Alicante. He downloaded the boarding pass and slipped the phone back into his pocket.

Then he pointed towards the comatose Russian and the Syrian whore who was polishing off the remnants of a bottle of champagne. The Russian handler standing nearby nodded an OK at him.

LUKAS PETRASKAS REACHED the urbanisation outside Alicante ten minutes later. The woman in the bed woke and spoke to him sleepily in Russian. 'Where are you going?'

'I have to travel again. Couple of days and I'll be back.'

He opened the wardrobe, took out a couple of fresh shirts and threw them in his backpack.

'Will that job ever be over?' The woman sounded annoyed now. She leaned on her elbow and reached over for the packet of cigarettes. She passed one to Lukas, and they lit up. He sat on the side of the bed and stroked her hair gently.

'When this is done, this is done. I won't owe any more money. I'm free.'

'You said that two months ago, Lukas.'

'This is it. I know.' He was getting a little vexed now. It wasn't as if he didn't provide all that was needed. And more. Lukas Petraskas stood up slowly and did a final check of his passports and papers. He heard the car pull up outside.

The woman dragged deeply on the cigarette. 'Why are you going back there this time?'

'Better you don't know. Now, go back to sleep. See you in a few days.' He leaned over and kissed the woman in the bed; then he made his way downstairs.

The taxi dropped him at Alicante airport a short while later, and he boarded the Belfast flight under his new alias: Carlos Santos, with his slightly weathered Spanish EU passport.

53

A SUDDEN SUMMER SQUALL HIT THE M50 AS LUCY AND SULLIVAN drove south. Sheets of warm summer rain swept across the motorway, and they could hardly see in front of them as they cruised along. It was after ten by the time they reached Garda headquarters in the Phoenix Park headquarters. In the basement in the back of the complex, Terry, the IT technician, brought them into a room full of computers and assorted monitoring equipment.

Lucy sat down in front of the bank of computers. 'So we don't really know if our man got the message on the shortwave radio?'

The techie smiled. 'No. But we don't know he didn't either.'

Lucy nodded. 'OK. Maybe he did and maybe he didn't. If he did, he's already in the loop. If he didn't, the forum should stir it up and pull him in. Or reinforce the shortwave broadcast.'

'Exactly. He won't be able to ignore the forum. I'm sure of it.'

Lucy pointed at the screen. 'So, have you access to this online forum now?'

'I've managed to bypass the triple lock security.'

Lucy smiled. 'OK, spare me the cyber talk. We're just simple down-home folk.'

The computer screen flickered into life. A graphic displaying a virtual round table and chairs appeared. The techie tapped the screen. 'As each one logs in, the chairs light up. It's sort of cute.'

Lucy smiled. 'Real cute, alright. But no one yet?'

The techie smiled politely. 'Too early. Tonight, Friday night, is forum night. They don't do beer and curries like the rest of the world.'

Lucy nodded at the screen. 'So what do they chat about?'

'Academic rows. Funding. A little personal stuff, too.'

Lucy glanced around at Sullivan. 'So, twenty-five in all?'

'Not all of them log on to each session. But we know who's who. Except for our special guest, of course.'

'Der Sammler?'

'I'm sorry, Detective O'Hara?' The techie's face was puzzled.

Lucy smiled. 'It's just a German handle we think he uses.'

'Oh, right. Well, we're hoping he'll take the bait when Ms Carlton does her bit.'

'So are we. Right. Thank you.' Lucy turned back to Sullivan. 'I'm off to Windgap now. Be ready to get in position with Peter and the others by three.'

Sullivan nodded and sat down in front of the screen with the techie. 'Just run through how this should work again.'

JOYCE CARLTON WAS SITTING at the wrought-iron table, sipping tea. Lucy sat down and patted the retriever on the head. 'You just carry on doing whatever you would normally do. Bar leaving the house, that is, Ms Carlton.'

Joyce Carlton smiled politely. 'Of course. Do you think we

might start calling one another by our first names? Seeing as we are facing the same lunatics together.'

Lucy returned the serve softly. 'Alright then, Joyce. Fine by me.'

Joyce Carlton leaned forward. 'And my David? Are you sure he's alright?'

'He's under close protection outside Marseille with his partner.'

Joyce Carlton burst out laughing. 'His bloody partner? I don't give a tinker's curse for that unctuous little frog! I just want to make sure my son is safe.'

Lucy smiled and stood up. 'He is. Look, I should go inside, out of sight.'

Joyce Carlton angled her head. 'Aren't you going to eat or drink something?'

'Later. We need to go through the system when we're inside. The play hasn't started just yet.'

Joyce Carlton stood up. 'We're in the Green Room, you might say.'

Lucy smiled. 'Waiting for our cue.' Lucy started to make her way indoors, followed by Joyce Carlton.

'So who gives us our cue, Detective?'

'The bad guys. That's usually system.'

It was dark when Lucy helped Joyce Carlton to log onto the forum in Philip Carlton's study. The coloured graphic of the conference table came up, and the little seats were illuminated on the screen. Now there were fifteen.

Lucy watched the other woman move the mouse slowly and rested her hand on her shoulder. 'That's it. You're going in under Philip's old ID. See – his chair has lit up.'

They watched the chat pass back and forth for a while. It

was mostly about the Greek marbles in London and some new dig in Turkey that had just received major new funding.

Half an hour passed.

Half an hour later, Lucy touched Joyce Carlton's arm gently. 'Right. Let's start. I'll dictate it to you, nice and slowly, and you type it in.'

Joyce Carlton looked at her. 'Will whoever is reading know it's me?'

'We want them to. Especially our anonymous guest. That's the whole point.'

Lucy checked the silent panic button under her blouse again. 'OK. Here goes. Don't worry about typos. It will make it seem more natural. Now, click the red button.'

'Done. Bit like a game, isn't it?'

'Right. Start typing exactly what I call out to you. *I am writing as the closest relative of the late Philip Carlton, whose cruel death has traumatised all who knew him. I am a stranger to the forum, but I feel it is time to bring up some matters that my late brother was trying to raise before his untimely death. The story, insofar as he has told me, goes back to the 1970s and the 1980s...*'

Ten minutes later, Joyce Carlton took her fingers off the keyboard. There was a muted reaction from the other fifteen people logged onto the forum. A couple of 'sorrys' and a 'how tragic.' Lucy's phone rang.

It was the IT man in Phoenix Park. 'Nothing happening there yet. That chair is still empty on the screen. No! Wait!'

A little chair on the right-hand side of the screen lit up. The techie's voice suddenly grew excited at the other end of the line. 'That's him! That's the one hiding behind all the nodes.'

Lucy tapped Joyce Carlton's wrist gently. 'Now, just a few more sentences. Start. *Does no one want to listen to what I have to say? Is it because the person behind this evil will be found out? I hope so, because I have much to tell and old documents of my late broth-*

er's to back it up with. *I am too old to be afraid. Tomorrow night, I will share one of these important documents with the forum...*'

Lucy laid her hand on Joyce Carlton's shoulder. 'Right. That's enough. Log off.'

Lucy and Joyce Carlton looked at one another. Their eyes said the same thing: *the game has started.*

54

A NOISE INVEIGLED ITS WAY INTO LUCY'S SHALLOW SLEEP IN THE
big double bed in the Carlton house at Windgap. She opened
her eyes and listened carefully. There it was again: a noise like
the scraping of metal on the ground, below the window, out in
the yard. Then the sound of footsteps under the window, and
the old retriever barking. Someone was muttering something to
himself. 'Come on, you bastard!'

She drew the gun out from under the pillow in one fluid
movement and peeped through the heavy satin curtains. A
man was lying on the ground with something metal in his
hand. The retriever was sitting beside him, gnawing on a bone.

For a moment she didn't get it.

Then she smiled shamefacedly: man clearing drain. *Chill,
Lucy.*

Joyce Carlton called to her softly from the landing.
'Breakfast?'

She showered and made her way downstairs to the kitchen.
She whispered to Joyce Carlton, 'I'll stay in the study until that
workman's gone. You never know.'

In Philip Carlton's old study, she went through the bookshelves again. This wasn't Professor Rohan's classical world of Greece and Rome. Or her own library of language and linguistic books either. This was practical history: little digs and great excavations. Drawings of trenches and walls and finds. Dirty hands, muddy feet, sunburnt faces, from Anatolia, through Egypt, to the Americas and back again by way of China.

She took down an ancient tome on Egypt and Palestine, on Flinders Petrie's expeditions. There were places in Egypt there she had visited with her father and mother. Images of *fellahin* toiling in the midday sun, to dig up the bones of their long-dead ancestors.

Joyce Carlton appeared in with a tray and set it down on the desk. 'Philip would be tickled to know that the one who's hunting his killer is breakfasting in his study.'

Lucy smiled politely. 'I'm sure he would.'

Joyce Carlton looked around the walls. 'Was it all worth it?'

'All what, Joyce?'

Joyce Carlton waved her hand at the shelves groaning under the weight of books. 'All the study. Excavations. Ruminations. Call it what you like.'

Lucy frowned. 'It's our inheritance. Someone has to dig it up.'

Joyce Carlton took the lid off the teapot and gave it a quick stir. 'Hmm. Anyway, I'll leave you to it. I'll call you when the drain man has gone. These days, the only digging I'm interested in is done by the drain man and the gardeners.'

LUCY SPENT the afternoon between the study and the kitchen, keeping well away from the living room in case anyone happened to spot her through the window.

She was having coffee in the kitchen when her phone rang.

It was Sullivan. 'Myself and Peter are in the cabin at the

bottom of the neighbours' garden, on your right. The old couple have been moved out and the ones on the other side as well. The ERU guys are in position on the far side of the house. We have a telecom van parked near the front of the house with a couple more people in it to stop anyone, and a drone slightly off-site. There's a dummy traffic stop out on the main road as first line.'

'No hint of anything yet?'

Sullivan lowered his voice. 'No. But it'll soon be dark. That's when things might get iffy. And you two?'

'All in order.'

They drew the curtains before dusk. Lucy sat with Joyce Carlton in the living room. The phone glowed silently. The Phoenix Park IT man. 'Just to let you know, we've got a general fix on that shortwave radio now.'

Lucy perked up. 'Where?'

'West Cork. He contacted someone through the app system. We're using automated frequency scanners that work super fast, twenty-four seven. They bit on his frequency briefly. Very short burst.'

'West Cork? How close are you?' Lucy pulled up Google Maps on her phone.

'Fifty-square-mile radius, southwest of Cork city. We're hoping to narrow the location down further. But the activity suggests something has started.'

'Right.' She could feel a chill starting up now, somewhere south of her solar plexus. That old feeling of imminent threat. She ran through her protocols again, mentally, then turned back to the book she was reading for brief relief.

ADAM BIELSKI HADN'T SERVED in the Polish or Russian armies or sweated under sniper fire on the streets of Chechnya like Lukas Petraskas.

He was much too young for that.

But he had been well trained in firearms as a teenager, back in Bydgoszcz, in the North of Poland, by men whose fathers had fought Germans and Soviets in the '40s. The equipment he was carrying under his jacket along Morehampton Road, in Dublin 4, was par for the intervention the Lithuanian had ordered: an ancient Soviet Makarov pistol that had come in to Dublin port, in a job lot from a London Albanian coke crew.

He swept the sightlines carefully as he went along, presenting nothing more to the casual eye than a young man heading out on the prowl for the night. He passed the Embassy of Georgia, then crossed the road and turned up into Wellington Place. The street was practically empty, with only the odd car on the streets. He ran his hand over his right chest in a reflex action and felt the heavy metal of the Makarov under his jacket.

Then his eyes tracked towards the laneway with the mews B and B.

JENNY SAUNDERS HAD MADE up her mind now: she would fly back to London the following week. It was time to face the music: the first night back in the London flat without her mother. An old school friend would spend the first couple of weeks with her.

'You only really grow up when your mother dies...' Who said that, now? She knew she had read it somewhere, in some magazine or other. She would have to learn to live without her mother behind her, watching her every step. It would be a lesson, she suspected, that would take her the rest of her life. Or until she had her own child to fret and fuss over.

Someone new to circle around.

She dreaded the thought that one morning she might wake up and not think of her murdered mother first thing. And she felt strangely guilty in advance. A sort of down payment on righteous depression.

It made her feel better, for some reason.

The mirror in the B and B looked kindly on her. She appeared a lot better than she had in months. Something seemed to have softened in her, too. Strange, that. She would have expected the opposite.

She touched up her mascara lightly and decided: a couple of drinks in that pub off Grafton Street, to break up the evening. You couldn't hide forever from the world. And anyway, hadn't those bastards already got what they wanted – her mother and her father?

There was an odd sound to her right, like someone snapping a dry twig in half. At first she thought it might be a small bird tapping at the window. She turned her head towards the window, smiling, half-expecting to see a sparrow or a starling tip-tapping at the glass.

Then she spotted the tell-tale hole and spiderweb cracks in the glass.

'Jesus Christ!'

She dove onto the bed as two more bullets came pinging through the glass. Then she rolled onto the floor, screaming, and pressed the speed dial on her phone. She lay there, shaking, until the men in the black ballistics jackets came smashing through the door five minutes later.

Within half an hour, she was in the army barracks in Rathmines, with an army medic for company and two army Rangers at the door.

REESE'S VOICE was sombre on the phone. Lucy bit her lip and listened silently. If she tried to butt in at the wrong time, she would blow it all. 'That bastard could have killed her, Lucy. Do you realise that?'

'He didn't want to kill her. It's a distraction.'

Reese's voice cranked up a gear or two. 'Three bullets through a window is a distraction? Are we inhabiting the same planet?'

Lucy spoke calmly. But not with one of those creepy, Californian-style counselling voices Reese so detested. No feelings – just facts. Verb, subject, object. 'She's up on the second floor of the B and B. It's almost impossible to hit anyone with a pistol at that angle.'

Reese wasn't relenting. 'Oh, well, that's really comforting, that is. The words *almost impossible* and guns don't sit well together, you know. He hit the f'ing window three times.'

Lucy took a deep breath. 'And missed her three times. This is to throw us off and make us drop our guard on Joyce Carlton.'

Reese held fire for a moment. 'And what if this character uses a rifle, like with Jeremy Arkens and his wife?'

'There's no clear line of sight in Windgap. Brosnahan and Sullivan and the ERU guys would spot someone lining up a target a mile away. And the drone. It'll be close-up or nothing.'

Reese's laugh was cold and hard. 'So you and Joyce Carlton get shot at close quarters instead of through a telescopic sight.'

Lucy paused. 'I would put even money that our Lithuanian didn't do the shooting. Maybe he's already heading for Windgap. We can't pull out now.'

Reese fell silent for a moment. She pictured him in the basement in Phoenix Park, standing beside the little IT guy, who would know well enough to keep his mouth shut. She heard Reese cough that nervous cough. Then his footsteps retreating to some little Garden of Gethsemane in a corner of the room, to commune with himself.

It was like something clicked with Reese, then.

Or maybe he just wanted it all over and done with. There was no way of telling. But Reese's voice was calmer now when he came back on the phone. 'I'm just afraid for you, Lucy. That's all.'

Lucy swallowed hard. 'And I appreciate that. But Sullivan and Peter Brosnahan have my back, and there's an ERU unit and eyes in the sky. It will all work out.'

'Let's hope so.' The line went dead.

Lucy reached inside her jacket for the pistol and the silent alarm under her blouse, and smiled at Joyce Carlton, who had been listening silently all the time.

It would be a long night.

55

LUKAS PETRASKAS COULDN'T HELP ADMIRING THE YOUNG POLE now, for once. How he knew his way around the arcane world of zeros and ones. A world alien to the Lithuanian. Adam Bielski had hacked into Philip Carlton's cloud data in short order and found the Windgap maintenance schedules.

It was all straightforward enough. If you knew what to do.

Boiler maintenance was every six months, and gutter maintenance was annual. The drain man came every month because of the poor condition of the neglected pipes.

But Bridgewood gardeners called every week. That was the important thing.

Lukas Petraskas and Adam Bielski knew this as they waited in the little laneway behind Tibradden late on the Friday evening. All they knew was that that there was no need to permanently silence the old widower Charlie Bridgeman and his son, Ivan, who ran the Bridgewood company together.

Lukas slipped in through the back garden while Adam went to the front door. When Ivan Bridgeman answered the door, Lukas raced upstairs to the old man's bedroom and put the Makarov to his right temple. 'No move! No move!'

The rest was easy.

Ivan Bridgeman handed over the keys and didn't protest as the duct tape was put over his father's mouth. As long as his father got his heart tablets, he felt somehow that all would be well. It didn't seem like a terrorist operation, or personal or even religious. And, anyway, his own long-term, live-out girlfriend in Dun Laoghaire would raise the alarm when he didn't ring her by the following afternoon. And Ivan Bridgeman knew hard men when he saw them. Staying above ground seemed as good a deal as any, in the circumstances obtaining, as old Mr Bridgeman liked to say.

They hadn't put any tape over Ivan Bridgeman's mouth because he might have to talk, if and when a certain phone call came in. And Ivan Bridgeman knew what to say and how to say it.

Or else the little device sitting on the table between them would be activated.

Half an hour later, they drove down towards the coast for Windgap and the home of Joyce Carlton.

56

JENNY SAUNDERS SAT SNIFFLING ON THE GAUDY PURPLE SETTEE IN the basement of Cathal Brugha army barracks in Rathmines. The young army medic with the cute little lisp finished his checklist and smiled. 'You have no physical injuries, Ms Saunders, and everything is normal.'

'I can still hear those bullets...' Jenny Saunders wiped the tears from her eyes with her late mother's embroidered handkerchief.

The medic stood up and looked over at Reese. 'Those sedatives will kick in, in about half an hour.'

'Jenny...' Reese knelt down beside Jenny Saunders and took her arm. 'It's going to be alright. It will all work out.'

The big baby eyes looked up at him. 'How do you know?'

'Trust me... I know. And no one can get to you now.'

Reese spoke with the two Rangers on duty outside the door for a moment. Then, out of earshot, he rang Lucy in Windgap. 'Everything OK out there?'

'Fine. No stir so far. Everyone's in place.'

'I still don't like this, Lucy.'

'I know. Look, I've got to go. Perimeter check.' Best to get Reese off the blower before he started.

SHE STARTED the security sweep at the top of the house. First, the big room in the attic. The maid's room. Cold in winter, warm in summer.

There were still traces of lives lived there in Carlton senior's time. A framed religious tract on the wall and a couple of vanity mirrors. She set about the bedrooms on the third floor and then the bedrooms on the second floor. She had chosen the bedroom adjoining Joyce Carlton's, with the interconnecting door, to sleep in, for extra security. Finally, she scouted out the first floor, the ground floor and the cellar with the wine racks and the long-forgotten trunks.

They ate lasagne and a green salad together in the study. Joyce Carlton sat in the big Queen Anne chair with her tray on the ottoman while Lucy ate over at the desk, surrounded by the detritus of Philip Carlton's academic career.

She looked across at Lucy. 'You know what I told you about Derry?'

Lucy frowned. 'Well, yes. That Derry was behind Arkens's involvement in all the crooked deals.'

Joyce Carlton bit her lip. She was clearly finding it hard to say what she had to say. 'Well, what I have to say now is closer to today. To Philip's time.'

Lucy tried not to sound too eager. 'Go on...'

Joyce Carlton poured herself a cup of coffee. 'When Jenny Saunders was born, Philip paid support to Violet, in London. This went on for a few years.'

'This we know.'

Joyce Carlton took a sip of coffee and looked into the middle distance. 'He saw the child a couple of times in London, on the QT. But it could have brought scandal to the family and ruined Philip's career – getting a postgrad pregnant. Then he stopped paying maintenance a few years later.'

Lucy angled her head. 'So, what made him stop paying, then?'

Joyce Carlton gave a wicked little chuckle. 'Our very own Iago, Derry. He played the same game on Philip that he had played on Jeremy Arkens, over me.'

'Blackmailed him, you mean?'

Joyce Carlton nodded. 'Even better. Blackmail balanced with a bribe, like a shoe salesman. He told Philip that if he helped him secure this manuscript – some sort of early biblical text in Latin – he would give Philip enough money to buy off Violet Saunders.'

'How? What way?'

'By buying an apartment in London and giving her security. It had certain advantages for both Philip and Violet, of course.'

'So?'

Joyce Carlton's eyes focused on Lucy. 'He was weak, Philip. And a little selfish, let's face it. So he accepted.'

'And this is what is behind all this murder and mayhem?' Lucy's own voice had reached a pitch now.

Joyce Carlton grimaced. 'Yes. That was what kept Philip awake at night, in his old age. It killed him. Violet Saunders knew all the details. That's why she's dead too.'

Lucy froze. 'And Jenny? How much do you think she knows?'

Joyce Carlton shrugged her shoulders uncertainly. 'Who is to say?'

Lucy's walkie-talkie pinged. She picked it up and pressed receive.

An officer's voice came on the line. 'This is the traffic stop on the main road, Detective O'Hara. We have two men here from Bridgewood Gardens. They say they have an appointment to clear the back garden. They have ID, and we've checked them out with their office. What do you want us to do? Over.'

Lucy swung around. 'Were you expecting anyone?'

'The gardening company. I completely forgot to tell you! Bridgewood send a couple of chaps every week to do bits and pieces.'

Lucy turned back to the walkie-talkie. 'Go ahead. Let them in. Everything should appear normal if anyone is watching further back. Over.'

'Clear. They're going to drive in now.'

Lucy turned back to Joyce Carlton. 'I'll keep an eye on things from upstairs.'

Joyce Carlton made her way out of the room. Lucy slipped upstairs to one of the back bedrooms and watched the two men as they got out of the van at the back of the house. The younger of the two was talking to Joyce Carlton. She could hear the voices clearly from above. The younger man spoke first. She could hear the Dublin tone under his East European accent. 'Which rubbish you want first, Mrs Carlton?'

'Over near the pond. I'll show you.' Joyce Carlton pointed over to a corner of the garden.

The older man nodded at her. 'I'm finkin' is good idea, Mrs Carlton.'

Joyce Carlton started walking into the garden followed by the two men.

57

L̲ukas P̲etraskas and A̲dam B̲ielski made their way slowly
up the garden, past the fish pond with the plump Chinese carp.
Lukas glanced around him. This would be easy. She wouldn't
be expecting it. The high walls around the huge garden
screened them from view. The trellis would give them cover,
too. When the old lady came back out with the tea, that would
be the time to strike.

'Where this pergola thing?' Lukas looked at Adam.

'Back there. Near metal table.'

Lukas smiled. 'So, fix pergola thing and I sit table and have
cigarette. When she come with tea, I do it and we go. OK?'

He watched his companion head off with the toolbox for
the big wooden arch affair that had been damaged by the storm
the week before. Then he headed back towards the house and
took a seat at the metal table and lit up. The old woman had
said she would give them tea before starting. Good timing, old
lady. Get her into the garden, do it and then go. No hanging
about and increasing the odds.

He drew hard on his cigarette and watched the smoke curl

up into the air. Then he asked himself the same question he'd asked the night of Philip Carlton's death: why can't people keep just their mouths shut? But his question was interrupted by the voice of the old lady from the back door.

'Tea's coming. Take a seat, gentlemen.'

Shame, all the same. He pulled up a chair for the Pole and passed him a cigarette as the old lady reached them with the tray. *Wait until she leaves it down and turns to go.*

Then do it. Take her out from behind and she'll fall quietly on the grass. He had seen her put the gate zapper in her jacket pocket. So he'd grab it, open the gate and get out.

Lukas stood up to help the old lady with the tray. She smiled sweetly at him. 'There are still some gentlemen left in the world, thank God!'

There was a clatter of china as Lukas left the tray down on the table. The old lady started rabbiting on about the weather. He tugged at his collar and saw the Pole take the signal. Then he unzipped his jacket as the old lady poured the tea. The pistol with the silencer was sitting snugly over his heart.

Three minutes would do it. He would just finish pouring the tea. And...

And then something caught his eye on the back wall of the house.

Lukas Petraskas froze then set down the teapot on the iron table.

His eyes narrowed. It was hard to be sure, from the distance. He squinted hard, then nodded at Adam Bielski and threw his eyes in the direction of the wall.

Adam Bielski looked back towards the house. At the ivy-smothered back wall and the big old windows. His eyes moved slowly up the wall, then stopped suddenly. He focused hard for a moment, with the old lady blabbering away in his ear.

Then Adam Bielski turned to Lukas Petraskas and tapped

his right eyelid with his forefinger: camera. CCTV camera. Lukas Petraskas slowly zipped up his jacket again and tugged at his ear to signal 'cancel' to his companion. And 'get out in 5.'

Then he smiled up at the old lady and complimented her on her strong tea.

58

LUCY'S EYES TRACKED THE TWO WORKERS AS THEY SETTLED IN AT the metal table. It all seemed aboveboard. But she wouldn't be happy until they had left the premises. She watched the older one stand up and pour the tea. The two of them were smoking and chatting with Joyce Carlton as though they didn't have a care in the world.

Easy seeing they weren't working for a man.

She noticed the older one look back at the house then. What was he looking at? The dog? There was no one else in the house. What could it be?

It suddenly didn't seem right. And now the younger man was looking in the same direction. What were they looking at?

Then she saw the old dog wander up the steps into the garden, wagging its tail, and saunter over to them.

It was nothing. Still, better to be sure.

She called Sullivan for an update and continued looking out the window, through the net curtains. Brosnahan was out in the utility van and the ERU men were changing shift in the neighbours' house. The IT techie in the Park hadn't got any further with locating the signal in West Cork.

Lucy spoke softly into the walkie-talkie to Sullivan. 'By the way, there are two guys from Bridgewood Gardens clearing up rubbish in the back. They were checked out at the front.'

Sullivan didn't seem too put out. 'They're on the schedule David Carlton gave us, along with the drain guy who came earlier. I have eyes on them. They were already stopped at the traffic stop and checked out.'

Lucy kept her eye on the two men in the garden and pulled up the number of Bridgewood Gardens on the phone.

A rough-and-ready old Dublin accent answered the phone. 'Bridgewood Gardens. Ivan speaking.'

'Hello, Mr Bridgeman. Detective O'Hara here, from Boyne-bridge Garda station. Have you just had a call to check the ID of two workers here, at Windgap, in Foxrock?'

The voice at the other end sounded peeved. 'That's right. From your people, just a few minutes ago it was.'

'Could you describe them for me, please.' Lucy's eyes followed the younger one as he filled the wheelbarrow again. She knew the sort well. Polish worker who just went and did the job, took the money and left. Frugal Lidl shopper whose children always did their homework, went to bed on time and ate lots of fruit, vegetables and fish. Summer holidays back home and blonde, bilingual children.

'Aleksander is the younger guy. He's a bit lippy but a good worker. Jozef is the older guy. He doesn't speak much. Good worker too, though.'

'Any identifying marks?'

'Well... Aleksander has tight cropped hair. And Jozef has a scar on his right arm. If you like, you can call into the office, Detective.'

Lucy looked away from the garden. 'No. That won't be necessary. OK. Thanks for your help.'

'Is there anything else you need, Detective?'

'Sorry?' Lucy frowned. Her antennae were up now. It was

the sort of thing someone with a guilty conscience might say. Like a drunk being over-chummy at a roadblock. Maybe good old Ivan Bridgeman had had a run-in with the law before. Not important now, though. Could check it out later.

'No. That's fine. Thank you, Mr Bridgeman.' She knocked off the phone and slipped back into one of the front bedrooms to have a quick look about. The telecom van with the second ERU unit was still parked at the front, a little down from the house.

All was in place.

59

IVAN BRIDGEMAN CLOSED HIS EYES FOR A MOMENT AND THOUGHT hard. When he opened his eyes, his gaze settled on the plastic lunchbox on the table. He could make out a little circuit board now and a lump of what must be explosive (or was it just plasticine? No point in taking chances) and a wire connected to the lid.

He caught his father's eyes looking at him. 'It'll be alright, Dad. They're just after money.' It wouldn't help matters to say any more.

It was then that he spotted the *pièce de résistance*: the ancient-looking Nokia 3310 beside the circuit board. That meant it could be remotely activated and it had a booby trap. It was at that point that he finally decided against phoning the detective woman back.

But he couldn't help feeling guilty about the real focus of the bad boys' intentions. Surely it couldn't be old Joyce Carlton? What had she ever done to anyone?

LUCY CHECKED HER SIDEARM AGAIN.

Maybe it would all come to nothing. Maybe the man at the top of the chain had already disappeared back into the woodwork with his criminal cohorts. Back to first positions, wherever they were.

She might go online again, on the forum, and get the IT crowd to broadcast something more inflammatory. A pincer movement, like old Professor Rohan had said.

The old man's face was back in her mind now. She hoped he was alright, wherever he was. Hoped that she hadn't been too neglectful by not insisting on an address for him in the UK. It wasn't beyond the bounds of possibility that they could reach him there, of course. If they really wanted to. But he was off the island, like Saoirse and David Carlton. That was the best option. Long odds. She hoped against hope that she hadn't miscalculated with the elderly man.

She frowned suddenly, when she thought of Saoirse.

Tried to put dark thoughts out of her mind but couldn't. She slipped back downstairs to the study and sat into the Queen Anne armchair with one of Philip Carlton's books on language and lore in Mesopotamia to distract herself. The land where writing began. Bean counters, poets, warriors, lawyers. The mundane way civilisation arose too. I have ten more cows than you, mate. My land stretches down to the Tigris, actually. My son will inherit this. My daughter will marry this one. Language and life. Maybe that's all we had, in the end. The three L's: life and language and, occasionally, love. The thought suddenly made her weary.

Without meaning to, she fell into a light sleep. Everything faded away and the book fell from her hands onto the hardwood floor. There was a patchy dream. Berlin. She was on a cruise on the Spree canal with her mother and father. A song was playing on the Tannoy. 'Schneewalzer'. That jolly, kitschy German tune her father used to sing to her as a child.

'*Du mit mir und ich mit dir...*'

There was a knock on the door. Joyce Carlton popped her head in. 'They're gone, Lucy.'

Lucy heard the Bridgewood van pull away down the driveway and the gates close behind it a few moments later. She stood up and shook herself awake. 'How long have I been asleep?'

'Best part of an hour, dear. They've finished everything. Very dependable company. Anyway...'

Lucy stretched herself slowly. 'Look, I'll stay in here until it gets dark. Then I'll join you in the living room.'

'Coffee?'

'Please.' She slipped over to the downstairs bathroom and sloshed water on her face. It was on her mind again now: Saoirse.

Back in the study, she tried to phone Gerhard, then Saoirse, but their phones just rang out. A sliver of fear slipped into her heart now. Surely nothing could happen over there? But it played on her mind so much that she phoned Professor Schliemann in Kiel.

Schliemann tried to reassure her gently. 'I'll keep trying him, Lucy. I have a couple of friends in Hamburg, and I'll get them to check at the apartment.'

It was suddenly hard to focus. The odds were that everything was all very well, of course. Like with old Professor Rohan. But this was her own flesh and blood. If she heard nothing in an hour, she would get Anna to contact the German police directly – screw liaison – and hit the panic button.

Then, just as the sun went down, as Joyce Carlton was drawing the curtains, the phone rang.

60

LUCY GRABBED THE PHONE AND SHOUTED INTO IT, 'WHERE WERE you, Gerhard? I asked you to let me know if you were going to be out of contact.'

'Sorry. We were at the movies and had the phones off. Is everything OK there?'

Lucy caught her breath. She was silent for a moment, trying to stifle the sob in her throat. 'Fine. I was just worried.'

'I'm sorry. Really.' Gerhard's voice was nervy now, reading between the silences.

Lucy took a breath. 'It's getting close to Dad's anniversary, you know. That's all.' Lucy took the glass of water Joyce Carlton poured for her. 'Let me have a word with Saoirse, Gerhard. Just... just don't leave me hanging like that again.'

She heard Saoirse's feet running towards the phone and broke into a smile. She just wanted to hold her. To squeeze her. To take her into a room far, far away and never leave her again.

SHE SAT into the living room with Joyce Carlton and they watched an old movie about a man disappearing from his old life. It suddenly seemed a good idea – to duck into the earth on one part of the planet and resurface in another.

A new life.

Darkness had fallen now. It was the second night. She realised that things were more likely to happen tonight. That it was probably tonight or not at all. She took out her pistol, excusing herself to the woman in front of her, and checked it. Joyce Carlton looked at the gun curiously. 'We used to shoot rabbits with Dad around here, years ago. Hardly shoot a rabbit at a hundred yards with that little thing, though.'

Lucy laughed. 'Personally speaking, I'd prefer not to shoot anything. It's just a thing with me.'

'Had a bad experience?'

Lucy smiled awkwardly. 'You might say that.'

At around ten o'clock, Joyce Carlton excused herself and headed up to bed on the first floor, overlooking the front garden. Lucy was alone now. She did a check-in with Sullivan in the little shed next door, at the end of the next-door garden.

Sullivan was sanguine. 'They may have decided the price is too high.'

'Maybe. Maybe not. OK, my phone and walkie-talkie are open. Hear anything, let me know.'

It was around midnight when she felt tiredness suddenly tug at her again. She checked all the doors and the alarm system and checked in again with Sullivan. Then she headed up the stairs slowly to the bed in the room next to Joyce Carlton's. She peeped in through the adjoining door. Joyce Carlton was slumbering deeply.

SHE WOKE SOMEWHERE around three in the morning with a feeling that something was wrong. Very, very wrong. At first she thought it was the trace memory of Ivan Bridgeman's voice that had got under her skin. The needy sort of tone. But that was ridiculous. It had to be something else. What was it, then?

It was the quiet.

The way a baby wakes when there's too much silence. Subliminal startle reflex. And that odd feeling that came with it. It was that same feeling she had had in the Black Hills a few weeks before. Why hadn't the attacker arrived? She closed her eyes to get back to sleep, but her mind wouldn't let her.

And that was exactly when the voice of Ivan Bridgeman faded away and the voice of the older worker from Bridgewood Gardens filtered back into her mind again, like a random YouTube video.

'*I'm finkin' is good idea, Mrs Carlton.*'

The th-fronting in 'think.' The Cockney 'f' substitution for 'th'.

Bollox! The blood started to drain from her face. *No, it wasn't possible, was it?*

She thought of Schliemann's analysis of the voice. The Cockney underlay beneath the Baltic-Slavic. Why hadn't she sussed it earlier? That weird melange, like a Connemara man gone Cockney, or a Dublin flat-dweller gone California. She saw the sound before her eyes now, couched in the phonetic alphabet. Sound as symbol.

QE bloody D.

She grabbed the pistol and tiptoed down into the living room. On the TV, the CCTV playback showed the drain man there with his dog. Then the van with the two gardeners arriving. She skipped forward through the footage. She stopped at the part where they were sitting at the wrought-iron table drinking tea. There they were looking back at the house. It was suddenly clear what they had been looking at: the CCTV camera on the wall. Not the dog.

They seemed suddenly anxious to finish the pergola work. Anxious to scarper before they were rumbled. The camera at the front of the house caught the van as it swung around to drive back down the little avenue.

She peered at the screen and rewound it a dozen times to make sure. Then she froze the screen and looked at it up close.

There was no mistaking it.

There was only one person in the van. Sullivan might have counted them out secretly from the back garden, but one man was missing by the time the van reached the front gate. The older one.

She suddenly jerked upright.

That meant he had to be in the house somewhere. She closed her eyes and played the audio memory over in her mind again.

She pressed the silent alarm under her top. Once, twice, three times. Then she started running up the stairs.

Get her down and out the back door.

That was when she heard it: the footsteps tiptoeing down from the third floor. Maybe he had been hiding up in the maid's old room, in the attic. Had slipped up there while Joyce Carlton was in the garden and she was keeping herself hidden in the study.

The footsteps started up slowly again now.

She hit the panic alarm under her top again. Then she said a silent prayer to whoever.

But there was no guarantee that anyone was listening in heaven or on earth.

61

JOYCE CARLTON SAT UP IN THE BED AND STARED AT THE PISTOL IN Lucy's right hand. 'What is it?'

Lucy glanced at the bedside locker. Booze and tablets, a starlet's supper. She whispered into the older woman's ear, 'Get up, Joyce! Now!'

Lucy swung around – the footsteps had stopped again suddenly. She grabbed the older woman by the sleeve and dragged her along. She checked the landing: clear. They started slowly down the stairs.

Don't fall. Trip and you're both dead. Hold focus.

They were on the ground floor now. What if the Lithuanian had slipped ahead of her? If she could just get Joyce Carlton down and out through the back door.

She pushed open the living room door, swept the room with the pistol, then grabbed Joyce Carlton again. 'Stay close to me!' Lucy rushed past the study and shouldered open the door to the kitchen.

'Down!' Joyce Carlton ducked. Lucy crept in at hip height to the kitchen with the other woman following her, still half asleep.

She raced across the kitchen floor with Joyce Carlton to the back door. Where was the key she had left in the lock? She fumbled about in the dark for a second looking for it.

He's locked us in.

She crossed to the sink window and threw it open, but no house alarm sounded.

He's suppressed the alarm some way.

Get her down to the cellar.

She threw open the cellar door and switched on the light. She hesitated just for a moment – then closed the door after her and guided Joyce Carlton down the steps. Joyce Carlton shivered, still half asleep. 'I hate the cellar! Spiders!'

'Screw the spiders! Get in behind those trunks over there and don't move. I'm going back upstairs.'

Joyce Carlton touched her shoulder. 'Please be careful! Please!'

Lucy pressed the panic button again, but still there was no sound of footsteps running to help. She would have to stay in the kitchen with the gun pointed at the hallway until Sullivan and the team arrived. She raced back up the cellar stairs and closed the door behind her. Then she braced herself against the sink, at an angle to the door leading into the corridor.

Can fire right into the door from there. Three shots across the centre panel.

She started having second thoughts now. No point in waiting to be shot, and for Joyce Carlton to be killed. She could fire a shot with no silencer alright, and they might all come running, but then they might get caught in the crossfire then.

She took a deep breath, checked her gun, then started back towards the door leading into the corridor.

At the foot of the stairs, the lights suddenly went out, and she found herself staring into pitch darkness now. She strained to hear.

He's on the first floor. He realises Joyce is in the cellar and knows I'm coming for him. He has the advantage – the high ground.

She crouched down and advanced up the stairs to the return on the first floor. Then she lay down on the floor again and listened hard. She closed her eyes for a millisecond. Then she caught it. Just the faintest creaking of a floorboard above her head. She stood up slowly, with her back to the wall, and braced herself in the dark, trying to catch the slightest source of light.

She steadied herself and pointed the gun at the staircase.

IT FELT like a car smashing into her legs as Lukas Petraskas rolled into her. She tumbled over his crouching body in the darkness and came down heavily on her shoulder. A terrible pain shot through her whole body.

Kill the pain, isolate it. Shut it off.

She dragged herself to her feet and grabbed the pistol from the floor. He had reached the ground floor now. This was Special Forces military training: primary target first.

Joyce Carlton.

She clenched the pistol tightly and raced down the stairs. In the hall, she crouched down and pushed open the door to the kitchen slowly.

Zing!

A bullet winged its way just over her head. He was still going for his primary target, alright. And then he turned slowly towards her, and the light of the slimline torch in his hand flooded her eyes, blinding her.

She threw herself forward into the kitchen, out of the arc of the light beam. In the reflected light, she glimpsed the face for the first time now. The blue-cold eyes. Then it was darkness again and she lost her target.

She scurried under the old hardwood table. Lukas Petraskas swung around and drew a tight bead on the table.

Three metres. Clean shot. This is where I die.

I won't ever see my daughter again.

Help me, Father... help me...

62

THE BULLET PASSED THROUGH THE ANCIENT HARDWOOD AND TORE into the tiled floor with a wild screech. Lucy slammed against the leg of the table, and the gun was knocked out of her hand. She scrabbled about but couldn't put her hand on it. She could hear the Lithuanian counting as he steadied himself for the *coup de grace*.

Do something!

Her hand chanced on the heavy fire shovel by the table. She rolled out of the far side of the table and turned to face her attacker. She drew back her arm and then flung the shovel with all her might at the figure bearing down on her.

The Lithuanian ducked and his second shot ploughed into the ceiling.

She threw herself at his legs in the dark and heard his gun skitter across the tiled floor and the torch glass shatter. There was a scream of rage. Suddenly he was on top of her, trying to slam her head against the tiled floor.

With a superhuman effort, she jerked the upper part of her body up painfully and rammed the fingers of her right hand into Lukas Petraskas's mouth. His head jerked back and he started gagging for breath.

You have bought ten seconds. Twenty, maybe. Where the fuck is everyone?

It was then that she saw it: just behind the Lithuanian, a dim glimmer as the cellar door opened slowly. A faint white light pulsing in the darkness. The creaking sound caught the ears of the man above her, and he swung around towards the cellar door.

Out of the gloom, a woman's voice spoke calmly, with the stubborn authority of age and station. 'Are you the one who killed my brother, sir?'

But the voice in the half-dark didn't wait for an answer.

There was a loud bang and a muzzle flash, and a 22.250 round tore into Lukas Petraskas's arm, flinging him back against the sink in agony. Lucy pressed her back against the far wall. Her eyes started slowly adjusting to the light now.

Silhouetted in the failsafe lamp of the cellar door, Lucy saw the figure of Joyce Carlton cradling the ancient Carlton deer hunting rifle.

She was about to say something over the screams of the wounded man when a sledgehammer started chomping its way through the kitchen door, and then the door caved in. A man's voice called out her name, and another voice shouted, 'Everyone down on the floor! Now! Everyone down on the floor now!'

In the gloom, she saw Joyce Carlton lie down slowly and lay the rifle genteelly to one side. Then a mobile arc light on someone's backpack flooded the room like a football stadium.

Lukas Petraskas, his arm bleeding heavily, looked up groggily into the barrel of the Sig Sauer P226 nuzzling into his flat forehead.

63

IN THE BLINDING GLARE OF THE ARC LIGHT, LUCY LOOKED UP AT Sullivan. His fingers touched her shoulder and she winced in pain. 'Probably just bruised. We can get the medic to look at it.'

He glanced over at Joyce Carlton, who was starting to move. 'Just stay right where you are, please, Ms Carlton.'

Joyce Carlton smiled over sweetly at Sullivan, but said nothing. Sullivan turned back to the Lithuanian and the second ERU man beside him. 'And you don't move either! Understand?'

The wolfish eyes narrowed. Sullivan repeated the question in Russian. '*Ponimayesh?*'

The Lithuanian grunted. '*Da...*'

Sullivan nodded to the second ERU man. 'Patch him up. If he moves, shoot the fucker. I'll pay for the bullet.'

Lucy stood up stiffly and put her hand to her shoulder. She glanced over at the wounded man lying against the sink presses. 'He's not going to tell us anything right now, and we're on the clock. Search him, Gerry.'

Sullivan went through the Lithuanian's pockets and passed the phone to her. She trawled through the phone and found the app buried inside a couple of folders. She glanced over her shoulder at the ERU man with the Lithuanian. 'No ID, naturally. Are you done with him?'

'It'll hold until we get him to hospital. She just winged him.'

Lucy nodded at them. 'Right. All of you outside, including you, Joyce. Leave that rifle where it is, for ballistics, or there'll be a big legal kick up.'

The men in black glanced at one another, unsure. Sullivan spoke first. 'Detective O'Hara has operational seniority here.' The ERU man with the Lithuanian stood up slowly and signalled to the other two. They moved out into the garden with Joyce Carlton between them.

Lucy turned to Sullivan. 'Maybe a little bit of clarification for our friend here.'

Sullivan knelt down slowly and poked his pistol between the man's legs. Lukas Petraskas jerked back in pain. 'My gun fires, your happiness is gone. OK?'

Lucy tapped the shortwave app and set the phone to speaker. 'That's very uncouth of you, Detective Sullivan.'

'Couth would be wasted on this toerag.'

'Now...' Lucy kept her eyes on the Lithuanian. She heard the app kick in after a couple of clicks and put the phone on speaker. A voice came over the line. It was the sort of suave, slightly throaty voice a mid-ranking bank manager might cultivate in a Home Counties bank. She held the phone to the Lithuanian's mouth.

The Lithuanian closed his eyes. Sullivan jabbed him in the groin again. Lukas Petraskas's eyes were suddenly wide open now and full of pain, but he didn't make a sound.

The voice at the far end of the phone spoke. 'Is it all done? Hello?'

The Lithuanian took a deep breath. 'Is done. Is all done.'

'Very good. Tell your people our business is finally finished. Do you understand?'

Lucy took the phone and put her finger to her lips. The voice at the other end started up again. 'Hello? Hello? Are you still there? Speak to me! Are you still there?'

There was a click as the app cut out. Lucy turned to Sullivan. 'Let's hope that's enough for the boys in the Park.'

Sullivan motioned to the Lithuanian to get up. Lukas Petraskas struggled to his feet and scowled at them. Sullivan walked him to the kitchen door and nodded to the nearest ERU man. 'You two boys hold him here for the moment. Ms Carlton, I think you can come back in now.'

JOYCE CARLTON SAT on the edge of the sofa, sipping black tea. 'And you're quite sure my David is alright?'

Sullivan spoke. 'He's fine. You'll be able to contact him in a few minutes. We're going to keep a detail on the house here tonight, though.'

Lucy's phone rang. The IT man's voice was high. 'We've narrowed the signal down, Detective O'Hara. To a definite location in West Cork, not far from the Old Head of Kinsale. We're getting a drone to the area to firm things up.'

'Good. I'll get back to you.' Lucy phoned Reese. Reese's sombre voice came on the line. 'Well done. Did our friend talk?'

Lucy hesitated a moment. 'He did. The techies have a definite location in West Cork, George. Somewhere near Kinsale.'

There was no equivocation in Reese's voice now. 'OK. I want you in on this.'

Lucy fell silent for a moment. 'Don't you think this is more an ERU job?'

'RSU, from down in Cork, and an ERU unit will pull a joint operation. You're senior officer in Dublin and Cork. Get over to Baldonnel with Gerry Sullivan, and an Air Corps helicopter will take you from there. The local Munster unit will be on standby in Cork city.'

'I understand.' Lucy turned back to Sullivan. 'Right, we're riding out.' She glanced back at Joyce Carlton. 'The officers will stay with you until your niece comes. I'll be in touch later.'

Joyce Carlton frowned for a moment, then spoke slowly. 'I could have killed that man.'

Lucy smiled. 'Never mind. There's always next time.'

Lucy slipped back into the kitchen and signalled to the ERU men. The last thing she saw of Lukas Petraskas was his Cheshire Cat smirk as he was hauled into the Toyota Land Cruiser.

Then she joined Brosnahan and Sullivan and headed off across the city.

64

THE AIR CORPS HELICOPTER CUT WEST OVER CORK CITY AND described a great arc before turning east, toward the Irish Sea and Kinsale. Lucy looked down at the patchwork of fields. 'Where do we land?'

'About twenty miles back. There might be scouts.'

A voice cut in over the comms. 'Pilot here. We'll be putting down at a point south-west of Kinsale. The combination team are already in place.'

Sullivan passed over the iPad to Lucy. It showed a spectacular view of a windswept clifftop retreat and an immaculately groomed front lawn. Sullivan pointed at a little copse to the right, at the back. 'That's where the assault team will be. We'll be on the far side. There's a little wooded area there, too.'

Lucy ran her finger over the map. 'Have they identified him yet?'

'Locals thought he might be German. Almost never saw him. The thing was, the original owner actually was German. We think this guy just stepped into the dead man's shoes and assumed his identity.'

'Ah...'

Sullivan pointed at the house on the headland on the iPad. 'Built with NATO money in case of a Soviet invasion.'

Lucy laughed. 'I didn't realise the Soviets liked Cork so much.'

Sullivan tapped the screen again. 'And it's got a nuclear, biological, chemical bunker beneath. Generic NBC construction. The Germans have just sent us over old blueprints from similar NATO bunkers.'

'And we can't even run a train on time. So, how do you get to the bunker itself?'

Sullivan ran his finger along the perimeter of the house. 'Through the cellar. See that little concrete box at the side of the house? That's the vent shaft the drone's infrared picked up.'

Lucy sat back in the seat and thought for a moment. 'It couldn't be a suicide scenario, could it? I mean, if this fellow is mad enough to order all these deaths, maybe he has no intention of being taken alive...'

Sullivan shrugged his shoulders. 'Never know. But we have sniper cover on both sides. The old UK Kratos rules apply, off the record. Head shot to the brain stem and bye-bye. Do a body shot and the electromagnetic pulse could set off an IED. But you won't have to decide.'

'Heard that song before.' Lucy looked out over the landscape as the helicopter tilted to the right.

A voice cut in over the headphones. 'Three minutes to landing.'

The helicopter banked again and started to make its descent.

THE LITTLE BIRD was made of bronze. Not a lifelike creature at all, but the Collector loved it all the more for that. Took pity on its long dead creator. Its provenance was clear, the alloy and the style, along with the carbon dating, told that. Syro-Palestine. It had been carried across the Mediterranean and into the Aegean on a boat, sometime around 1,000 BC. Its similarity to Celtic designs in illuminated manuscripts was probably what had attracted him to it in the first place.

'Someone must have loved you, little bird. A long, long time ago.'

And it was, after all, the first piece he had secured for his collection.

The first piece that Jeremy Arkens had tracked down with the help of Derry Carlton's international connections through his father. Where would the whole collection have ended up without their contributions? Scattered to the four winds, that was where. The possession of semi-literate know-nothings, all over the globe, whose only entitlement to the priceless objects was the size of their purses.

He kissed the little bronze bird and smiled. All the way from Syro-Palestine, by way of Ancient Greece, to a bunker in West Cork. He passed through the various rooms now, checking and counting. The little collection of golden torcs in what had once been the old dining quarters. The wooden crucifixes in the sleeping quarters. Crosses carved by poor penitents in the shadow of the Great Hunger.

He slipped into the radio room and looked at the glowing dials on the shortwave radio. He would leave it on. Not much point in pretending to himself now. The game was over. He had one last throw of the dice, though.

Ars longa, vita brevis.

He would take the treasure with hm. Would not suffer it to fall into the hands of ignoramuses whose taste was shaped by television and the crass internet.

He left the Latin manuscript to last, as he always did. He drew up a chair and sat in front of the glass case with the Genesis of St Fergal. Then he pressed the button. There was a little whish of air as the vacuum device flipped the page. He read *sotto voce,* savouring every sweet syllable of the ancient Latin.

Yes, they would be arriving soon. He accepted that now. But still he was dallying unreasonably, as if to stave off the inevitable. Leaving it to the last moment. He shut the bunker door after him and pulled down the locking handle.

There was a heavy clang of metal.

The Collector grunted to himself and made his way up the stairs into the kitchen.

65

THE SIX-MAN ASSAULT TEAM SQUATTED DOWN IN THE LITTLE copse to the right of the house. The drone hanging in the sky gave a good image of the back of the house. Lucy watched them all on the iPad. 'Where are our snipers?'

Sullivan whispered to her, 'There's one in the front of the house and one at the back, behind the bushes.'

Reese's voice broke in through her earpiece. 'Lucy, I have control of the shooters. But you may have to make an executive decision. Real world and real time.'

Lucy glanced across at the house again and squinted through the binoculars. 'I realise that.'

'So I am formally authorising you to do that, *in extremis*.'

Lucy smiled. 'Love the dog Latin.'

'I'm making a legal point here, Detective O'Hara. For the record, mine and yours.'

'I understand. *In extremis*.' Lucy looked through the trees. There seemed to be movement inside the kitchen now. She thought she could see something through the big glass doors. 'I'm go! Over.'

Lucy tapped Sullivan on the shoulder. 'Give me the feed

from the drone.' Lucy looked at the image on the iPad. 'The sun is on the patio door glass. It's impossible to see what's going on inside.'

She spoke into her mike. 'All units hold. All units hold.'

The patio doors started to open slowly. An elderly man stepped out gingerly onto the patio and looked about. He was dressed in a well-pressed pair of jeans and a green gilet with a tartan cap pulled down over his forehead. He glanced about him diffidently, then turned towards the right-hand side of the house.

He might have been popping out to take in the milk.

Lucy spoke into her mike again. 'Rear sniper locate subject. Seems unarmed. No sign of bulky clothing. Wait!'

The man at the kitchen door turned and glanced around him; then he made for a little box set into the back wall of the house, at knee height.

Sullivan turned to her. 'What's he up to?'

Lucy refocused the binoculars. 'I think it's the system the Germans told us about. Last one out burns the bunker. Fire and water. Very biblical.'

'Right.'

Lucy suddenly gasped. 'What the...?' She took the binoculars away from her eyes for a moment, as though to wake herself up, then put them back to her eyes again. 'He's taken off his hat. Jesus Christ! Look!'

'What?' Sullivan put the binoculars back to his eyes.

Lucy spoke out of the side of her mouth. 'Am I seeing right?'

'It can't be, can it?' Sullivan turned to her.

Lucy left down her binoculars slowly and started to stand up. 'I'm going over there.'

Sullivan grabbed her arm. 'No, Lucy! You don't know what frame of mind he's in!'

Lucy spoke softly into the mike. 'Rear unit sniper cover,

track me and keep eyes on subject. I'm taking authorisation for fire.'

Reese's voice broke in. 'You have authorisation, Detective O'Hara.'

Lucy started walking slowly out of the woods. She tipped over the bone-dry drain and kept her eyes fixed firmly on the figure of the elderly man at the wall. She watched as he lifted the Perspex panel on the box. It all seemed a bit unreal to her, all of a sudden. Like a blurred dream.

She stood stock-still on the lawn at the edge of the patio and waited for a moment. Then her right hand moved towards the pistol in her shoulder holster. The salt sea wind was on her face now, and she could hear bird calls from the little copse to the right of the house, where the second unit was hidden. Her sense of everything around her was suddenly heightened.

For a moment, she hesitated, almost feeling foolish. Could this all be wrong? A terrible mistake?

She started walking slowly to the edge of the patio. Then, just as her feet touched the concrete, the elderly man turned from where he was squatting, his hand hovering over the red button under the plastic cover. Lucy stopped short and took a deep breath. '*Guten Abend, Herr Doktor Sammler.*'

The man leaned forward to press the button as though he hadn't heard her. Lucy's voice suddenly hardened now. 'Please don't, Professor Rohan. It's all over now.'

The man gave a little laugh.

Lucy O'Hara raised the pistol slowly. 'I said don't!'

Professor Rohan glanced over his shoulder, then turned his eyes back to the switch again. 'Going to risk another Bateman, are you?'

He gave another little chuckle. She began to wonder now whether he was goading her into shooting him. Death by cop in the West Cork countryside.

She lowered the pistol slowly and spoke slowly and carefully into her mouthpiece. 'Sniper hold. I have the shot now.'

'Copy that. You have the shot, Detective O'Hara.'

'I have the shot.'

The old man turned around and looked up at her with polite disbelief in his eyes. He seemed to be on the point of saying something, but she wasn't sure what. Lucy raised the pistol again, slowly, like someone signalling the start of some sort of ancient ceremony. Then, without hesitating, she squeezed the trigger.

There was a thud as the bullet hit home and a choking smell of cordite and burning plastic came to her nostrils. The elderly man slumped sideways onto the grass.

Detective Lucy Divonne O'Hara, PhD, lowered the pistol and spoke into her mouthpiece. 'All stand down. Scene clear. Medics forward.'

66

THE .345 ROUND LODGED IN THE CENTRE OF THE CONTROL PANEL, exactly where she had placed it, and smashed through the side of the box, shattering the cabling to the basement. The shocked eyes of Emeritus Professor Rohan looked up at her from the ground. He was breathing heavily, but otherwise unharmed. Lucy glanced up at the sky and spotted the drone hovering above her head. Reese would be watching her, she knew.

Good...

She holstered her gun and knelt down slowly. The elderly man looked up at her now with something she couldn't quite read. It wasn't anger or spleen, but something more like disgust. Disgust for her and the rest of the world, she suspected.

He gave a tired smile. 'Feel like some sort of war goddess now? Athena, perhaps?'

Lucy smiled sweetly. 'More like Nemesis, Professor Rohan. Know her? She's the one who gives people their comeuppance.'

She beckoned to the medic to come out of the trees and spoke into the mike. 'Snipers, keep eyes on. Both teams, secure the perimeter.' She looked over her shoulder as Sullivan approached. 'Cuff him, Gerry, and have him checked. Stay with him. I'm going inside the house to have a quick look-see.'

She waved at one of the ERU team and the ordnance officer to follow her. She put on a pair of forensic gloves and did a quick first recce of the house, opening drawers, checking closets and photographing items. In the main bedroom, off the enormous bathroom, Lucy stumbled on what she wasn't really looking for.

On what she hadn't even expected to find. She scanned the words. This was the original, alright.

It was just lying there, on top of a chest of drawers as though its author had wanted it found. She pulled out an evidence bag, slipped the document into it and put it into her shoulder satchel. Then she continued through the rooms until she got the all-clear from the ordnance officer in the bunker.

She thought of the elderly man handcuffed outside. This was the man who had given the order to kill herself and her daughter. Who had Philip Carlton and Violet Saunders and Jeremy Arkens and his wife killed. Who played her like a fiddle, because of her father.

She took the evidence back out of her satchel and read through it again. She wasn't going to let him walk away to detention that easily.

Dear Joyce and David,

It is with great regret I write these sad words. By the time you read this, I will be gone to my eternal rest, sadly. Of late, things have become more and more difficult. My health is failing, I no longer seem to have any purpose in life, and I feel it is time for me to make my exit. I am not doing this lightly. I have given it much thought. To those who have loved me and whom I have loved, I would like to say sorry, from the bottom of my heart. Joyce, you have been a good sister to me; David, you have been an honourable brother to me. I can no longer face the darkening days and have decided that I

*must not burden the rest of the world anymore with my declining
health.*

Please forgive me.

With all my love,

Now she knew what she needed to do. What she must do.

She made her way slowly down to the cellar. The ordnance
officer looked up from his phone. 'All clear. No heat signals of
anyone else about either. That handle in the recess opens the
bunker door. I've just checked it.'

She made her way back upstairs to where Professor Rohan
was sitting by the patio door on a low chair. 'He's coming down
with me for walkies and talkies.'

The unit officer looked around him. 'We have orders to fly
him directly to Dublin.'

'I'm SIO here, lads. Now, uncuff him.'

She watched the old eyes as the handcuffs were taken off.
Professor Rohan seemed to be having a little conversation with
someone offstage now. She nodded at the two officers. 'Follow
me down to the cellar and bring him with you.'

They descended to the cellar and crossed to the bunker
door. Lucy turned around to the others. 'Right, everyone else
up and out. Myself and the professor here are going to go
walkabout.'

Sullivan suddenly appeared at her shoulder, breathless. 'Are
you serious?'

Lucy grinned. 'Never seriouser. I'm getting the nice
gentleman to show me 'round his collection. I have a little
surprise for him. Now, boys, chop-chop!' She watched the ERU
men in the helmets clunk their way back up the cellar steps.
Sullivan made his way upstairs silently behind them.

She waited until she heard the kitchen door slam shut.
'Now, let's have a little look-see at your man cave, Professor
Rohan.'

The eyes fixed on her sullenly in the low light of the cellar. She opened the bunker door and found the light switch. Her eyes fell on the glass case with the Genesis of St Fergal. Was this the manuscript Joyce Carlton had mentioned?

'Walk...' She followed the tired footsteps to the glass case.

The croaky old voice spoke beside her. 'Read Latin, do you?' Lucy's eyes traversed the illuminated page and she read a couple of words.

'I'm very impressed.' There was a sour sort of smile on the wrinkled face.

'It's only knowledge, Professor Rohan. Mr and Mrs Google know far more than we will ever know.'

The old face smiled. 'Only knowledge? The medieval scribes and scholars would have been fascinated by that idea.'

'Walk on...' She followed Professor Rohan to the door of the next room. She glanced inside for a moment and spotted the radio. Then they proceeded on to the other rooms. Past the wooden crucifixes and silver crucifixes, golden torcs and rings and cloak pins and a room with clay metal pots. At the furthest room, she stopped and looked at the man beside her.

She thought of Joyce Carlton's question again. 'Was it worth it all?'

'Was what worth what, Detective?'

'All the murder... mayhem... cheating... lying... stealing worth it, for this?'

The man beside her hesitated for a moment; then he spoke. There was no warmth in his words, though. He might have been reading a racing report. 'It rather depends on your point of view, Detective. The Akkadians overwhelmed the Sumerians. The Assyrians disposed of the Hittites. The Celts overran the pre-Celts. All possession is theft or transfer, you know. It's all relative, you know.'

Lucy smiled politely. 'You're beginning to sound like an old hippy. And, besides that, you're starting to bore me. Come on. You have a helicopter to catch.'

They walked back past the rooms into the main chamber. Lucy stopped at the glass case with the manuscript. 'Greed. That's it, isn't it? And arrogance.'

The old voice sounded tired now. 'Love, Detective O'Hara. But then, you wouldn't understand that. We have different values, you see.'

Lucy stared at him. 'Really? Like what?'

Professor Rohan looked at her. 'Like love and respect for one's heritage. A love that is beyond you.'

Lucy stopped suddenly and placed her hand on the old man's shoulder. She looked into the eyes of Professor Rohan. 'Oh, dear! I almost forgot!' She gave a big smile.

'I'm sorry?'

Lucy grinned. 'The most important manuscript of all. In your case, anyway.'

She took out the evidence bag with the typed letter and held it up in its plastic cover. 'Recognise this, Professor Rohan? Strictly speaking, not a manuscript at all. It's typed. Let me read the first line.'

The eyes clouded over. 'Do we really need this circus act?'

'It's the very least I can do. Now...'

She began to read in a low voice. *'It is with great regret that I write these sad words. By the time you read this, I will be gone to my eternal rest, sadly.* Do you recognise those words, Professor? You should. They're yours. Before your killer read them out to Philip Carlton, and he bowdlerised them to blow your little scheme out of the water. Hoist by your own petard, Professor Rohan.'

'What's your point? You're getting tiresome.'

'*Vanitas vanitatem.* Ecclesiastes 1:1. You didn't reckon with a clever man like Philip Carlton up against a dumb cut-throat.

The dead, whom you admire so much, have come back and snookered you.'

The rheumy eyes looked out at her silently, sullenly. Then they started slowly towards the bunker door.

A SEASONAL SUMMER rain was falling steadily in Cathal Brugha barracks in Dublin the following morning. A flash of lightning lit up the evening sky as Jenny Saunders stood with Lucy in the porch of the admin building.

Jenny Saunders grabbed Lucy's shoulder. 'I thought that was a shot!'

Lucy took her by the arm. 'All that's over. You'll be escorted to your London flight tonight and met at the far side. We have the organ grinder and the monkey under lock and key now.'

'Thank you, Detective O'Hara.'

'Look, we'll be in touch soon about the criminal case. But, in the meantime, you can ring anytime for a catch-up. Fair enough?'

'Alright.'

Lucy left Jenny Saunders with the other detective and raced across the barracks yard in the rain, to where Sullivan was waiting in the car. They drove along the rain-lashed Grand Canal, then swung south onto the M50 interchange for Boyne-bridge, on the coast. They were on the motorway north before either spoke.

Sullivan stared out through the window. 'There's often a dip after a case like this. But you know that, of course.'

Lucy glanced over at him. 'I just want to see my daughter. Then I'll be fine.'

'Of course. I mean...'

Lucy frowned. 'Spit it out, Sullivan.'

'It's not really a nice way to spend your life, is it? Ever think of that?'

Lucy laughed to herself. 'Someone has to pick up the poo.'

'Point tastefully made, as always.' Sullivan smiled silently and they slewed on through the rain.

THE TEAM WERE all in the incident room with Reese in Boynebridge. Trays of doughnuts sporting colours not normally found in nature – radioactive reds, cobalt blues and psychedelic purples – were set out on one of the desks with a couple of pots of coffee.

Anna Crowley waved her phone at them as they entered. 'Brits have just lifted our Polish friend in a port on the east coast.'

Lucy clapped. 'So, our little family is complete.'

Reese crossed over to Lucy and shook her hand, then Sullivan's. 'Well done all.' Reese nodded towards the door. 'Little word with you offside?'

'Sure.' She followed Reese down the stairs to one of the interview suites. He left his superintendent's cap down on the table and pulled up a chair for her.

Lucy ran her hand through her hair and smiled. 'You going to interrogate me?'

'Wouldn't like that particular job.' Reese went all serious then. Or as serious as he could muster. 'It has been conveyed to me, from on high, that the great and the good want to reinstate you as forensic linguist.'

Lucy glanced around the walls of the interview room. At the clock on the wall and the video camera up in the corner. Then she turned back slowly to Reese. 'Do they now?'

Reese looked as pleased as a puppy with a burst ball. 'Oh, yes. With full entitlements, etcetera, and retrospective payments. I've been told to tell you that.'

Lucy grinned at him. 'Well, I don't want it, George. Tell them thanks anyway.'

'I'm sorry?' Reese looked puzzled.

'The Bateman slate is clean. I'm happy with that. I just don't want to go back to semi-academic work in an office, that's all.'

'Really?'

Lucy picked up Reese's hat and ran her finger around the sweatband inside. 'Really. I'd like to stay local with special tasking. That sort of thing, you know.'

Reese gave a little chuckle. 'You're saying you want us to create a special post for you?'

Lucy smiled. '*Au contraire.* I'm saying let me carry on with what I've been doing for the past couple of months. Local with special expertise and secondable on demand.'

Reese laughed cautiously. 'Secondable? Is that even a Scrabble word? You mean a *have gun will travel* sort of thing?'

'More a *have forensic linguistics degree will travel* sort of thing.'

Reese sat back in the chair. 'It would appeal to the bean counters, I suppose. Two jobs for one salary cheque. And you're doing it anyway, as you say.'

Lucy stood up slowly. 'So there you have it, George, in a nutshell. Now, I have to get back upstairs and devour a few of those dodgy-looking doughnuts.'

Lucy stood up slowly and started walking towards the door. Then she took out her phone and swiped Saoirse's number, in Germany.

67

THE MERMAID CALLED *BETSY* GROANED A LITTLE THEN SWUNG sharply southwards. The sun was setting in the west now and a cool breeze had sprung up. Lucy leaned over and started zipping up Saoirse's windcheater. 'It's getting chilly.'

'But we're still going to *Mémé's*, aren't we?'

'*Bien sûr!* We'll berth near the yacht club and walk up. You sound like you're getting fond of your grandmother.'

There was a shrugging of shoulders. 'Maybe...'

Lucy turned back to the tiller and glanced northwards over her shoulder towards Boynebridge and the estuary of the Boyne. She pictured, once again, Philip Carlton's cold body lying over the desk in the portacabin. The letter dictated to him by Lukas Petraskas. The sad, final moments of Philip Carlton's life, which she couldn't even bring herself to think about.

It all seemed an age ago, suddenly. A summer of strife. But Reese had come back with the good news that morning: she could stay put with on-demand secondment. Two irreconcilables satisfied: She hated changed; she wanted change.

There would be another Philip Carlton, she knew that much. And another Violet Saunders too. Could be anywhere in

the country. But she would have the best of both bad worlds:
stay put in the Black Hills and travel when needed. A voice
spoke to her somewhere beyond the horizon. She assumed it
was her father. It was the time of evening when he usually
signalled to her. She listened but didn't look up.

There are worse lives, Lucy.

'You take the tiller, Saoirse. Steady now. I'll take it back
when we're coming in.'

A short while later, they passed the main harbour in Rush
and berthed in front of the little boatyard in the estuary. It was
a short walk from there to the bungalow facing the beach. Her
mother was sitting out in the back garden when they arrived.
'You are staying for the night? It's too late to go back.'

'We are indeed.'

They ate a light salad and Elisette Divonne uncorked a
bottle of Bordeaux. 'Before you start with that Spanish vinegar
of yours.'

Just before the sun finally slipped below the horizon, and
the first hint of an end-of-summer chill set in, Lucy's phone
rang. It seemed like it was coming from another world. A world
from just a few weeks before. She glanced about to make sure
no one was listening. 'Detective Sullivan, what can I do for
you?'

'I've been up in Boynebridge going over some files. I'm
heading home and I thought you might like to join me for a
quick drink. Say about nine.'

'Might could, I suppose.' She glanced around her again.
Her mother was busy in the kitchen. Saoirse was playing with
the pet rabbit in the garden.

'I thought you didn't mix modal verbs, Detective O'Hara?'

'All depends on the company. I'm in Rush, by the way. But
then, you probably guessed that already.'

'So, let's mix a few modals in that big bar down at the
harbour.'

Lucy smiled. 'Sounds good. Say, nine?'

She knocked off the phone. The light on the rocks at the end of the garden caught her eye all of a sudden now. The sinking sun still caressed the warm stone. She thought of Cairo again, and the deep rosy hue when the evening sun struck the bricks of the old buildings in the late evening. A light she had always loved. A local light. Another time, another place, another life.

Then she saluted the late summer sky with her empty glass and made her way back into the kitchen, where her mother was struggling with a fussy soufflé and a hungry child.

WE HOPE YOU ENJOYED THIS BOOK

If you could spend a moment to write an honest review, no matter how short, we would be extremely grateful. They really do help readers discover new authors.

Leave a Review

If you want to contact John, he can be reached via his website at www.johnmaherwriter.com He would love to hear from you.

Published by Inkubator Books
www.inkubatorbooks.com

Printed in Poland
by Amazon Fulfillment
Poland Sp. z o.o., Wrocław

60957332R10216